"I'VE DONE SOMETHING BAD."

The girls drove over to River Falls Mall in Clarksville to pick up Amanda. Melinda was crying for most of the ride.

"I've done something bad," she cried to Amanda as soon as she saw her.

Amanda waited silently for an explanation.

"Everybody just wait until we get back to Melinda's house," Laurie told them.

Back in Melinda's living room, they sat Amanda down and told her the story. About the kidnapping of Shanda. About holding her prisoner in the trunk of the car. About the beatings. About the final terrible act of murder.

Melinda was crying hysterically. Amanda gave her a hug. She didn't really believe that any part of the story was true.

Until she let them show her the bloodstains in the trunk of the car.

BOOK YOUR PLACE ON OUR WEBSITE AND MAKE THE READING CONNECTION!

We've created a customized website just for our very special readers, where you can get the inside scoop on everything that's going on with Zebra, Pinnacle and Kensington books.

When you come online, you'll have the exciting opportunity to:

- View covers of upcoming books
- Read sample chapters
- Learn about our future publishing schedule (listed by publication month *and author*)
- Find out when your favorite authors will be visiting a city near you
- Search for and order backlist books from our online catalog
- Check out author bios and background information
- Send e-mail to your favorite authors
- Meet the Kensington staff online
- Join us in weekly chats with authors, readers and other guests
- Get writing guidelines
- AND MUCH MORE!

**Visit our website at
http://www.pinnaclebooks.com**

CRUEL SACRIFICE

APHRODITE JONES

Pinnacle Books
Kensington Publishing Corp.

http://www.pinnaclebooks.com

For my Mother and Father

PINNACLE BOOKS are published by

Kensington Publishing Corp.
850 Third Avenue
New York, NY 10022

Pinnacle and the P logo Reg. U.S. Pat. & TM Off.

First Pinnacle Printing: January, 1994

30 29 28 27 26 25 24 23

Printed in the United States of America

AUTHOR'S NOTE

Cruel Sacrifice is not a fictionalized version of the Shanda Sharer murder case. The narrative is based on more than five thousand pages of documents and hundreds of hours of taped interviews. Documentation includes police transcripts, the defendants' psychiatric records, and other proven sources of journalistic research.

Some of the names of people mentioned have been changed to protect their privacy.

AUTHOR'S NOTE

ACKNOWLEDGEMENTS

Nonfiction is the result of a collective energy. This book could not have been researched without the cooperation of Judge Ted Todd and his staff; without Detective Steve Henry and Sheriff Buck Shippley and other members of the Indiana State Police whose names already appear in the main text, and who were equally important in the development of *Cruel Sacrifice*.

I would like to thank Donna Norton, my transcriber and proofreading assistant, whose efforts were an immeasurable help; Paul Dinas, my editor at Pinnacle, for his belief in my writing; Peter Miller, my agent, for his timely and essential input into this project; author Mike McGrady, for his positive criticism; and attorney Hughes Walker, for his legal expertise and continuing support.

Above all, I would like to thank my friends and family for their love and patience; especially my sister, Janet Jones, who is the one person in the world that I have been able to depend on.

And finally, I express my gratitude to all of the people who cooperated with me on this book, from members of the media to Steve Brock, who was largely responsible for getting the Loveless girls to publicly admit the abuse they suffered, and of course to the countless people who took the time to talk to me about this horrible tragedy in the hopes that somehow, we can learn from it and make this place a safer world.

Prologue

It was a freezing cold day in the dead of January when the three girls got to New Albany. They left Madison right after school let out that afternoon, and had lied to their parents about their plans for the night. No one knew they were on their way to Louisville, more than fifty miles away from their quaint Indiana hometown.

All Toni knew was that they were going to a punk rock concert, but first they had to make a quick stop in New Albany. Soon they'd be crossing the Ohio River and the state line, and they'd be on their way.

"Did you tell her yet?" Laurie asked Hope on the ride down.

"Tell her what?" Hope asked, playing dumb.

When they pulled up to Melinda's house on Charlestown Road, everyone was silent. Melinda opened the door, she already had her trench coat on, but the three stepped inside for a few minutes just to warm up. Of the four teenagers, Laurie was the oldest, the only one with a car and a driver's license. Although she was just seventeen, she seemed to be in control of things. Anyone who knew her for even a short time knew that Laurie had an attitude problem, that she tried very hard to be different, to be daring, that she desperately wanted to be accepted, and that she wanted her friends to follow her example.

Melinda was a very different type of person. While Laurie's demeanor was quiet and mysterious, Melinda was hyper and seemed excited to see them. Even physically, Melinda was the opposite of Laurie in every way. In contrast to Laurie's hard square jaw, chunky body, and cropped head of bleached hair, sixteen-year-old Melinda had a seductive smile, a perfect figure, and a thick head of flowing light brown curls. Melinda wore more conventional teen clothes; Laurie was a "punker," usually dressed in solid black clothing. Hope and Toni asked if they could borrow some of Melinda's clothes to wear for the night, and the four girls followed each other upstairs.

No one else seemed to be home so they made themselves comfortable in Melinda's bedroom, sorting through her array of shoes and jeans, admiring her closetful of jackets, and eyeballing her purses on the inside door. They looked over some of her T-shirts, piled neatly in a stack of milk crates, and inspected her collection of tapes, mostly bubblegum music like New Kids On The Block, Paula Abdul, and George Michael. There was the usual teenage paraphernalia hanging on Melinda's walls: family photos, stuffed animals in various nets, posters of idols, including a few of Elvis in *Jailhouse Rock*.

Toni picked out a pair of shoes and slipped them on. Hope found a pair of Melinda's jeans to wear and some shoes to match.

"This is the knife I'm going to use," Melinda said gleefully as she reached in her purse and pulled out a big old kitchen knife.

Melinda said she was going to scare Shanda with it. She had Shanda's number and address written down on a piece of paper and she decided to call there one last time before they took off, just to be sure Shanda was home.

Nobody said a word. They stayed there giggling and primping for about a half hour, carefully appraising themselves in front of Melinda's mirror.

Even though
all about Melinda
to "teach her a less

Melinda kept tryin
on the machine. All t
other two girls in. Hope
They were impressed with M
her bravado, and her story. It
to conjure up an image of Sha
hated with such a passion. Shand
nice butt; she wore tight jeans an
Shanda was a copycat, she was tryl
linda. She was wearing the same kind
hairstyle. She was, Melinda told them wi

As they listened to Melinda rage on, La
bit antsy. She knew the history all too well — N
lesbian, and Shanda was stealing away her girl
linda wanted Shanda out of her life. But Laurie
of hearing it. She just wanted to get going.

The four left a few minutes later, and Laurie had
take over the wheel. Hope only had a learner's permit,
Laurie trusted her. Melinda had a piece of paper with th
words "Capitol Hill" written down, and she was looking
for Shanda's dad's house in nearby Jeffersonville. She
knew it was near Jeffersonville High School somewhere
but she couldn't figure out where the street was. They
pulled into a McDonald's and Hope and Toni went in for
directions. While they were there, they ordered some
Chicken McNuggets.

Capitol Hills Drive, they learned, was a tucked-away
street in a middle-class subdivision. It was getting pretty
close to dark by the time Hope parked the car about a half
a block away from Shanda's house. Melinda told Hope to
go up to the door with Toni and introduce themselves as
friends of Amanda.

"Just say Amanda wants to see you," Melinda whis-

Laurie had never met Shanda, Laurie knew
...'s plan to scare Shanda, to beat her up,
...on."
... Shanda's number and hanging up
... while, she was busy filling the
... Shanda's number ... both age fifteen.
... and Toni were ... her cursing,
... Melinda's cool talk, ... for Melinda
... didn't take long for Melinda
...nda, the cute little girl she
...a was a blond; she had a
...d too much makeup.
...ng to look like Me-
... of shoes, the same
...h disgust, a slut.
...rie got a little
...Melinda was a
...friend. Me-
...was sick

...ake," Shanda
... around midnight and
... Amanda with you when you
...her with you. Have her spend the night
... something . . ."

When Shanda went back into the house, she told her
father that it was just some girls who wanted her to go to
the mall. They argued briefly about it. Shanda told her
dad to calm down, and ultimately he did. Since he had
divorced her mother, Steve generally saw Shanda only on
the weekends. He wanted his little girl to be happy. He
must have realized he was getting nowhere by arguing with
her that night.

In the meantime, Hope and Toni went back down the
road to Laurie's car and explained the situation to Melinda. At first, she was mad because they didn't manage to
lure Shanda out of her house. The two girls assured her
that they could come back and get Shanda later, and they

12

headed for Louisville to hear some music.

It took them a while to find the place where the concert was being held, the A-1 Skate Park. It was a place where skateboarders hung out, really just a warehouse with skate ramps where skaters could show off their various maneuvers. On Fridays, punk rock bands played there, and people used the concrete as a dance floor.

The minute Hope pulled up at the park, a bunch of young men approached the car and one of them started flirting with Melinda. Laurie wanted to get some booze, and the guys said they'd lead them to a nearby liquor store. The girls followed them in their car through the Louisville streets, only to wind up in the back parking lot of a deserted school. Once there, the guys tried to intimidate them by bumping into Laurie's car, but eventually the four girls made it back to the skate park. They stood in line to get tickets to the concert.

As it turned out, after about ten minutes, Hope and Toni decided they had enough of the loud music, the heat, and the slam dancing. Toni saw Melinda pinch a girl on the butt and thought it was time for her to get out of there. She and Hope asked Laurie if they could wait for them in the car, and Laurie handed over the keys. As soon as they walked outside, they met a couple of cute guys who introduced themselves as Jimmy and Brandon.

Melinda and Laurie stayed at the slam dance concert for at least two hours, so there was plenty of time for the four teens to get to know each other outside in the car. As the jam box blasted loudly in the backseat, Jimmy and Brandon were both making advances.

Hope and Toni must have gotten comfortable with them quickly because after a few kisses, Toni suddenly blurted out, "The two girls that we're with are planning on killing somebody tonight."

Part One

The Ordeal

One

It was going to be a very busy and hectic weekend over at the Sharer house. Steve had his father-in-law, his dad, and a few other relatives staying over to help take a wall down in the living room to enlarge the space. On top of that, there was his wife Sharon, his stepdaughter Sandy, and his daughter Shanda, all crowded into the tiny home.

It wasn't too long after Hope and Toni left when the phone rang. It was a neighborhood girl who invited Shanda to a party, and even though he was hesitant about letting his little girl stay out late, Steve agreed to let Shanda go, provided she be home by 10:30 P.M. He reminded her that they were going to be tearing that wall down early the next morning and he needed her help.

It was after 11:15 P.M. when she waltzed through the door, and she had her friend Michelle with her. Shanda asked if she could stay over.

"Look, we're going to be cramped for space," Steve insisted.

"Please, Dad?"

"No."

Steve called the girl's mother and arranged for her to pick Michelle up. A few minutes later, he decided he was too tired to wait for the woman to arrive. He told the girls there was some pizza in the kitchen and said they could watch TV for thirty minutes. Then he turned in.

They must have watched until almost midnight, and Steve finally came out of his bedroom.

"Cool it. Turn it off. Let's hit it," he told them, meaning it was time for lights out. For Steve, that was it for the night. He fell asleep and never heard the door close when Michelle left.

Across the bridge over in Louisville, Melinda and Laurie decided they had enough of the concert. When they came out of the skate park and found Hope and Toni making out with some guys in the car, they figured it was a good time to use the nearby pay phone to make a few calls. They were gone a good long while. They'd called Shanda's house a few times but all they got was the answering machine. They called Amanda, too. When they returned to the car, Toni was waiting outside.

Hope was still in the car with Brandon so the three girls went next door to Long John Silver's to use the restroom and kill some time. Once Brandon was gone, Hope got the car started, and Melinda told her to drive back to Shanda's; but on the way out of Louisville, Hope got confused and was driving in the wrong direction, heading toward Tennessee.

While they circled the interstates, Melinda discussed her plans.

"God I can't wait to kill her," Melinda shrieked with glee.

She mentioned the knife and explained that she intended to tease Shanda with it. She said that she thought Shanda was cute, that she'd like to have sex with Shanda, that she was going to run the knife up and down her stomach and play with her.

It took them a while to figure out the interstates but they finally made it back to Shanda's. Melinda wanted

18

Hope and Toni to go back up to the door but Toni was refusing. No one could persuade her. Even Hope tried to get Toni to go but she said it was too cold out, that she was freezing. Melinda couldn't go herself because if Shanda saw her, she'd get scared. Melinda had threatened her many times; she was not a face Shanda wanted to see at 12:30 A.M.

Eventually Hope and Laurie agreed to go. Melinda got down on the floorboard in the backseat. Before she got out of the car, Laurie helped cover Melinda with a red blanket and handed her the knife. She and Hope went up the driveway and disappeared behind Shanda's house.

As the two girls got around the corner, they saw some guy coming out of Shanda's house, a young guy. He was saying goodbye to Shanda. They ducked behind Shanda's garage for a minute. They knew the guy probably saw them out of the corner of his eye but he took off in his truck just seconds later. They were nervous about approaching the side door, but Shanda made it easy for them. She was right there waiting.

"Hi, are you going to go with us?" Hope wanted to know.

Shanda seemed glad to see them. Laurie was a new face, but Shanda wasn't concerned about that. She just wanted to hear what Hope had to say about Amanda. Hope told her that Amanda was waiting for her at The Witches' Castle. Amanda wanted her to come out. The three talked for about five minutes. Hope was having trouble convincing Shanda that she should go along. Shanda said she didn't have the right clothes on, so Hope volunteered to go inside with her and help her pick out something to change into and Laurie went back to the other girls.

Standing out near the car, Laurie opened the back door, reached into the backseat, and adjusted the blanket over Melinda. She added a few items of clothing and some fast-food bags on top to camouflage her further.

19

"Hope's bringing her," Laurie said quietly as she adjusted the blanket one last time. Before they knew it, Hope and Shanda came bouncing toward the car. Laurie told Toni to get out of the front passenger's side to let Shanda in the middle.

"Where's Amanda?" Shanda asked as she sandwiched herself between Hope and Toni.

"At The Witches' Castle," Laurie said with a reassuring voice.

"What's she wearing? Does she look cute?" Shanda asked.

Having met Amanda once before, Hope knew enough to make up an outfit that would fit Amanda's style: loose baggy shorts, a baseball cap, basically a "skater" look.

By then, the car was rolling, and they were on their way to Utica, to the "castle." It's a place better known to Utica residents as Mistletoe Falls because of the mistletoe on the property. Once a nice home, today it's just the stone remains. Even in the daylight, sitting up in a wooded hillside in an isolated spot that faces the Ohio River, the place is spooky, with its serpentine walls, foot bridges, and burned-out fireplace. To the girls, it seemed even more ominous that night.

Legend surrounding the castle says that it was once inhabited by nine witches who controlled the town of Utica. It had been burned by townsfolk who tried to destroy the witches. At least, this is the legend Laurie believed, and she was eager to talk about it with others. In fact, Laurie had taken Toni and Hope up to see it just the day before. It was one of the stops they made on the ride down to Melinda's.

Laurie had been going up there for some time. She had taken Melinda and Amanda up there, too. Laurie showed them what she called "the mausoleum" where she believed the nine witches were buried. She also showed them the "dungeon" and an altar-like place where there was an inscription that said something about death. She told them she felt the presence of witches there.

Twisting through the country roads toward Utica, Hope engaged Shanda in further conversation about Amanda. It was a discussion that she knew would cause trouble.

"Do you know Melinda?" Hope asked.

"Yeah."

"Did you know that Amanda and Melinda broke up?"

"Well, I think me and Amanda have been going together for about four months now," Shanda said proudly.

In the backseat, Laurie tapped Melinda under the blanket, giving her the signal to appear. With that, Melinda jumped up, pulled Shanda's hair back, and put the knife to her throat.

"Surprise! I guess you weren't expecting to see me!" Melinda squealed.

"Please don't hurt me!" Shanda yelped and started crying.

"Shut up, bitch!" Melinda told her as she pressed the dull of the knife even harder into Shanda's neck.

"I just want to talk about Amanda. I want you to tell me the truth about Amanda. I'm not going to hurt you, I just want to talk."

Shanda just kept crying.

Melinda had the knife to Shanda's neck for the entire ride to The Witches' Castle as she continued her interrogation.

"Are you and Amanda going together?"

"No!"

"You're lying to me! I just heard you!"

"No, I was just saying that!"

"Did you go to the Harvest Homecoming with her?"

"No! Please don't hurt me, Melinda!"

"You better tell me the truth or I'll slit your throat!"

"I won't talk to Amanda anymore!" Shanda cried.

"Are you and Amanda writing to each other?"

"Yes."

"Did you go to the haunted house with Amanda?"

"Yes."

"Did you and Amanda have sex?"

"Yes."

"You're a liar!"

Shanda was hyperventilating.

"And Amanda knows I'm going to kill you . . . Amanda said she wants you dead just as much as I do!"

By then, they had turned the final corner, and they were at the foot of the castle. All five girls got out of the car and Melinda took one of Shanda's arms, Laurie took the other, and they led her up to the dungeon. Hope and Toni followed closely behind, using lighters to illuminate their path. Once in the dungeon, Laurie produced a couple of pieces of rope from her pocket and tied Shanda's ankles while Melinda tied her wrists. They sat her down on a bench. Hope and Toni kept two lighters going which produced eerie shadows on the fallen stone walls.

Melinda began to mock Shanda's looks, asking why she wore her hair that way, why she wore the shoes she wore. She hated the attitude Shanda had about her looks. She hated that Shanda was somehow trying to copy her.

Hope held the knife now, and was harassing Shanda with it. She made Shanda take off her rings and her Mickey Mouse watch. The watch played music and Hope thought it was fun, so she put it on and pressed the button a few times, laughing at Shanda.

"Doesn't she have pretty hair?" Hope teased.

"Yes, Shanda does have pretty hair, and I'm going to cut it off!" Melinda said.

It was a threat she made more than once.

Laurie pointed to the back of the dark dungeon and told Shanda there were bones buried back there.

"It could be you next," she said with a taunting glance. Toni went back down to the car with Laurie and re-

22

turned with a black T-shirt which they tried to set ablaze. It was a black T-shirt with a picture of a yellow smiley face with a bullet in its head. Laurie dowsed it with whiskey and was able to start a small fire.

"That's what you're going to look like, Shanda," Laurie told her.

Shanda couldn't say anything. She was still crying.

All of a sudden, about six cars went by at once and the girls got scared. The castle is private property, and they didn't want to get caught up there. Laurie was afraid people were going to see the flames.

"I know a better place where we can go," Laurie told them, "let's go to this place by my house." Everyone agreed; it was time to get out of The Witches' Castle, and Laurie and Melinda untied Shanda, grabbed hold of her arms, and escorted her back to the car.

Hope was driving, Toni was in the passenger's seat, and Melinda and Laurie had Shanda wedged between them in the back.

"We need gas, we're almost out," Hope said.

But nobody knew where a gas station was.

Shanda told them where she thought there might be an open gas station, Five Star, right near her dad's house. Shanda gave them the directions. Shanda must have felt safer being close to home, perhaps hoping she could recognize somebody and signal for help. But Laurie was one step ahead of her. Just before they pulled in, she covered Shanda with a blanket and she and Melinda stayed in the car to see that Shanda didn't make a move.

Hope pumped the gas, she and Toni went in to pay for it, and they ran into a couple of good-looking guys in a blue convertible on their way back. They struck up a conversation and Toni joked about them taking her home with them, asking if they were headed toward Madison. The guys said they weren't. Hope was getting nervous, thinking Laurie and Melinda might become suspicious about their

23

being gone so long, so they cut the conversation short and hightailed it back to the car.

After they took off, however, they realized they didn't have their bearings. They didn't know how to get back to Madison. They had to stop at another gas station. At the second station, Toni got out and called a friend of hers, Mike, someone she had planned to look up in Louisville. Toni talked with him for a couple of minutes, just chit-chat. Meanwhile, Hope got directions back to Jefferson-ville, and from there she knew she could find their way.

It was about an hour's drive on the isolated country road Route 62, and along the way, Laurie played strange music, industrial punk music, and the other girls got spooked because Laurie started to act strange. Laurie screamed, she cried, she laughed her "Devil" laugh. It was so unusual for Laurie, all these outbursts, she usually showed hardly any emotion at all.

Melinda clutched the knife, holding it in full view. The tip of it reached Toni's back up in the front seat. Shanda was sobbing quietly.

"I just want to talk to you, Shanda," Melinda said in a consoling voice. "I'm not going to hurt you."

When the girls arrived in Madison, Laurie directed Hope to drive down Broad Road, a gravel road that led just past Laurie's house. It was a heavily wooded area, sparsely populated and lightly travelled. After they drove for a few miles, Laurie told Hope to turn down a logging road. It was actually a dirt path, and barely visible at that, and Hope drove through the brambles and dirt until they reached a clearing which was used as a garbage dump.

Everybody got out of the car and walked around for a minute. Toni gave Shanda a hug and said she was sorry.

"Tell them not to hurt me," Shanda pleaded.

Toni turned to Melinda and asked her to take Shanda home.

"Shut up!" Melinda's voice boomed.

Toni was frightened. She and Hope got back in the car. They watched Laurie and Melinda make Shanda take off her clothes. Melinda came running back to the car with the items in her hands.

"I'm going to keep them for souvenirs!" Melinda said as she threw the sweatshirt, jeans, and bra in. Melinda grabbed one of Hope's T-shirts and took it for Shanda to wear. Hope took Shanda's white polka-dotted bra and put it on. She and Toni turned up both available radios, the jam box and the one on the car dashboard. They didn't want to listen to what was going on outside but they couldn't help themselves from watching through the windshield.

"Hit her!" Laurie commanded, holding Shanda's hands behind her back to give Melinda more leverage.

"Melinda, help me . . . please stop . . . don't do this to me," Shanda cried, "I'll stay away from Amanda, please . . ."

"Shut the fuck up!" Melinda howled.

Melinda punched Shanda in the stomach and the little girl went down, holding her stomach, gasping for air.

"Please stop! I have asthma! I can't breathe!" Shanda whimpered.

With Laurie egging her on, Melinda took Shanda's head and slammed it into her knee a couple of times. Shanda's mouth started to bleed profusely.

Then Melinda and Laurie each took one of Shanda's arms and Melinda tried to cut Shanda's throat. Melinda tried to use her foot to push the knife into Shanda's neck, but the knife was too dull. At that point Hope jumped out of the car and tried to hold Shanda down. When she got back in the car, Toni asked her why she was helping them. Hope didn't say anything.

When Toni looked back out the window, Laurie was sitting on Shanda's stomach and Melinda was sitting on her legs. Laurie was trying to strangle her but Shanda was still

25

struggling. Melinda got out the rope and handed it to Laurie. She helped Laurie put it around Shanda's neck. They each took hold of it and pulled as tightly as they could until Shanda was unconscious.

A few minutes went by before Laurie came and tapped on the car window and said that Shanda was knocked out. She needed the keys to the trunk. Hope handed them to her, and Laurie asked that the two of them assist but neither girl budged. They watched as Laurie and Melinda opened the trunk and dragged Shanda; when they put her in, there was a loud thud.

Hope started to cry.

"Is she dead?" Hope asked.

"Yeah," Melinda told her.

"Oh, God! Oh, God!" Hope cried hysterically. She floored the gas pedal, driving frantically to get them out of the woods. Along the way, she hit a log or a bump, and it tore the muffler off the car.

"Oh, shit!" Laurie yelled. The car engine roared in the background.

The girls stopped over at Laurie's house. Laurie went into the kitchen, got some Pepsi and brought it up to her bedroom for everybody to drink. Laurie had on a long dark-colored trench coat similar to Melinda's. There was some blood splattered on it and she quickly washed up in the bathroom.

Hope and Toni were lying on the bed; they told Melinda they were tired. They wanted to go to sleep and wake up and find out that this was all just a bad dream. Just about then, Laurie's dog started barking outside and it startled the girls. All of a sudden—it was barely perceptible—they heard Shanda's muffled screams from the trunk.

"I'll take care of it," Laurie told them.

She raced from the house with a small paring knife in her hand which she had taken from her mother's kitchen.

Moments later, Laurie reappeared with more blood on

her. Shanda's screams had stopped.

After Laurie washed her hands again, she came back to her room, pulled out a velvet pouch which contained Rune "stones" and poured them out onto the bed. She pulled a book out and began reading Melinda's future. Based on the ancient Rune magic which dates back to pagan Viking times, the stones are inscribed with messages, encoded with occult meaning. For Laurie, the stones were better than Tarot cards.

"Everything's going to be okay," she told Melinda.

Laurie made a quick phone call and the others overheard her saying, "It doesn't matter what I need it for! I just need it!"

When she hung up, she suggested that they all go out "country cruisin'." By then, it was after 2:30 in the morning, and Hope and Toni weren't interested. They didn't want to go and Laurie didn't push the issue.

Laurie grabbed her coat, and she and Melinda took off. Their first stop was the garbage burn pile next to Laurie's house. The girls were arguing about what to do with Shanda, and suddenly they heard kicking and screaming coming from the trunk. Somehow, they quieted her.

Laurie was getting nervous about her neighbors because she saw the lights on in their trailer. She figured they might have heard something, so she left Melinda out there in charge of Shanda and decided to go check out the situation. The people there had a working Coke machine on their front porch, and Laurie knocked and asked for change of a dollar, saying she was thirsty.

Her neighbor thought Laurie looked extremely upset, and he asked her if everything was alright. She explained about her muffler being torn off, saying she was going to get in trouble over it. She bought a Coke and left.

Minutes later, Laurie got into the driver's seat and started off toward Canaan, a nearby town. She suggested that they just stay up and drive around all night so Shanda could die slowly. She took them on isolated country roads, Melinda had no idea where they were. Then Shanda started kicking and screaming again, this time clawing at the insides of the trunk.

"I'll make her quiet," Laurie said as she pulled over, taking the trunk key from the ring, directing Melinda to get into the driver's seat.

Melinda was looking in the rearview mirror, watching Laurie open the trunk, and then she saw Laurie throwing punches and she heard Shanda screaming. There was a struggle going on between them, a lot of commotion. Melinda kept her foot on the pedal to drown it out. Suddenly she heard a thump and Laurie slammed the trunk down and came running back inside the car.

"You should have felt it!" Laurie yelped as she banged a black tire tool down on the dashboard. "It was so cool! I went like this and I could feel her head caving in!"

"Smell it!" Laurie said, and she stuck the tire tool up to Melinda's face.

"That's sick! I don't want to smell it!" Melinda protested. The tool was dripping with blood.

Laurie said she'd take over the driving again and they drove for a while. They were thinking about burning Shanda. They stopped the car again and both went back to the trunk to assess the situation.

As the trunk opened, both girls became startled. Shanda sat straight up. Melinda could see the whites of Shanda's eyes; they rolled back up into her head. She was covered in blood. Her hair wasn't blond anymore . . . it was red.

"Mommy," they heard her say as they closed the lid.

After that, Shanda wasn't moaning, she wasn't talking; she was like a zombie. They stopped again and were going to throw her over the bridge, but before they could get her out of the trunk, they saw headlights approaching. Melinda threw the knife down and Laurie quickly slammed the trunk on Shanda.

They continued driving and Shanda started kicking again but this time they couldn't hear any screaming, all they heard was gurgling. They stopped and opened the trunk again and Shanda said "Melinda."

They closed it and kept driving until they heard the banging again. Laurie went back to the trunk by herself. When she came back, Melinda asked what happened.

"You've got to see her, she's soaked with blood. She's red," Laurie yelled.

TWO

The sun was rising and it was almost daylight by the time Laurie and Melinda pulled up at Laurie's house. Hope and Toni heard the dogs barking and jumped out of bed.

"Where's the little girl?" Hope asked as soon as they walked in the bedroom.

"There's no little girl," Laurie said with a twisted look, "it was just a nightmare."

They both had blood on their hands and Melinda had blood on her face. They went to the bathroom to clean up.

When they came back, Hope quizzed them about what they did with Shanda. Eventually, Laurie couldn't contain her glee.

"Every time she screamed, we opened the trunk and hit her over the head with a tire tool!" Laurie told them, laughing.

"We must have hit her like about sixty times!" Melinda bragged, joining Laurie in laughter.

Their conversation woke Laurie's mom; they heard her stirring out in the hallway, and Laurie went out there. Her mom wanted to know who was at the house, and they got into a fight about her being out so late and bringing home a houseful of girls.

Laurie finally said she would take the girls home, and she stormed into the bedroom and got the others moving. She told her mother they were hungry, and that they were going to McDonald's for some breakfast.

They drove over to the burn pile and were talking about burning Shanda, but it was really cold out and the burn pile had a coat of frost on it so they didn't know if it would work. Laurie wanted to show Shanda's body to Hope and Toni but only Hope would get out to look at her. Toni stayed in the front seat and cried to herself as she looked at the girls through the rearview mirror. All she could see was blood and legs. Toni revved the car engine to drown out Shanda's screams.

Hope took a bloodied bottle of Windex from the trunk and sprayed it on Shanda's wounds.

"You're not looking so hot now, are you?" she muttered.

The girls decided they would try to burn Shanda.

Laurie closed the trunk, the girls got in the car, and with Laurie behind the wheel, they headed for town. Their destination: the Clark gas station on Route 62, just a short distance from Madison High School.

Hope pumped some gas into the tank and Toni and Laurie went in to pay for it. Toni wanted to buy some Pepsi and Laurie told her to get a two-liter bottle.

Toni hardly had time to let Hope and Melinda have a sip of the Pepsi before Laurie ordered her to turn the bottle over. Laurie dumped the whole thing out right there at the pumps and then filled it with gasoline. She handed it over to Melinda and went in and paid the fifty-five cents extra that she owed the station.

As she got behind the wheel, Hope was already suggesting a place where they could go to burn Shanda's body. She directed Laurie past the Jefferson Proving Ground site onto a gravel road, Campmeeting Road, located about eight miles outside of Madison. Hope had a friend who lived in that area and she knew the desolate spot well.

They wound up on Lemon Road, a place in the middle of nowhere. It was untouched country, just a lot of farming fields and woods with only an abandoned farmhouse nearby.

Laurie backed the car into the cornfield. The ditch she backed into had frozen over with ice, and she had a bit of trouble maneuvering but she made it. Everybody got out of the car and looked around. Toni got frightened when it came time to open the trunk and she went back into the car, lying down in the backseat so she wouldn't have to watch.

The three girls opened the trunk and saw that Shanda was bleeding badly. Melinda was grossed out, she didn't want to touch her, and Hope finally agreed to help. They wrapped her in the red blanket and lifted her onto the ground. Shanda was clutching the blanket for dear life but she wasn't talking.

"Pour the gasoline on her, Hope," Laurie commanded, handing Hope the two-liter bottle.

"No, you!" Hope handed the bottle back.

"Just do it real quick! Just hurry up and pour it!" Laurie roared.

Hope poured a good amount of the gas on Shanda.

Within seconds, Shanda was on fire.

The girls jumped in the car, got up to a T-intersection in the woods, and Melinda suddenly asked them to stop. She told Laurie to turn the car around, to head back to Shanda. She was afraid the body wasn't burned enough. She wanted to make sure.

There was still some gas left in the Pepsi bottle, and Melinda poured it onto the smoldering body. She stood there for a second and watched it flame up again, then she threw the Pepsi bottle down. She told the girls that Shanda's tongue was going in and out of her mouth and she made

32

fun about that when she got back in the car.

"You should have seen it. It was so funny" Melinda said. "I'm glad she's dead! I'm glad she's out of me and Amanda's life!"

No one said much. Toni was biting her hand as hard as she could. She almost drew blood.

Hope suggested they go to McDonald's to get something to eat so they made their way back to civilization. It was 9:30 A.M. when Laurie and Melinda went up to the fast-food counter; meanwhile, Toni used the McDonald's phone to call her friend Mikel, who was "covering" for her that particular night. Toni just wanted to check to see if her mom had called Mikel's place. Toni was talking real fast, nervously saying she was on her way home.

"Toni, what's wrong?" Mikel asked.

"Nothing."

"I know you better than that! Something's wrong, Toni. What is it?" she prodded.

"Well, I went out with Laurie and Hope and Melinda and something bad happened."

"What happened?"

"Well . . ."

"Was it a car wreck?"

"No, worse than that . . ."

"Okay, what?"

"They killed somebody."

"Who?"

"It was a girl named Shanda . . . and they beat her with a crowbar and they tried to slit her throat . . ."

Toni started reeling off the events so quickly that Mikel could hardly understand her.

"And they made me look in the trunk to see this girl's body . . . there was blood everywhere . . ."

Toni couldn't talk anymore. She was afraid that the other girls would catch her, so she hung up with Mikel and joined the others at their table. Laurie wasn't eating much

33

and she agreed that it was time to drop Toni off at home. She dropped Hope off at home, too, and then headed back over to her house. She needed to get the car fixed up before she could drive much farther.

When they got inside, Laurie's parents were having breakfast at the table, and Laurie and Melinda sat down with them. Melinda thought Laurie's mom was very sweet and she tried to have a friendly conversation with the lady, all the while nervously picking at her nails.

Laurie asked her mother if she could stay over at Melinda's that night.

"Is it okay with you Melinda? Did you call your mom?" her mother asked.

Melinda lied and said yes.

Laurie asked her dad to get under the car and fix the muffler for her. While he was busy doing that, Melinda cleaned out the inside of the car, taking articles of clothing, fast-food paper bags, and other things, throwing them onto the burn pile for immediate disposal. Through it all, Melinda was a nervous wreck.

After her dad fixed the muffler, the two girls drove around to the side of the house and got a hose, opened the trunk, and sprayed all the blood out. Laurie found something that looked like a bloody piece of skin, and she picked it up and was feeling it and looking at it.

"Look, it's a piece of her head," Laurie said.

Melinda hit Laurie's hand and it dropped to the ground.

Laurie called Hope, finding out that she wanted the two of them to come over right away. She was home alone and she was afraid. The two girls got to Hope's house just a short while later, discovering that Hope was in a state of panic. No one was there to let them in, and all they could hear was sobbing coming from Hope's back bedroom.

They walked back there and Hope was sitting on her bed crying, saying she couldn't believe it. She was holding Shanda's Mickey Mouse watch, just staring at it. They were trying to calm her down, and Hope finally placed the watch on her dresser. In an attempt to keep Hope quiet, Laurie decided to pull the "stones" out to do a reading. She threw them out on the bed and studied them a while.

"Everything's going to be okay, Hope. We're all going to be alright," she assured her.

They all went and sat in the living room to watch TV. Hope's mom came home shortly thereafter with her tiny grandchild, Hope's nephew, in her arms. They watched television for about a half hour, Laurie was talking to Hope's mom and Hope was holding the baby, and everything was peaceful.

Melinda called her mother to say that she was doing okay, and not long after, she and Laurie were on their way back to New Albany. At about 3:00 P.M. that afternoon, they arrived at Melinda's house. No one was home, and Laurie clicked MTV on as Melinda headed for the phone.

The first person Melinda called was her best friend Crystal Wathen, telling her to come over right away. She wouldn't talk details over the telephone. When Melinda called Amanda's house a little while later, her dad said Amanda was at the mall, so she called the mall and had Amanda paged. Within minutes, the phone rang. It was a collect call from Amanda.

"Can we come pick you up? Something really bad has happened. I need to talk to you, I need to be with you," Melinda was sobbing.

"What?"

"Shanda is dead."

"You're joking! You're stupid!" Amanda said in disbelief.

"No, she's really dead."

Amanda agreed to let Melinda pick her up, and they arranged a meeting place and an approximate time. By then, Crystal walked through the door and Melinda ran up and hugged her.

"You know you're my best friend," she told Crystal. "I love you . . . There's somebody in the living room I want you to meet, it's Laurie."

Laurie was lying on the couch with a blanket wrapped around her just blankly staring at the TV. Melinda introduced them, and the two girls seemed to hit if off right away. As Melinda and Laurie started describing the whole ordeal to Crystal, both of them were talking at once and sometimes they'd argue about what happened.

It was a story that lasted all day long. The two of them went over every detail and then they'd remember something else and go back and add that in. They told Crystal that Shanda was trying to claw her way through the trunk to the backseat, and they all got scared and sat up in the front seat together. They said Shanda was screaming and hollering through the back of the trunk, and it was coming through into the car. They said when they opened the trunk, Shanda sat up and was rocking back and forth.

Crystal thought they were playing with her, but in the middle of their conversation, Laurie took the knife out of her trench coat pocket and showed it to Crystal. She said it was her mom's kitchen knife. She said they used it to stab Shanda in the back of the head.

After Crystal heard these initial particulars, the three of them drove over to the River Falls Mall in Clarksville, about ten minutes away, to pick up Amanda. Crystal drove the car because Laurie said she was too shaken up to drive, and Melinda was crying for most of the ride.

"I've done something bad," she cried to Amanda as soon as she saw her.

Amanda waited silently for an explanation.

"Everybody just wait until we get back to Melinda's house," Laurie told them.

Back in Melinda's living room, they sat Amanda down and started to go over it again. This time, the story became even more confusing because all three people were talking to her at once. Then Melinda started crying hysterically, and she and Amanda went upstairs alone together to talk in private.

"You're not mad, are you?" Melinda wanted to know.

"No," Amanda told her.

"I feel like it's my fault," Melinda cried.

"It's not, baby. It's going to be okay," Amanda said.

Amanda gave her a hug. She really didn't believe that any part of the story was true.

When they went back downstairs, Laurie was insisting on showing everyone the trunk. She could see that neither Crystal nor Amanda were taking the whole thing too seriously, and she wanted to prove it to them.

Even though it had been hosed down, the trunk still had blood all over it. The four girls could even make out Shanda's bloody handprints on the inside lid. Shanda's socks were in there; they were covered with blood.

"Now do you believe it?" Laurie asked.

"I just wanted to beat Shanda up and scare her, but we just got carried away," Melinda said.

Amanda felt sick to her stomach. She walked away and tried to puke on the side of the house and came back a minute later and told them to take her home. Laurie drove, giving the evil eye to Amanda through the rearview mirror.

When the three girls got back, Melinda's stepdad was home, so the details had to continue quietly upstairs. Crystal stayed for hours, and the day passed quickly because none of them could stop talking about each gory thing that happened. Melinda's phone rang a lot; she was telling her friends that something happened but she couldn't say what. She'd disappear every so often and take a shower, then come back to the bedroom and start crying hysterically again.

"Will God forgive me?" Melinda asked her friend.

"God will forgive you for anything if you're really remorseful for what you've done," Crystal promised.

"I don't believe in God," Laurie started laughing. "And I don't feel bad anymore about killing Shanda."

Steve Sharer had been up since 4:30 A.M. At that time he noticed that the back door was slightly open, but he figured it was his stepson Larry who didn't shut the door all the way. He went and pushed it closed and locked it and looked around in the bedrooms and didn't see Shanda, but he guessed that Shanda was probably asleep in the family room in the basement. He didn't think much about it.

He dozed off for a few more hours. It was about 7:00 A.M. when he got dressed and started the coffee, and his wife Sharon came into the kitchen.

"Is Shanda in here?"

"No, I think she's downstairs but I haven't gone down there."

Sharon quickly went down to check. There was no Shanda.

They went over what Steve did at 4:30 A.M. that morning and finally he said, "I locked that door . . . you know, if she had stepped out she probably got locked out."

Steve and Sharon went outside and looked in his van and their other car. Steve noticed that his rottweiler was limping, acting like she had been hurt in her hindquarter. He thought maybe the dog had been struck.

"What in the heck's going on here," Steve asked out loud.

He called over to Michelle's house, thinking that perhaps Shanda decided to spend the night over there, but Michelle had no idea where Shanda was. Steve concluded it would just be a process of elimination. He started calling all of Shanda's friends, but he was having no luck. The people he called were growing increasingly concerned and by that afternoon, many of them were calling him back to see if Shanda had been found.

At 1:00 P.M. Steve finally called Shanda's mother, Jackie. She arrived minutes later, and the two of them decided to file a missing person's report. Someone from the local Sheriff's Department came over and took the information. After he left, Jackie suggested that they comb the area, so they went down to New Albany and looked around the Hazelwood schoolyard and any other place they could think of, but they found no signs of Shanda.

Three

Saturday, January 11, 1992, was a crisp sunny day. Donn Foley and his brother Ralph had left Canaan early to go hunting for quail. They went over to the Jefferson Proving Ground, a government facility where ammunition is tested. After winding through the fields and farms on County Road 1133 for about eight miles, Ralph spotted something that looked like a burned pile of rags on the roadside. But as they got nearer, Donn thought it might be one of those blow-up plastic dolls that somebody burned as a prank.

The brothers stopped the truck to take a closer look.

Donn decided he'd have to touch it to tell for sure, and he scratched the toenail. Standing in an open field next to a pool of water, he suddenly realized he had come upon the burned corpse of a young woman. It was the kind of sight he hadn't seen since his days in Vietnam.

Her face and upper body were charred beyond recognition. Some layers of skin flapped in the wind. As he knelt at her side, the Foleys looked in horror at the flesh that was still visible on the lower half of her body. Her legs were bloodied and spread wide open. She was nude except for a pair of blue panties which had been pulled to one side.

It was 10:55 A.M. by the time the brothers got back to

Canaan and called the police. They were asked to return to the body until the deputy sheriff, Randle Spry, could arrive, and within a half hour, the deputy reached the scene, marking off the tire tracks that ran through the edge of the field by the body. Both the body and the tracks were in a mud hole which had frozen over.

When Jefferson County Sheriff Buck Shippley arrived, he called the Indiana State Police and requested a technician and a detective for a detail. It was just before noon when Trooper Detective Steve Henry received a phone call at his home from a sergeant at the Sellersburg Post. Forensic expert Sergeant Curtis Wells received a call at the same time.

It would take each man an hour to travel to the northern part of Jefferson County. They dropped everything to get there, both arriving simultaneously just minutes after 1:00 P.M. Deputy Spry informed the men that he had Lemon Road blocked off to secure the scene of the crime.

Both Curtis Wells and Steve Henry thought someone was playing a practical joke when they looked over at what was lying on the south side of the roadway.

"We drive around and I get out and I look. . . . Because I know the sheriff—he and I used to be state troopers together—I know he likes to pull pranks sometimes," Wells recalled, "and I'm thinking surely he wouldn't do this to me on a Saturday morning."

"What kind of joke is this?" Wells said. "That's a mannequin!"

"No, it isn't," Shippley told him.

As the men got closer, it was apparent that it was the dead body of a young white female. She had been badly burned in the face and both hands were charred. A flammable substance had been used in an attempt to make the face and fingerprints unidentifiable.

There was a pool of blood underneath her head. Her legs were slightly bent and raised at the knees; her hands

41

were in the classic clinched "boxer" position associated with a fire victim, tightened up from the reaction to the intense heat. Both the hands were partially covered in a pseudo-casting material; whatever material she was holding had melted down, forming red casts. Along with the face and upper torso, the hair had obvious thermal damage. There were clumps of hair that had burned off. There were other clumps that were blackened, matted, and stiff like a paintbrush.

Lesser thermal damage existed on the lower torso of the body but it was an equally horrifying sight. She had some blistering on her legs from the heat, and the victim's blue panties were only partially burned; they appeared to be purposely pulled slightly to the left side around the vagina. The anus of the deceased had an unusually wide opening, and the body appeared to be "posed" in a sexual way which suggested some kind of sick molestation.

"They wanted her body found in that position. I think it was because they wanted to show that she was a bad girl," Wells later said. "There's no doubt in my mind the body was posed. When I first looked at that I thought the panties could have been moved to the side in order for them to insert something."

Wells took video footage of the surrounding area and the primary scene. He also took 35mm photographs and some Polaroid shots. He marked and photographed the tire prints on the gravel road as well as the tire print left in the muddy grass area near the body. A single shoe print, also located near the body, was photographed and videotaped. Plaster casts were then made. The tire print closest to the body, the one that made police think that a vehicle pulled in and dumped the body out, turned out to be from a truck tire.

Just to the north of the body was a blackened, melted plastic bottle which appeared to be a soft drink container. It was burned beyond recognition, so no fingerprints would be identifiable from it. A partially melted plastic bottle top was also located.

Before the deputy coroner of Jefferson County took custody of the body, Wells collected hair samples from a scalp that was wet with blood. From the right hand, a slightly charred Jeffersonville High School girl's class ring, with the initials SGH, was removed. From the left ear, a gold-colored post earring was detached. The feet, hands, and head were bagged to protect and preserve any trace evidence, and then the two men lifted the corpse into a body bag. The body was taken to Jefferson County Morgue pending autopsy at the Kentucky State Medical Examiner's Office in Louisville. Examination of the body prior to its removal discovered no obvious wounds associated with a stabbing or shooting victim.

Sheriff Shippley spotted tire prints at the intersection of Jefferson Church Road and Lemon Road which had the same class characteristics of some of those found near the primary scene. Wells and Shippley came to the conclusion that the suspect vehicle had turned south onto Jefferson Church Road then appeared to come to a quick stop at the intersection, as evidenced by the skid marks in the gravel near the intersection.

Approximately one tenth of a mile south of the intersection in a curved portion of the road, investigators found additional tire prints. Wells took photographs of these areas and then called an accident reconstructionist who assisted him in the crime scene drawing. From the little they had to go on, Wells was certain that the only conclusive evidence would come from obtaining a search warrant and going through the vehicle itself — once they found it.

After completing all the technical work at the scene, Curtis Wells, Steve Henry, and Buck Shippley stopped for something to eat. All three men were longtime buddies and had been on the force for many years, but none of them had ever seen anything as shocking as this. For Steve

Henry, who had recently been promoted to detective, it would be his first murder case. Shippley surmised the body belonged to a woman in her twenties. He was convinced that the woman was not from Madison or anywhere nearby. After all, crimes like that didn't happen in Madison. Besides, they didn't have any missing person's reports.

The three law officials thought that maybe the killing was a result of a drug deal gone wrong in nearby Indianapolis and that the victim had been brought to this rural district and pushed out of the car by a gang of thugs. "I had to assume the body dumped here came from another part of the world," Shippley later told the press. "It was a crime that had all the markings of a big-city slaying."

What they couldn't understand was why the killers didn't try to hide their crime in any way. The corpse had been left just a few feet off the side of the road in an open cornfield. The killers could have moved the body just a couple of yards into a patch of dense forest where it might not have been discovered for months. It was almost like they wanted the first passer-by to see it.

At 8:20 P.M. that night, just minutes after they walked in the door, a fifteen-year-old boy, Shawn Pyles, came down to the jail to report a disturbing conversation he overheard at Andersons Bowling Alley, the local teen hangout. He heard a couple of girls saying that they'd witnessed a murder. The girls were kind of bragging about it but they seemed nervous. He thought they might be serious.

As the three lawmen were digesting Pyles's statement, the Madison police called and interrupted their interview. One of the girls from the bowling alley, fifteen-year-old Toni Lawrence, had shown up at the local police station. She was hysterical, saying she wanted to talk about the case. She was directed to go to the Sheriff's Department, and she arrived moments later, accompanied by her parents.

A delicate girl with large glasses and mousy brown hair, Toni's rambling came out in confused bits at first. Toni told the lawmen that the victim, Shanda, was from New Albany. She said she thought Shanda was thirteen. By now she had calmed down somewhat and she was ready to make a statement to Henry and Shippley. She was read her rights, her parents signed a waiver for her, and Toni and her father Clifton sat down in the sheriff's small office.

From time to time, one of the two men would break from the interview to report information to Wells, asking him to make some follow-up phone calls. Wells made contact with the New Albany Police Department and was advised that there was no missing person's report of a teenage girl utilizing the first name Shanda. The Floyd County Sheriff's Department in New Albany was also contacted, but the dispatcher on duty had no such missing person's report filed.

Back in the sheriff's office, Steve Henry turned on the tape recorder and listened to the rest of Toni Lawrence's statement about the events of January 10 and 11, 1992. Toni told the police that the previous evening she had gone to New Albany, Indiana, about forty miles south along the Ohio River, with two friends, fifteen-year-old Hope Rippey and seventeen-year-old Laurie Tackett. They drove in Tackett's beige car and picked up a friend of Laurie's. Toni did not know the exact address of Laurie's friend in New Albany. Her name was Melinda. That's all she knew. She did not know her last name. She believed Melinda was about sixteen years old, but she wasn't sure. Toni had never seen her before.

In her original statement, Toni said that when they left Melinda's residence, Laurie was driving and they went to a hard-core punk rock show on Preston Highway in Louisville. She explained to Henry that after leaving Louisville, Melinda started talking about Shanda, saying that Shanda was trying to steal her girlfriend, saying that she would like to kill Shanda.

"Is that when she started talking about this Shanda . . . after you went to Louisville?" Henry asked.

"She started talking about her when we were in Louisville. . . . She said she just wanted to teach her a lesson. . . . Okay, Melinda is a lesbian," Toni said.

"Okay."

"And Melinda's girlfriend is Amanda and Shanda has been messing around with Amanda."

"Wait a minute, Melinda's girlfriend is who?"

"Amanda."

"Amanda from?"

"New Albany."

It was hard for Toni to get the times and names and places straight herself, but Toni finally did get specific about Shanda's residence, telling them that she thought the address was 509 Capitol Hills Drive in Jeffersonville. Immediately, Henry took another break in the interview, giving Wells the new information whereupon Wells contacted the Jeffersonville Police Department.

Jeffersonville had a missing person's report on a female juvenile, but it was several days old and did not appear to match. However when Wells called the Clark County Sheriff's Department, he discovered that Lieutenant Terry Hubler had taken a missing person's report from 905 Capitol Hills Drive in Jeffersonville, on Shanda Renee Sharer, white female, date of birth, age *twelve*.

Born in the East Kentucky mountain town, Pineville, Shanda was five feet tall, weighed one hundred pounds, and had last been seen wearing stone-washed jeans, a black sweatshirt, and brown suede shoes.

Wells called Detective Howard Henry at the Sellersburg Post and updated him on the investigation. There was no positive identification of the body yet, but Wells asked Henry to go over to the Capitol Hills subdivision and talk to Steve Sharer to see what additional information he could come up with. He advised Henry to be careful about what he said because even though they felt they had the right person, all of the information didn't match up exactly. The address was flip-flopped, Toni said it was 509 instead of 905, and that the girl was thirteen, not twelve. He couldn't let Henry walk in there and say "your daughter is dead" when it was still possible that she might walk through the door an hour later.

Detective Howard Henry was as non-alarmist as possible when he went over to ask some basic questions about the circumstances surrounding Shanda's departure. He was trying to get information about the girls Toni mentioned, what they looked like, what kind of car they drove, but Steve had little to tell him.

"Is anything missing from her room?" the detective asked.

But a search of the room Shanda slept in proved to be fruitless. Henry discovered that Shanda stayed with her mother in New Albany most of the time, and would later request to search Shanda's room there as well. He obtained the dental records under the premise that he was investigating a missing person.

Back in Madison, between Toni's sobs and hysterics, she managed to tell the authorities her version of what happened the night before. She talked about Melinda hiding herself on the floorboard, about Hope Rippey and Laurie Tackett going up to Shanda's door. She said Shanda voluntarily left the residence with them. She went over the incident in the car when Melinda came up out of the backseat and put a knife to Shanda's throat. She explained that they took Shanda to a witches' castle on Utica Pike, she wasn't sure what town it was. Unfortunately, her graphic description of what went on there turned into a kind of rambling that sounded like plain teenage dribble, and the police weren't getting a clear picture.

"At The Witches' Castle, we walked up there . . . they took her up there and Laurie tied her legs and hands. . . . they said they were going to cut her hair off . . . and the whole time Shanda's crying saying 'please don't do this Laurie. Please. Please don't kill me.' And then Shanda goes, 'Well my brother will come out looking for me and when he comes and doesn't find me there.' And then Melinda goes, 'Are you trying to scare us?' and Shanda goes, 'No.' Then Melinda goes, 'Well just shut up.' "

"Did you get the impression that these girls had been to The Witches' Castle before?" Henry asked.

"Laurie said she had."

"Okay, but why, why would they go there?"

"Laurie, she used to be a Pentecostal, and she quit and then she got back into church and then she quit again and then she got in all these cults . . . and they drink . . . blood."

"They drink what?"

"Each other's blood."

Henry and Shippley were speechless.

Toni told the authorities that after the castle, they went to a place near Laurie Tackett's house, and she and Hope stayed in the car while Laurie and Melinda tried to strangle Shanda.

"But she wasn't dead yet . . ." Toni said, moving the story along, "we all went up to Laurie's house and Laurie read Melinda's stones or something. Like this weird cult thing that Laurie's into. And then me and Hope went to sleep and Laurie and Melinda left and they didn't tell us where they were going."

She said that when they got back, Laurie and Melinda were talking about how they hit Shanda in the head with a crowbar. Then they said they were going to burn Shanda, but first they said they would drop Toni off at home.

"After they dropped you off they were going to burn her?" Toni's father interrupted.

"Yes."

"After they dropped you off this morning?" Henry wanted to know.

"They even went and got gasoline."

"On the way home . . . on the way to bring you home?" her father asked.

"They stopped at Clark."

"They got gasoline on the way?" he prodded.

"On the way to my house."

"This morning?" Henry asked.

Toni shook her head yes, and Buck Shippley picked up the line of questioning.

"When you left Laurie's house, did they take you to your house?"

"Yeah."

"Did Hope go with you when they took you home?"

"Yeah."

"And they did not say to you what they did after they left the house?"

"They said they beat her in the head and they were going to burn her."

"Okay, at what point did they drop you off at your house?"

"At 9:45 A.M. this morning. I didn't come home until this morning."

Then Toni's father spoke up again.

"When they said they was going to burn her, was that after they dropped you off or before?" he asked.

"Before."

"And they dropped you off and they were going to burn her?" he rephrased the question.

"Yes," Toni said.

"They took you home . . . what time did you arrive home again?" Shippley asked.

Toni sat thinking.

The sheriff reminded her, "Quarter till ten . . . and they stopped at the Clark station on the way."

Toni shook her head yes.

"And when did you see in the trunk?" her father interjected.

"When they had her on the ground. They took her out on the ground because Laurie had a butcher knife and that's when . . . God . . . they were going to stab her or something . . . they didn't stab her, they beat her over the head and then I looked up and . . . the blood was on the trunk."

"Did Shanda appear to be alive?" Henry asked.

"Yes."

"This morning?"

"Yes."

And that concluded the first interview with Toni.

When the men came out of the office, they learned that Curtis Wells had identified the car and had also contacted a Floyd County probation officer, Virgil Seay, who informed him that he had a complaint made against a young lesbian, Melinda Loveless, filed by Amanda Heavrin's father. Seay had in his possession letters written by Melinda Loveless to Amanda Heavrin.

A Positive ID came in from the dental records of Shanda Sharer.

Within minutes, Detective Howard Henry was on his way to talk to the dead girl's parents.

Part Two

The Girls

Four

New Albany sits in a cluster of three Indiana cities, along with Clarksville and Jeffersonville, all of which are considered a part of the Louisville metropolitan area. There is a pleasant downtown area with one or two antique stores, a couple of specialty shops, and a farmer's market, all of which give it an old-world charm. For the most part, the prevailing atmosphere is family-oriented which tends to make even a visitor feel safe and sound.

Back in the mid-sixties, when Marjorie Lasley married Larry Loveless, she was sure she had married her way into the all-American dream. She was just sixteen and a junior in high school; he was twenty. To Margie, Larry was a dream come true. She was in awe of his brand-new 1966 Oldsmobile, the first car that she had ever been out on a date in.

Having lived in New Albany all her life, Margie had a big church wedding at the Speed Memorial Church. The affair was quite elegant, with the whole bridal party wearing white, the ushers and groom in white jackets and black bow ties. The bride was a bit plump, as were her bridesmaids, and the groom looked a little too young, as did his best man, but Margie and Larry had nothing but high hopes for the future. They had already found a small apartment on McDonald Avenue, not far from Margie's parents.

Their honeymoon was at the Colonial Inn in nearby Clarksville, where the young lovers spent a hot summer weekend. For Margie it was somewhat like a fairy tale.

"Here I was, this bride, I had all these fancy negligees, he carried me over the threshold, he did all that," she recalled.

But one thing bothered her. Larry was too sex-oriented, and having been a virgin when she met him, she didn't know how to handle it. All weekend, not once did he take her out for a romantic dinner, all he wanted to do was stay in bed and have food sent up to the room.

Still, when they moved into their one-room place, things were looking good for them. Larry worked at the Fine Shirt Factory in New Albany and promised her they'd have lots of money one day. Meanwhile she put fifty-nine cent Banquet TV dinners in the oven and was satisfied with going out to eat at Frisch's, a local coffee house, once a week. She was still in high school, hoping to go on to become a nurse.

But after just four months of marriage, the first real sign of trouble occurred when Larry started following Margie to school, tracking her down in the hallways, making all kinds of accusations. He became so jealous and enraged by the thought that she was getting attention from other boys that Margie finally quit before graduating.

Even more alarming, an awful incident occurred when Larry's brother Danny came over to spend the weekend with one of his girlfriends. Margie said she found her new husband attacking her brother-in-law's date.

"I go to sleep, and I heard some noise, I wake up, and there's Larry Loveless at the foot of the bed on the floor with this girl, and they were kissing, and I went nuts," Margie said. "No telling what he did to her. I never saw her again."

Within the first year of their marriage, Larry Loveless

got drafted into the army. In May of 1967, he completed training in Fort Knox, and was on his way to Vietnam. Margie cried a lot because she didn't want him to leave, she had just discovered she was pregnant and she was scared. She decided she would return to her parent's home, shutting down the little studio apartment. Larry agreed to send her his paycheck every month, which he did faithfully. While in Nam, Larry wrote to her often, "Make sure you're a good little girl, that you're staying at home," he'd tell her.

While he was over there he even sent for Margie once, asking her to meet him in Hawaii by herself, and she went, leaving her newborn girl, Michelle, behind in New Albany. It was her first time on a plane and the whole trip was a big thrill for her, seeing Larry and showing him pictures of their baby, going out for exotic drinks, and of course, making up for a lot of lost time in bed. But Larry managed to put a damper on things by accusing Margie of cheating on him. He questioned her relentlessly about it.

After a thirteen-month tour of duty, Larry still had six months left to serve when he returned to the States. He was a hero when he got to New Albany. There was a write-up about him in the local paper.

Margie and Michelle went with him to Fort Hood, Texas, while he completed his military service. They lived in a one-room hotel apartment, and it was the only time Margie ever lived out of the New Albany area, so she felt very much out of her element. She was also discovering that Larry was somehow different — often he'd stay out all night, claiming he was on field trips, but she knew he was lying. When she asked him where he'd been, she was told not to question him.

One of the first things Larry did upon his return was to have all of his teeth pulled. Even though his teeth were fine and the dentist was against the idea, Larry insisted that it be done because some of his back teeth were bothering him. Since the Army was footing the bill, he wanted them all out. He claimed they were rotting away, and he wanted a perfect smile. He was happier with dentures.

All along, Margie grew increasingly homesick. She was trying to adjust to dealing with a baby, and Larry just made things harder for her because all he wanted to do was get her drunk and have sex. He was acting weird, doing strange things around the apartment. More than once, she caught him laying in bed, wearing her underwear; often he was forcing himself on her in the baby's presence.

"Some of our biggest arguments were over sex because I just wouldn't do it if Michelle was awake," Margie reflected. "It was then I knew he was a pervert, because I'd be missing my underwear, they wouldn't be where I had put them, they'd be moved."

In addition, Margie was finding out that her husband had a mean streak. At one point, he chased down a neighbor, beating the man with a broomstick because the guy had talked to Margie in a slightly provocative way. He was so jealous and possessive that he became suspicious of her every last move, constantly threatening to leave her in Texas with no money and no way back to Indiana. He wasn't the person she thought she had married, but yet she had a commitment and a child. She felt locked in.

When they returned to New Albany, Margie couldn't have been more relieved. She found a duplex apartment on McDonald Avenue, even closer to her parents this time, but her problems with Larry only got worse. In addition to his jealousy, Larry had also developed a big chip on his shoulder about being a veteran. It was a ploy he used to get his way.

What compounded the matter was that everybody treated him like a hero, especially his parents and his in-laws. He was cocky about it, saying that he fought for his country, now he'd do whatever he wanted to, bragging that he killed a lot of people over there—men, women, and children. He had a worldly air all of a sudden, claiming that he had seen it all, done it all, that he had even tortured people.

Suddenly Larry had a great fascination with guns and was regularly going target shooting at a range, The Shell Farm, sometimes insisting that Margie join him. He started to collect guns, spending every spare dime on them. He began sleeping with a gun under his pillow.

Larry was also becoming a compulsive neat freak. When she first met him, Margie was proud that he cleaned his car every day, shining and polishing the chrome, rubbing it down inside and out. But now, in their apartment, Larry was insisting that the place be organized his way. He was very particular about everything, down to the finest detail. The way his pillow was laid on the bed, for instance—it had to be just so. He didn't want anything moved out of its spot. One time Margie decided to rearrange the living-room furniture, just to have a change, and Larry came home and threw an absolute fit.

Margie finally confronted him about his neurotic behavior and Larry blamed it on his mother's cleaning disease. She'd make him wear white ironed shirts all the time and if he would get dirty, or if he messed up his room, he'd get punished, he told her.

"I always thought Larry was beat as a child by his mother, because Larry told me that she used to lock him in the closet," Margie said. "She was real strict on him about being clean. He said she'd lock him in there for a couple hours, and this went on until he was thirteen. He said she'd whip him with a belt."

And then there was the problem with Michelle. He treated the baby badly, hitting her for crying even though she was just an infant. (One of Michelle's earliest memories is of being hit in the head in a crib.) Later, when it came time for potty training, Larry beat Michelle up so many times that he himself felt compelled to apologize to his daughter about it when she got old enough to "understand." Although he would perform some fatherly duties, such as bathing her and changing her diapers, it was odd the way he would touch her private parts or fondle certain areas.

But Marjorie said nothing. Even though she suspected that his behavior was inappropriate, she was a naive seventeen-year-old who never had sex education, who grew up in an era when people said sex was something you did to have babies. She loved her husband — he always told her she meant the world to him — and she didn't want to believe that he would do anything that would cause harm to their child.

As for the rest of her family, none of them got along with Larry. They didn't appreciate the fact that Larry didn't properly support his family. Too often, he'd go to his parents for money, or have Margie go to them. It wasn't that he didn't earn enough, it was that he was too busy buying toys for himself, mostly guns and motorcycles. As for Margie's three sisters, they wanted little or nothing to do with Larry or his family. This was especially the case for her closest sister, Freda, who had a bad feeling about the Loveless clan right from the start.

"Marjorie and Larry were married and the first time I met his dad, he laid a kiss on me, like, he threw his tongue down my throat," Freda recalled. "And I thought, well, my God! To me, it made me sick."

According to Freda, his mom wasn't much of a prize either. She classified her as a fruitcake, as someone who had a compulsive cleaning sickness. She was impossible to be around, cleaning up under the very plate you were still eating from.

The final blow for Freda came the night she stayed over at Larry and Margie's apartment when she was just thirteen years old. Larry invited her to sleep in their bed with them. She thought it was a curious request, but being so young, she went along with the idea because Larry was telling her that he was her brother, that they were all family. After the lights went out and Margie fell asleep, Larry reached over and put his hand down Freda's panties. She jumped up, woke Margie, asked to be taken home, claiming she didn't feel well, and that was the last time she ever got too near him.

As for Margie, who was highly suspicious of Larry's every move at that point, it came as no surprise when she discovered that Larry had his first full-blown affair. They hadn't been back in New Albany for long. When the woman came to Margie and confessed about it, Margie cried and cried and then questioned Larry, but he denied it and slammed her up against the door. That's when the real violence started, as well as the verbal abuse, but by then Margie was pregnant again, and would soon give birth to another beautiful girl, Melissa.

After she came home from the hospital, Larry told her she was ugly, that she was fat, that nobody would have her anymore. In the same breath, he'd accuse her of being a whore. Margie finally realized that she needed her independence, that she would have to get away from Larry's insanity and cruelty, but not before she could support herself and the children. It would take her years to finish a high-school equivalency program and, with the help of her parents, nursing school. In the interim, however, Margie stayed with Larry and managed to have her first affair. He was a neighbor who paid some attention to Margie, someone who was nice to her, gentle with her.

Larry had worked at Sears since he'd returned to New Albany. In 1971, he landed himself a job at Southern Railroad in Louisville, and finally started making good money. He discovered the Louisville bar scene, and he began taking Margie out to singles bars, always introducing her as his girlfriend. He'd ask her to dress up in miniskirts, high heels, and black stockings. He'd tell people he was a doctor or a dentist, always somebody important, and usually claimed to be from Texas, even though he had no Texan accent. On their way to the bars, Larry would break out his flask of cheap whiskey and have Margie swallow a few gulps. Then, if she wouldn't agree to go home with a couple and switch partners, it would lead to a big argument, one that she always would lose in the end.

Larry's control over her completely erased any semblance of her self-esteem. She wasn't Margie, she was Larry's robot; it made other people around her cringe.

"I knew about how Larry liked to watch her having sex with other men. She told me about that," Freda confided. "I remember how he would beat her up, then make her go out and get drunk and dress up like a slut."

But Margie didn't really see herself. She lived for her two little daughters and the prophecy of fulfilling the American dream: the house, the two-car garage, the clothes, and everybody happy.

Within a year of Larry's employment at the railroad, Larry decided to buy their first home. He and Margie picked out a brand-new place, and Margie was ecstatic. By that time, Michelle was becoming a little lady, almost four, and their second girl, Melissa, was still in diapers, cute as a button.

Larry's parents, Harold and June, gave them the $800 down payment for a three-bedroom brick house at 2216 Palmer Court. It was near a woodsy area on the outskirts of town, with a big park nearby where Larry would take the girls on "walks."

The house on Palmer Court sat at the end of a cul-de-sac, which Margie thought would be perfect for the kids. They could play, and she wouldn't have to be worried about cars. Even though it was a quiet neighborhood, not long after they moved in, Larry insisted on fencing in the backyard, and oddly enough, he failed to put in a gate. The only way the girls could get off the property was to go through the garage.

But Margie didn't even think about that. She loved her big country kitchen and large utility room, and she was busy decorating, picking avocado green for the carpeting and floors. They bought a brand-new living-room set and new bedroom sets; Larry felt comfortable living on credit.

It didn't take long for him to cultivate some bosom buddies at the railroad, and he started bringing them home. He worked the second shift, until 11:00 P.M., and then he'd go out and get drunk, staggering through the door between midnight and 1:00 A.M. Margie had usually fallen asleep on the couch by then, but she'd hear them come in, and play hostess as best she could. There was one friend in particular, Pete, who began to come over on a regular basis. At first they were just friendly calls, but it didn't take long for it to turn into something quite different.

"Larry told me to have a drink, and he'd pinch me, hard, and I knew if I didn't we'd have a big fight, so I'd give in. Then he'd say, Pete, it's okay, it's okay. I'd have two, three drinks, he'd always have music on, rock music, Rolling Stones, Doobie Brothers, and he'd say, 'Pete, it's okay, she's my wife and you're my best friend and I'll share her with you.' That's what he always said. And then he'd pinch me again, and tell me to be a good girl, and then before you know it, I was fucking Pete," Margie remembered. "He was fat, big, a big heavyset man. I hated him. I thought we were gonna be friends, you know, social, I even met his wife, and I liked her. They had two little girls."

The "parties" with Pete became more frequent. There were at least a dozen sex scenes with Pete, during which Larry started engaging in homosexual activity, something which Margie witnessed and participated in. She was mortified, but it wasn't until her four-year-old daughter Michelle came out of the room and caught them one night, that Margie became disgusted enough to say anything. It was something that Michelle would never forget. She heard them from her bedroom and got scared. She couldn't go back to sleep. There was too much noise.

"I heard moaning and groaning, and it scared me," Michelle confided. "So I crawled out of bed, and I crawled, and I opened the door and I crawled down the hall. I stayed pretty low. I don't know, I peeked around the corner into the living room at the couch on that wall, and I just seen. I knew what was going on. I just remember seeing my dad and Pete and my mom. And after that, well, I mean, I learned to stay in my room."

When Margie saw Michelle in the hallway and she told Larry, he acted like he didn't believe her. He didn't care.

"It's never going to happen again, I'll be good," Larry promised.

After the Michelle incident, Larry started taking the girls to his parents' house to spend weekends. Margie argued with him and begged him to stop bringing people home, but he carried on with his orgies, pretending like nothing ever happened the next day.

Margie wanted to get away from Larry, she dreaded every weekend, and she confided everything to her sister Freda. She filed divorce papers but she wasn't strong enough to leave.

"She started talking about the switching when they was on Palmer Court. I don't remember the year, I'd say five years they had already been married," Freda recalled. "I gave her my opinion, I said how could you stand this? Then she would go to lawyers and file for divorce and never go through with it. She would pay her money, she was kind of a joke after a while, going to so many lawyers."

Somehow Larry would always win Margie back, writing her little notes and telling her he was sorry. The apologies always came after one of their "party" weekends, when Margie refused to sleep in the same bed with him. He would promise to try harder in their marriage, saying he couldn't live without her.

He was spending more time drinking, more time out, and more time partying. As a result, during his first year of employment at the railroad, in the early part of 1972, he wound up getting laid off. It just so happened that the New Albany Police Department had an ad in the paper that same week. They were enlarging their department and were looking for people. Larry Loveless went down there, impressing them with war stories, and before he knew it, with a few short weeks in training at Bloomington under his belt, Larry found himself in uniform as a probationary police officer.

Margie and his parents were so proud. However, his daughters were of a different opinion. At age four, Michelle was already frightened of him. Melissa was just two, but even in infancy, she learned to be cautious. Larry had always waved his guns around, often using them to threaten Margie. Now he had a legal reason to carry one, and it made him even more bold. He liked the feeling of authority. He would go out in uniform even when he was off duty, wearing it to go shopping, to go out to eat. And this feeling of power carried over into the home. Often, when Margie was either out or asleep, he would do strange things with the girls.

"He had his handcuffs and he would tie me to my bedposts with them," Michelle remembers. "I had twin beds, they were bunk-beds and he would tie me like sometimes on the top bunk but the handcuffs would go down to the second bunk and one time I fell off and I had a bump on my head cause I fell from the top bunk to the bottom cause the handcuffs slid down the pole."

Michelle says that her father would take her out to the garage and threaten to hit her with his brass knuckles. He would get out a piece of 2 x 4 wood and demonstrate what kind of damage they could do.

"You want this to happen to your face?" Larry asked.

But he never used them to harm her.

At the same time, his sexual behavior with Margie took new forms. Margie says she would come home from shopping and find him masturbating in her underwear, wearing her lingerie, wearing her makeup. She says that in bed, he started inserting vegetables inside her: cucumbers, bananas, and carrots.

"It's not going to hurt, it's not going to bother you," she can still hear him saying.

If she fought with him, he would physically hold her down and have his way. He even inserted his night stick inside her on a few occasions. He liked seeing Margie scream.

Loveless was on the police force for well over six months, and things went along just fine for him, that is until a late Friday afternoon in April, when something happened that made Larry mad. He had just gotten off work, he had gone home and changed into his street clothes and was taking Margie and the girls out for a hamburger. On the way home, stopped at a red light, the man in the next car smiled and waved at Margie. It was a black man. Margie recognized him and just as the light changed, she smiled and waved back.

"Who the hell was that?" Larry growled.

"It was someone, I think I went to school with," Margie said.

Margie thought it was nothing. But Larry dwelled on it all the way home. With the girls in the backseat, Margie shuddered as she watched him get angrier and angrier, his face turning red. But he waited until they got home before he said anything more.

"Have you fucked him? You fucked him, didn't you?" Larry screamed as soon as they walked through the door.

"What?" Margie was outraged. "What are you talking about? I'm not even sure if I knew the guy, I mean, I waved, it was just a reflex!"

But Larry wouldn't let it go. He kept ranting and raving. Then, he got quiet. He started pacing.

"I just kept saying no, I don't know this guy. I mean, I never slept with this man," Margie remembers. "And he was just so crazy jealous."

"Well, I'll fix him," Larry said aloud to himself. "I'll take care of him."

It didn't take long for Larry to pick up the phone and dial his partner, Pete Stasser, who, along with Loveless, had been on the force for about eight months. Margie was in the next room with the kids, so she really couldn't hear what was being said. Larry never wanted her around when he talked police business and she had learned to tune him out whenever he was on the phone.

Within days, the front page of *The Tribune* had a headline which read "Suspend Two Policemen." The April 29, 1973 article reported that the two probationary officers, Larry Loveless and David Stasser, had been suspended from duty due to an incident that occurred at 8:15 the previous Friday night on Woodland Drive in a New Albany city housing project. Michael Buchanan, age twenty-two, of the same housing project, was taken to Floyd Memorial Hospital with a head wound at about 9:00 P.M. He was later bandaged and released.

According to the paper, an eye witness, Kenneth Bailey, saw the whole incident and reported it to the police. The men were off duty at the time of the alleged assault on Buchanan, and they were out of uniform, but were equipped with night sticks and guns, and were wearing their badges. After the trouble occurred, the two policemen brought Buchanan down to headquarters. It was because the other officers saw his wound that Buchanan was sent to the hospital.

A preliminary investigation confirmed that the trouble was between Loveless and Buchanan. The paper reported it was the Mayor's understanding that Loveless had a confrontation with Buchanan earlier that afternoon. The two men were awaiting a hearing on the matter, but both resigned from the force before the scheduled hearing date. Some months later, according to Margie Loveless, the NAACP filed a $100,000 lawsuit on Larry Loveless, but nothing ever came of it.

This time, when Margie threatened to leave him, it wasn't a sob story that kept her there. They had a big argument, and Larry got out one of his guns.

"If I can't have you nobody can have you. You're dead. *I'll blow your brains out,*" he threatened.

Five

Larry and Margie were going through hard times. Larry was working back at the railroad again, carousing more than ever, and then Margie caught him in bed with one of her good friends, Debbie, a neighbor at Palmer Court. Margie walked in on them, both half dressed. "It's not what you think!" Debbie told her, but she later confessed to everything. Debbie's husband wound up divorcing her, and they sold the house and moved. Margie and Larry finally decided that an open marriage would be appropriate. They were hitting the bars, separately and together.

By then, Margie had completed her high school equivalency program and had received a paramedical scholarship from the Kappa Kappa Kappa sorority to study at the Prosser Vocational Center in New Albany. In 1974, she became a Licensed Practical Nurse and, even though Larry protested, she was hired at Floyd Memorial Hospital. Dedicated to her work, she earned Nurse-of-the-Year honors. But she was hardly at home anymore. Instead, she had her ten-year-old niece Teddy baby-sitting whenever possible. Teddy practically lived there for a while, using the guest bedroom as her own.

She hadn't been working long before she discovered she was pregnant again, and she couldn't understand it. She was taking birth control pills, and she had no plans to have any more children. She had a big future planned for herself, one that would take her away from Larry Loveless and his problems. She cried about it at first, and even called a doctor to ask if there was something she could do to terminate the pregnancy. Then she talked to a priest and did a complete turnaround. She realized that it was a blessing.

At work, the nursing staff was really good to her, feeding her milk shakes, making her smile, treating her like a queen. But when she got home, it would be a different story. Larry said Margie ruined things by getting pregnant. They couldn't have their "parties" anymore and he hated her for that. She was just starting to look good, he told her, now she was all bloated and obese. Throughout her pregnancy, he kept calling her a whore, saying she got pregnant from somebody else.

On a cloudy day in October of 1975, Margie gave birth to her third child, Melinda. When she brought her into the world, she felt ashamed of herself for ever thinking that she didn't want this child. Melinda was so beautiful, so precious, with chubby cheeks and lots of hair. Larry was drunk when he went to visit her at the hospital, and she later found out he was seen on his motorcycle riding around town with another woman. Margie was devastated and cried to herself, but by that time, she truly believed she couldn't make it without him. Margie's mom, Waneta, was the one who stayed with her during her recuperation in the hospital. It was also Wan-eta who brought Michelle and Melissa to see their tiny baby sister.

Margie only took a six-week leave from work when she had Melinda because she was so worried about finances. She now had three mouths to feed. Even though Larry made the house payments, he wasn't turning over his income to her as he'd done in the past. What's more, he wasn't making as much money as he once did because he would take days off to party. He only worked when he wanted to. When he got paid, he would cash his checks and buy booze, buy himself things, leaving Margie to take most of the responsibility for the upkeep of the children.

Instead of trying to help her, he would do things to hurt the children. When Melissa was just a young child, he had her out with him shooting guns and drinking beer. For a while there, Melissa was always drunk, but only Michelle knew about it. Margie was too busy working to know what was going on with her girls, often pulling double shifts to make ends meet.

At the same time, Michelle was getting old enough to become a little mother figure for her two sisters, she was trying to look out for them, especially for her infant sister Melinda. Because neither of her parents were home much, Michelle had to learn how to care for her sisters. She felt that Melinda was her personal responsibility, and by the time Melinda could speak, she was calling Michelle "Mom."

The relationship was not the normal "older sister" syndrome, where one plays mom to the other. In this instance, their father had twisted Michelle's thinking by continually telling her that Melinda was "theirs."

"See my father made me feel like Melinda was mine and his baby. And I was only eight years old when Melinda was born. And I knew that I wasn't pregnant and that I did not have the baby, that Mom did. But in my head from being told this that Melinda was our baby, it became where I felt like, I don't know, that she was," Michelle explained. "And he would say, 'She looks just like you.' And she did."

But Larry made a different claim to his wife. From the day Melinda was born, Larry insisted that she was not his child. It was true that Melinda did not have the same dark hair coloring shared by both Larry and Margie, and also true that Melinda's facial features were prettier than the other two girls, but Margie knew that the child was Larry's, and she even had blood tests to prove it to him. Larry was never convinced.

Margie felt sure that Larry also repeatedly said this to his parents, and they must have taken him seriously because they never invited Melinda on any outings. It was strictly Michelle and Melissa who had the privilege of being spoiled by their grandparents. Harold and June used the excuse that Melinda was too young, that three were too many to handle, that Melinda was a bedwetter. They rarely would have Melinda around. Michelle said she and Melissa felt bad about leaving their baby sister behind, but at the same time, there were so many arguments in their home, so much fighting, they welcomed the chance to have some peace.

It was rare that Michelle would ever have friends over because she was always nervous about what her father might do. On one occasion, when Michelle was in the second or third grade, she had her little friend Tina over, just to play outside. Larry went out there, sat himself down with them, and proceeded to tell them the facts of life. When Margie returned home later, she got a phone call from Tina's mother, who was extremely upset.

Michelle and Melissa learned that they had to fight over having pets, let alone friends. They'd bring home a stray cat or dog, it would stay with them for a while, and then it would just disappear. Michelle remembers running down the street, searching for her animals, yelling out their names, and her father would stand at the end of the driveway, laughing. Michelle had a black rabbit back then, which her mom let her keep in her room, and one day when she came running home from school to see her pet, it was gone. Larry said he had to bury it, that the animal just died.

When they were little kids, Melinda was still an infant, their cousin Teddy was on the scene more than ever, filling in as a big sister and a "mom" for all three girls, but she was also subject to bad treatment from Larry. Teddy was just a kid herself, just a few years older than Michelle, but she felt responsible for her cousins, and frightened for them as well. Larry was sleeping with Melissa then, but none of the girls felt safe there. They knew Larry was capable of coming into their rooms and doing something to them while they were asleep. Sometimes, they'd wake up and see him standing there, staring at them from the doorway. They all got to a point where they were sleeping in the same room together, hoping there would be safety in numbers.

Somewhere in that time period, Teddy's mother Charlotte called Margie to ask some questions about Larry. Margie went over to discuss it in person, and while Charlotte wasn't actually accusing Larry of anything, she was concerned.

"I think he's bothered the girls," Charlotte said, referring to her two daughters, Edie and Teddy.

Margie and her sister sat down with Charlotte's two children and tried to get some answers. At first, the girls just started crying. Teddy refused to talk about it and Edie told them that nothing really happened. It was just that Larry would bundle them in his arms and hug them.

Later that day, Margie brought it up to Larry.

"Charlotte had me over and said the girls told her you had bothered them," she said.

Larry flew into a rage. He literally picked Margie up, slammed her against the door.

"Don't you ever accuse me of child molesting! You're crazy!" Larry yelled. "Don't you ever accuse me! That's the sickest thing in the world!"

"But why would these little girls, why would Edie say something like that, Larry? Why? Where did this come from?" Margie asked him.

Larry accused Charlotte and her family of being liars. They were white trash with filthy minds, he told her.

Since the girls never brought the subject up again, Char-

71

lotte and Margie both dropped it. Whenever they'd visit Charlotte, one thing Margie noticed was that Larry would go and take naps around the girls. Nobody ever thought there was anything wrong with that; he'd just go lie down in the basement, in the family room where they were playing. If it was the girls' nap time, Larry would stay there and say, "I'm just laying here with the girls." It was just accepted as part of Larry's overall laziness. He slept so much of the day because he worked the late shift. Eventually Margie put it out of her mind. Teddy was over baby-sitting every weekend, and there seemed to be no problem.

Margie loved Teddy, as did Michelle. All the girls thought Teddy was wonderful. She was the one who cooked for them, cleaned house, played games with them, listened to music with them; they idolized her. She practically raised Melinda, carrying the baby on her hip from the time she was an infant until she was six years old.

But Michelle was worried about Teddy because Larry was so mean to her. Years later, Teddy would reveal that Larry was taking her off to the woods nearby and doing things to her; it went on for years, probably until Teddy was fourteen. Michelle didn't really understand what was going on between her dad and Teddy. However, there came a day when Larry finally did something that made Teddy disappear from their lives.

"He burned her head. He caught her hair on fire," Michelle confided. "He caught her hair on fire and then he said, 'oh, don't worry about it, I'll cut it and fix it for you.' He cut her bald. And the next thing I know, Teddy is out of our house, out of our home. She just got out of the house one night and we didn't have anything to do with her, her mom, her brothers. She didn't come over, we didn't go over there. We weren't allowed to have nothing to do with them."

But it wasn't only Teddy who had bad things happen to her. Melissa had become his favorite, the one Larry spent a lot of time alone together with, his tomboy whom he adored. It was Michelle whom he disliked, who he called "bitch" and "whore." Countless times he locked her in the closet in her room for punishment. When she couldn't say her "A B Cs," she got locked in. When she asked him to leave her alone in the bathroom, she got locked in. Larry would leave Michelle locked up for hours at a time, and, knowing that she was afraid of the dark, he'd remove the lightbulb in the closet before he locked the door. Sometimes she stayed in there so long, she'd have to urinate on the floor. She'd use her clothes to wipe it up and then throw the things out once she was free again. Other times, as Michelle got older, he'd go to her bedroom window at night, tapping on it and frightening her.

Margie never knew any of this was going on because Larry would threaten to do worse harm to Michelle if she ever told, and Michelle believed him. But Margie recalls a night when seven-year-old Michelle walked into their bedroom and Larry just picked his head up and pulled his gun out from under his pillow and shot at her, missing Michelle's head by inches. Of course Margie got hysterical, running after Michelle to console her. She came back to bed and confronted Larry.

"I'm sorry, I'm sorry. It was an *accident*. I thought I was in Vietnam," he claimed.

After they had lived at Palmer Court for six years, Margie and Larry decided it was time to move to a bigger house. He had managed to alienate all of the neighbors anyway, picking petty fights over fences and dogs, anything to cause a problem. Melinda had just turned two years old. With two salaries coming in, they could afford a place on Floyd Knobs, a slightly more affluent area up the hill just outside of town. "Snob Knob," some people call it.

The house sat on corner, a bi-level with three bedrooms upstairs, three baths, a full basement, half of which was the family room (complete with a fireplace) the other half of which was a partially finished bedroom, where Michelle eventually slept. They bought new furniture, gold tone, and hung a large mirror over the couch in the living room. The girls were able to pick the colors for their rooms upstairs, and it was a cheery abode, mostly done in blues and beiges. It had a big eat-in kitchen and a lot of space.

Larry insisted on keeping the curtains closed in his bedroom. He kept it dark so he could sleep all day. He had gotten in the habit of using old army blankets to cover the bedroom windows back at Palmer Court, something which embarrassed Margie whenever people came over, but as much as she argued with Larry about it, it did no good. He insisted the blankets kept the house cooler in the summer, warmer in the winter. He was adamant about having them up. "The sun hurts my eyes," he'd tell her, and he started to sleep in the basement occasionally, where it was cool and dark.

And after they'd moved, they began to have real money problems. Larry was taking more days off from work. He just lay drunk in the house most of the time. Margie's salary alone was hardly enough to support them. The first time that Larry filed for bankruptcy, Melinda was only about four years old. She didn't understand that her father was a bum. All Melinda knew was that he stayed home with her, that he loved her, that sometimes he slept with her at night.

The bankruptcy claim only erased their debts, it did nothing to put food on the table. Margie was trying to find someone to rescue them. She couldn't go to Freda. For one thing, Freda was very poor herself; for another, they had really lost touch because Freda's husband wouldn't let her go near the Loveless household. Margie was forced to go to her older sister Janet, who knew very little about Margie's life but who cared about her.

Janet and her husband Bob were devoted, church-going

74

people. They tried to do what they could to help, but at the same time, they resented Larry. They had a family of their own to support and were not wealthy by any means, so they didn't need the extra strain. Still, they felt that if they didn't do something, Marjorie, Michelle, Melissa, and Melinda would all starve to death. Larry was not a provider.

"For long periods of time, he played like a kid. He thought it was a game I think, and he was in charge of it. He always wanted guns and motorcycles and cars. Everybody has wants, but you don't just go out and spend it when you need food and clothes and stuff for your kids," Bob later said. "If he wanted a four hundred dollar gun, he would order it. If he wanted a new car, he would buy it. If he wanted a motorcycle, he would buy it, and then after the whim was over, he would want to sell it. Nothing to eat, very little, that's why they would come here. They would come here off and on and say they were hungry."

Janet and Bob belonged to the Graceland Baptist Church in New Albany, a plush congregation on eighty acres of beautiful landscaped grounds which had its own schools, including a college and an Evangelistic Lay Ministry. Bob was a deacon there at the time, and he convinced Margie to start attending. She even got Larry to go with her on a few occasions, usually after a big fight where she would threaten to leave him if he didn't stop forcing her into his sordid sex games. All along, Larry was still bringing home people to switch partners.

One rare weekend when the Loveless grandparents had agreed to take all three kids, Larry staggered in drunk with an unsightly couple on his arm. There was a joint sex scene and afterwards Larry went down to the family room with the woman by himself. Since the other man had passed out, Margie crawled to the basement stairway to look down the stairs. When she saw Larry in the act with this other woman, something clicked within her. She went upstairs in the bathroom and tried to drown herself. After the people left, Larry found Margie upstairs half conscious. She told him she just didn't want any part of his perversion anymore.

A short time thereafter, Margie came down with encephalitis, a viral infection which doctors said she possibly got it from a mosquito bite. She started having seizures, and she ended up in the hospital. All along, Larry stayed home taking care of the girls.

Margie stayed in the hospital for quite a while. Part of her problem, the doctors told her, was narcolepsy, the sleeping disorder where people sleep unusually long hours. They put her on heavy medications, including phenobarbital. When she finally returned home, she remained on the medication for six months, and it made her helpless. She couldn't work, couldn't drive, all she could do was lie in bed. Even though Larry's parents pitched in at the house, looking after Margie and the girls, Larry often opted to stay home as well.

Toward the end of Margie's illness, Larry suddenly decided that everything was going to have to change. There would be no more drinking, no more sex parties, nothing. He had a vision that God was with him, that they were going to work out their problems and try to make the marriage work. He said he wanted to become a faithful husband.

For years they hardly went to church at all. Now, as soon as she recovered, Margie found herself at Graceland with Larry. They made a full confession of their sins, speaking separately and together to one of the deacons. Larry Loveless seemed truly different.

Because Loveless's testimony was so overwhelming, because he had quit drinking cold turkey and seemed truly touched by the spirit of the Lord, the Graceland people reached out to him, offering the family a house to live in temporarily. The bank had begun foreclosure proceedings on the house at Floyd Knobs.

Margie was filled with anger over losing the house, she just didn't want to give it up. The girls were crying; they didn't want to leave their friends. But within a matter of weeks, they packed all their belongings and moved into a small four-bedroom place owned by the church and located on nearby Greenfield Drive. They could hardly pay the rent; for a few months, parishioners donated the money until they could get on their feet. By then Melinda was five years old. Graceland Baptist would comprise her earliest memories.

Six

During church services, with Margie standing up behind him, Larry would get up and testify. Under the watchful gaze of hundreds of believers (the sanctuary seated two thousand) Loveless proved himself to be a man of God, eventually joining the staff as a lay preacher, going out on the "circuit" to spread the word. Sometimes there would be "healing" services where people in wheelchairs would be brought forward to the altar. In the two years that the Loveless family was there, neither Margie nor the girls ever saw anyone get healed. But Larry was passionate about it. On one occasion he took off his eyeglasses and smashed them to the ground, claiming that his perfect eyesight had been restored. Two days later, he wound up buying new glasses because he couldn't see to drive.

Regardless, the Loveless family were the new stars of the congregation, and everybody paid attention to what Larry and Margie had to say. People couldn't get over how they made it through all the drinking and fighting.

"He would say how we had been delivered from the hands of the devil. Then he would start crying, saying that he's got his family back together, that he was an alcoholic, and that he no longer drinks." Margie remembers it well. "He would say we were into sex and everything that you could think of, and it's all over. We've been delivered and God has set us free."

Then Margie would back Larry's story up, saying yes, he was an alcoholic; yes, there were no more affairs, no more sex, that kind of thing. And she would start crying too because she was so happy, thinking, "Oh, boy, we're going to be this normal 'Leave It To Beaver' family."

Melinda was enrolled in the Graceland kindergarten class. All three girls went to school there and Margie became the school nurse on a full-time basis; it was the only way they could afford the tuition. At age five, Melinda carried her Bible everywhere she went. She was a precious little thing who worshipped the ground her father walked on. Her older sisters weren't quite as submissive and compliant, but they went along with the program.

It didn't take long for Larry to get himself involved with a select group of people, the real insiders who believed the power of God could allow them to do anything. These were people who believed in demons and exorcisms, people who would come over to the house to shout and scream out demons. Michelle remembers Larry once talking about having the power to raise the dead, claiming that her father actually tried to do it. Larry became a fanatic, and in the process, he cut off everybody, even his parents, because they weren't "saved." It wasn't really a matter of demonstrating the power of God; it was, perhaps, a matter of Larry demonstrating the power he had *over* God.

He had Margie throw away any and all of her clothes that were "inappropriate." The dress code did not include miniskirts, jeans, or the like. As for the girls, there wasn't much of a problem with their clothes—it was their stuffed animals, their records, and their books that had to be destroyed, had to be burned in the incinerator for "purity's sake."

Melinda had a three-foot doll, Patty, that she loved. Patty was her best friend. She had blond hair. She could hold her hand and she would take steps, she could make Patty move. It was a forty dollar doll, something completely extravagant she'd had awhile, and Melinda loved her. She dressed Patty up in her own clothes. She even slept with her.

Because the doll had strange eyes, Larry decided it was possessed by demons and had to be destroyed.

"Larry tells her he's going to take it and burn it," Margie said. "She thought it was a person."

"How could you do that to Patty?" Melinda asked, and she just cried and cried.

Margie went out searching for the doll and she bought Melinda another one just like her, but it wasn't the same.

Melinda never got over it.

"That was my best friend . . . I hated him for that," Melinda remembers. "That was my favorite, I talked with her and I played with her and he just took it, he always ended up taking my stuff. I used to love Michael Jackson and he would tear down the posters and throw them away. They was satanic or something."

In her first year at Graceland, it was decided that Melinda would be exorcised. The rest of the Loveless family had already gone through it on numerous occasions. With Melinda, however, it would be done a little differently. She wasn't exorcised in the Greenfield house like everyone else. The five-year-old was taken to a motel and left with a fifty-year-old man for about five hours. Melinda didn't really remember what happened. She told Michelle that she just took a nap.

Margie didn't question any of this. She was so happy that Larry had quit drinking, had quit the abuse and the sex parties, she would put up with just about anything. She was asked to wear a veil to show her submission, and on certain occasions, she did. She was asked to throw out all of her makeup, and she did that, too. She was attending church almost every single day, either for a service or for a social function. She was extremely involved, cooking for potluck dinners, attending prayer meetings, taking her kids to the recreational facilities on the compound.

"She wasn't into what the Bible says, she was into Dad," Melinda recalls. "She never talked to me about God and the Bible. Dad was her God! 'Do whatever daddy says, just be quiet and do what he says.'"

When Larry suggested it was time they renewed their wedding vows, Margie thought it was a wonderful idea. Even Larry's mother and sister came to the event. It was a big ceremony, and all the girls played a part. Margie threw her bouquet, there was a buffet meal served afterwards, and their life was off to a new start.

Jayne Davis, the woman who had the wedding reception for them, had been the basketball coach at the Graceland school, and she knew the Loveless girls. She saw them as God-fearing Christians, and she was particularly fond of little Melinda. To her, Larry appeared to be the perfect father, even though he did admit to many things about his sordid past.

Barbara McDonald, another parishioner back in the years when Margie and Larry were members, also had problems with Graceland. A voluptuous blond who was having marriage difficulties, she had been led to believe that as long as she had faith, God would take care of her problems. She was told if her marriage wasn't getting any better, it was because there was sin in her life.

"They concentrate a lot on demonic possession. They had regular exorcisms in trailers and that kind of thing," Barbara confided. "Everybody whose thinking wasn't quite what Graceland's thinking was had to go through exorcism. They would take children out of school for exorcisms. Take them out of the learning system for exorcism for the way they was thinking about something, for maybe lustful thoughts."

Barbara went through exorcisms a half-dozen times herself in the three or so years she was at Graceland. For her, they began when she went to one of the preachers, complaining about some of the Graceland practices.

"I started questioning the church because of the whippings the kids took. My daughter, in particular, came home one day and said one of the teachers had knocked a kid up against one of the lockers," she explained, "slammed him up against one of the lockers, and no matter how Christian or non-Christian you are, that's indecency. I started questioning at that point, and the fact that I started questioning, then I became demon possessed."

Michelle was tired of the whole religion, tired of going to school and being forced to pray. She was sick of everyone praying over her, sick of people telling her what to do. She didn't understand the concept of speaking in tongues. Michelle wanted out.

One of the things she hated the most was the movies Graceland would show of the Rapture, the day the world would end. Michelle says they were shown once a month, on Wednesday nights, and some of them scared her to death. She would watch in horror as she learned that the devil would come to rule the Earth for a thousand years, that people who had the 666 mark would be part of the devil. She just couldn't take it anymore. She had been exorcised on countless occasions, for every trivial thing she did, it seemed.

"One time I wouldn't run an extra lap at basketball. They were just picking on me. They wanted me to run and I had already run ten extra laps than the other girls," Michelle recalled. "I just went home, so when I got home, at dinner we had peas and I said 'I'm not eating them damn peas' . . . I ran to my room and before I knew it, ten people from the church were there putting olive oil crosses on my door.

"Don't come in here! It's the devil's room! Just leave me alone!" Michelle yelled.

"They put olive oil on my forehead, in a cross shape. Finally, they thought they had won cause I had gotten so exhausted from crying and screaming that I just went to sleep," Michelle said. "I guess they thought they had finally got the demons out of me. I was just laughing thinking, I'm just worn out."

Larry had everyone brainwashed, and other than Michelle, only outsiders could see the insanity of the situation. Freda had tried to talk some sense into Margie, but it did no good. On one Halloween, when she took her girls over to their house to visit, Margie just sat there and watched as Larry threw Freda out, saying that she was worshiping the devil, that it was the witches' night.

"Margie, these are my kids, I'm just trick-or-treating! Where did you go? Don't you remember when we used to dress up?" Freda cried. "Mother used to make popcorn balls and it was a big event!" But Margie said nothing. After that, Freda was determined to keep her nose out of the Loveless business. For years, she stayed completely away.

By the end of their second year there, someone at Graceland decided to let Larry start counseling others. While Margie was nervously eating her way into oblivion, reaching over two hundred pounds, Larry was spending all his time with women who were having marriage problems and women who were getting divorced. For Margie, he had very few words, he'd just look at her and say, "You're obese, you're sickening." He would hardly touch her anymore. Eventually she decided to do something about it. Even though she was not someone who had been overweight all her life, even though she was not really a candidate for the surgery, Margie decided to have a gastric bypass. It was an idea that Larry came up with.

Then the gossip started. A few different women finally went to Margie to say that Larry had been "dropping in" on them too often. Without going into too much detail, they were implying things about Larry. One told Margie that Larry made her feel "uncomfortable." Another said

Larry tried to kiss her. Margie got a sick feeling in her gut.

"Would you ask him not to come by?" one of them requested.

When Margie mentioned it to Larry, he threw a fit. He said the women were whores who needed to be healed.

One of the women he went to counsel was Barbara McDonald. Larry didn't discuss Barbara's divorce when he went over to see her, he talked to Barbara about her own personal growth, her Christian growth. He read Bible verses to her and said that she needed to get back to the church, back to the fellowship, that God was still her redeemer. Many people at the church had shunned Barbara for going through with a divorce, and Larry was there to tell her that she was still a good person, that they all still cared about her.

"We were sitting at the dining room table and I think our chairs was real close and I think he was holding onto my hand. Larry was a real *touchy, feely* person and he would pat me a lot," Barbara remembers. "I thought that day in particular, I felt kind of funny around him."

Barbara decided to call off the meeting a little bit sooner. It was the first time that he had come over by himself and she wanted him to leave. She had to lie and say she had an appointment because he wouldn't take the hint. But as they were walking to the door, Larry suddenly pulled an about-face.

"He said that it's been a while since I had a man, since I was divorced, and he said that he would be the person to take care of that," Barbara recounted.

"I was a lot bigger than Larry, he was a little guy, and when he started with that stuff, he started unbuttoning my blouse and I remember trying to push him out the door and he wasn't going out the door, and I am saying, 'Larry if you don't leave, I am going to call Marjorie,' and he's pulling at me, tugging at my clothes, he's trying to get my clothes off and I pushed him out the door."

"If you call Marjorie, I'll come back and shoot you," Larry told her.

But that didn't frighten Barbara at all. She immediately called Margie and told her what happened. Margie was stunned.

She knew things had been slowly slipping all along. Larry was sneaking beer; first it was just one here and there, then it was whole six-packs. Melinda was eight when she caught her father drinking again, and it just broke her heart.

"Don't drink, Daddy, don't drink again, please! It's the devil! It's the devil in you," Melinda wailed.

By that time, Larry had already moved his family to another location. The payments at Greenfield were too high, so they went to Sellersburg, a small town where they rented a country house. That place didn't work out either, so after just a few months, they moved out to a farmhouse in Hamburg, an area that was even more isolated. Margie and the girls felt trapped.

All along, Larry was grumbling about the church; they should have been providing more for him, he thought. He wasn't being paid near what the "regular" staffers were. He was very bitter about it. He had a select group of friends, including another preaching assistant, who all followed him in his thinking. Larry didn't like the way the church was spending money. They had bought new cars and houses for the top people and he was jealous.

One Sunday morning, he stood up in church in front of a big service and said that he disagreed with the way they were all spending God's money for their luxury. Someone told him to sit down, but he just repeated himself, then said he wanted to take his membership away. He wanted his membership card torn up and burned.

Margie was embarrassed to death. She had her kids in their schools and she was the nurse there, and suddenly the Loveless family had been excommunicated.

Seven

With each move, more of their possessions were sold, misplaced, or damaged. And all along, the three girls were being shuffled from one school to another, especially Melinda.

With no income coming in, Margie turned again to her sister Janet for help. They lived in Janet and Bob's basement for about two months, free of charge, only contributing a few dollars a week for groceries. But they all hated it there. Janet was very frugal and strict, two qualities that the Loveless girls knew nothing about.

"They were real good to us," Margie admitted. "Janet was real protective of the girls, but she made them do things like the dishes, which I didn't like because I didn't make them do anything, I always did all the housework." Margie spoiled the girls rotten, she says, because she was always trying to make up for all the fighting and the terrible things that Larry did.

It was a difficult situation for everyone, but Larry made things worse because all he did was lay around. He didn't help Bob cut the grass, he didn't do any chores, didn't budge from the couch and the TV.

One of Larry's acquaintances from Graceland finally came up with a loan of $5000 which allowed Loveless to put a down payment on a house. Larry treated it as a gift, and they moved into a place on Genung Drive back in New Albany. It was a dingy little house but Margie was glad to be close to people in town again and close to work. Margie got her job back at Floyd Memorial, and Larry went back to the railroad. The girls were left by themselves a lot, but they were busy in school, making new friends. Michelle had gotten her driver's license and her grandparents bought her a car, so she had some freedom. Still, she was subject to Larry's whims whenever he walked through the door.

"Larry was a very mean, selfish, distorted man," Michelle said. "When I got older, he would still smack me on the butt, and try to kiss me on the mouth. I was fifteen, sixteen years old and he would still pull my pants down and he would whip me on the butt. He would take me and lay me out on the picnic table without no shirt on, to pop my pimples. That was a big thing he did to us girls. He used to make me scream and cry."

"You're sick," Michelle would tell him.

"You'd better shut up and watch your mouth," Larry would say with an angry grin.

Even though things were becoming more and more perverted in their house, the children thought it was just normal play. They would all laugh when Larry would grab Margie's crotch in front of them, putting his hand down her pants, then smelling his fingers. Eventually he started putting his fingers to his daughter's noses, saying, "Doesn't your mom stink!" And after a while, it got to be a family joke. The girls would just grab each other, goose each other, and smell each other. Larry would never touch the girls in front of Margie, but he'd come downstairs with a pair of their dirty underwear, smelling the crotch and saying "Whose is this?" as he held it to his nose with a funny look. He thought it was amusing. It was something he did everyday.

Larry was getting drunk more than ever, at which times he forced Margie into new and more exotic sex acts with vegetables, using them on her in a way that was violent and rough. He would tell her he was just being "creative." Margie went along with it, thinking it was the only way to keep him faithful.

Through it all, Margie still worked hard. She went to PTA meetings by herself, trying to hold down the fort. One day, she came home from work and Michelle told her that their father was making them all stay outside at night while he was having this neighbor woman over for tea. It turned out to be the mother of Melinda's little friend. Larry had been using Melinda as a go-between.

"Mommy, I don't want to go outside and play all night till it gets dark. Mosquitoes bite," Melinda complained.

And right then, Margie knew. She confronted Larry and at first he denied it but then he admitted that the woman wanted to marry him and take care of him.

"He was telling me this on the front steps of Genung Drive. She would marry him and pay all his bills and take care of him. And my initial reaction was, I laughed," Margie said. "I thought it was so funny."

Margie went to the woman and had a talk, finally telling her, "You can have him." The woman, however, never made another move. After that, Margie and Larry went back to an open marriage arrangement.

They stayed in the house on Genung for only one year. They had to move out because, again, they couldn't afford the payments. Larry was still not working steadily. They took a loss on the house, and Larry used most of the money to buy himself a new Harley. Because of their financial crisis, they had to move into an apartment set-up this time, a three-bedroom town house.

The Sheffield Square Complex had a pool, and in the summer, Melinda made a few friends there. Larry seemed to have a problem with that. He didn't like her spending time with others. He wanted her all to himself. He treated her like she was his little wife, taking her out with him, glued to Melinda at all times. Margie just couldn't understand it. Instead of working, Larry spent all day at the pool with the girls. When Margie would lay out there, she'd question him about it.

"Doesn't it bother you to be the only man out here? Can't you see you don't belong?" she asked.

Throughout the first year at Sheffield, Melinda spent all of her spare time with Larry. She was nine years old and had developed into a young dark-haired beauty. Nothing could have pleased him more when everyone who laid eyes on his daughter would comment on her extraordinary looks. Larry always had a "place" where he and Melinda would be off to. He told Margie he was taking her hunting to the Clark County State Forest or out horseback riding. He had a whole host of locations, but later Melinda would not remember much about doing anything like that.

Margie was never home anymore. She was either working or out in search of men. She knew it wasn't fair to the girls for her to be gone so much, but she wanted to pay Larry back. She needed to have some affairs of her own to make him jealous. Really, she hoped she'd find some white knight to take care of her and her girls. Still, she had to be realistic, so she tolerated Larry. She would try to patch things up here and there, for the children's sake, especially for Melinda, who remained incredibly attached to him.

Larry, all the while, was threatening to blackmail Margie, saying that if she tried to leave him, he'd tell the girls all about her escapades, all about how many men (and women) Margie had been with. At the same time that he was threatening to do this, he was busy telling the girls that their mother was a slut, a whore, a no-good, giving them all kinds of details about Margie's sexual practices. He would have each one of them call to check up on her at work, only to learn their mother wasn't there half the time.

As time went on, their minds were turned against her. They thought that she encouraged Larry's behavior by her own cheating and lying. Larry would tell them that their mother just didn't love them.

"Most of her time, you know, twenty-five years with Larry Loveless, she couldn't see that he did any wrong, always pleasing him and keeping the peace in the family," Michelle said. "She always took Larry's side, and upheld men over us girls. Whether it be dad or someone she was dating, I felt like she always put them first, and never us girls. I always felt like she never cared about us. I guess I just wanted her to have the mutual respect for us that we had. A male always occupied her time or her energy or her life."

Melinda was particularly horrified by her mother's behavior. She viewed her father as a saint for putting up with it. When Margie would talk about divorce, Melinda would panic. She felt that the only person she had, really, was Larry, and she couldn't bear the thought of being separated from him.

"He was getting the girls to hate my guts, all because he knew I just wanted to get rid of him," Margie said. "I prayed that he would die. I prayed that he would have a car wreck coming home drunk. I used to tell him that I wished he was dead."

Even though Melinda reveled in Larry's attention, she finally reached a phase where she just wanted to watch cartoons, play with her dolls, and talk to her friends on the phone. She was going on ten now, and she was tired of going off with her father on his "walks" in the woods.

"She got real bored. She didn't want to go," Margie recalled. "And the few times she told him that she didn't want to go, he was mad at her all day. He would be mad at me the whole day. He didn't talk to her. He wouldn't speak to nobody. The silent treatment was big in our house."

Whenever she tried to refuse Larry's offers, Melinda would wind up spending the day with him anyway, usually at her mother's insistence. "Go hunting with him, go with him, go for the ride. Please, please go with him," Margie would beg. "He would say that I'd turned her against him or something. It was craziness. Just pure craziness."

Whenever Michelle or Melissa wouldn't comply with Larry's demands, it would be a similar scenario. "I'd get on my hands and knees, I would. I'd say, 'Girls, you mind him, please do what he says.' Because I knew that I was going to get it, you know, later, or they would get it," Margie confided.

But Larry didn't really need Margie's help; Larry was the ultimate dominator on all fronts. He had complete control over everyone and everything in his home. None of them had any rights or any privacy. Whenever he felt like it, Larry would walk in on them in the bathroom or in the bedroom. He made their lives impossible.

"Boundaries were crossed every day, you know, he'd want to go into your bedroom and get your underwear or wear your clothes," Michelle revealed. "All my books I had, he marked in them. Even in my college dictionary, he put 'Jesus loves you.' He'd put footnotes all in my books. He took my perfume. I had to hide my makeup because he'd wear it. My foundation, my blush, he'd use to deepen his cheekbones. . . . If he wanted to sleep in your room, he could."

"Your room's cooler. I work. You don't," Larry would say.

When Melissa and Michelle got old enough, however, they didn't stand for it. If Larry came into their bed, they just got up and went into a different room. But Melinda was different, she was the baby, she was easygoing. Off and on, she slept with Larry until the day he left. Even, at times, toward the end, when she really didn't want to.

Larry controlled every square inch of the dwelling, keeping it so cold that sometimes Michelle could go into the house and see her own breath. He kept green army blankets on all the windows and wanted no lights on except a reading light. The place was like a tomb. He kept the TV tuned to the stations that he liked. It was always Westerns or karate flicks, never anything the girls might enjoy. He wouldn't allow the girls to play their music, not even on a portable radio.

The only time there was music in the house was when Larry wasn't there, or when he was feeling sentimental, playing songs from the early seventies. If he was in one of those moods, he would call Melinda downstairs and sing to her. Sometimes he'd have Margie there, too.

"Mom and Melinda were the only people who could be around him when he was mushy and playing music," Michelle said. "It was always sad stuff, like 'Killing Me Softly' . . ."

Through it all, the fights between Larry and Margie were taking their toll on Melinda. She would get so upset, crying for her poor father, that she couldn't function. She would be sick, refusing to see any of her friends. She just hung around Larry and tried to make him feel better until finally, Margie wound up going back to him and apologizing.

"Oh, she ran to her room. She'd run to her room, turn up the music, and sometimes cry. Usually curl up in a little fetus position. Curl up and shake or cry," Margie recalls. "I always loved her. I'd always give her a kiss. We'd get a dollar and go and get ice cream or something."

In the meantime, Margie was sneaking off to get counseling at a human resources clinic. The counselors emphasized that the violence in her home was affecting every member of the family and told her she'd have to break away, if for no other reason, for the girls. She understood that Larry was maintaining control over her as a way of coping with his own frustrations and jealousies. It would take a long time for her to see that she was sick herself, that she was co-dependent; day by day, though, she was getting slightly stronger. Sometimes, she'd manage to talk back to Larry, eventually calling him names when he told her she was fat and stupid.

"I called him a loser all the time," Margie said. "Because I wasn't afraid at the time. I was getting better."

But Margie still had plenty to be afraid of. Guns always stayed in their bedroom. Larry kept a couple of pistols in the closet and a sawed-off shotgun or rifle under the bed. He kept the guns close to him, pulling one out to threaten Margie whenever he got the impulse.

Of course Margie had more than just herself to be concerned about. For one thing, Larry was now slapping Michelle around, especially on the occasions when Michelle would try to physically prevent her father from hurting Margie. One day, when Larry was trying to choke Margie in the bathroom, Michelle broke into the fight, and he turned his anger on her with full force.

"I thought I was going to be killed cause they were screaming and he was angry, and I thought, this is it," Michelle remembers. "And he just threw me on the ground and choked me until I lost consciousness. I mean, I don't remember, I blacked out or something, cause he was on top of me. And the next thing I know, you know, I get it together. I stood up. And he's just standing there like *what's your problem?*"

This was typical for Larry. He would do something monstrous and expect all to be forgiven moments later. Afterward, everyone would go out to eat, just like nothing happened. Margie was used to it. She had become almost numb to it all. For years, she suffered the kind of abuse someone in a concentration camp might have to endure. One time Larry took her to a railroad party, where Larry allowed twenty or so men to have their way with his wife while he watched.

That ordeal lasted until almost six in the morning. When she got home, Margie tried to drown herself in the bathtub but Larry rushed in and pulled her out by the hair as he had done so many times before.

Instead of asking for a divorce, Margie decided to sow her wild oats, refusing Larry sex and making sure to tell him about all of her lovers when she'd come home late at night. For about a month or so after the railroad party, Margie wouldn't let Larry touch her. But Larry soon got fed up with that treatment because one day he stumbled into the town house, and, as his daughters stood in the hallway listening in horror, he violently raped Margie in the bathroom.

"My girls heard it, they were home. Melinda was crying. He had my head locked [between] the sink and the toilet somehow and he did his thing," Margie said. "What I remember is him telling me he hates my guts and I'm his and he can fuck me whenever he wants to. I'm his wife. He owns me. And I'm screaming, crying, and I mean, I know they're out there."

From then on, in a desperate attempt to protect herself and her girls, Margie started to call the police whenever there was a problem. Larry's reaction was to call the department himself, trying to make Margie out to be the cause of the squabble. The Loveless household was a regular stop for the officers who handled domestic violence. Because many of them knew Larry from his short stint on the force, Larry stopped hurting Margie for a while. He was worried about his reputation.

But Margie was determined to make it on her own. She was talking positively for the first time in her life. As much as he tried, Larry couldn't defeat her. By chance, Barbara McDonald had moved into the apartment complex, and Barbara became one of Margie's support people. She and Barbara were starting to go out together, and

Margie opened up and confessed some things. She even told Barbara that she suspected there might be incest going on, but then she denied it in the next breath.

"Everyday it was something, everyday it was something about guns and threats," Barbara recalls. "She would come to me. I was there saying, 'Marjorie you can do it, you can do it, you can get a divorce.' She was scared to death to get a divorce because she really truly believed that he was going to kill every single one of them. He even threatened to shoot me if Marjorie and I went anywhere."

Because Larry didn't want Margie associating with Barbara, she was afraid to go over to Barbara's apartment. Instead, they would meet at the pool. Sometimes Larry would see them talking, and he would insert himself into the pool scene. Barbara always thought his behavior with Melinda was inappropriate there.

"He catered to Melinda unbelievably. The way he sat and looked at Melinda is how a guy would sit and look at his brand-new girlfriend and say, 'Isn't she pretty? Look at her walk!' " Barbara recalled. "That's the way he always was with Melinda. He never said anything like that about Margie."

That was the summer of 1986. At that point, Larry had pretty much dumped Margie, devoting almost all of his energy toward his daughter. He would spend time with Margie, only when he decided it was time to go out for some "adult" fun. One night, he told Margie he wanted to take her to dinner and a movie; of course he took her to a sleazy bar instead. He was putting on his "dentist" act again, but this time, he decided to leave the place with two women, strolling out into the parking lot with them. When Margie followed him out there, they started a fight. Margie insisted that he take her home, and Larry agreed, pushing her into their jeep and driving off.

The next thing Margie knew, she had a fist in her face. Larry pounded her as hard as he could. Then he opened the passenger's door and threw her out into the road. Some passers-by spotted her, and when they pulled over, they thought she had been hit by a car because she was covered in blood.

Margie was taken by ambulance to the Clark County Hospital where she received eighteen stitches in her mouth. Because of her multiple bruises, she was admitted for treatment. Someone from a New Albany spouse abuse center took a Polaroid picture of Margie's battered face. They recommended that Margie press charges, and she did. In the meantime, Larry had gone home and cleaned up. After he changed his clothes, he went down to the police station to report the incident himself. When he arrived there, on August 6, 1986, he was arrested and charged with battery, a Class D felony, and then released on $2500 bond.

The next day Margie filed for divorce again. This time they both went together to the lawyer's office. Larry wanted out of the marriage, too. But within an hour, right in front of the attorney, they made up and left arm in arm. Margie dropped the charges, and things were quiet at home for a while.

However, the financial status of the family remained bleak. When the railroad would call Larry to work the day shift, he would turn them down. He only wanted to work night shifts when he could be drunk on the job. There were many days where there was no money for groceries. Margie and the girls lived from pay check to pay check. They were struggling, but an outsider would never perceive that. Larry and Margie had good jobs, both drove nice cars, although one or two of them got repossessed along the way, and the girls always looked well-groomed.

Even though he was in top shape (he jogged every day and continued his karate) Larry filed for full disability, complaining about his legs, his back, and mental depression. He had a small disability check coming in from the government for posttraumatic stress disorder, but now he wanted more. He spent much of his time going to doctors at the Veterans' hospital in Louisville, trying to document how disabled he was.

At home, things had deteriorated a little further. Larry was now packing his bags every other week, walking out on the family as he threatened to leave for good. Nothing could have pleased Margie and her two older daughters more, but Larry's actions had Melinda so torn up, she'd cry herself to sleep at night.

Melinda still idolized the man. She knew that he mistreated her mom, that he mistreated her sisters, but she couldn't help that. She was Larry's favorite, they had a special understanding, a special kind of love that took precedence over all else. She was his "Sissy," his "baby," his "Lindystar." Melinda would rub his head, rub his arms, wash his feet, and just pamper Larry every night. When Margie began to take more serious steps toward the divorce, Melinda was deeply disturbed. She begged her mother to hold the family together.

In the fall of 1986, it just so happened that Southern Railroad, the company where Larry worked for fifteen years off and on, gave him a form of early retirement. The company was paying people off because they were in the process of a merger. Loveless negotiated for a lump sum of $45,000 and wound up with $28,000 cash after taxes.

Right away, Margie made plans to buy a house. In the back of her mind, she knew she would leave Larry, but she wanted her daughters to have a home of their own first. She had always promised them that.

Within a week, Larry put $15,000 down on a three-bedroom brick house, located directly across from a cemetery, and the family soon moved to Charlestown Road. Before the deal went down, Larry had agreed to straighten up his act a bit. He would leave Margie alone, let her sleep on the couch, and he would stop picking on Michelle and Melissa. It was a suitable arrangement.

But it didn't last.

Eight

The house was cheerful. It was a relief to all of them to feel the sense of roots again, and things seemed to be back on the right track. Melinda had developed a lot of friends, so there were always a bunch of little girls sitting outside on the stoop, talking, playing, and listening to their music. Her best friend Crystal Wathen was always there. Crystal and Melinda were as close as two girls could be.

"All the time, we played dolls, Barbie dolls, we would play games, we would play house, everything little girls would do," Crystal recalled. "We would sit back and pretend we were radio stations and tape ourselves and all kinds of stuff, we did all kinds of crazy stuff."

Because Crystal became like one of the family, she never questioned Larry's behavior; in fact, she got along pretty well with him. "We've been through everything together," Melinda would later say. "Crystal practically lived in my house, opened the refrigerator, got what she wanted, walked around in her underwear. She was like another kid there."

Larry was attracted to Crystal in his own way. He took pictures of Crystal and Melinda in their bathing suits. He teased and played with both of them all the time. Still, his behavior was erratic, and Crystal really couldn't quite figure him out.

"Really, he was a very attractive man. If you met him, you would never think anything about him. You had to know him personally, and know his problems. One time he would be drunk, next time he would be sweet, next time he would be like back to the old days when he was a gentleman," Crystal said. "He would set us down and show us how a man was supposed to treat a woman. You were supposed to pull the chair out and set the woman in and push her in the chair and talk to them and hold their hand and be really sweet to them. All this little stuff he would show us. Then the next time he would be really overruling and overprotective, and you would be in bed by nine o'clock, radio off, lights off."

Margie liked Crystal, too. She'd come in from work and hear Melinda and Crystal giggling, talking about boys and trying on makeup. Margie gave Melinda a lot of free space. She was pleased to see her daughter happy. She wanted her to have a successful, normal life. She wanted that for all her girls. Whenever Margie wasn't working or sleeping, she'd be at Melinda's beck and call, chauffeuring her daughter and her friends over to the Greentree Mall or to the movies.

"I love Marjorie, I love Marjorie to death, she's like my mom," Crystal would later say. "She went into a stage of a teenage bopster, and we thought that was so neat. She would always want us to wear cute clothes to make us look pretty, and wanted us to do our hair to look pretty. She wanted us to be teenagers and we loved that in her."

When Melinda was twelve, she had her first little "boyfriend." It was the boy next door, he was just about her age, and the two of them spent time together playing ball and bike riding. Margie decided it was time to explain to Melinda about the facts of life, but instead of sitting down with her, she bought Melinda a book that detailed everything about menstruation, venereal disease, and pregnancy.

A year later, it was Michelle who revealed the realities about AIDS, condoms, and multiple partners to Melinda. Even though Michelle had turned against men, she understood her sister's seductiveness. At that early age, boys flocked to Melinda, stared at her, and came on to her. Melinda was only in the sixth grade, and she already had older boys coming around, trying to date her. Michelle threatened to call the police on one boy, a nineteen-year-old whom she threw off the property. Melinda had plenty of boys around to occupy her thoughts with, boys she met at school. She would come home all excited, describing someone she thought was real cute. It bothered Larry.

"My little girl's growing up and leaving me," he whined.

"No, I'm not, I've just got friends," Melinda assured him.

Larry was still spending time alone with Melinda, although it wasn't as frequent anymore. She'd still go with him to the Shell Farm in Sellersburg, his old stomping ground where he'd target shoot, but Melinda was getting tired of it and she started to tell him so. She was meeting new friends, getting more involved in school. She was growing up. But Larry wouldn't acknowledge that. Instead, he blamed Margie.

"You're turning her against me, you told her she can't go," Larry howled.

When she was with Larry, Melinda always thought of herself as a tomboy, as somewhat masculine. Even though Larry would tell her how beautiful she was, he would box with her, sometimes hitting her rather hard; he would show her how to be aggressive. Melinda felt he was molding her into a little boy. She was in a confusion about her sexuality, about her identity.

"I just watched him clean guns and he would go shoot them and he would take me and my friend with him, whoever was my friend at that time," Melinda explained. "I thought it was for protection, to be safe, because he'd say

101

you've got to protect yourself. He let me carry a thing of Mace and he gave me a little knife, a hand knife, and I kept that in my purse."

Apparently Melinda wasn't the only one in the family who lived through a state of confused gender identity, because just before Christmas of that year, Michelle came into the house and quietly announced that she was a lesbian. Larry paid it no attention; he was in his glory, busy spending the balance of his money on himself and his women friends. He did, however, make it a point to bring home a Christmas present for each person in the family, except Michelle.

"He laid all their presents out, and he had them all wrapped, and he just said, 'I didn't get you anything, Shelly,' " she remembers. "I guess it hurt my feelings to some extent because the only time he ever bought any Christmas gifts or anything was that one time."

Margie's reaction to Michelle's news was devastation. Michelle had been popular with boys, she had plenty of dates and boyfriends. It just came as a complete shock. She didn't believe her ears at first.

At that time, Margie was working on a new unit at Floyd Memorial, the chemical dependency unit, and one of her colleagues, Susan Chandler, remembers how upset Margie was when she came on shift.

"I think she felt betrayed, because she thought her daughters shared everything with her," Chandler said. "She kept talking about how she wasn't sure how she felt about Michelle anymore. For my part, I wondered at the time if Michelle had been abused sexually, but, having no evidence to go on, I didn't say anything."

Eventually, Margie got over the shock and she accepted Michelle's girlfriend, Kitty, into the home. Kitty was someone whom all the girls loved and trusted. She quickly became like one of the family, and at first, Kitty thought everything appeared to be normal. It would take her six months to discover how bizarre the family situation was. Among other things, she realized that Larry was very immature, operating on the level of a sixteen-year-old. There were a lot of things about Larry that she didn't like. She watched Larry hit Michelle on the backside one time too many, and she thought it was perverse. She observed the harsh treatment Margie received for little or no reason. Larry would constantly belittle her.

"That's okay, I love you that way. I like women with big butts," Larry would tell Margie with a snicker.

Still, Kitty didn't feel sorry for Margie because she viewed her as an unfit mother, as someone who was also responsible for the dysfunction in the house.

When Kitty saw Larry going off to sleep with Melinda at night, she finally opened her mouth and tried to put a stop to it. When Kitty asked Melinda if Larry was touching her when they slept together, Melinda said no.

"She told Melinda that she doesn't need to be sleeping with her father, that she was too old, and just to say no," Michelle remembers. "And at one time, she confronted Larry with it. He told her to mind her own business."

"While Larry was in the home I remember being plagued with the idea of whether or not to report Margie and Larry to social services," Kitty said years later. "Michelle and I talked very often about the possibility of Melinda being sexually abused. Michelle asked me not to call social services, and at that time I thought that foster homes were all corrupt. I was afraid it would be worse for Melinda in foster care."

The worst part of it was that Larry would flip from being degrading and perverted to being this "perfect" father, putting them down in one breath, saying "I love you, Sis" in the next. Kitty would get crazy listening to all the girls trying to defend him. Melinda never wanted to hear anyone say a bad word about her father.

Melinda was an enigma. Sometimes, she acted like a thirty-year-old woman. Other times, she was just a sweet little girl, thirteen years old, spending a lot of time alone in her imaginary world. Her "playroom" was a cubbyhole carved out under the stairwell. It was a laundry chute, actually, about six feet by four feet, and she kept all of her favorite dolls and toys there. For her friends, it was a clubhouse. No one bothered Melinda when she was in there, so she and her friends had real privacy. They could do whatever they wanted. They even wrote graffiti on the inside walls.

When she played DJ with Crystal, she would sing the George Michael song about a father figure quite often, but she also would make things up, make up words, make up scenes on tape, that usually had a sexual or devious slant.

But as much as Melinda tried to hide from reality, she couldn't hide from Margie's and Larry's constant battles. Their arguments were getting more heated, and Larry was using the situation to torment Melinda. He'd sit her down and have one of his serious discussions with her, something that Michelle and Kitty witnessed often. After one particular occasion when Larry took Margie's brand-new jeep out for a drive, banging it up and vomiting all over the new plush interior, Margie threw Larry out.

"Sissy, your mommy isn't being good to me and daddy's going to have to leave," Larry told Melinda, bringing her to tears. "Now, Sissy, I don't know when you're going to see me again, but *remember I love you and they can't take that away . . .*"

Melinda got hysterical.

As usual, when Larry took off, he left Melinda sobbing, begging her mother to take him back. It was just one of the many times he would pack his car, drive off for a few hours, and then return in the night.

But Larry was only making things worse for the other

girls. Melissa was repressing everything. She spent most of her time away from the home, out drinking and carrying on with her buddies. When an argument would break out in the house, Michelle and Melinda would sit in the living room, their hands shaking and their hearts pounding. After it was over, they'd both just sit there staring at the TV with blank expressions. They were good at gazing off into space, pretending they were somewhere else.

When Melissa, who had been successful with the boys in high school, informed the family about her decision to turn gay, Margie thought it was strange, two gay girls in one household, but she was comfortable with the concept by then, and she didn't make any waves. She even allowed Melissa's girlfriend to live with them for almost a year. Larry disliked Melissa's girlfriend, calling her a whore, whenever she wasn't around. But the girls loved her. Of course, there were a few incidents that occurred between Melissa's girlfriend and Larry. Toward the end, Michelle walked in when Larry had the girl on the ground. He was on top of her, all over her, and she looked scared to death.

In 1988, Larry Loveless got hired by the Louisville Postal Service as a mailman. Melinda was so proud of him, she liked seeing him in his uniform, and Margie was relieved to have him off her back financially. Being a postal worker meant having a job for life, she thought. Michelle and Melissa were both working, so to some extent, they were both contributing to the household as well. Finally, Margie could do something for herself, so she enrolled in college, registering for twelve hours, desperate to get her RN, which she saw as a step in the direction of leaving Loveless once and for all.

But Larry wasn't a mailman for long. After about four weeks on the job, he would bitch and get drunk, claiming that the job was too hard on him, that he couldn't deliver the mail. Even though he was still doing his karate and jogging, he told Margie his legs hurt.

"What is wrong with you? You've got a good job, a future," Margie told him. But he had a list of excuses for her. Dogs bit at him, it was too hot, anything he could think of.

"Melinda felt sorry for him. She massaged his feet a lot during this time because he was whining that his legs hurt. So she would rub lotion on his legs and he would lay there and it was so sickening," Margie confided. "Then it got where he was unloading stuff in the basement and garage, sneakingly. I noticed when he'd come home from work, he'd unload stuff out of his trunk."

Larry was unloading duffle bags of mail in his basement. At first, when Margie went down to do some laundry, she thought he was just sorting out the mail; she didn't know why he was going through it. But then she realized something was up.

"You didn't see nothing," he said, telling her it was only stuff that people throw away. "It's junk mail, but if you tell, I'll go to jail or something and so will you. Because you know about it, too."

Larry asked Margie to help him but she refused. One night, she peeked through a bag and saw a few post cards in there. Later she watched him tearing the bag of mail into little pieces. Most of the time, he took the sacks and emptied them in a Dumpster. More than once, he burned it in a container outside the garage door. Margie saw it, but she never reported him. He threatened to kill her if she ever breathed a word to anyone.

However, it didn't take long for Larry to get cocky, tearing mail up in front of Margie's brother-in-law Bob and also in front of her sister Freda. Freda just couldn't believe what was going on. As much as she had learned to say nothing around him, she finally got her nerve up and confronted him.

"You know Larry, that's a federal offense," Freda warned.

"It's just junk mail, coupons, it's just Wednesday's flyers of sales around," Larry told her.

"I don't give a shit! What if some old lady was waiting for that sale at Walgreen's to get her something?"

But Larry just laughed.

He lasted at the postal service for three months. He quit and lazed around the house for a while, and eventually began training to become a truck driver. He started to go out driving with other truckers, so he was gone a lot, sometimes for a week at a time. Melinda would be upset whenever Larry was gone. He'd send her post cards from faraway places like California or Florida, and promise to bring her with him one day.

Melinda was now meeting boys at the mall and, of course, she was still hanging around with Crystal Wathen. She and Crystal were so close they did everything together. They took pictures of each other in lingerie. They even experimented sexually together. When they met a few boys they thought were cute, Crystal and Melinda would make out with them together. But they considered it no big deal because no intercourse occurred. Melinda was just like that. Sexuality was something you shared with others, she believed.

Margie had no idea what her daughter was doing. All she saw was a fresh-faced kid whom she'd take to Hardees every morning when she got off her shift. Melinda wanted to be a model, but Margie didn't have enough money to pay for the portfolio, and then Melinda talked about wanting to become a nurse, and Margie got her a place as a candy striper at Floyd Memorial. Melinda worked with geriatric patients in the summers of her seventh and eighth grade years; she was well liked by the hospital staff.

After the school year started, in the fall of 1989, Larry decided to take a little vacation and go visit his parents in Florida. He wanted to take Melinda out of school so that she could accompany him, and Margie was furious about it. They argued over it, but one night, she came home from work and Larry had the car packed.

"I begged him not to take her. I was crying," Margie recalled. "He said he didn't know if he would be back. To me that was kidnapping."

Larry and Melinda were gone for just only a week. When they returned, Melinda never showed any signs of problems. As long as Larry was in the picture, as long as Margie said nothing about divorce, everything was okay on the surface.

Melinda entered Hazelwood Junior High School that year, where she performed as a slightly less-than-average student. Melinda was one year older than the other kids in her class, having been held back in kindergarten at the Graceland Baptist school; she had a hard time making good grades. She just didn't know a lot of the "basics" that she should have already learned. The only thing she excelled in according to her report card was "handwriting." Still, she was happy because she was extremely popular. Everyone told her she was beautiful. Everyone complimented her taste in clothes.

However, one of her recorded tapes reveals the troubled mind which lay behind the angelic face. In a sweet singing voice, Melinda came up with a song she called "A Night I Can't Remember."

"This was a night, a night I can't remember. Children were sleeping, and they begin to cry. I checked on my children, but suddenly, they didn't move. They were all dead . . .

"Went to my mama, said, oh Mama, dear, help me. She was dead too . . . shall I kill myself? This was a night, a night I shall not remember. I went to honey, he honeyed on me . . . I said, oh husband, go fix me tea . . .

"He went to the kitchen, I heard this sound. He

came back here bleeding. I said, dear, can I help you? He was dead, too. I said, dear husband, don't die on me now. The children are dead and the mother is, too. I cried, oh dear God, help me . . .

"This scary night, was October 20, my birthday. This was a night, a night to remember. The children are dead, my mom, and my boyfriend . . .

"I said help me, the police came in a hurry. But I wasn't afraid. My eyes got watery, I cried, please take me to a funny farm . . .

"They said I have bad news, oh dear, you can't remember. I said what, they said you killed them all. I said yes, oh my gosh, killed my whole family. . . ."

Nine

In mid-November 1990, when her cousin Lisa was planning to spend the night, Melinda begged her father to take them swimming at the nearby Holiday Inn. Melinda kept complaining that Larry never took her anywhere with her friends, and eventually the three of them took off. Larry went in jeans, using his cane as he pretended to hobble inside the pool area.

"Melinda kept saying why don't you get in the pool with us and he said, 'No, I don't have my swim trunks just my underwear.' So he started unbuttoning his pants and he was pulling down his jeans like you know he was going to take his jeans off," Lisa recounted. "I guess he had watched us sit down or something and he pulled his pants up, and he started poking the cane in the water with us."

Larry was just having a ball, poking at the girls, humiliating them in public. All the while he was laughing. They finally decided it was time to leave. They went to wash off and change.

"I took a shower and Melinda was in there with me and when I walked out, my stuff was gone and her stuff was gone, it was off the chair and I looked around, and I was like 'Where is it?' I heard laughing and I looked up and he was standing on the chair. He was standing on something, looking over the boy's shower room where you could see over," Lisa said. "And he was holding our stuff. So I ran into the other room so he couldn't see me. Then I started crying."

was telling Mom that I hated her and it was her fault."

Margie felt so distraught over the scene, she went upstairs and made another suicide attempt. This time, she swallowed a bottle of Larry's tranquilizers.

"I wrote this letter apologizing, cause I felt guilty. I didn't know at the time how bad it was. I thought I hurt him real bad," Margie explained. "I thought I cut his hand off maybe or something."

The girls found their mother out cold on the floor with their baby pictures strewn around her. Again, they called 911. They also called Freda and told her a few bits and pieces. By the time Freda got down to the emergency room, Margie's stomach had been pumped. She was being admitted, but she was going to be okay. Freda left to get her daughter from Charlestown Road, and on her way, Freda happened to see Larry. He was on foot, his hand was bandaged up (it turned out he had needed only two stitches) and he was carrying a cup of coffee as he walked.

"What the fuck's going on?" Freda just went off on him, "You're a low-life dog!"

Larry just kept walking. Freda cornered him with her car.

"This is not over with! You will pay! You'll pay for what you did with Lisa," she said in a rage, "you're not messing with Marjorie or your kids, you're messing with somebody else!"

Larry threw the hot coffee in Freda's face, and she spit at him. "I took my car, and he tried to walk away, and I just kept aiming for him," Freda said. "He kind of fell on my hood with his hands and things, I don't think his feet was touching the ground, but I drove him almost a block on the hood of my car. I was going to do him in. That was it."

In the meantime, back at Charlestown Road, the Loveless girls were filling Lisa in on some of the strange things they knew about Larry.

"They was just talking about what all he had did to them, and what all had happened to them. He made them pee in

Both Melinda and Lisa were stark naked, and Larry was laughing, calling to Melinda from the pool area, "if you want it, come out and get it." Lisa was in tears and Melinda was trying to stifle her, because down the hallway at the end of the shower stalls, she could see that a pool attendant was picking up a phone.

"Hush," Melinda kept telling her, "he's been drinking and he just acts funny. Keep quiet, or she's going to call the police."

Because she was afraid Larry might get caught, Melinda ran out to the pool and grabbed the clothes from her father. When the girls got dressed and rejoined him, for the first time in her life, Melinda showed her anger toward Larry.

"Dad, you're just drunk, quit, just take us home."

Lisa was crying in the background. In the car, Melinda tried to calm Lisa down, but Lisa was inconsolable. The minute they pulled up to the house, Lisa spotted Margie walking the dog and she ran to her aunt, just hysterical, reporting the whole event.

Margie had been putting up with Larry for almost twenty-five years, she had seen him in her underwear, in her slips, using dildos on himself, she had seen it all, but when her twelve-year-old niece came to her in tears, Margie reached her breaking point.

"Mom, he was just drunk, maybe he didn't mean it," Melinda told her as she followed Margie into the house.

"Okay, girls, go on up and change clothes and just get upstairs and I'll take care of it," Margie said.

Larry staggered in a few moments later. Margie was in the kitchen, busy chopping lettuce.

"Why did you take the girls? You're drunk! What are you doing to them?"

"Nothing, bitch!"

"You were peeking on them while they were getting dressed weren't you?"

Larry said nothing.

111

was sexually perverted, he did perverted things to me and I would lay there and let him do them to me. I would always pretend I was somewhere else and pray that what he was doing to me would be over soon," Margie admitted. "I look back in horror at what I allowed to happen, what I endured. I was afraid of him. He had convinced me that I was worthless and had no rights in our home."

The next day, from her hospital bed, she finalized the divorce proceedings. At the same time, she got a restraining order to keep Larry away from the house because she was afraid that Loveless would reappear to get revenge. However, Larry never returned to New Albany. He seemed settled and happy in Florida, writing to Melinda often, updating her on his life.

Just days before Margie's release, after a family session, a counselor noted the "bizarre illness of husband demonstrated by a card he sent to Margie's 14 year old daughter."

When Margie first got home, she took the blankets off the windows, she opened up all the curtains, and the house was filled with light. Everything was different. The girls all had friends over, and they watched whatever they wanted on TV. They blasted the radio, and, for the first time in their lives, they got to know their mother as an individual.

But by the time Christmas rolled around, Melinda was having severe separation problems, always complaining to her sisters and friends about how much she missed Larry. She hated her mother for divorcing him, and she constantly implored her to take him back. Margie hoped that if she handled Melinda with kid gloves, she would straighten out eventually. But, with each passing day, Melinda was getting worse. Margie knew she would have to get her into counseling.

All along, Larry was writing letters and notes to Melinda, asking, "How's your mom?" Playing the loving husband and father, he sent flowers to both Melinda and Margie. He begged Margie to take him back, and Margie was even considering it. She and Melinda used to cry together sometimes, because they both missed Larry terribly. Larry was now sending Melinda pictures of himself, which she would tack up next to her bed. Whenever Melinda received something from him, she would be moody and depressed all day. On several occasions, Larry even called her, telling Melinda he was going to bring her to Florida to live with him.

But within six months, all of that stopped. Melinda wasn't hearing anything from Larry. When the final divorce papers were signed, Melinda felt entirely abandoned.

"He's not writing me, he's not calling me, I can't believe him," she confided to Crystal. "Well, fuck him, if he don't want to call me or write me, that's fine."

But it wasn't. What made matters worse was that almost immediately after the divorce went through, Larry got remarried. He sent a photo of himself and his new bride kissing on their honeymoon cruise to the Bahamas. "Here's your new step mom," Larry wrote on the back.

"I don't remember the woman's name, I don't remember what she looked like, but I remember Melinda showing me the letter and getting mad," Crystal said. "She felt that this woman was taking her place. He wasn't calling her or writing her. She felt like he was neglecting her or leaving her behind, like she didn't have him anymore. He didn't even invite her to the wedding."

In a desperate attempt to replace Larry, Melinda started dating anybody who showed an interest in her. Between her frenzied dating, her unrequited love for her father, and her hate for her mother, she had a summer of pure hell. By that time, Margie had become serious with someone, Michael Donahue, whom Melinda resented terribly. Michael had all but moved into the house, and soon he and Margie became engaged. Melinda couldn't deal with it.

"She was having problems, major problems, nervous, constantly upset all the time," Crystal remembers. "She wanted to find somebody to be with to get her away from all that, so she started going out and she would always find the wrong kind of guy to go out with, I mean drunk and everything. But she didn't realize what she was doing. They were all male chauvinist pigs. All guys want is sex and everything, and I guess that's what Melinda thought, they was all dogs."

That summer, all Melinda talked about was one bad experience after another. According to Melinda, her first sexual encounter with a boy ended terribly. After sex was over, he slapped her, treating her like she was scum. Soon she decided she would become bisexual, and that made Melinda happier. She still went out with guys, but she realized increasingly that girls could satisfy her needs more.

Eventually, her cousin Lisa introduced Melinda to Amanda Heavrin.

"Everybody thought she was a boy. She dresses like a boy, she wears boys' shoes, boys' haircut, short," Lisa said, describing Heavrin. "She wears guys' clothes, she hangs out with the guys. She's in basketball, she's just rough. She gets into fights with boys. She just does everything boyish."

According to Lisa, it was Amanda who made the first move, asking many questions about Melinda.

"She kept talking about this girl and she said, 'Oh, she's so pretty,' and she said, 'Lisa, do you know who she is?' " Lisa recalled. "She kept saying things like, she has real long, curly hair, and she dresses like Madonna and stuff, and I said, 'Well show her to me,' and I said, 'That's my cousin.' "

That weekend, Amanda and Melinda were introduced at a pep rally. The two of them really hit it off. Melinda thought Amanda looked just like her father in certain ways. She even told Amanda that while showing her a home video of Larry doing karate moves. Amanda was into karate, which Melinda saw as a "sign."

Melinda hung around with Amanda for a few weeks before they actually did anything. Amanda was so shy and inexperienced; at first, Melinda wasn't sure about the whole thing.

"I don't know where she got her experience, but when she kissed me forcefully, it was awful. Melinda later said, "I thought this girl can't kiss. I've got to do some practice, teach her. I went home and cried to Kitty, 'She's so cute, but she can't kiss and I don't think it's going to work out!' But she was gay cause she kissed me and I was so happy."

When Melinda brought Amanda over to her house to spend Christmas 1991, Margie thought Amanda was a little boy.

"She goes, 'Who's your little boyfriend?' and I was, like, 'God, it's a *girl*,' " Melinda remembers.

Even though Amanda was very shy and quiet, everyone seemed to like her. Amanda felt comfortable in the household, especially because she and Melinda shared a lot of private time together upstairs. Melinda thought Amanda was funny. Amanda was a sweetheart, she would sing to her and be very romantic. Because neither one of them had come out of the closet about being gay, they decided to keep everything a secret. It was the first real love affair for each of them, and their love life became intense.

"We used to go up to my room and just sit and talk and listen to music," Melinda confided. "We talked about what we liked and stuff and I think when it first happened, well, I don't know. We've done it in so many different places, down to a graveyard in the snow, right across from my house. It was snowing and that was my idea. I said, 'Come on I've got a surprise for you!' It was on impulse, I mean in a chair, everywhere, I don't remember when the first time was or how. But I just know she came on to me."

When the two girls became inseparable, Melinda and Crystal had a fight over it at first. But eventually, Crystal had a serious boyfriend, a football player, so they were both busy, each involved in their own thing. So if that's what Melinda wanted, it was cool with her. Regardless, Crystal and Melinda still called each other all the time and remained "best friends."

"She used to get me on the phone and say, listen to Amanda sing, and Melinda would say 'Sing for me Amanda,' and Amanda would start singing," Crystal remembers. "She told me Amanda wore real cute clothes, that she had an excellent body, with a perfect shape, not like everyone thinks, not real boyish. She said that Amanda's got a real pretty shape."

While all this was happening, unbeknownst to anyone in the family, Margie and Michael went off and got married. It was just days before New Year's, December 29, 1991. It was a simple ceremony, with only the two of them and a witness. She and Michael went out to a quiet dinner afterward. Margie was just ecstatic, thinking that she would have this normal family. She could hardly believe she had found someone who treated her nicely, who was good to both her and the girls. But Melinda was shocked, devastated, when she heard the news. She was all the more resentful because Margie got married without telling her.

"It was supposed to be a surprise," Margie told her. But Melinda just started crying and ran up the stairs.

"Melinda, why are you ruining this day for me? I am married now and we can be a normal family. I can stay home and cook and clean," Margie explained.

"I hate you!" Melinda said through her sobs. "I wish you were dead!"

"I kept going up and trying to talk with her, I begged her to come down. I think she finally did, but she wasn't very friendly," Margie remembers. "Michael told her many times that he wasn't there to replace her dad. She didn't want to give him a chance. She didn't want to give either one of us a chance to show her what a normal life could have been."

As Melinda's relationship with Amanda continued, she confided in her, expressing all the hate she had for her mother. She told Amanda about her mother's sex parties, about her mother's sleeping around. She complained about living in the same house with her. But Amanda was powerless to do anything about it. All she could be was a sounding board, responding to Melinda's moods by catering to her in bed. "Sexual wise, she would sing and she was romantic, soft, tender, sweet," Melinda said. "And then she can be very, very aggressive and rough when I want that."

But things became rocky for the two of them, because Melinda was taking out her anger on Amanda in a number of ways. They were picking on each other and bickering.

By early February, 1991, Melinda was so depressed, hiding in her room, crying herself to sleep every night, Margie decided to take her to the Lifespring Mental Health Center for outpatient counseling. Lifespring was a place that Michelle had been voluntarily going to since the year before. Melinda went, kicking and screaming, only because Margie threatened to ground her if she didn't comply. Ultimately, it was agreed that they would all go for counseling at the same time, partly for Melinda's benefit. Their counselor at Lifespring was Mina Thevenin, but unfortunately she was someone that none of them really liked. Apparently, they had trouble opening up to her.

Thevenin noted that Melinda suffered from low self-esteem, and given the history of the family, she thought it was possible that Melinda had been molested. Melinda was obsessed with Larry; she even tried to imitate his clothes and mannerisms, the counselor discovered. Melinda confessed her same-sex relationship, talked about her guilt feelings about her father, blaming herself for his disappearance, and expressed great shock and anxiety when she learned that her two sisters alleged they were sexually abused by Larry.

Just weeks after she began the sessions at Lifespring, Melinda started having real problems at school. Rumors were flying that she and Amanda were lesbians, and she was getting into fights over it. Crystal and Amanda were part of that scene as well.

"People were already saying they're gay," Crystal recalls. "I got in a fight with these two twin girls, one of them called

Melinda a lesbian and I jumped up and was going to fight. Amanda got into it too and we was all going to fight." The fighting got so heightened that at one point, Melinda used her Mace to squirt some boys who were mocking Amanda.

"We didn't hold hands in school. Never. Not only that, we both had reputations, we had to keep whatever we did to us," Amanda said. "Nobody ever picked on me cause I wasn't afraid to stand up to them, but Melinda wasn't the type of person. Stuff started going around about us. I just said don't worry about it. If you show them they don't bug you, after a while, they'll quit."

But the fighting didn't quit. In fact, it continually got worse, because in addition to the outside pressure, Melinda and Amanda had both become very possessive and jealous. The two girls picked fights with each other, and someone usually wound up being hurt, if not physically then emotionally.

On the morning of March 4, as Margie was driving Melinda to school, she happened to notice hickeys on her daughter's neck. After much arguing, Melinda finally told her mother she was gay. Margie was furious about it. There was a major confrontation between them. That afternoon, in the middle of the crowded school lunchroom, Melinda started crying and screaming that she wanted to kill herself, that she wanted to die, that she had no reason for living. She couldn't stand her mother. She couldn't stand the peer pressure. She was just fed up with everybody. One day at school she went to see a counselor and was asked to sign a "suicide pact" because she was so depressed she didn't want to live anymore.

After a few weeks, Melinda calmed down. She decided she didn't care if people knew she was gay or not. She knew her mom didn't accept her, but her sisters understood and loved her, and that made life somewhat bearable. Still, she missed Larry and cried over him all the time, playing sad songs in her room, locking everyone out of her life, even Amanda.

In early April, Larry sent Melinda another letter telling her of his plans to remarry. Apparently, his second marriage broke up. Later that day, Michelle found Melinda hanging over the sink in the bathroom. She had her mouth filled with B-12 vitamins, which Michelle made her spit out.

Because she refused to go back to Lifespring, Melinda's counseling ended on May 22, 1991. In one of her last sessions, the counselor was able to get Melinda to admit that she had a nightmare about her father molesting her, but Melinda denied that any sexual abuse actually took place.

Thevenin thought otherwise, because she had prior information about this from her talks with Michelle as far back as 1990. At that time, Michelle had discussed her fear about Larry molesting Melinda, and Thevenin made out a report to the Department of Welfare, asking them to check on the household. She had a record of that report in her notes, yet there was no follow-up from Welfare. Because there was no documented proof, and because Melinda refused to talk, Thevenin's hands were tied. Melinda's final diagnosis was Dysthymia (depression) and Identity Disorder.

That summer, Melinda's emotional problems became even more pronounced. At the age of fifteen, she was still wetting the bed, watching cartoons, and playing with toys. Sexually, she was extremely advanced, yet she functioned on the level of a nine-year-old. Her relationship with Amanda grew more intense, and often she would secretly meet Amanda in the St. Mary's cemetery (across the street from her house) and cry on her shoulder. Melinda felt comfortable at the cemetery because it was a place where she spent a lot of time with Larry. But even with Amanda, Melinda was moody. At times she could be very mean to her, making comments that cut like a knife. She knew what buttons to press to hurt people.

As the summer months dwindled, Melinda's depression was turning to anger. She was beginning to take things out on Amanda physically, sometimes getting rough with her in bed.

"I was basically in control, sex wise," Melinda confided. "I would tell her, I would give demands and stuff, orders. I controlled her that way. I was always wanting to have sex and if she wouldn't, I would get mad and I would forcibly make her. She would end up crying and say, 'God, not like this. . . . '"

Part of Melinda's problem was that she had a fixation about a home life that never existed. She romanticized everything about Larry, recreating a childhood and a family that was perfect, just everyday normal. Having Michael around made her uneasy. She could hardly tolerate him, especially because he was questioning her about things like grades and homework. Her father never did that. In the past, when Melinda had a math problem to solve, Larry would hand her a calculator and they would both laugh as she used it.

Her stepdad was a real thorn in Melinda's side. He was concerned that she had a problem with reading, a problem with her attention span. He saw her watching only kiddie shows, and he wondered why she never watched the news, how she could be so completely oblivious to the world at large. She did not know what the Persian Gulf War was about; she hardly knew who George Bush was.

"You tell me what the fuck is going on today besides Amanda!" Michael finally blew up at her one day. "There is more to this fucking school than talking on this fucking phone!"

When Michael took Melinda's phone privileges away for a week, Melinda never really forgave him. That kind of punishment was foreign to her. Michael did all the things that any average parent would do, taking her along to company picnics, taking an interest in her schooling, attending parents' meetings with Margie. But Melinda never truly accepted him. For Melinda, the relationship with Michael

123

became a game. If she acted the part, she got away with doing whatever she wanted.

Melinda would be big buddies with Michael for weeks, and then something would remind her of Larry, and her whole attitude would change.

"She would tear her room apart, take stuff down, put her dad's pictures up, stay in her room, cried, moped, take three or four showers a day," Michael recalls. "I would talk to her and ask what's up? 'I didn't get a card from my dad.' I would say your dad is your dad. Me and you are best friends, okay?"

But Michael couldn't fill the void. Melinda decided it was time to find a new group of friends, people who were more sophisticated than she, people who were into hard core and punk, and who could show her a good time. She still spent her days with Amanda, but she had a whole new crowd with whom she'd hang with at night, usually going over to Louisville, getting drunk and wild.

Ten

When Shanda Sharer moved to New Albany with her mom in the summer of 1991, she was the one who insisted on going to public school. She was tired of wearing uniforms, she said. She had attended St. Paul Catholic School in Louisville for years, and she was ready for a change of pace.

Shanda Sharer was just like so many other twelve-year-olds in America. She liked going to the mall, talking on the phone, and meeting boys. She was a sensitive girl who didn't like to hurt anyone's feelings, who was loved dearly by both her parents and her stepparents. Her older half sister, Paige, had been more of a disciplinary problem growing up, but not Shanda. By her mother's own admission, Paige was somebody who got punished a number of times, but with Shanda, that kind of thing was never necessary. She was an easygoing kid. Shanda liked to help people and she had big plans for the future. She wanted to become a nurse, just like her older sister.

Still, it was a tough time for Shanda. She was a bit nervous about the transition to the public school system, and on top of everything, her mother, Jackie, was going through her third divorce. Shanda's parents had already married and divorced twice, and the child was filled with mixed emotions.

On August 1, 1991, Shanda sat down and wrote about some of her fears and hopes:

Dear Diary,

I can't believe it, but it's true. It's time for a new school year. Let me tell you what I'm looking forward to the most and what I'm dreading the most. Well, this year, I'm going to a different school. I'm sort of scared I won't fit in because I heard that there are hoods, pretty girls, and all those guys. I wish my mom would understand that I don't want to be 12. I want to be 13. I wish I could tell people I was 13 and my mom would go along with that but I know how my mom is. She's not that kind of person, but I would love it if she would. I would work hard, but I'm already going to do that. I love my mom very much but she doesn't understand how much that I want to be 13 and have people spend the night on school nights and . . . talk on the phone past ten o'clock . . .

Love, Shanda

Shanda liked to dress as a teenager, and because she was already well developed, she fooled most people. Her mother let her wear makeup and tight jeans, nothing too outrageous, nothing, really, that many girls her age hadn't already begun experimenting with. But Shanda wanted to date. Shanda wanted to be treated like an adult. Her mother wouldn't allow it. "I wish I could go with anybody," she wrote in her diary, "I wish I could live with my dad and have as much fun as possible." Shanda spent weekends with her dad, during which time she had a bit more freedom.

In late August, when Shanda arrived at Hazelwood

Junior High, she was a cute blond with a beautiful smile and a good grade point average. At St. Paul Shanda had been involved in all kinds of sports (basketball, softball, gymnastics, and cheerleading), she was the typical all-American girl. She had even been a Girl Scout.

But Shanda's Girl Scout image was something that she quickly shed once she entered the mix at Hazelwood, and it showed in every facet of her life. For one thing, she didn't go out for sports, all of that ended, in part, because her grades had dropped; she was too preoccupied with other things.

Shanda had attracted a lot of attention, from both boys and girls, particularly Amanda. "Why are you staring at her?" Melinda would ask in an outraged tone. Melinda couldn't stand the idea that Amanda found Shanda attractive. Melinda started to make fun of Shanda in the lunchroom, picking on her in front of everyone. Even her cousin Lisa witnessed it.

"I ate lunch with Melinda one day and she was like being mean to her. She was just making fun of her hair. She was saying, 'Look at her boobs,' " Lisa recalls. "Shanda had gotten in trouble or something and she was cleaning the tables. Whenever she would clean another table, Melinda was making fun of her, calling her 'ugly girl' and stuff like that, because she thought she was trying to take Amanda away from her. She just made it known that she didn't like her."

Around the same time, Amanda saw her cousin Nathan arguing with Shanda in one of the hallways, and she jumped in to break up the fight. Amanda and Shanda both wound up having to spend a week "in school suspension." (ISS, the girls call it.) On September 6, Melinda purposely was tardy so she could be put in ISS, too. She told Margie that she had to stay after school to help decorate for a party.

But after just a few days in detention together, even though Melinda tried to intervene, the two girls became friends. Amanda apologized to Shanda, telling her to call anytime, handing over her phone number in one of her first letters to Shanda. Apparently, Shanda did call, repeated times, even though it was against her mother's wishes. Shanda's mother would later tell *Indianapolis* magazine that she did not approve of Amanda, that she thought Amanda was a boy when she first saw her. "I told Shanda that this was not the type of person she needed to be with," Jackie later said in an interview, "but Shanda had no friends there, so I decided to give the kid a chance."

Shanda and Amanda exchanged lists of their class schedules with each other, making plans to meet in the cafeteria or in the hallway between classes. Amanda told Shanda that she had no locker partner, and asked Shanda to slip any notes she might write through the locker vents. She eventually asked for the combination to Shanda's locker; seducing the twelve-year-old with a succession of letters and gifts. In one of the earliest letters to Shanda, whose name she couldn't even spell correctly at first, she hints around about being a lesbian.

9/13/91

Shana,

Sorry I didn't call. I forgot. Could you give me your number & your classes again please.

Hey, so how do you like ISS? I guess it's OK. . . . I don't want you to think I'm a bad person or anything. I don't like to fight. I hate fighting. It's just when I had you on the ground getting ready to hit you I couldn't because you looked so helpless down there. But then you swung at me so I started hitting and you started pulling my hair. . . .

Well I'm laying in bed about 10:00 P.M. time for me to go to bed. Listen, OK, Shanda, I know the way you are now. . . . Either [you're] putting an act on me and saying you like me or you're putting an act on your friends. You act so different around your friends than you do me. Whats UP? Your so nice to me.

Please tell me because friends just don't tell me their classes for the *hell* of it. So there's got to be a reason. I have a question to ask you. I know this is going to sound dumb. But do you kinda in a way like girls? If so I think it's so cool cause it's so different. Is that why you're so nice to me? Do you think I'm cute or something?

Please tell me the truth. I won't laugh cause I think it's cool.

Your Friend,
Amanda H.

PS: Please tell me if you do cause I would really like to know. Melinda said she asked you about that but you said it was cool. And you wrote me and said it's nice. Please tell me.

Footnote: The letters written by Melinda, Amanda and Shanda included here were taken from court documents.

At around the same time, Melinda wrote her first warning to Shanda. She was concerned, and she was trying, in a friendly way, to dissuade her.

Shanda,
Don't be mad at me please! I want to be your friend. I just don't like when you speak to Amanda

when I'm not there! I mean, why can't we all three be friends? You act as if you got something going with her!

Amanda & I are going together & she loves me & I love her & she only wants to be friends with you. You need to accept that! Shanda, Amanda told me you're going through bad times. Well if you need someone to talk with you can always talk with me! I don't want you sneaking behind my back! Why don't you speak to Amanda when she's with me? You need to find you a boyfriend cause Amanda is mine. You can even ask her! Please talk to both of us or you can forget about Amanda!

You, me, & Amanda need to have a talk together and get this squared away then we could all be friends! Sorry I'm writing so sloppy! Can you meet us at lunch?

Your Friend,
Mel.

Apparently, the three of them did talk, but nothing was resolved. Just days later, Amanda wrote Shanda a letter filled with sexual innuendo.

9/16/91

Shanda,

Hey, girlfriend what's up? Please don't let Melinda bother you. Please don't stop liking me because of her.

I tried to call you about 3 times but your mom said you couldn't talk I said ok. Thanks.

I was wondering do you still like me? If so I'm glad. I have a lot in store Fri or Sat. Something you've been talking about for a while now. Do you know what I mean.

I'm just joking or do you want me not to joke. Do you want to happen what I got in store? If so answer back yes if I see you Fri or Sat. ok?

So how you and Ray doing I saw you all walking in the halls holding hands kissing each other.

good bye

I walked behind you yesterday to Mrs. Walker room last, yesterday. well gotta go.

Love, Amanda

PS: I think I'm starting to like someone. You know her.

As evidenced in the mid-September notes, Shanda was spending a lot of time flirting with her male friend, Ray; yet at the same time, she was claiming to be interested in Amanda. Ultimately, Amanda broke down and wrote to Shanda, trying to determine whether to pursue the issue for real.

Shanda,

Hey, I'm in Band 6th and I saw you today coming out from fire drill . . . I thought you looked very cute.

Listen Sat. maybe we can work something out like you meet me somewhere a we'll hang out.

I'll talk to you about it.

Love,

Amanda

P.S. Yes, I will flirt. Will I have sex or make love with you—that's a big question for such a little girl. Can you back up your word?

Amanda wasn't sure what to think. She verbalized her puzzlement in a letter written to Shanda on September 19, "I still can't beleive all that stuff you said, God . . .

want to kiss me have sex well love with me god. the reason I always leave when you with Ray is I get jealous." Later, Amanda wrote a list of questions for her, asking Shanda if she was serious about wanting to kiss, if she wanted to start a relationship: "Do you want to have sex with me, is that what you want?"

Amanda felt like she was caught in the middle of a web. She was torn between the two girls. She wasn't sure that Shanda really cared about her. At the same time, she knew Melinda loved her, but her girlfriend was just too overbearing and possessive. Melinda was already beginning to threaten to leave her:

Amanda,
Why did you write her fucking name on your folder! It hurt so much when I saw it! I didn't think you would put her ugly name on your folder & you wrote it!! You must have liked her enough to write her name! Why? Well I'm gone!
                                        Melinda
P.S. Just tell me you like her once cause I know!

Amanda was spending a lot of time on the phone, trying to appease both of them, evidently making Shanda upset at one point, then writing two separate letters in an effort to set things right again.

                                8:23 P.M. 9/20/91
Shanda,
    Sorry about Nathan. Sometimes he can be a bother to me. Sorry I slipped & said some bad words.
    Well as you know I got grounded. I'm always grounded. So don't call, I'll call you, ok? . . . I will come over when ever I get a chance, so I'll proba-

bly write a lot of letters. When I'm grounded I write a lot of letters. I hate my dad sometimes. He doesn't want me to hang around with Nathan. Sorry you had to hear him yelling. I hate it, too. . . . Ok, got to tell you. I can't hold nothing back from you, Shanda. I went back to [Melinda's] house. She asked me to go back with her. I probably wouldn't of got grounded if we didn't stop off at Melinda's house.

What kills me is I want to go with both of you when do you go to your dads Fri. Well, if I'm not doing anything and you want me to go I will if my dad lets me.

Well I gotta take a shower be back after I take it. 8:30.

It's 8:45 I'm back. As you can see that's what I mean when I say I'm confused cause I LOVE YOU BOTH.

Shanda I love you
(23)c

Well, listen if I'm not busy, I'll write you again tonight.

Love ya,
Amanda Poo

Amanda Loves Shanda

finish	start
10:27 P.M.	10:05 P.M.

Shanda,

Hey girley, were you mad at me when I let you go. It seemed as if you were cause you slammed your phone down. . . . Well, you wanted to know if I'm in love. . . . You think you love me but deep down you probably really don't. Like you said you may not ever stop liking me. I hope not cause I might have to shoot you up. No just joking. Don't get me wrong I like you and everything but I like Melinda, too. But you got to understand I knew her a lot longer. About a year. She says the same thing. She says she in love with me & she didn't really know till about 2 or 3 months after she knew me.

But I'm not saying I wouldn't kiss you. I would love to. I never said I wouldn't make love to you. I don't know what to do. I have two beautiful girls who like me & I don't know what to do, Shanda. I can't say I love you because I just don't know. I like you. . . . I don't want you to be mad at me. I hope you never stop liking me cause I look forward to a good future with you.

Please still like me. OK? Please try to write back or talk to me & tell me what you think. But Shanda I never want you to quit loving me. I think it's sweet you say you love me. I love it when you said I love you in 6th per.

Please don't stop saying it.

When her pleas to Shanda produced no solid results, Amanda must have had some second thoughts about becoming involved. Writing Shanda, she comtemplated, "Hey, if you want to have a relationship that's alot," and questioned her about whose big neck chain Shanda was wearing. In the meantime, Amanda's relationship with Melinda was starting to fade, and Melinda was growing anxious about it.

"She always writes me letters at school, love letters and sticks them in my locker. That stopped. And I'm like, 'What's going on?' " Melinda later said. "Things weren't going great. I just noticed this big difference. She wasn't walking me to class. When I would yell for her, she was with the blond all the time. I said 'What's up?' cause I knew something. I couldn't take it cause she was mine. I molded her. She was my little Mandy, everything I ever wanted. It was like I was obsessed with her."

Melinda just couldn't understand it. Even though she had found a whole new group to hang around with, people like Kary Pope and the Leatherbury brothers (her "punker" friends who were older and more worldly), she never slighted Amanda for their sake. She only saw them when Amanda was grounded or after hours, when Amanda had to be home for curfew.

For over a year, she and Amanda had shared so much together. They weren't just lovers; they were best friends. And now Melinda was being totally ignored. She was extremely hurt. She felt betrayed. Before she knew it, Amanda was spending nights over at Shanda's. Melinda had her friend Kary Pope drive her by the place on Capitol Hills one night. She jumped out for a few minutes to talk to Amanda and Shanda in the front yard. When she got back in the car, she told Kary that the three of them had agreed to be friends. She thought they had reached an understanding.

But obviously, Shanda was unmoved by Melinda's requests and demands and met Amanda whenever possible. By the end of September, when it came time for a big school dance, Melinda wrote to both Shanda and Amanda, hoping to take control of the situation.

9/27/91

Shanda,

Hey girl, what's up?

I'm in study hall being real bored! Amanda was outside my door so I played it off and got something to drink. (Dumb-ass teacher)

Well, have you decided if you're going to attend

135

the dance? I'm not! I'll probably go up to the mall and see a fucking lame movie or something. Well, I've bored you enough so I'll see ya later, babe!!

Love Ya,
Melinda

Amanda,

I love my hair! It feels so much better!

I really don't want you to go to the dance but if you really have to go I just want to go with you. I don't want you to go without me.

We can talk about Friday at lunch time.

I don't really want to wait around Friday so I might go out with Kary Pope & then have her drop me off at Hazelwood at a certain time. Well, I'll talk to ya later.

Love,
Melinda

Melinda
loves

— — — — —

You fill in the blanks.

Shanda and Amanda went to the dance at Hazelwood together. When they came outside, Melinda was there waiting for them. She had Kary Pope drive her by the schoolyard at just about the time the dance would end. She confronted Amanda and slapped her, then chased Shanda around the building, threatening Shanda, warning her to stay away.

The next day at school, Melinda ran to Amanda in tears, begging for a hug in the hallway. Amanda comforted her, but Melinda could tell that the hug wasn't really sincere. Shanda was the one Amanda cared about. Shanda was filling her shoes — literally, Melinda thought — because Shanda was even starting to dress like her, mimicking her Madonna-look. Later that day, Amanda wrote a note explaining and apologizing to Shanda about hugging Melinda. She sent Shanda some poems, asking her not to be mad.

Melinda, meanwhile, had taken about as much as she could stand. In her mind, all she had were her looks, and anyone trying to outdo or duplicate that was a major problem. During the first week in October, she and Shanda had a number of confrontations over it.

"I mean Shanda just had this airy attitude about her. I mean when I would talk to her she was real, real sweet and nice, she just laughed, had fun, she was kiddish," Melinda said. "We would walk around, she would wear real, real tight jeans. She started dressing like me, doing her hair like me, to please Amanda I guess. I would yell at her and threaten, I would just say stuff like, 'Trying to look like me now' and just, you know. She would get on my nerves wearing these tight jeans and shaking her butt around school and Amanda would stare and I would be right there with Amanda and that's disrespect to me."

Melinda was just about to turn sixteen and she was getting tired of playing childish games. One day, when she discovered some torn-up letters from Shanda in Amanda's jacket, she pieced them back together, read them, and threw a fit. "You're sick! You're a whore! You're sleeping with a baby!" Melinda shrieked, striking Amanda in the face. Finally Melinda gave her an ultimatum.

"Manda, you have to have me or Shanda. You can't have your cake and eat it, too."

But Amanda never made a decision, and Melinda was obsessing over the situation. Her sister, Melissa, decided it was time for Melinda to meet someone else, someone who could divert her, with whom she could go out and have a good time. She introduced Melinda to Carrie East, one of her friends, an attractive young woman with very short hair, a muscular frame, and a deep voice. Melinda categorized her as a dyke, and she wasn't crazy about that type. Still, East had a new sports car; she came from a nice family; she had money to burn. Melinda decided to give it a shot. She had to do something because her depression was just getting worse.

"I just tried to escape from Amanda and get her off my mind and go on but . . . that's why I always played sick, I didn't go to school or nothing," Melinda said. "For a minute Amanda would ignore Shanda and Shanda would get mad. Shanda would slam lockers and get mad because Amanda started to ignore her and pay attention to me. Amanda knew she was losing me, so therefore she would put roses in my locker, and put notes, and try to talk to me and I would just ignore her like she was not there and keep walking, keep stepping, and say something smart like 'Go on to Shanda' or something."

While Melinda spent her time being wined and dined by East, going to fancy restaurants, going out driving and drinking, Amanda and Shanda grew much tighter. Amanda was regularly inviting Shanda to spend the night, saying "I love you" in many of her letters. And the two girls developed their own secret code, their own language that no one could decipher should any of their letters be found. For example, they both started writing the number "23" on the bottom of their notes.

On October 7, she wrote a note explaining her fear about getting close to someone again. She didn't want to get hurt. "I've been thinking alot about that letter," she told Shanda, "& I do believe it. Its just Im scared to get in a relationship." In an undated letter, Amanda described her predicament more fully.

Shanda,

Hey, honey, your cousin seems to really care about you. That's good. She's sweet. Tell her I said 'Hi' OK?

My feelings for you are getting stronger & stronger each day. I know sometimes it may seem like I really don't give a damn about you — like I don't even know you. Its just I'm scared of treating you the wrong way. I just don't want to do something wrong and fuck up us. Right now I just don't know about relationships with anyone because I already got hurt in one, plus we haven't even gone together for that long. I didn't ask Melinda to go steady with me till about 6 or 9 months after we have been going together. You know I do care about you. It's just I have mixed emotions. In a way I still love Melinda. I think I always will.

I think that's something that will never change about me, Shanda. So I guess you will just have to grow to love me like that. I mean I still get jealous over Melinda when she talks with other people. I'm just not over her yet. It will take awhile cause love takes time. If you think you can wait it out, it will prove how much love you really got for me.

But deep down inside is like maybe your only doing this because it's something *NEW*. There's one big question I need to ask you. . . . I know s e x is fun. But how come you wanna have it every time I'm over there. Love's not

Sometime during all of this, in the month of October, Melinda became so distraught that she felt compelled to go have a talk with Edwin Ellmers, the assistant principal at Hazelwood. Even though Ellmers was a middle-aged man and someone she hardly knew, she needed someone to talk to about her problems.

"Melinda came to me one day in the hall and she said she wanted to talk to me and I asked her what was the problem and she told me that she wanted to talk about her mother, that her mother would not accept her," Ellmers explained.

Behind closed doors, Melinda told Mr. Ellmers that she liked girls, that she was gay; she was concerned because her parents didn't understand her. In Ellmers's twenty-year experience as assistant principal, it was the first time he had ever heard anything like that. Ellmers didn't know how to handle the situation. He gave Melinda a book on interracial dating and then he called Melinda's mother, who came in and confided that they were already in professional counseling. Ellmers let the situation drop.

detention slip, and Jackie blew up about it, confronting Shanda, arranging a meeting between Shanda, herself, and some school counselors at Hazelwood. "After the meeting," Vaught claimed in a *Courier Journal* article, "Shanda told her that she wanted to get rid of her new friends, but was afraid of the consequences." According to the newspaper, her mother forbid Shanda from seeing Amanda and Melinda, then hired a tutor to help improve Shanda's grades. She did not realize that Amanda continued the relationship through third party dialing and letters.

All along, Melinda had been crying about the failed relationship to one of her friends, Kristie Brodfuehrer, who acted as a go-between for Melinda. She called Amanda for her, then let Melinda get on the phone to talk. Kristie knew Melinda was very distraught. She was there on one occasion when she watched Melinda call and say, "Amanda, you're destroying me, I just want to kill myself! I can't take it anymore, why are you doing this to me?" And Kristie was becoming seriously concerned about her friend. "Amanda ain't worth all this," she told her, "you need to get your shit together! Go to school and worry about your grades!"

But Melinda was only concerned about getting back together with Amanda; she missed her, and she had reason to believe that Amanda felt the same way. "I started talking to her and she gave me these pretty little roses in this glass dish-like, it snapped shut, she left it in my locker and my heart just melted, so I said okay and we went and we had a talk," Melinda remembers. "I said I know you're still fucking her, Amanda . . . I wouldn't touch her, she made me sick. She was messing around with a little girl. I was, like, 'You should be baby-sitting her' if anything."

On Tuesday, October 22, Melinda and Amanda agreed to skip school together with Kary Pope. They picked up two other girls, Diane and Renee, and took off to Louisville for the day, hanging out on Bardstown Road, where they checked out the newest CDs, posters, and T-shirts. They dropped by the "spirit" shop, a place Kary knew about which had healing stones and other "magical" items. They all took No Doze, so the day just sped by. When they got home that afternoon, they were "busted"; Kary had to answer to the administrators at New Albany High School, where she was a junior; Amanda and Melinda were put in ISS at Hazelwood, and later got grounded by their parents.

Because it was the first time Amanda had ever skipped school, her father, Jerry Heavrin, was alarmed. He snooped around his daughter's room looking for clues, trying to find a reason for all the hang-up calls, for all the trouble Amanda was having.

It didn't take him long to find a few letters from Melinda to Amanda. As he sat down and read them, he couldn't believe the tone. It was overtly sexual. He questioned Amanda about it, but she refused to admit that anything was going on. Heavrin decided it was time to keep Melinda away from his daughter, reporting Loveless to the local juvenile probation officer, Virgil Seay. He requested a restraining order against Loveless, leaving the letters there on file.

Meanwhile, Carrie East found out that Melinda and Amanda were possibly reuniting. East was in love with Melinda, and she was ready to fight for her, if it came to that.

"Carrie found out and so I was in a position now, I had to choose," Melinda said, "I didn't want to hurt Carrie cause she had said that she loved me and would do anything, she would cry and get on her knees. And I couldn't just play with someone's heart just to get back, to make someone jealous because they're making me jealous. I felt bad, and I said okay, okay, just give me time."

But East didn't give Melinda a chance to think about it. East knew Melinda really wanted Amanda; Amanda was her true love. East got so angry about the prospect of losing Melinda that she arranged for Kary Pope to drive the girls to the Community Park in New Albany that night. She was ready to beat Amanda up.

"This car has been following us all night and it's Carrie East," Melinda recounted, "we were at the park and she's saying she's in love with me. What's Amanda got that she don't? She can give me more, she's older, far more experienced. . . . I saved Amanda's butt actually because Carrie was charging her with a bat. Amanda's, like, you know she's scared, she's in the car, she ain't even trying to help me. So I say to Carrie if you're going to hit anyone, you're going to hit me. So I push her and I tell her to grow up, because it's immature to come out there to beat a little girl up. So I get in the car with my wife, my woman, you know, Amanda, and we take off."

But of course Amanda wasn't interested in belonging solely to Melinda. And after the scene at Community Park, Shanda was probably looking better to her all the time.

On October 24 when "Harvest Homecoming" weekend began (Harvest Homecoming is a month-long annual New Albany event that culminates with a traditional small-town festival), Amanda told Shanda not to make plans with anyone else; she invited her to sleep over. At first, her mom, Jackie Vaught, told Shanda she couldn't go, but then she changed her mind. That weekend, Shanda and Amanda went to the "Haunted House" together with Shanda's father Steve and his wife Sharon. They all had a good time, just kidding around, scaring each other in the "haunted" building on the grounds of Culbertson Mansion, a state historic site on Main Street. It was one of those grand old houses with painted ceilings and marble fireplaces, a real anomaly in New Albany.

After a day of food booths and rides, the girls spent the night together.

Shanda,
I really had a great time with you last night.
I look forward to more.
Please don't cry no more, Ok?

Love,
Amanda

Amanda,
I loved last night, too. I want more too and always. . . . Can I have something to remember you by? I want what we had last night. If you want. Will you accept my ring if I give it to you?

Love,
Shanda

It didn't take long for the word about the "homecoming" to get back to Melinda. Her "girlfriend" was sneaking out behind her back and she was furious. That very weekend, Melinda ran to Kristie in a panic, reporting her latest news.

"Guess what! Remember the girl at that dance?" Melinda asked.

"Yeah. What about her?"

"Amanda's going out with her," Melinda said in a desperate tone.

"Just leave her alone! She's just a little kid!" Kristie told her.

"I think they went to the haunted house together. Let's find out. Do you have her number?" Melinda asked, begging Kristie to call Shanda. And even though Kristie had never met Shanda, she looked the number up and introduced herself on the telephone. She acted as if she were looking for Amanda, getting Shanda to admit that she and Amanda had gone to the homecoming together.

"I'd just like to beat her up," Melinda said when she heard the confirmation, "I'd just like to *kill* her."

Five minutes later, when she called Amanda to quiz her about the homecoming, Amanda denied having gone, claiming she hadn't seen Shanda at all. The fact that Amanda lied about it got to Melinda the most. She wanted revenge; she wanted to go get Shanda right then. But Kristie convinced her that it wasn't Shanda she should be mad at; really, Amanda was the one to blame.

That night, Kristie and Melinda made a plan to go pick Amanda up and maybe beat her up. But it didn't work out. Instead, she and Kristie wound up with a bunch of guys until the wee hours of the morning.

However, Melinda wasn't about to let things slide. The next day, she called Crystal, asking what she should do about Shanda, about how she could get rid of her. At first, Crystal just took it as angry chatter. "We talked about killing people all the time, just kill them and get it over with," Crystal remembers, "but then you get to the point where, hey, they ain't worth it, and you go on with your life."

But Melinda wouldn't drop the subject. After she ranted and raved long enough, she convinced Crystal that she had to get rid of this little girl, and Crystal encouraged her. "She tried and tried and tried to get this girl to stay away from Amanda, and Shanda wouldn't do it, and Melinda couldn't take it no more," Crystal explained. "When Melinda started telling how much she hated Shanda and what Shanda was doing to her, I said I'm tired of this shit, Melinda. . . . Fuck people, fuck everybody. I'm tired of people's shit and I'm tired of putting up with it. Fucking kill the fucking bitch! She fucking deserves to die. She shouldn't be messing around with your girlfriend anyways. You done told her once, twice; three times is too many. Now do something to get her to stop."

At school, Melinda continued to threaten Shanda, telling her she would beat her up bad, causing a couple of scenes out on Buerk Field, the football field near New Albany High School where kids would meet. But all of the fights and problems with these streetwise kids had transformed Shanda. Shanda would fight back; she stood up to Melinda, and was doing a good job of defending herself.

"She changed completely within a matter of a month," Jackie Vaught later told *The Courier Journal*. "Shanda had always been a leader. But these kids were older and rougher, and she got herself into a situation where she was no longer a leader; she was a follower. I watched her just dwindle. She went from this robust child who could never do enough to this child who didn't even want to talk, that would close the door to her room and not come out all night."

Shanda was now spending weekends with Amanda, confiding things to her about difficulties at home. "She said she saved a lot of lunch money, she was supposed to run away with a bunch of friends to Florida or something like that . . . I told her she wasn't going to get very far on sixty or seventy dollars."

All along, the notes Amanda wrote became more loving in their tone (she signed them Amanda poo, the nickname Melinda had come up with). She told Shanda of the many feelings she had for her, now that they were "going together."

Amanda wrote several notes telling her "I'm all yours." She gave Shanda flowers, drew her hearts, and even drew a "Rose of Love." She also wrote (or copied) sweet poems for her. One mushy poem, entitled "Thoughts," tells Shanda, "My precious one, I love you so, and with each day, that love will grow, until it's height reach to the sky, even then it will not die."

By October 28, Melinda's sixteenth birthday, Amanda and Shanda's relationship reached its height. The girls were sending perfumed notes to each other, writing

"Shanda loves Amanda" and "Amanda loves Shanda," filling whole sheets of paper with just those few words.

Melinda had written to Amanda just days before, asking to talk things out, but she got no response. She just got stonewalled.

The year before, Amanda was buying Melinda little gifts all the time. She had even given her a gold "panda" ring, something Melinda wore almost like a wedding band. But this birthday, her sweet sixteen, passed without even a word from Amanda. Melinda was dumbfounded. Making things even worse, her father hadn't sent so much as a card to her.

By October 29, Amanda and Shanda exchanged pictures of each other. "Do I look like a boy or what," Amanda asked in one note. On the same day, Shanda wrote a letter back, professing her love and devotion. "So do you get jealous when I talk or look at Dana. You really shouldn't because. . . . I love you 2 much. I just want you and only you," Shanda wrote. "I promise I would never lie 2 you. Please don't think that I like that girl [Dana]."

Reportedly, Jackie Vaught found one of the romantic letters from Amanda to Shanda, and she tried to arrange a meeting for herself, her present husband, and her ex, Steve, also Amanda's father, Jerry, and the two girls. She wanted to have some clear answers, to get the situation sized out once and for all. She didn't know what to think because Shanda denied that the letters meant anything to her. But unfortunately, the meeting didn't take place because Jerry Heavrin felt that three adults against him was unfair; he felt he was being ganged up on and decided to back out at the last minute.

While waiting for Heavrin to show, Jackie decided to question her daughter about the nature of the relationship she had with Amanda. "I asked her if Amanda had ever touched her in a way that she should not, and she emphatically told me no," Jackie later said in an interview with

Indianapolis magazine. "I told her, this letter leads me to believe that you and Amanda have more than just a friendship, and she said, 'No mom, we don't. It's just that Amanda needed a friend. I wanted to be a good friend.' "

Jackie and her daughter had a good cry together, and agreed to a new beginning for both of them. "I don't know if anything physical happened between Shanda and Amanda," Vaught told the reporter, "maybe it did . . . I know that Shanda felt bad about what happened and she wanted to start over again. She slept with me every night after the night we talked."

With Steve Sharer's financial input, the last week in November, Shanda was enrolled at Our Lady of Perpetual Help in New Albany. The school would offer Shanda a religious educational program that Jackie was very familiar with, having attended there as a young girl herself. Reportedly, Shanda immediately became a part of the girl's basketball team; she was well received by the students there. Her parents thought they had the problem solved.

But all along, Amanda had kept in touch with Shanda. Amanda still wore Shanda's ring; Amanda promised that she wasn't paying any attention to Melinda, that she wasn't even reading Melinda's letters to her. There was another dance coming up at Hazelwood, and even though Shanda was no longer a student there, she intended to go, writing to Amanda, asking about the dance, explaining that she would be spending the night with her cousin, Amanda Edrington, that Friday.

It was a short note, which Shanda ended with, "We would have fun if I was spending the night with you? Remember the dance in my room! HA." At the bottom, she wrote "Melinda is gone" putting an X through Melinda's name.

On November 22, Friday night, Shanda's cousin, Amanda, and her girlfriend, Amanda, both students at Hazelwood, tried to sneak Shanda into the dance. "You had to have an activity ticket to get into the dance and she was not a member of school anymore so they wouldn't let her in, so we got her an activity ticket and tried to get her in and they recognized her and made her go back out," Shanda's cousin said.

Because she was not allowed on school property, Shanda was forced to stand across the street with a bunch of other kids. She wasn't waiting for long, however; within minutes, they were all regrouped and on their way into someone's car. Then suddenly, Melinda appeared, commanding Amanda to tell Shanda that she didn't love her, that she never wanted to see her again.

Heavrin complied.

Then Melinda turned to Shanda: "If you even try to talk to Amanda again I'm going to fucking kill you."

Not long after, Shanda received a copy of the Hazelwood yearbook along with a letter from Amanda, detailing the page numbers where certain pictures had been circled. There were pictures of Shanda and Amanda circled in colored ink. At the end of a brief note inside, Amanda mentioned a girl who wanted to beat Shanda up, trying to tell her to stay away, to warn her about the danger ahead for both of them if they continued the relationship.

By December 12, Amanda decided to type a letter to Shanda. On her part, it was a serious attempt to put an end to things. In the letter Amanda promised Shanda Sharer that she'd always be there for her in a time of need. She told Shanda that she knew she was having a "little love game" with Ray, and basically indicated that she wanted to end their relationship because of it.

Shanda wrote her a five-page letter back. In it, she complained about "Our Lady," reporting her class schedule and her uneasiness there, wishing that Amanda could be in her classes with her and saying that she didn't feel as smart as the other kids, "yeah I'm smart, but not this

151

smart ya-know."

Shanda was curious about what was going on at Hazelwood, asking Amanda to take care of her cousin. "Because people sometimes can take advantage of her," Shanda wrote. She ended the letter with a poem that closed with verses:

You make me feel like the whole world is singing.
And when you make me cry
I feel left out but in a happy way.
I want you 2, 2 feel like I do. I will always love
the person who loves me most.

Twelve

Throughout the fall of 1991, Melinda Loveless had culti-
vated a number of girlfriends, mostly in an attempt to divert
herself from her problems. Among them, she was the center
of attention; they all thought she was beautiful enough to be
on the cover of *Vogue*. People wanted to be around her, and
she knew it.

"If you ever watch movies and see, like, these love god-
desses with, like, long hair and they're all dressed up in white
and their bodies are just perfect and face structure is just perfect and their hair's just perfect, that's Melinda," Kary Pope
said. "Everything about her is beautiful, you can't find one
thing on that girl that is not beautiful."

But what attracted people to Melinda even more was her
zany personality and her blunt ways. Melinda would go up to
strangers and grab them on the butt; she'd talk about sex all
the time. "I bet she has a big bush!" they would hear Melinda
say as she walked by someone in the mall. Her friends
thought she was an outrage; they loved it.

For a while, Melinda and Kary Pope had a pseudo romance
going on. They never actually had sex, but they did make out
on the floor of someone's house once, and they acted like
they were "going together" for a certain period of time. Melinda thought it might make Amanda jealous.

"She'd hold my hand when we were in the car, she would
act like we were going out," Kary confided, "and then later on
in our relationship after that, she'd always tell me she loved

153

me and that she missed me and I would just come over to her house and see her."

Kary Pope was not the kind of person Margie wanted her daughter hanging around with. Kary had half of the hair on her head shaved off; she wore black clothes and spiked leather accessories; she was a hard-core punk. Her friends, Larry and Terry Leatherbury, twin bisexual brothers, were even more punked out, donning mohawks, dog collars, and nose rings. Melinda never brought them around; she knew her mother would never approve. She tried to keep her punk friends in a separate universe, seeing them mostly in Louisville, hanging out in Cherokee Park off Eastern Highway, in a spot known as "Fag Hill."

"It's a gay people hang out," Kary explained, "people have sex in the bushes or they pick up *trade*. If you want a car to follow you, you blink your lights."

The Leatherburys were from Madison, over an hour away, but they spent a lot of time in Louisville, mostly because Madison had nothing to really offer them. Kary Pope had met them in 1990. They had a comradery based on their "alternative" life-style and had developed their own network of gay people. They looked out for each other.

One day, along about the second week of October 1991, Kary and Melinda happened to be at Kary's grandmother's house in New Albany when Laurie Tackett called. Through the Leatherburys, Laurie was getting to know the Louisville scene. They had introduced her to Crystal Lyles, who told Laurie about Kary Pope, and Laurie was anxious to make her acquaintance.

Laurie was sick of Madison. She had just turned seventeen and was desperate to leave home. She needed to find new friends, and she was calling to see if Kary could possibly rescue her.

"Hello, my name's Laurie. I'm a friend of Crystal Lyles.

She gave me your number," a soft voice said.

Kary had no idea who she was talking to, but the girl sounded nice.

"I don't know you. I'm supposed to come down there and stay with her for a couple of days, but I don't have a car. She told me you were cool. She said you would help me out. I'm having problems with my family. Would you come and pick me up? I'll give you some money."

When Kary hung up just a few minutes later, she asked Melinda if she would go with her to Madison. "We thought, well, if she's too weird-looking, we'll just drive off and let it be an adventure to go up there," Kary remembers.

Kary and Melinda got as far as Hanover, about a ten-minute drive from Laurie's house. They were lost, and stopped there to call for directions. Eventually, George Tackett drove his daughter over to Hanover, dropping her off at the gas station where the girls waited.

Laurie really impressed the girls. The minute they laid eyes on her, they knew she was one of them. She was drinking Seagram's wine coolers and was already half drunk when she got into the car. She had a bagful of clothes with her and she told them she was moving out. The three of them talked about things they had in common, general chatter, getting to know each other on the drive down.

When they arrived in New Albany, however, they discovered that Crystal Lyles didn't have a place for Laurie to stay after all. After much pleading, Kary finally agreed to have Laurie stay with her at her grandmother's, just for one night. Melinda and Laurie didn't seem to like each other at first, but Kary had found a new friend.

After they dropped Melinda off, Laurie confided to Kary that she was bisexual, showing her a picture of her girlfriend, Diane Norton, who she said was moving to Utah. Laurie had just broken up with the girl, and she was distraught over it.

Laurie and Kary were attracted to each other; they struck up an immediate bond. One night turned into three, during

155

which time Laurie and Kary learned that they had similar likes and wants. They were both into the "alternative" scene. They followed the music of Sinéad O'Connor, Siouxsie and the Banshees, and The Cure; they both wore punk clothes; they were both dabbling in the occult. The other thing they had in common: They both hated their families.

"Her grandmother was rude. She just seemed like she wasn't a happy person, and she was on Kary about everything," Laurie said. "Kary wasn't going to school and she would come in and she would say, 'Well, if you're not going to school, I'm going to call the police on you,' just threatening her."

"Do you want me to leave?" Laurie asked on the second day, reacting to the tension in the house.

"No, no, my grandmother won't do anything," Kary assured her.

The third day of Laurie's stay, Kary swallowed thirty speed tablets and that night she panicked. She thought she was dying. She thought her heart was going to stop.

"I was wigging-out and she was holding me in her arms and she says, 'Kary, you're not going to die,' " Kary remembered. "She took my arm and she held my arm and she called out this name, Lucinda. And she just kept saying Lucinda, Lucinda, over and over again, and somehow she made me feel better."

Laurie was "channeling" a spirit, and Kary was fascinated by the prospect. The Leatherbury twins were into channeling as well. Channeling, a modern term for "spirit guides" or "mediums," became a popular term because of the activities of people like actress Shirley MacLaine. Kary knew all about the spiritualist concept, and she was intrigued to discover that Laurie was a part of it.

From the Leatherburys, Laurie had already heard about the place called The Witches' Castle. She told Kary she wanted to see it, and the next day they made plans to go up there. Soon it became a regular occurrence. The group of them would go to Utica, bringing white candles and lighters to hold seances on the grounds. Kary's grandmother eventually insisted that Laurie find someplace else to stay, and Kary drove her back up to Madison, helping Laurie gather the rest of her clothes, then arranging for Laurie to get temporarily settled over at Crystal Lyles's place.

Just days later, Kary Pope was admitted into Jefferson Hospital for drug rehabilitation. At just seventeen, Kary was addicted to cocaine; the girl was strung out.

During her few weeks of treatment in November 1991, Kary was out of the picture, not knowing who Laurie was spending her time with or what was happening with her friends in New Albany. Unfortunately, the hospital stay didn't do much good. As soon as she was released, Kary was back on the street, hanging out with Laurie again, dropping acid on occasion, and dabbling in witchcraft more than ever.

By then Laurie and Crystal were sharing an apartment, but Laurie had no job, no car, and little money. She spent her days combing the streets of New Albany by foot, looking for any kind of employment, finding that she didn't have the skills necessary to land a decent job. Still, Laurie didn't mind her financial difficulties too much; she was just happy to be living in New Albany. She and Crystal became inseparable, hanging out with Crystal's friends and the Leatherbury twins. She was in with a new crowd; she had found acceptance.

"Madison is such a small town, it's so conservative, I hated it," Laurie said. "Nobody understood me, and I felt I was the only gay girl in Madison. Larry and Terry were gay, but they were guys and I just needed to be with people like me. In New Albany, we had a whole bunch of people who were gay that we hung around with."

It was not until the end of November that Laurie and Melinda became friends. Up until that time, each had kept her distance. They had received mixed signals from each other. Laurie didn't believe Melinda was really gay at first; Melinda didn't act gay. Melinda had her own misgivings about Laurie as well. She heard too many strange things about Laurie, and she didn't like the way Laurie behaved.

"Every time I went out with Kary, Laurie was almost always with her," Melinda said, "and what I seen and heard from Laurie, I thought she was really weird. I heard she once sacrificed some animal, I think a cat. I later came to learn that Laurie worshiped the devil."

Laurie Tackett was born on October 5, 1974, brought into the world with the given name, Mary Laurine. For the first three or four months, because she cried so much at night, her parents, George and Peggy, tried to have their newborn baby sleep between them. However, being in their bed only caused Laurie to cry more, and her parents ultimately decided to let her cry herself to sleep, alone in her crib.

In many ways, Peggy and George were from two different worlds. From the time she was a young child, Peggy suffered a history of seizures; she was on medication, and she was very fragile. Her only involvement outside the home was at the Pentecostal church, where she was a devout member. George however, had a troubled youth. On January 19, 1961, he was sentenced to serve two to five years at the reformatory in Pendleton, Indiana, for second degree burglary. On April 28, 1964, he was sentenced to serve one year in a minimum security facility in Greencastle, Indiana, for theft by exerting unauthorized control.

Still, by the time Laurie was born, ten years later, George Tackett had gotten his life in order. He was a factory worker at the Reliance Electric Company in Madison, and he spent most of his days working overtime to support his family. Peggy remained a housewife and a pious church-goer, giving birth to their second child, George, Junior, who they nicknamed Bubby. But even though they had a new family together, things really weren't right in the household. George wasn't "saved," he refused to go to church, and he and his wife didn't see eye to eye about it.

There were also problems with Laurie. She didn't seem to be a happy child. Peggy noticed she was a self-absorbed little girl who tended to stay away from other children. She saw, too, that Laurie was moody; without any notice, she would switch very quickly from being cheerful to being depressed or angry.

According to Laurie, there were only two instances which she would remember from childhood; in both cases, she claims a molestation occurred. These incidents allegedly happened when she was age five and age twelve, respectively. Outside of those traumatic events, Laurie claims to remember little or nothing of her childhood. "Ninety-nine percent of it is blocked out," she insists.

"I don't remember my childhood, just nightmares and dreams," Laurie explained. "All of my memories are violent. One of the only things I remember is a hallucination I had when I was five. Hands the colors of the rainbow were coming out of the floor. Then gray ones, all wrinkled up, were straining to get further out of the floor, trying to grab me."

When Laurie was six, she had a dream about an army of men dressed in black armor who were fighting naked children. She remembers the "black" army stabbing the children. She emphasizes that this is her most vivid memory of her childhood, that she remembers nothing else, really, before the age of twelve.

Other schoolchildren would later categorize Laurie as someone who was withdrawn, as someone who sat alone on the bus and didn't have many friends. As per her mother's orders, she looked like a church girl, donning long dresses and long hair, and the other kids rejected her because of it. Peggy Tackett belonged to a fundamental church, The Lighthouse on the Hill in Madison, which forbid its members to wear makeup, jewelry, or jeans. It was a place where people often spoke in tongues, where miraculous healings transpired, where people had visions. It was a place that Laurie grew to loathe, especially because her mother was so fanatical about it.

"Everything I did, I was told I was going to hell for it," Laurie said. "That's all they preached, going to hell and burning. If you don't receive the Holy Ghost, you're going into eternal fire."

By the time Laurie reached puberty, at about the age of thirteen, she and her mother were fighting bitterly over the ideologies of the church. Laurie wanted to wear "normal" clothes, she wanted to listen to rock music, but her mother wouldn't hear of it. Even medical care was beyond the realm of Peggy Tackett's scope; medicine was something that only sinners needed, not people of God. Whenever Laurie got sick, except for two or three times when she had an ear infection, her mother wouldn't take her to the doctor. Laurie had a jaw disorder, her teeth came in too early when she was a baby, but her mother wouldn't allow her to have surgery. Laurie suffered massive headaches from the disorder, missing many days of school over it.

"When I was at home, I was never allowed to express myself," Laurie complained. "My mom's weird. She doesn't try to help herself. She prays to God and believes God will take care of everything."

At age fourteen, Laurie stopped going to church. She told her mother that she didn't believe in the Holy Ghost, and she refused to accompany her on Sunday mornings. Laurie stayed away for almost a year, during which time she began smuggling clothes to school, changing from her dresses into jeans, and then back into dresses for her return home. She also began to drink heavily, sneaking wine and whiskey into her room every day. Laurie got away with that routine for almost six months; however, one Monday afternoon in May 1989, Peggy caught her daughter wearing jeans and there was hell to pay.

That night at the dinner table, Peggy threw a fit, telling

Laurie that people would think she was a "bad mother" for letting her wear jeans, telling Laurie that she was going to be a "bad person" when she grew up. In a rage, Peggy jerked her daughter out of her chair and Laurie fell to the floor. Laurie jumped up from under the table, ran to her room, shut the door and leaned against it, but her mother beat the door down, hitting her daughter, then trying to strangle her.

Laurie was able to get away and run to a neighbor's house, where she waited for her mom to calm down. The next day, the neighbor called the Indiana State Department of Public Welfare, asking them to investigate possible child abuse in the Tackett house.

On May 12, the day after the report was filed, Jill Larimore, a social worker, went to Madison Junior High, requested the use of a counselor's office, and spoke with Laurie. She asked Laurie about the large bruise on her face, and Laurie told the caseworker that her mother hit her. Laurie showed Ms. Larimore some scratches on her neck and a faint bruise on her arm. Photographs were taken of all three wounds.

Laurie also had a bandage on her arm, the caseworker noticed, but Laurie said that her mother wasn't responsible for it, explaining that she had cut herself by accident the year before, when she had taken a knife and tried to scrape a tattoo off her arm.

That same morning, the caseworker, went out to the Tacketts' home with an escort from the local Sheriff's Department. Peggy wasn't home, but George Tackett agreed to accompany his wife to the sheriff's office as soon as she returned. At 11:30 A.M., they arrived along with the Reverend Sims, who was there to provide the Tacketts with moral support.

Officer Jones read Peggy Tackett her rights. She was very tense and angry throughout the interview, but eventually she admitted that she had hit her daughter, stating that she "prayed to God that she would never do this again."

On May 16, 1989, Peggy and George Tackett appeared before Jefferson County Circuit Judge Ted Todd, signing a consent for the implementation of an "informal adjustment," whereby an officer of the juvenile court would assume supervision over Laurie for a period of six months. The agreement would allow Laurie to live at home, but required that the family would cooperate with unannounced visits from a social worker.

On June 6, Larimore made one call to the Tackett home to see how they were doing. During the visit, Mrs. Tackett told her that her daughter was extremely demanding and manipulating, complaining that she was spending weekends away from home, and was refusing to get a job.

Larimore made two follow-up phone calls to the Tackett home that month. On June 9, she spoke to Laurie, who said that she had called one or two places for a job, but no place was hiring. Laurie had a long list of establishments that Larimore had suggested for employment, and she was told to continue her search.

On June 22, when Larimore called again, Mrs. Tackett informed her that Laurie was spending the night at a friend's. She told Larimore that things were better at home, but complained that Laurie never followed through with her job pursuit, that Laurie only wanted to "run" constantly.

It wasn't until November of 1989 that Larimore made another contact with the Tacketts, this time, for the last time. She and another social worker made a home visit on November 13, at which time she noticed two things: Laurie's hair had been cut short, and she was wearing colorful clothes. Laurie explained that she and her parents had had a talk, and that they agreed to give her money to buy jeans and get her ears pierced.

Since Larimore was familiar with the practices of Peggy's strict religion, she took Laurie's appearance as a positive sign. She thought things had worked themselves out. That same day, she made the decision to terminate the "adjustment" and

wanted to believe it, cause I wanted to get out of reality."

The society used Ouija boards and tarot cards to gain access to other worlds and spirits. Following Julia's example, Laurie soon started channeling, going into trances and pulling spirits into her body, one of which she called "Deanna the vampire."

"The Ouija board is supposed to be a gateway to spirits, and Laurie would go to letters. She spelled Deanna an awful lot," Larry said. "Laurie would close her eyes and sometimes she would start shaking a little bit, and then she would do a transfer."

During these trances, Laurie's body would become limp, she would start crying, then she would fall onto the floor, talking about things she could see. One time she described dead babies, other times she would talk of a vampire woman, saying *"Come to me"*. "We all had a fascination about vampires because vampirism entails immortality," Larry said. "Immortality was something Laurie desired."

But Larry and Terry thought that Laurie was always faking it. They never believed her "trances" because they seemed rehearsed. It was just something she was doing to get attention. They patronized her, pretending to go along with her, never thinking it was authentic. Moreover, they thought Laurie was carrying the "evil" element too far. Their group was mostly based on the power of mental telepathy and on spiritual energies, not on evil forces.

"When people think about the occult, they automatically think devil worship. I was never into things like that," Terry explained. "Occult things were part of our peer group, but it wasn't bad occult things. It was basically just spiritual, trying to expand ourselves and deal with our own pain. Basically, it was a support group for us all."

But Laurie's behavior was deranged in Peggy's eyes. She became convinced that her daughter was possessed by demons; she began telling Laurie that she could see demons flying around her head.

turnaround papers were mailed to the state.

But just weeks later, right around Christmas, Peggy Tackett suffered a serious seizure (she had stopped taking her medication) and she decided that God was speaking to her. Suddenly, she became even more devout, again imposing the rules of the church on Laurie.

"It's my life! I have got to live my own life! This religion is not for me!" Laurie protested.

But Peggy Tackett told her daughter that she would obey.

"My mom, she made me want to be evil," Laurie said. "I mean, I was never into satan, I just wanted to be the opposite of her, because I hated her. I resented her. I wanted to be the evilest person on Earth."

By then, Laurie had turned fifteen, and she began to go overboard with her rebellion, cutting her hair shorter and shorter, dressing in more "alternative" ways. She began to paint her face with purple lipstick and heavy black eyeliner. She discovered that, supposedly, Jefferson County was one of the top nine counties in the country known for witchcraft, and she was spending a lot of time alone behind her house, where she said there were peculiar woods that gave her "peace."

She decided to absorb as much as she could about the occult. She started out small, learning about the role-playing game, Dungeons & Dragons, from her neighbor, Brian Teague. She borrowed playing manuals from Teague; these were books about dragons and wizards which promised to provide her with "an arsenal of magical items."

"You can go on a journey in your mind, you pick the character you want to be," Laurie described. "You're fighting off the evil power. It's kind of like Nintendo, you're fighting off evil to get to a destination."

But Dungeons & Dragons didn't hold Laurie's interest for long. She was much more fascinated by "real" witches and sorcerers. Eventually Teague taught Laurie how to read "stones." He had a set of rune stones which he later gave to found her diary, in which she wrote: "I want to be a boy" and "I hate God." Bubby reported the information to Peggy, who dragged Laurie to a sermon at the Lighthouse, where the preacher ranted that all homosexuals would go to hell. Laurie never stepped foot inside a church again.

Rumors started flying about her. When people questioned her belief in God, Laurie simply said she was an atheist: "I just dressed in black and I didn't talk that much and I had a fuck-you attitude towards everything."

Terry Leatherbury noticed a change in Laurie himself; she was more antisocial. "She started to act really strange, kind of withdrawn," Terry remembers. "She would just sit there and she'd get this look in her eyes. I could always tell that there was something wrong, and I just felt she was eccentric. She started hitting me for no reason. One time I was just sitting there, and she ran towards me, she started scratching me."

Laurie was crying more frequently, talking about her nightmares. She often spoke of one dream in particular she called "Desolation," where she saw the end of the world. It was a vision of dead bodies everywhere . . . and dead babies hanging from trees.

Thirteen

All along, Laurie was having serious problems at school. Her teachers noted a change in her academic performance, and she began to fail. She had to repeat seventh grade. Laurie suffered on a personal level at school; she was abandoned by the few childhood friends she had. Most of them did not approve of her physical transformation, her appearance was frightening to them, and they stayed away.

That is, with the exception of Hope Rippey, whom Laurie treated as a younger sister. Hope was the one person whom Laurie could trust. The two girls had a sense of love for each other that transcended all physical boundaries. "I've always had sisterly love for Hope. She's just a baby and I would do anything for her," Laurie later proclaimed.

Hope was a timid child, the fourth of four children. Born June 1976, she was a child who sought protection and love, who was terribly frightened whenever her father went away on a business trip, always running to him for a kiss or hug and a promise that he would return home soon. Her father, Carl, had moved to Madison in 1969, where he became employed as a testing engineer at Indiana/Kentucky Electric, a power plant. Carl handled the new designs and performance of equipment, checking the performance levels for efficiency, safety, and economy.

Melinda's parents, Larry and Marjorie Loveless,
on their wedding day, July 15, 1966.

Larry and Margie Loveless, Easter Sunday, 1969.

The Loveless Family in 1975: (left to right) Michelle, 10;
Margie holding Melinda, three months old;
Larry holding Melissa, 6.

Melinda singing "White Christmas" at
her school play in 1985.

Melinda Loveless
at age 10.

Larry, his motorcycle, and his "girls" in 1985.

Larry in his postal uniform.

Melinda embraced by her father, Larry Loveless.

The Loveless home at 2211 Charlestown Road,
New Albany, Indiana.

Melinda and her friend, Crystal Wathen.

Larry Loveless at home.

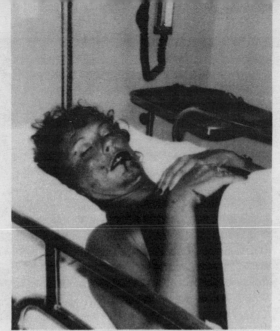

Marjorie Loveless at Clark County Hospital in
1986 after her beating by Larry Loveless.

Melinda's room.

Melinda on her fifteenth birthday with her mother.

Melinda, Michelle and Melissa Loveless.

Madison Junior High School.

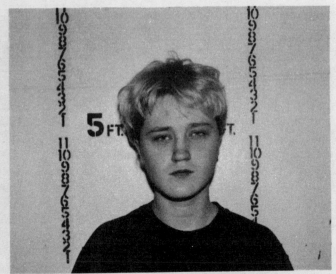

Mary Laurine Tackett shortly after her arrest.

The Tackett home in Madison, Indiana.

The Lighthouse on the Hill Pentecostal Church attended
by the Loveless family.

Kary Pope in her "punk" days.

Hope Rippey at 14.

Hope Rippey shortly after her arrest.

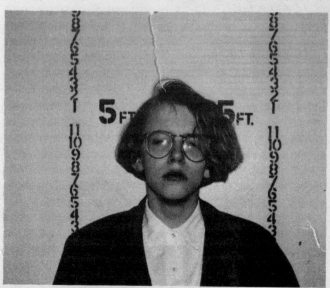

Toni Lawrence shortly after her arrest.

Hazelwood Junior High School.

Shanda Sharer
as she appeared
in junior high school.

The Witches' Castle.

The muddy ground off Lemon Road
where Shanda's body was found.

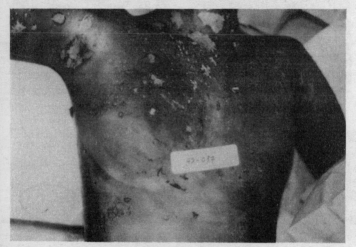

Upper torso scars.

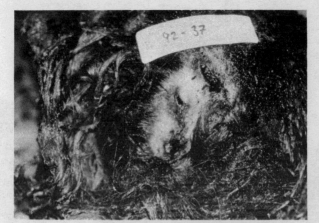

Head wounds.

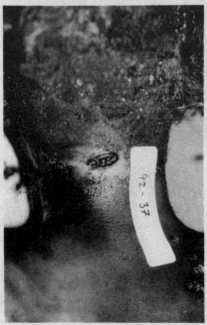

Neck wound.

Detective Steve Henry on the steps of St. Joseph Superior Court in South Bend, Indiana.

Jackie Vaught and Steve Sharer address the media after Hope Rippey's sentencing.

Prosecutor Guy Townsend holds a press conference after the four girls have been sentenced.

"She didn't want to be separated," Carl recalls. "She always thought I wouldn't come back from business trips."

Hope's two older brothers, Dan and John, born four years apart, were in constant fistfights at home; it was something that started when they were little kids, and it caused Hope a lot of grief. Because neither her parents nor her older sister did anything to dissuade the boys from fighting, Hope was always trying to get in between them, trying to make peace in her house, using any means necessary to get them to stop.

"Hope would get in there and physically try to hold these boys away from each other," Carl said. "She was a feisty little kid."

In February of 1984, when Hope was just seven years old, her parents, Carl and Gloria, got divorced. The divorce caused a tremendous upset in Hope's life. At first, Gloria and the kids lived at the house in Madison, and Carl stayed with his parents, who also were Madison residents. Soon they discovered that this was not a suitable situation, and Gloria moved back to Michigan, her home state, taking the children with her.

For three years, Hope lived in Quincy, Michigan, known as "the magic capital of the world" where commercial wizardry is invented. It was 250 miles away from Madison, and, while she had some trouble adjusting at first, with the love and support of both her parents (her father came to visit regularly), she managed to fit right into the school system in nearby Bronson. She played the flute in band, she took piano lessons, she was even chosen to play Dorothy in the school production of *The Wizard of Oz*.

In 1987, primarily because Hope was homesick, and also because she and her siblings were still upset about their parents' divorce, Gloria and Carl reunited. They didn't officially get married, but Gloria moved back to Madison with the kids, setting up house in their original residence.

Hope was entering seventh grade at the time. That fall, she enrolled in Madison Junior High School and rejoined her childhood friends. Her friendship with Laurie was intact, as was her friendship with Toni Lawrence, to whom she had been close since preschool. She was happy to be back home.

Hope was an average student who never posed a disciplinary problem. (Although her school counselor did say that Hope was somewhat argumentative at school, taking up causes and later participating in a student walk-out.) Hope was active in many aspects of school life. She made the Junior High basketball team, and she ran track. Although she didn't set any records, she did receive ribbons for her efforts, and her parents went to her sporting events to cheer her on.

For the most part, she had a stable home life. There were still difficulties within the family, but her father did whatever he could to see that Hope was happy. Her father took Hope and her friends to Lexington and Indianapolis, treating them to days at the zoo and the amusement park. He has pictures of Hope and her pals at Kings Island, the Cincinnati theme park which was always her favorite. Her idols were The New Kids On The Block, and Carl went out of his way to take Hope and a bunch of her friends to the Louisville Fair Grounds so they could see them in person.

Laurie was not included in that trip. By that time, Hope had somewhat separated herself from Laurie, feeling that they didn't have that much in common anymore. She knew Laurie was someone Carl didn't totally approve of. He especially didn't like Laurie's new style of dress; he had no use for the "alternative" look. He told Hope that he didn't want her following in Laurie's footsteps, and Hope promised that she wouldn't, insisting that the main reason she remained friends with Laurie was that Laurie was being shunned by the other kids at school. She felt sorry for her.

One day, Laurie went to Carl, very upset about the possibility of losing Hope's friendship. Carl assured Laurie that Hope still cared about her.

"Hope was someone Laurie could come to and I didn't deny her. I thought Hope could always make the right choice," Carl said.

Though he was always somewhat hesitant, Carl took Hope to Laurie's house on a number of occasions, deciding that it was all right for his daughter to have friends from different walks of life. He trusted Hope. He believed she would always act sensibly.

Laurie was thinking about dropping out of school, and Hope was concerned for her friend. She encouraged Laurie to stick with it. Laurie actually did drop out of classes for a few days here and there, and Hope was the one to convince her to give it another try.

Carl knew that Laurie was having problems with her mother, and he knew the woman was unreasonable, because he had been through a scene with her himself. Their run-in occurred just after he had taken Hope and Laurie shopping in Louisville, at which time he purchased them a Ouija board. Carl had played the game himself when he was a little kid, and he bought it for the girls, explaining that it was an illusion, that it was not something that physically happened. The girls said they understood that.

The next day, Peggy Tackett went to the Rippey house and confronted Carl about it. He told her he saw nothing wrong with his purchase, but she was extremely upset. He could do nothing to calm her down.

"She said the Ouija board was against their religion and she discussed it with their minister and that the only way to get rid of that evil was to have the thing burned," Carl remembers. "I gave it to her to do whatever she wanted to do with it. I said, okay with me if you burn it."

But Peggy didn't only want the board, she also wanted the Rippey house to be exorcised.

"She wanted to have someone come from her church,"

Carl said. "She felt that because we had the board stored here, we were endangered. She was very adamant about it."

That afternoon, Carl allowed Mrs. Tackett and some of her church people onto his property and the exorcism of the house was performed. Laurie and Hope were both witnesses. They thought it was ridiculous, as did Carl, but he felt that if it would appease the woman, it was no skin off his back.

Regardless of all the turmoil in Laurie's life, she and Hope remained close. Still, Hope did not consider Laurie her best friend by any means. In fact, it was Toni Lawrence who she preferred to spend the majority of her time with. Toni was from one of Madison's more affluent neighborhoods; her father, who was a boilermaker, provided his family with a comfortable existence.

Born on February 14, 1976, Toni was the youngest of four children. By the time she was fifteen, two of her older sisters were already married with children of their own; still, Toni enjoyed the status of being the family "baby." A petite girl who wore thick glasses, she was rather spoiled by her parents, and Hope liked going over to the Lawrences' brick ranch-style home, where basically she had the freedom to do anything she wished.

"They were like sisters. Toni came and spent the night and Hope went there," Carl said. "Toni's parents accepted Hope coming over and liked Hope because she wasn't a noisy person, and she didn't defy anyone. I never had any problem with Toni. She was like a daughter. She would come over and play with toys and watch TV."

Hope's house was one place that Toni felt comfortable. She didn't feel the same way in school; in fact, Toni usually just clammed up. While she seemed to be of average intelligence, receiving Bs and Cs in most classes, her teachers noticed that she wasn't someone to readily participate in class. She had to be called on specifically before she would offer any input.

Teachers also noticed that Toni was a bit of a prima donna. It was just little things that called their attention to it; for instance, even though she lived just a stone's throw from the junior high, Toni required her mother to drive her back and forth to school. One teacher in particular, Jim Lee, had a little problem with Toni because of her attitude. Toni treated his class like it was her forum, coming in late whenever she felt like it, and he confronted her about it.

"She didn't expect me to be saying anything to her about being late, because I think she was treated much that way at home," Lee said. "She was never given any reprimands for things that she did that she shouldn't be doing."

In the eyes of their parents, neither Toni nor Hope did anything that necessitated a reprimand. Both girls were volunteering at a nearby nursing home two days a week, reading to patients and taking them for walks; they were good little girls. Hope's father, Carl, said the only problem he ever had with her was that she didn't keep her room straightened up. Toni's father, Clifton, saw his little girl as someone who had never done anything "really bad."

"The worst thing she did was lie about where she was staying one night," Clifton said.

Toni had many interests: She liked to write poetry; she liked to draw; she liked to read. She had aspirations about going on to college. School counselor, Jack Dwyer, remembers Toni coming in and talking to him about that. She seemed to have a good head on her shoulders, and he expected her to have a bright future.

Even though she was quiet and somewhat introverted, she was well liked. She had many friends; they called her "Toni-Roni." She enjoyed doing all the normal things, like going to the movies, cruising for guys, and playing pool at the teenage hangout. She was not an outgoing person, but she was quite active. No one really knew how very depressed she was.

In 1990, she had been raped by a boy who attacked her, threatening to hurt her, telling her to lie still and do whatever he said. She was in eighth grade at the time, and she wasn't going to report the incident, but her mother, Glenda, found a letter Toni wrote to her friend which detailed what happened. The next day, Toni and her father went down to the police department and tried to press charges, but all the police could do was issue an order to keep the attacker fifty feet away from her. Toni was so upset that, for the first time in her life, her parents brought her to the Lifespring counseling facility in Madison. Unfortunately, it didn't help her. After just one visit, Toni never went back.

Toni just kept things to herself; she was inwardly sad most of the time. At school, people found out about what happened, and certain people twisted things around and began to label her a slut. She responded to the taunts from peers by becoming "wild" with the boys, racking up boyfriends as easily as she racked up pool balls. She became self-destructive. She was drinking and smoking pot and was having unprotected sex with multiple partners.

But the boyfriends didn't take away any of Toni's pain. Really, she had turned off to men a long time before; allegedly, at the tender age of nine, she was sexually abused by a family relation. She never told anyone about it back then. It was something she just kept bottled up.

Sometime during eighth grade, Toni tried to hurt herself by slashing her wrists. It was one of a couple of reported incidents involving Toni's problem with self-mutilation and suicidal thoughts.

Actually, among Madison teens, Toni was only one of a number of people who were in the habit of cutting their wrists. Laurie's friend, Diane Norton, a beautiful dark-haired girl who had recently transferred to Madison, was the supposed brain behind this self-mutilation concept. She told people that cutting her flesh worked as a tension release.

Laurie thought she was intriguing and she wanted to follow in Diane's footsteps. The thing which attracted Laurie to Diane most was the girl's cold personality. When Larry Leatherbury met her, he described Diane as someone who was horribly cruel, who was without emotion. He could see that Laurie was extremely attached to her; in fact they all put Diane on a pedestal, calling her "the ice princess."

Not long after they met, in the first part of 1991, Laurie fell in love with Diane, deciding that sexually, she probably preferred women. For a while, Laurie kept her boyfriend, Aaron Hall, and figured that maybe she was bisexual. Soon, however, she got rid of Aaron, calling Larry up one day, saying, "Guess what I did! Guess what me and Diane did!" She was uncontrollably laughing about her conquest.

Diane's idea about self-mutilation appealed to Laurie, and the Leatherburys observed the two girls engaging in this practice openly. They noticed that whenever Diane cut herself, Laurie did it, too.

"Laurie's an extremely co-dependent person. You know, she tries to be like everyone else she meets," Larry said. "Like Diane, for instance. Diane's head was shaved except for her bangs. Laurie got the exact same haircut."

Soon Larry and Terry joined the girls, cutting themselves on numerous occasions. Usually, they used razors or pins and just made surface cuts; they wanted to see blood, to watch it ooze. Diane was an absolute expert at it, she had scars running all the way up her arms.

"You could feel the blood coming out, and it felt so good. It was to relieve tension," Larry explained. "I mean, I jab myself with this big, huge safety pin that I have. I jab myself with that to get rid of tension. That way I would have physical pain to concentrate on instead of emotional pain."

For Laurie, who was sixteen by then, the practice of cutting herself turned into a physically and emotionally damaging event. She began to disfigure herself alone in her room at night, not just when she was in front of others and trying to impress people.

"I didn't cut myself for the fun of it. I was always upset when I did it and I was crying and I felt like I had to cut myself for the release," Laurie said. "When I first saw Diane and Larry doing it, it made me sick to my stomach. But, see when I grew up I was never allowed to hurt, I was never allowed to show how I really felt. I could never yell or tell my parents how I felt, cause they never listened. This was one way I could get the pain out. When I did it, that's how I felt, like I was getting all the pain out."

All the while, Laurie continued her friendship with Hope and had gradually become buddies with Toni. She introduced them to Diane, and they thought the new girl was cool. She had New Age ideas.

At the time, Toni was really a part of the preppy scene at the junior high school; her friends were all very straight-laced Madison kids. She still remained close to certain people from that clique, but overall Toni had grown tired of that group. She was looking for people who could somehow share her torment, not for people who lived to shop.

According to Laurie, during school and during classes, she, Toni, and Hope made little paper cuts and razor cuts on their arms. These were very minor cuts, things that would heal in a day or two. Laurie asserts that other kids witnessed all three of them doing this, claiming that people saw them but no one said anything about it.

"If people were going to question it, they wouldn't have come to me, cause I think most of the people were leery of me and they didn't like me and they were afraid of me or something," Laurie commented.

On Monday, March 18, 1991, while in her morning first period classroom, Laurie inflicted some superficial cuts on her hands. No one at school noticed it, but the next day, the Tacketts saw the cuts and became concerned. They took Laurie to King's Daughter Hospital in Madison for an overnight stay.

On March 20, Laurie was seen by a psychiatrist, Dr. Gwen Heaton, and Laurie reported that the week before she had an altercation with her former boyfriend Aaron, telling the doctor that she did not want to continue the relationship, even on a friendship basis.

Dr. Heaton recommended that Laurie begin therapy with a local counselor and prescribed Desipramine, an antidepressant which she instructed her to take daily.

Just two days later, on a Friday night, Toni asked Diane and Laurie to sleep over. Up in her room, someone pulled out a pack of new razors. Laurie took one out, claiming that she was just trying to show off. "I was making motions like I was going to cut the back of my hand and I guess my hand went too far, and I did cut the back of my hand and I didn't mean to," Laurie explained.

Blood was gushing everywhere. Toni brought Laurie into the bathroom and the bleeding continued. The cut was deep enough that they could see Laurie's bone. Toni didn't know what to do. She was freaking out, she thought Laurie was going to die. She wanted to tell her parents, but Laurie convinced her not to. Diane, meanwhile, took out a camera and was trying to take pictures of the wound.

It was about 7:30 P.M. when Toni brought the cellular phone into the bathroom and Laurie called her dad, who rushed to the Lawrence residence. He took Laurie to King's Daughter Hospital and she underwent surgical repair of the dorsum of her left hand. The self-inflicted laceration was about four-inches long. It was deep enough to lacerate a tendon. George Tackett decided to sign papers to admit Laurie into the psychiatric unit at Jefferson Hospital in Jeffersonville, where she would soon be transferred for treatment.

"I did it so fast, I was in shock," Laurie said. "They sewed it up then my dad said I was going to Jefferson Hospital, and I started screaming and yelling at him and calling him names. They came in and they had to put IVs in me, and they had to shoot me up twice with Thorazine, cause they did it once and I didn't feel nothing, and then they did it again, and it all just hit me at once. I couldn't move."

Laurie was admitted to Jefferson Hospital the next day, March 23, 1991. George Tackett told the attending physician that Laurie's behavior had deteriorated after she struck up a friendship with a new girl in school. Apparently, it was this girl, Diane, who had gone to him and first informed him of Laurie's self-mutilation. "She may have been trying to fit in," Tackett tried to explain.

During her initial interview, Laurie told Dr. Kevin Conlee that she wasn't suicidal, explaining that there were five or six other schoolmates who had also cut themselves, not in suicide attempts as a tension release. She told the psychologist that her friend, Stacie, also cut herself in school on March 18. She added that another girlfriend, Hope, had severely cut herself about three weeks earlier.

Fourteen

Laurie described herself in the personal profile she gave to Jefferson Hospital as someone who enjoyed gymnastics and ice skating, who liked to draw and write, and whose biggest concern was "trying to be a good friend to my friends."

She reported that she wasn't on drugs, that she hadn't had any kind of liquor for over a year, and had never been arrested. She did not deny that she was sexually active, but said there was no way she could be pregnant. She glossed over information about her troublesome sexual feelings.

She had been working at Burger King for three months, Laurie stated, and she considered herself a "kind and caring hard worker." The only problem she said she ever had was one fight that had occurred at school three years prior.

To the written question, "Why are you at Jefferson Hospital?," she responded: "Really I don't need help. Everybody tries something once."

Laurie claimed to be getting along well with her thirteen-year-old brother and said that there had been no severe disturbances between her and her parents. (The psychologist noted that Laurie's mother had not yet been to see her at either hospital.) She willingly described herself as depressed, saying she was feeling lonely, sad, and bored. She expressed her concerns for approval from her peers, and denied that she felt any irritability or anger.

She explained to Dr. Conlee that for the past two weeks, she had been able to get "lost" by reading some fiction that her friends had recommended to her. One of the novels included a story about a character who was unhappy and suffering who managed to get away from a certain environment and thus relieve her suffering. She also reported that she had been lent some psychology books from a friend who was older, a college student, which she found somewhat interesting.

Laurie insisted that she had no intentions of killing herself, stating that she felt sad and frightened at the implications of being in a hospital with children who appeared to be mentally ill. She said she did not consider herself to be as ill as these children, and insisted that she did not need treatment or confinement in a hospital.

As she continued speaking, Laurie's facial expression grew sad. Her eyes filled with tears.

"I don't need to be here," she told the doctor.

The hospital staff didn't agree, however, and for the first three days of her hospitalization, Laurie was kept under maximum suicide precautions, with nurses checking on her every fifteen minutes. She was administered antibiotics to prevent infection of her hand and was also given the previously prescribed antidepressant. This time, the dose was doubled.

On March 26, George and Peggy Tackett visited the hospital and had a formal interview with a family therapist, Rod Linton. They indicated that Laurie was extremely oppositional to any redirection they would offer. Laurie had recently told them that she would no longer attend school, and they said they had no control over her actions. "I feel helpless and don't do anything," Peggy told Linton. "She can do what she wants."

The initial impression of the family counselor was that the Tackett family was covering up problems. He noted that while the parents sat in the lobby, waiting for the family session to begin, they held each other very tightly by the arm; while walking back to the adolescent unit, they walked with their arms around each other; however, when they entered the therapy room, they sat down in the chairs farthest apart from one another.

It was revealed that both Tackett parents suffered from low self-esteem, and that both had a very small circle of friends; they were antisocial. George told the therapist that Laurie suffered from extremely low self-esteem as well.

"Some people stand out in a crowd. I could shout out in a crowd and not be noticed. She may have to learn that she is the same way," George said.

After the family history was taken, Laurie was brought into the room, and George drew his chair up behind his daughter and began to pat her hair and back. When asked why there was such a problem with disciplining his daughter, George responded, "Perhaps I love her too much."

Laurie was asked what she hoped to achieve in family therapy.

"For my mom and dad to trust me more," she said.

Three days after the family session, Laurie opened up to her therapist a little more, admitting that she had been involved in "white witchcraft." She made a differentiation between that and satanic worshiping, telling him that she had been involved with Ouija boards from the age of thirteen, at which time she channeled a spirit from Egypt which she said was "after her." She also told him that at that time, she became involved with many people who were part of a cult and she carved the initials of her boyfriend in her arm. She showed her therapist, Larry Freudenberger, her scars.

Later in their discussion, she casually mentioned that her father was contemplating taking her out of the hospital.

Apparently, Laurie was experiencing a lot of anxiety about being in the hospital; she was hyperventilating and exhibiting other panic symptoms. She had called her father and convinced him to come and get her.

The next day, Laurie went through a battery of psychological tests involving personality assessment which concluded that beneath her cooperative and controlled facade, Laurie suffered from a borderline personality disorder.

After a week in the hospital, Laurie had become comfortable enough with Freudenberger to divulge some of her secrets. Among other things, she reported visual and auditory hallucinations, recalling "imaginary friends" with great detail. At age six or seven, she said, she had visions of two "little men" who would "talk to me and cheer me up." And she remembered a fear being associated with her bedroom, stating that at the ages of eight or nine, she was so frightened that she slept on the living-room couch.

She said that she often experienced a sense of time loss of up to three or four hours, where she had no memory whatsoever of what had transpired. On some occasions when this would occur, she would find herself at a different location, not knowing how she got there. Laurie said she had this problem since her early childhood.

She talked about a sexual abuse incident that occurred when she was eight or nine, when she visited a fifty- or sixty-year-old neighbor and he fondled her breasts. She also hinted that she was abused by her parents in the past, saying, "It's there. I know I was hit. But I can't remember it."

On March 30, George Tackett spoke to Dr. Steven Shelton and wanted Laurie discharged immediately, saying that he wanted to have her home. The doctors finally convinced Tackett that Laurie needed to remain hospitalized for further evaluation, and reminded him of her depressed condition. Up until then, Laurie had denied being suicidal to both her parents and to therapists.

On Easter Sunday, March 31, Laurie ran to the nurses' desk. She was holding her hand to her heart, yelling, "My heart is beating real fast and it hurts!"

The panic attack, her doctor concluded, was a result of two stressors: her parents not coming to visit her for the Easter brunch, and another patient calling her a name while in gym that day. The next morning, Laurie was still extremely upset and tearful. She took an educational assessment test that day, and while she was cooperative, she was very solemn.

"I'm not very smart," she said before the test began.

Although she became frustrated at not being able to answer all of the questions, stating that her depression was keeping her from remembering things she had learned, she performed quite well.

On April 2, the Tackett family came in for a group family session, participating without Laurie present in the first half of the meeting. Their son, Bubby, stated that a neighbor of theirs had convinced his sister that she was carrying the soul of an extraterrestrial being. Bubby told therapist Rod Linton that he and Laurie went over to their neighbor's house often, where they had been told that the Creotians (extraterrestrial entities) had their spaceship disintegrate in the Earth's atmosphere, and they had to project themselves into Earth beings (called Terretians).

According to her brother, Laurie was told that in the next two months, the Creotians were going to come and take back the souls that were projected into Terretian bodies. Bubby also stated that while he was over at this girl's house, she demonstrated how she allowed other souls to speak through her and showed them how she could walk around the room in an invisible state.

"Bubby firmly believes that these things are taking place and he believes in astro-projection and other forms of cult practice," Linton remarked in his family therapy progress notes.

In the second part of the family session, Peggy broke down in tears and cried quite intensely as she talked about what was wrong within their family and what needed to change in order for Laurie to come home. She told the therapist that, at the moment, all of her thoughts were focused on Bubby, who was becoming increasingly hard to manage.

"He treats me like a dog," Peggy cried. "He just tells me what to do and then walks all over me."

With Laurie now in the room, all four of them began talking about the problems that existed in the family, agreeing about many things. At one point, Laurie complained that her mother continually told her "You'll never amount to anything." Laurie later said she didn't understand why she had to be in the hospital, since it was her family that had the problem. Peggy became angry, claiming the hospital was unfairly trying to blame her.

The Tacketts were then told a metaphorical story about a little girl who was hurt because she didn't change a bandage on a wound that she had. After they heard the story, feelings of hopelessness seemed to flow out of every family member.

The next day, during his meeting with Laurie, Dr. Shelton noticed something interesting about her which had never occurred to him before. In his report, he indicated that Laurie's face seemed to be asymmetric, with one eye appearing higher than the other. "The patient covers this well with hair styling," Dr. Shelton wrote. (By that time Laurie's reddish-blond hair had grown back in, and she had rather long bangs.) Shelton also indicated that he was waiting for the results of a brain scan.

But the doctor didn't need to wait for the test results; that night, Laurie had a casual conversation with a health care worker which proved to be a helpful gauge of her mental state.

"If I tell Dr. Shelton that it was an accident, do you think he'll believe me and let me go home?" she asked.

The worker asked how Laurie was planning to handle her depression and other problems.

"This place is not stopping me from hurting myself,"

Laurie said. "I could go back in my room anytime and cut my wrists with a broken lipstick case or stab myself with a pencil."

With this new information, Dr. Shelton decided to prolong Laurie's hospital stay, much to the dismay of both Laurie and her father.

"I can't stand being in here. I'm going to have to pull all of my hair out if I stay here," Laurie told her therapist as her body began to visibly shake. "I can't stand being away from my family."

Because she was making such a fuss, Laurie was asked if she wanted to go to the "quiet room" to get her anger out.

"No! I'm not angry! I'm not crazy!" Laurie wailed. "I don't need to go in some room by myself!"

Laurie continued to display a tearful affectation in her therapy sessions, yet she was always quick to point out that her goal was to be discharged. She told her psychiatrist that she felt her treatment team had provided her with specific recommendations which she would follow when she was back home, repeatedly asking to be released.

On April 5, Laurie's multidisciplinary treatment team had a meeting, summarizing Laurie's problem list as:

1) Depression
2) Family dysfunction
3) Time loss

Her brain scan returned normal, as did her EEG, another neurological test.

On April 7, Laurie had a pleasant visit with both her parents; apparently, the Tacketts listened to her and held her. Laurie liked this. She would say later that she was able to "get everything out" with them, crying, "I can't talk to no one here!"

The next day, when he got another call from Laurie during one of her panic attacks, George Tackett returned to the hospital, asking that his daughter be discharged. It took a one-hour meeting with Dr. Shelton for him to change his mind.

Laurie was still extremely depressed and teary, remaining quite focused on her discharge and the manipulation of her parents to remove her from the hospital prior to the discharge date. She seemed to still be somewhat resistant to therapy; however, there were some signs of recovery. Her compliance with treatment appeared to be improving every day.

Toward the end of her hospitalization, Laurie was seen for a sixty-minute individual therapy session. Also during that week, a difficult family therapy session was held, at which time Bubby stated that his dad hit him in the groin from the front seat of the car while they were on their way to the hospital. When they questioned George about it, he said, "No comment." Bubby also reported that his dad threw a glass bottle at him when he tried to get out of the car. (The hospital later filed a report with the Welfare Department regarding this event.) George was angry that Bubby brought this up; he said he might make Bubby leave the house if his behavior didn't change. Laurie sided with her dad throughout the meeting.

A few days later, April 12, 1991, Laurie was sent home. When she was discharged from the adolescent psychiatric unit of Jefferson Hospital, the laceration to her left hand was almost healed. Laurie was still sad and teary, but continued to deny any suicidal or homicidal feelings. She already had some therapeutic "trial visits" to her home the prior weekend, and she was diagnosed as being ready for outpatient therapy. A follow-up appointment had been made for her with Dr. Gwen Heaton, whose office was located in Madison.

Throughout her two-week stay at the hospital, Laurie's parents had made arrangements with Madison Junior High and had brought books and materials to her. She had read pages from *Romeo and Juliet,* had studied basic algebra and biology, and had been tested on European exploration.

However, as soon as she returned home, she decided that she had no interest in going back to the classroom, claiming that the other children would only make fun of her. She refused to go to school, and she got involved in home study instead, taking a correspondence class. Around the middle of May, her parents brought Laurie in to see Jack Dwyer at school. Even though Laurie was quite resistant, she agreed to make a whole new start of it, being moved forward to tenth grade at Madison High School come August.

In June of 1991, Laurie was determined to run away from home, hiding out at the Leatherbury household for two weeks before police were able to track her down. As a precautionary method, Peggy had police place her on a one-year probation period before she would take Laurie back into her custody.

For one month, Laurie lived under her mother's strict rule, and it was obviously affecting her, making her feel suicidal and helpless. On July 23, Laurie made an appointment to see Dr. Heaton, where she talked about her depressive symptoms that were starting again. Laurie was put on the antidepressant, Prozac. She kept two appointments with Heaton after that, telling the doctor that the medication seemed to help her; however, she was not really interested in the therapy.

She stopped seeing Heaton in the beginning of August, at which time she said she wanted to get out of her home situation, that she wanted to move to a larger city, but she had no realistic plans about how she would do that. On August 27, just after school had started, Heaton received a phone call from George Tackett, who reported that Laurie was cutting her wrists again. Laurie returned for one final visit that same day, saying that she found school too stressful. She was feeling angry at the other students, feeling alienated from them and from the school system, explaining that this was the reason she cut her wrists.

She was not happy with her classes at the high school,

Laurie said, and she would sit at the back of the classroom and cut herself because she felt she couldn't stand school anymore. The two of them discussed the possibility of Laurie continuing school on a part-time basis, and Heaton made a call to Laurie's school counselor, but afterward Heaton never saw Laurie again.

Laurie dropped out of school in September, but stayed with her parents for a few weeks, all the while begging her father to give her the money to leave home. She was about to turn seventeen, and she felt she was old enough to make her own way in the world. In early October, when the opportunity arose for her to go to New York with her cousin, her father gave her a hundred dollars in the hopes that she could try to make a new life for herself there.

But things didn't work out for Laurie in New York; she was only there for a week or so. She didn't like it there anyway, she thought the people were rude. When her cousin had a fight with her New York friend, the two were thrown out, and they soon hightailed it back to Madison.

Days later, Laurie placed the call to Kary Pope.

Laurie thought life in New Albany was much more her speed. One of the things she and her new friends did was go to see *Rocky Horror* on weekends, an audience participation cult movie event at the Vogue theater in Louisville. Over time, it was something she'd see Melinda Loveless at on occasion, as she began to fit more into the circle.

She went to "parties" quite a bit, usually they were small gatherings, sometimes they would hold a seance, sometimes they would drop acid, and she was excited about her new existence, for the most part. She had even found a job at a Kroger's store in New Albany. But her big problem was that she didn't have a car. In November, she called her father and explained her predicament, but he refused to help her. By the end of the month, Laurie finally agreed to return home, transferring her job from the Kroger's in New Albany to the Kroger's in Madison, on the promise that her father would buy her some wheels.

Laurie moved back home and George Tackett paid $1500 to purchase a 1984 Celebrity four-door; the two of them decided that Laurie would pay him fifty dollars a week out of her earnings as a cashier. But Laurie was terribly unhappy in Madison. By then, Diane had moved back West, her friend Larry had moved to Louisville, so being in Madison was sheer hell for her. She had nothing to do, nothing to look forward to.

Unbeknownst to her family, she spent every spare minute driving back and forth to New Albany and Louisville. She thought the people there understood her, but mostly they just tolerated her. As the people in New Albany got to know Laurie, they all agreed that she was a little too strange; she acted crazy all the time, often in inappropriate ways. Sometimes she'd do a transfer and become an extra-terrestrial. Sometimes she claimed the Earth was being invaded by extraterrestrials. Other times she'd channel a fairy and start prancing around the room. She did anything for attention, they discovered.

While they often didn't believe she was for real, her act did seem somewhat authentic; she was good at convincing people, getting them to believe in almost anything.

"Laurie could get into someone's mind, and fuck your mind up so badly that you would believe this floor would catch on fire if you sat and watched it for a few minutes," Kary said.

Eventually, Laurie was beginning to frighten the girls in New Albany. She talked a lot about death and killing and her whole personality would change; her voice would change, her eyes, and she'd become someone else.

Kary Pope described a night when Laurie insisted they all go out to the woods. There were dogs barking and Laurie said they would all be killed by coyotes. Another time, at a party, Laurie wanted to cut the wrists of Kary's girlfriend. A number of people witnessed that, including the Leatherburys.

"We were all in this big basement, you could play Nintendo there or play pool or watch movies or whatever, everybody was doing something," Kary said. "And I'm sitting there, and Laurie is asking my girlfriend if she could cut her, because Laurie wanted to suck her blood."

Allegedly, Laurie sucked the blood out of a scab on her girlfriend's leg that night. It was something that the Leatherburys say they witnessed more than once.

"Well, she would suck other people's blood or her own," Terry confided. "She would give herself a cut and she would say *'Oooh, I just love the taste of blood.'* "

In December, because Kary and Laurie had a fight over this incident, Laurie started to hang around with Melinda.

Part Three

The Outcome

Fifteen

On Saturday afternoon, January 11, 1992, over at the Rippey house, Toni and Hope were crying hysterically, telling Gloria that they were witnesses to a murder. Gloria called Carl at work and said, "I think you'd better come home."

Earlier that day, Carl had stopped at his house for a few minutes. He was just passing through on his way back to the job. The four girls were all there at the time, and his son John pulled him aside and said, "Something happened to Hope. I think she saw an accident." Carl thought his son was talking about a car accident, and knowing that his daughter was so sensitive and squeamish, he didn't pay much attention to it.

When he walked in the door, Hope and Toni both started telling him bits and pieces of what happened. Carl could not believe what was being said.

"I didn't know what kind of involvement Hope had. The whole story was not expressed," he recalls. "I'm told there is a girl who has been killed and they witnessed it."

The girls told Carl that they had gone to the bowling alley and had consulted a friend there; he suggested they get a lawyer, giving them the name of a Madison attorney, Darrel Auxier. Hope told her father that she had already called him, and Carl, in disbelief, called Auxier's office to confirm it. The attorney said that police had found the body and were looking for the girls.

"If the police come to the house, tell them they have to go through me," Auxier said.

Toni hadn't made any contact with the attorney. She was too scared to tell her parents, no less another adult. She was just frantic. Carl and Gloria really had trouble calming her down. Finally, Toni said she wanted to tell her parents, but she needed someone there with her. The Rippeys agreed to accompany her to the Lawrence house and remain present as she made her confession.

"Toni explains to her mother and father what had happened. Her mother almost passes out, and her father says to Toni, *'Get the hell out of my house!'* " Carl recalls. "We tried to calm him down and give her mother some support."

That same afternoon, over at the Loveless residence, Marjorie had returned from work, only to find Melinda and Laurie hanging out in her living room. Melinda asked her mom for hugs and kisses, whispering that Laurie was going to spend the night. Marjorie didn't approve of Laurie, and she told Melinda that Laurie could not stay. But Melinda was adamant about it.

"She has to! She has to stay," Melinda begged. "She had a big fight with her family."

Marjorie eventually gave in.

All day, Marjorie noticed that Melinda was acting strange. Melinda was in hiding. She was locked up in her room with Laurie and Crystal for hours. When Marjorie would call her downstairs, Laurie would call for Melinda to come back up. The three of them were sticking close together. Before bedtime, Marjorie checked on the girls. Crystal had left hours before. Laurie and Melinda were up in Melissa's room, watching a horror movie. Marjorie sensed that something was wrong. She asked her daughter if everything was all right, and Melinda said that the movie was scaring her. Marjorie suggested that they turn the TV off, and she tucked Melinda in and gave her a hug.

* * *

That same evening, over in Jeffersonville, Howard Henry went in and sat down with Steve Sharer and Jackie Vaught at Steve's kitchen table. It was his third meeting with them.

"I'm sorry I've had to ask you all of these personal questions and put you through all this, but I have some bad news for you," Henry said. "We have discovered Shanda's body and she has been murdered."

Jackie Vaught got up from the table. She seemed dazed and became fairly hysterical and went into the living room where some other relatives were trying to console her. Steve stayed at the table with the detective and asked a few basic questions.

"Did she die instantly?" Steve asked.

"Well, I don't know, but it appears that she probably did," Henry said.

He had already made the decision not to give him any more information than he absolutely had to, trying to spare the man from hearing the details all at once.

When he left the house, he radioed in and discovered that a trooper had gone by the Loveless residence just an hour before, and had spotted a Chevrolet Celebrity four-door parked down the block. The trooper was directed to stay with the vehicle until a search warrant could be obtained. Howard Henry was also informed that Judge Ted Todd had issued arrest warrants for Melinda Loveless and Laurie Tackett. Steve Henry and Buck Shippley were already in progress to 2211 Charlestown Road.

It was almost 2:30 A.M. when the police cars pulled up, surrounding the Loveless house with their lights flashing. Steve and Buck had a couple of uniformed officers along as backup, and about five men went to the door.

"They beat the door down," Marjorie remembers. "They

just barged in the house. They asked me did Melinda Loveless live here. I said yes. I was scared. I didn't know who they were and I'm screaming. They just barged through, they was just going all through the house. I was crying and screaming, saying, 'What do you all want?' "

When the officers said that Melinda Loveless and Mary Laurine Tackett were being arrested for murder, Marjorie was bewildered. She asked to see their badges before she allowed the men up to the bedroom.

Upstairs, Steve Henry and Buck Shippley found Melinda and Laurie asleep in bed. When they first laid eyes on Melinda, they were shocked. In taking the statement from Toni Lawrence, their imaginations had run wild. They were expecting a great, big, heavy girl. They were surprised to see how little she was. The two men woke the girls, had them get dressed, and escorted them to the living room.

"They came down and Melinda's just silent, Tackett is silent," Marjorie remembers.

"Did you do something to Amanda?" she asked her daughter, thinking that maybe Melinda beat Amanda up. But there was no response.

The officers began reading the girls their rights, and just as they finished, Laurie interrupted them.

"Can I ask you a question?"

"Sure," Shippley said.

"Are we on 'Candid Camera'?"

"No. This is really happening."

They handcuffed the girls, and Marjorie looked on in utter amazement. She was sure the whole thing was a mistake. She hugged and kissed Melinda and promised, "I'll get you in the morning."

As they walked out the door, Steve Henry turned around and looked at Marjorie's frightened face.

"Ma'am, all I can say is I have a daughter the same age and she has a room just like Melinda's and I'm sorry," he said. "I'm sorry for you, but get a good lawyer."

The girls were transported in separate vehicles, and they were quiet on the drive over to Madison. When they arrived at the jail, Laurie put on her "tough" act, scowling at the officers, trying to appear like a hardened criminal. Melinda, on the other hand, just looked like a frightened little girl.

"I remember the night we arrested them, I thought Melinda was going to pass out. She started sliding down the wall and I caught her," Henry said. "It's hitting her and I could see it. I was watching her because her mother said she could be suicidal. Her eyes were kind of rolling back and she's shaking."

"Are you all right?" Henry asked.

"Can I call my mama?"

"Yeah, just come on in."

At that point the police hadn't asked any questions yet. They hadn't mentioned Shanda. They hadn't done anything other than book the girls and take mug shots and fingerprints.

When Melinda called home, they overheard her end of the conversation, and they got a glimpse into the bizarre reality they were facing. Her stepdad, Michael, was the one who picked up the line.

"I'm sorry, Mike! Tell Mom I'm sorry!" she cried.

No response.

"Mike?"

"Yes."

"It was a friend at school named Shanda. Shanda's dead."

"Shanda is dead."

"Yes."

"Did you kill Shanda?"

"I didn't kill her. I just meant to feel good and beat her up! It went too far, it got out of hand!"

"How did you kill her? You cut her?"

"Well, I punched her in the stomach, then someone got a knife out. They cut some of her."

"Did you stab her? How did you kill her?"

"It was terrible! I didn't mean for this to happen. I'm a

197

good person. I can't talk anymore. I have got to go!"

"Look, we're going to make it! We'll get a lawyer and we'll get through this shit!"

"Mike, don't feel pity for me. This is all my fault."

The next morning, Sunday, January 11, the officers sat down with each of the girls, speaking to them in an informal way. From the start, the two men had differing opinions of Laurie Tackett. Shippley saw her as a hard, calloused individual who was completely unremorseful. Henry saw a whole different side of her. He found her to be an okay kid. When he and Laurie talked, just the two of them, about Laurie's interests, her face lit up. She had a pretty smile.

"I enjoyed talking to her. She's intelligent," Steve Henry said. "We talked about movies, and we talked about life and we talked about everything for a while, other than this case."

However, the officers didn't have differing opinions about Melinda. To both men, Melinda was an extremely attractive young lady, who they believed could manipulate people because of her looks. She was seductive, and she was obviously aware of that. During their initial conversation, she tried to butter the men up by flirting with them, leaning forward in her chair so they could get a view of her breasts.

They found her to be almost the opposite of Laurie in every way. Melinda seemed to be functioning on a very low intelligence level. She was pleasant, but difficult to converse with because she didn't make a lot of sense.

"If you took Melinda back over to the McDonald's at Allison Lane, where they asked directions to Shanda's, I don't think she could find her way back home," Henry later commented.

Curtis Wells went to Louisville to the Kentucky State Medical Examiner's office for the autopsy that same day. It was conducted by Dr. George Nichols, who was assisted by Dr. Mark Bernstein and Sergeant Wells.

The autopsy revealed that the body had multiple injuries; lacerations to the head, neck, and legs; ligature marks on the wrists, which meant she had been tied, but there was no corroboration of Toni Lawrence's contention that Shanda had been strangled.

It was evident that the victim was still alive when she was burned; soot was found in the upper airway.

"Smoke didn't just float up her nose after she was dead. She had to breathe it," Wells said.

In the course of doing the autopsy, it was discovered that there were numerous lacerations inside the anus, with the largest one being at approximately twelve o'clock. The team used a standard victim rape kit and determined that there were no males involved in the molestation.

Because of the extensive thermal damage, however, the report was not conclusive.

By mid-morning, a preliminary hearing was held in the Circuit Court of Jefferson County in Madison, at which time a single count of murder was entered against Melinda Loveless and Mary Laurine Tackett. Counsel was appointed to represent each girl, supplied at the taxpayers' expense. In a separate procedure, both girls were waived from the juvenile court system; they would be tried as adults.

Within hours after the hearing, at Judge Ted Todd's request, Laurie Tackett was transferred to the Indiana Women's Prison in Indianapolis for psychiatric evaluation; a few days later, Melinda Loveless was transferred to the Clark County Jail in Jeffersonville, where she would await trial.

On Sunday night, the news of Shanda's murder hit the airwaves. WHAS, the ABC affiliate in Louisville, was the first to cover the story, reporting that a young girl's mutilated body was found on a Jefferson County road near Madison, that the cause of death was burning and smoke inhalation. "A sixteen-year veteran with the Indiana State Police said tears came to his eyes when he viewed the body," the brief newscast revealed.

By Monday, January 13, Indiana State Police released an affidavit to the media, quoting the chilling words of a fifteen-year-old witness to the murder. The girl had not yet been charged with a crime, but police said she was a possible suspect. That same morning, the grisly Shanda Sharer murder became the top news story on all local television stations, and was splashed on the front page of *The Courier Journal* and *The Indianapolis Star.*

The news sources reported that Jefferson County prosecutor, Guy Townsend, had already set trial dates, June 23 for Loveless, June 25 for Tackett. Because Townsend wanted to avoid pretrial publicity, he declined to give any further details on the case or to speculate on a motive. The story was broadcast throughout the day. At the top of the 6:00 P.M. hour, local stations rivaled each other with separate stories on Sharer, detailing the bizarre twists that police were uncovering in their investigation.

The initial television and newspaper accounts focused on the stunned reaction of Shanda's friends, family, and schoolmates. The school principal at Our Lady of Perpetual Help, Sister Sharon Marie Blank, was reportedly organizing a counseling team to help students and parents cope with the horror of Shanda's death. Five counselors were being brought in to console the school's 320 students, who would hold a memorial service for Shanda a few days later. The following Wednesday, the funeral service for Shanda Sharer would take place at the Our Lady of Perpetual Help Catholic Church.

Many of the young people who knew Shanda were in a state of denial. Brother Bill Reigel, a counselor for the Roman Catholic Archdiocese, told *The Courier Journal,* "Some have even dreamed that she is still alive. It's going to take a long time for this to pass."

The gruesome murder was leaving a trail of stunned people across southern Indiana and northern Kentucky. Not knowing all the facts, one of the things people questioned was the fact that teenagers were being tried as adults. Oddly enough, one of the most noted cases of a teenager being tried as an adult occurred in Indiana. Paula Cooper was fifteen years old when she stabbed an elderly Bible teacher to death. A Gary, Indiana, jury sentenced her to death, but in 1989, the Indiana Supreme Court overturned her death sentence, sentencing her to sixty-five years. The decision came about because of the onslaught of protests, including a protest by Pope John Paul II.

However, the issue of children being involved with violent crimes was by far the most compelling element of the story, and the Sharer case would become the focus of news stories for months, eventually receiving national coverage as well. In Louisville, the public was alarmed to discover that the Sharer murder was just indicative of the number of children involved in violent crimes in the area, which, they learned, was on the rise by an alarming rate.

Louisville probation officers told local television that their most recent crime reports showed an increase in violent youth crimes, saying that the most shocking statistic was that the youngsters involved were getting younger and younger. The probation officers attributed the problem to the breakdown of the family and the lack of concern for youth in today's society.

After watching a news broadcast early that morning, thirteen-year-old Jeffrey Stettenbenz presented himself at the Sellersburg Post that Monday, January 13. Two officers conducted an interview with the boy who had come, accompanied by his mother, to divulge some information about his friends, Amanda Heavrin and Melinda Loveless. Stettenbenz was the one who was with Amanda when she was paged to the phone at the River Falls Mall on Saturday the eleventh. In the interview, Jeffrey reported that a few days prior, he, Melinda, and Amanda held a three-way phone conversation, during which Melinda said she was going to kill Shanda.

"It was Friday. She called up around nine o'clock at Amanda's house," Stettenbenz told police.

"You were there at Amanda's residence when Melinda called?"

"Yes."

"Now, did Amanda tell you this or did you hear this yourself?"

"I heard it myself."

"Okay. And what exactly did she say?"

"She said, 'Amanda, I'm going to kill Shanda.' And Amanda said, 'Don't do it.' And she said, 'I'm going to do it. I have the rope.' And Amanda said, 'You'll get in a lot of trouble.' And she says, 'I don't care. I'm going to kill Shanda.' And she hung up."

Also on the thirteenth, Howard Henry responded to a phone call he received from Dale Gettings, a student at Jeffersonville High School who said he overheard Crystal Wathen and Thea Board discussing the murder. Henry went to the high school, requesting an interview with the two girls. He arrived at 1:30 P.M. in the afternoon, at which time he spoke to Crystal, telling her that he knew she had a conversation with Melinda Loveless about the murder.

"Whoever told you that is a liar!" Crystal said.

The detective explained that obstructing justice was something that she could be arrested for, but Crystal insisted that she did not know anything.

Minutes later, when he flashed his badge at Thea Board, the young girl reported that Crystal Wathen was withholding information.

Later that day, Howard Henry and Curtis Wells received permission from Jackie Vaught, to search Shanda's room. There, they discovered a couple of letters which implied a love triangle between Shanda, Amanda, and Melinda.

"It only takes a couple to get the gist of the idea," Howard Henry said. "I knew from those letters that Shanda was deeply involved. She was overwhelmed with it, with sex itself, particularly with members of the same sex."

Over in Madison, prosecutor Guy Townsend was trying to make a deal with Paul Baugh, the attorney that Toni Lawrence's family engaged. He was also talking with Darrel Auxier, Hope Rippey's counsel. Because the girls were juveniles, both fifteen-year-olds, and based on Toni's original statement which indicated that Hope and Toni's involvement was minimal, Townsend's original offer was to allow the two girls to be tried in juvenile court, in exchange for their cooperation of the prosecution of Melinda Loveless and Mary Laurine Tackett.

If Toni's and Hope's cases had been tried in juvenile court, the worst that could have happened to them was that they would have been found to be juvenile delinquents and sentenced to an indeterminate period in the Indiana State Girl's School, a reformatory, where they would have served a maximum of six years. Neither would have a criminal record.

Townsend's offer was made on the condition that Hope and Toni both pass a lie detector test. But neither girl came forward to do so at that early stage. In fact, neither girl would talk to authorities for some time.

At approximately noon, January 13, Buck Shippley received a call from Laurie's next-door neighbor, Jason Teague, Brian Teague's brother. He said that on January 11, at about 7:00 A.M., Laurie called him and asked if he had any gasoline, saying that her car had run out of gas. Teague reported that he told her all he had was kerosene, and Laurie said that would do, because she needed to burn some clothes. Teague said he did not give her any combustibles.

Earlier that morning, Steve Henry had been down at the Clark Station on Clifty Drive and had talked to Toni Nell Harmon, the manager who was on duty the morning of January 11. Harmon said that four girls pulled up in a light-colored car, had put some gas into either a can or a jar, and had also filled their tank. Harmon was shown a yearbook from Madison High School but was unable to identify any of the girls. Henry asked her to retain the cash register tape from that day, and he left, following the other slim leads he had.

That afternoon, Henry received a written statement from fifteen-year-old Tanya Liter, who presented herself at the sheriff's office, reporting that she had information about her friend, Toni Lawrence. Liter and Lawrence had a casual discussion on Friday, January 10, in science class. They talked about their plans for the upcoming weekend.

"She said they were leaving after school so they could see The Witches' Castle in the light," Liter wrote. "After they left The Witches' Castle they were going to go to Jeffersonville. She said Laurie said they were going to ride around town all night then come home the next morning. She said they were going to sleep in the car."

At about 5:00 P.M. that day, Aaron Hall, age fifteen, walked into the Jefferson County Jail with his father, claiming that he had information pertaining to the case. Hall told Steve Henry that he dated Laurie Tackett at one time. Hall's version of his situation with Laurie was that on Thursday, January 9, Laurie had come over to his house just after 10:00 P.M. She was very upset with her parents and wanted to talk to him outside. When he got into Laurie's car with her, she apologized to him for breaking up, and asked him to date her again. Hall said that when he refused, Laurie began crying, telling him that she was either going to kill herself or someone else.

Hall recounted to police that shortly after breaking up with Laurie, some months before, Laurie tried to run over him with her car in the Oak Hill subdivision in Madison. He also said that in his opinion, Laurie was bisexual, claiming that he had met Melinda Loveless in the past when she had been in Madison with Laurie.

By Tuesday, January 14, news coverage of the story heightened. Details about "the foursome" who drove Shanda to Madison, tying and beating her, and then burning her alive, filled news reports from Indianapolis to Louisville. The grief shared by Shanda's relatives, friends, and teachers was also in the public eye.

"She was a bubbly girl with lots of energy," her fifth grade teacher, Janice Douglas, told the press. "She wrote the most beautiful poems." The students at St. Paul Catholic School in Louisville, where Shanda was a former classmate, took the news very hard. They, too, were provided with counselors to try to help them cope with their fear and pain.

At the same time, police continued their investigation, uncovering more details as they prepared to go to trial. At the Sellersburg Post, Curtis Wells processed the suspect vehicle. Among the items that Wells seized from the car were handwritten notes, cigarette packs and lighters, and a brown steel rod. During the course of his search, hair, fingerprints, and bloodstains were extracted as well.

On Thursday, January 16, newspaper reports indicated that Hazelwood students were aware of a "feud" going on between Shanda Sharer and Melinda Loveless. April Manacle, age fourteen, and Christie Anderson, age fifteen, told *The Courier Journal* that Loveless and her best friend both picked on Shanda. Another classmate, Mike Basham, reported that the three of them "fought a lot at school."

The same article described close friends of Shanda's who expressed their sorrow.

"Shanda was so sweet. She never did anything to hurt anybody," Summer Kellams, a Hazelwood student, said.

"She had a lot of friends, but I think she got in with the wrong crowd," fifteen-year-old Jeremy Schlenker told the press. The newspaper mentioned that Schlenker, a student at Scribner Junior High, said he "dated Shanda several times."

Sixteen

On Thursday, January 16, just five days after the body had been found, Steve Henry and Buck Shippley conducted a one-hour interview with fifteen-year-old Amanda Heavrin at the law office of Steve Lomeyer in New Albany. Her father, Jerry, who was also present, had engaged Lomeyer to represent Amanda.

Amanda told police that she had known Melinda since seventh grade, and in the last year (eighth grade) Melinda had expressed a love interest in her. She said she had become friends with Shanda Sharer that past fall, explaining that Melinda was very jealous of Shanda. She got angry whenever she saw Amanda and Shanda talking in public.

"Were you romantically involved with Melinda?" Henry asked.

"No. Physically, no," Amanda said.

"How were you involved? I really need to know this in detail."

"Well, I don't know. I guess she found me attractive, and I thought she was a pretty young lady, for who she was."

"Did you accept this attention from her?"

"Yes."

"Did you feel the same way about her?"

"Not really. I just thought maybe she was going through some time about her dad, what her dad did . . ."

As the interview progressed, Amanda did not admit her real relationship with Melinda, but she did give information about the various threats that were made against Shanda by Melinda and others. Apparently, Shanda was the center of a couple of triangles, one involving a man named Steve from Louisville who threatened to burn down her house.

"Melinda is asking you where Shanda lives?" Henry asked.

"Yeah, later on, later on in the story."

"Okay, go ahead."

"She kept asking me where her dad lived and I told her I didn't know, cause I didn't."

Eventually, Amanda admitted that she received a phone call from Melinda on Friday, January 10. During that conversation, Melinda said she was at a slam dance party with Laurie, Hope, and Toni. The next day, while she was at the mall with her friend Jeff, she got paged to the customer service office where she was told she had an emergency phone call. She recounted her experience on Saturday, when she was picked up by Melinda, Laurie, and Crystal, telling police that Laurie and Melinda gave her every detail about what they did.

"They said that when they pulled her out of the car that she couldn't move or nothing because stuff rolled back into her eyes," Amanda said. "She was pale white and stuff, and they said they picked her up and Laurie made her take off her shirt and Melinda told her to put her shirt back on. Laurie said, 'No, I told her to take it off,' but she got to put her shirt back on, and they put her down. Really, Hope and Toni put her down on the ground and wrapped her up in a cover and poured gasoline on her and Laurie set it on fire. That's how they done it."

Amanda said that she didn't believe it at first, so they showed her the trunk, which she said was "bloody." She saw hand marks, little red finger marks, on the inside of the trunk, and there was a Windex bottle in there, which was covered with blood.

"Did they say why?" Shippley asked.

"No, sir, they didn't say why. They just kept it their little secret."

Henry asked Amanda about the significance of the number

"23," but Amanda claimed she had no idea what it meant. The number of Amanda's basketball jersey was twenty-five. When Henry asked her if Shanda liked girls, Amanda said no, that Shanda was "constantly with guys," naming a couple of Shanda's boyfriends, Ray Gresham and David Snow.

While the two men were interviewing Amanda, a call from Larry Leatherbury had come in to the Sellersburg Post. Leatherbury said he had information about the case, and later that afternoon, Henry and Shippley contacted the seventeen-year-old at his home in Louisville.

Leatherbury greeted the men, running down an alleyway toward them, wearing black shorts, a black T-shirt, black combat boots, and a long black cape that flowed behind him in the wind. When they got the young man in their car, he talked about Laurie and Melinda, showing them pictures of himself with the girls, which he handed over. He stated that he was homosexual, that Laurie was bisexual, and confided that he and Laurie had sex once in the past, when he was "straight," but it didn't work out. Mainly, the young man wanted to tell them that he had nothing to do with the murder, that he was out of town that night; he was in Lexington with a new boyfriend.

Leatherbury told police that Laurie dabbled in black magic and said that Laurie had come to him, asking that he put a spell on a girl, Diane Norton. The purpose of the spell was to ruin Diane's life because she was not returning Laurie's calls or writing to her. He stated that Laurie had a fascination with burning people and had often said that she wondered what it would be like to kill someone. He described a site in Utica, an old castle, where he had been with Laurie. According to Leatherbury, Laurie had once said the castle would be a good place to "sacrifice someone."

It was on that same day that Steve Henry met with Virgil Seay at the New Albany Police Department, serving a subpoena which commanded that Seay turn over the letters he had been given by Amanda Heavrin's father. Henry was stunned by the content. One letter read:

208

Amanda,

Yes! I think we should at least talk this out. If you
have noticed all these uncalled for fights have been because of Shanda! Yes I'm hurt & pissed at you! I can't
believe you! You better straighten your act up missy! I'm
sick of hearing & seeing Shanda!! I think we should let
me cool off cause I'm still let down with you. You have
not shown me no improvement yet. Shanda is not gone!
You haven't got rid of her. Its your problem not mine!
And until she stops calling me & her name & writing is
off of your shit, I'm not going to hang with you and your
problem. I'm real mad at you! I feel like I need to cry! I
want Shanda dead!!

Love,
Melinda

Eventually, Steve Henry turned over what evidence he collected to Curtis Wells, where it remained in custody at the Sellersburg Post. The items included a paring knife with a brown
wooden handle, located in a dark-colored trench coat worn by
Laurie Tackett on January 11, 1992; Laurie Tackett's trench
coat, with possible bloodstains; a butcher knife with a brown
wooden handle, located along route 250 in Jefferson County;
letters to Amanda Heavrin written by Melinda Loveless, and
letters to Kelly Downs written by Kristie Brodfuehrer.

Police still did not have enough evidence against either Hope
Rippey or Toni Lawrence for a solid case. Although Toni's
original confession would have been enough to arrest the girls,
there was the problem of hearsay with regard to Hope. As for
Toni, the prosecutor was still trying to make a deal with her attorney. Townsend believed Toni to be the least culpable of the
four, and he needed to try to give her a reasonable plea deal.
More than anything else, Toni Lawrence's testimony would as-
sure a conviction of Melinda Loveless and Laurie Tackett.

On Friday, January 17, Henry obtained a search warrant to allow him onto George and Peggy Tackett's property. His search turned up nothing of consequence to the case.

Immediately after the search, Steve Henry interviewed Peggy Tackett, who had very little to say. She told him that her husband had gone into Laurie's room at 2:00 A.M. on Saturday, the eleventh, finding Hope and Toni there. The girls told George that Laurie had taken Melinda out on a tour of Madison. She said she scolded Laurie and Melinda for staying out all night when they returned home, and had no further comment.

As he was leaving the Tackett property, Henry was approached by Jeff Goldsberry, the youth minister at the Pentecostal church where the Tacketts were members. Goldsberry informed him that James Wymsatt, a local man, had come to their trailer the week before, asking if it would be okay for him to look for a crowbar on the property behind their trailer. Steve Henry followed the lead, eventually tracking down Wymsatt's car, which had been repossessed and was located in an auto shop in Madison. In Wymsatt's trunk, he found a tire tool that did not fit any of the lug nuts on the wheels of the vehicle. The tool was placed in a paper bag and taken into custody. Wymsatt later admitted that he did look for a crowbar on the Tackett property, but claimed that he did not locate one.

At 7:00 P.M. that night, Mike Starkey, one of the tenants of the trailer on the Tackett property, called the Jefferson County Jail in reference to the case. From Starkey, Buck Shippley learned that on January 11, at approximately 3:00 A.M., Laurie had gone to his trailer and had spoken to his roommate, Ace Newman.

Ace Newman later talked to Shippley and Henry, telling them that at 2:30 A.M. in the morning, January 11, he was working on a sink in his trailer when he noticed a car pull up to the burn pile by his home. The car then went through the yard to the Tackett house, where it remained for a few minutes, and then returned to the burn pile. After staying at the burn pile for a while, Newman said, the car then went through the yard to Tackett's house again, then back to the burn pile a second time. Newman told police that at approximately 3:00 A.M. that morning, Laurie came to the trailer asking for change to buy a Coke. Laurie appeared to be upset at the time, and he asked her what was wrong. Laurie said that she had torn up the muffler on her car, but when he offered to help her, she refused his assistance. Newman said he gave Laurie the change to buy a Coke, and watched her as she walked back to the car, which was parked by the burn pile.

On January 21, following another lead, Steve Henry and Buck Shippley interviewed sixteen-year-old Valerie Hedge at her New Albany residence. Even though Hedge knew both Laurie and Melinda, at first she said, "All I know about the case is from the news."

Hedge said she met Melinda through Kristie, that she started hanging out with Melinda, Amanda Heavrin, and Kary Pope that past fall, going over to Louisville, over to Cherokee Park and Bardstown Road, where they often hooked up with the Leatherbury twins. She said that she herself wasn't gay, but confirmed that Amanda and Melinda were romantically involved.

Hedge told police that she first met Laurie at the Harvest Homecoming that past October. Laurie was with Kary Pope, Crystal Lyles, and the Leatherburys. Hedge said she joined them out by Kary's car; they were listening to tapes, Violent Femmes and The Cure, she recalled. That was her initial contact with Laurie and the Leatherburys, and they all quickly became friends, leaving the homecoming, and going to *The Rocky Horror Picture Show.* After that night, the five of them started spending a lot of time together, Hedge said, and she got to know Laurie's curious personality.

"Me and Larry and Terry and Kary were all talking one night, and Laurie said that she wanted to burn somebody," Hedge reported. "She always said she wanted to do that."

"Okay, when you are all sitting around talking, is anybody

dropping acid or anything?" Steve asked.

"No."

"Okay. Are you drinking, or . . . ?"

"No."

"Everybody's just sitting, talking."

"Yeah."

"Okay, where were you when she said that to you?"

"We were at Floyd Knobs. We were up on a hill."

It turned out that Valerie Hedge was at the Audubon Skate Park Friday night, January 11, and she confirmed seeing Laurie and Melinda there, saying she had a five-minute conversation with them at about 9:15 P.M. in the evening. They both acted perfectly normal, she told police, there was no sign of trouble.

On January 22, seventeen-year-old Kary Pope walked into the Sellersburg Post where she was interviewed by three officers, Steve Henry, Buck Shippley, and Officer Tony Downs of the New Albany Police Department. They asked Kary to tell them everything she knew about Shanda Sharer's murder, making it clear that they wanted the whole truth, exactly the truth, with no embellishments.

"Melinda would always come to my house and she would call Shanda on the phone and say, 'You better keep away from my girlfriend, I'm going to kill you, I'm going to beat you up,'" Kary reported. "And Shanda's dad got on the phone one day and said to Melinda, 'Shanda is not bothering you. She does not talk to Amanda. Amanda is not over here and Shanda don't have nothing to do with all you lowlifes. She's only twelve years old and she don't hang around sixteen- and seventeen-year-olds.'"

The story just flowed out of Kary. The officers didn't have to ask any questions. Kary was all too happy to talk about her friends, substantiating a number of things for the police.

"Melinda always wanted me to take her to Shanda's house and beat Shanda up," Kary told them. "I said, 'I'm not going to do it.' She said, 'I'm going to kill her, and I'll just have someone take me there that will help me beat the hell out of her.' Sometimes, she'd look at me and tell me, 'If you don't take me to her house, I'll just go on a rampage at school and just get suspended.'

"Melinda told me before that if she had the chance, she would kill Shanda," Kary said. "And Laurie was the type of person that she would probably do that for her, help her do that just to keep a friend.

"Me and Melinda got into a disagreement and she started hanging around with Laurie," Kary continued. "Melinda knew that Laurie had been telling everybody that she would enjoy killing somebody, that it would be her destiny to go out and kill somebody just to see what it felt like and just to hear someone screaming."

"Did you ever hear Laurie talk about killing somebody?" Henry asked.

"Yeah, she always told me and Larry and Terry how it would be fun just to kill somebody."

"What do you mean, always? How frequently does she discuss this?"

"We were all at this party and she was cutting on herself and saying that she loves hurting herself and everything, and she would love to do that to someone else, just like stick a knife through someone's stomach."

Kary also characterized Laurie's channeling experiences, telling police about "Deanna the Vampire," confiding that she thought Laurie was starting to control her mind.

"The first time I ever met Deanna, she told me that she was my goddess," Kary said, "and she would love me to become the dead with her, to become a vampire like her, and that scared me."

Kary talked about Laurie's fixation with fire, commenting that Laurie was always burning something, paper, matches, just anything she could get her hands on. Kary said that she had been to The Witches' Castle with Laurie and Melinda, and explained that at one time, Laurie described a killing that she envisioned had taken place there. She told them, too, that she had met Hope on one occasion, sometime in November or December 1991, and she had the impression that Laurie was trying to convert Hope into being gay.

When they asked her about the number "23," Kary said the only thing that came to mind was Michael Jordan. The men told Kary that Shanda's papers and notebooks at home were covered with the letters, NFL. They asked Kary if she knew what that stood for. They asked if it meant the National Federation of Lesbians, but Kary just laughed and said there was no such group that she was aware of. (NFL meant "Niggers for Life," she told others.)

Later that day, Steve Henry called Crystal Wathen's mother, asking that she bring Crystal down to the post for an interview. Mrs. Wathen explained that Crystal had already been interviewed by Melinda's attorney and had been advised that she did not have to speak to police if she didn't wish to. Mrs. Wathen notified Henry that a transcript of Crystal's interview would be made available at the prosecutor's office in Madison. Henry would later view the transcript; however, it was never included in his police report.

At 8:00 P.M. that night, Steve Henry conducted an interview with fourteen-year-old Leslie Jacobi, a friend of Melinda's and Laurie's, who, they learned, had direct knowledge of what happened the morning of January 11; not that Jacobi was there at the scene, but that she had been called by Melinda from the Jefferson County Jail on the day after the murder. Jacobi told them that Melinda admitted to "stabbing Shanda" and "burning evidence."

The next day, January 23, Sam Sarkinson of the New Albany Police interviewed Lisa Livergood, who was a friend of Shanda's during the fall of 1991. Livergood told police that Shanda had mentioned Amanda's interest in her, but Shanda said she was "not that kind of girl" and she "just wanted to be friends." Shanda knew that Melinda wanted to beat her up because of her friendship with Amanda, and she told her friend

Livergood that she avoided Melinda whenever she would see her. According to Livergood, Shanda had the idea that Melinda liked girls "because her parents used to make her do weird things, like undressing in front of windows."

During the next few days, two people voluntarily walked into the Sellersburg Post, offering information on the case. Detective Howard Henry was there to talk with them in an informal capacity. The first was a priest from Our Lady of Perpetual Help, who said nothing of relevance to the case, but who felt obligated to come in and describe the good student that Shanda had been, basically reporting that she seemed to be a well adjusted little girl.

Five minutes after the priest left, Howard Henry recalls, Carrie East waltzed in. Henry got the impression that East wanted to use someone as a sounding board, she wanted a shoulder to cry on, because she talked mostly about her own problems. East admitted her love affair with Melinda Loveless, but did not tell Howard Henry the whole truth at that time. She claimed to be in the middle of a triangle involving herself, Amanda, and Melinda, telling Henry that Amanda had threatened to "hurt" her if she didn't leave Melinda alone. But Howard Henry was already handling other cases by then, he jotted down the information and turned it over to his brother, Steve, and had no further contact with East or anyone else involved in the case.

On January 27, Melinda and Laurie were ordered to supply the police with handwriting and hair samples. They were also ordered to present themselves for inspection so that their footwear could be analyzed.

Also on that date, at 6:00 P.M. in the evening, fourteen-year-old Kristie Brodfuehrer was interviewed by Henry and Shippley at the Sellersburg Post. A frail, petite girl, Kristie described herself as a best friend of Melinda's, whom she had known since the third grade. She told police that Melinda was sweet and calm, a nice girl, who just acted wild and crazy sometimes. Kristie described Melinda and Amanda's relation-

215

ship as being "just real close friends," and contended that she wasn't sure they were lesbians.

"Had Melinda ever made plans to kill Amanda?" Steve Henry asked.

"No. She said one time she would beat her up. She couldn't do that."

"Did she talk to you about it?"

"Not really. She just kind of said that, you know, she was jealous because Amanda was spending all of her time with Shanda."

"When was this?"

"Back in October."

"If I made reference to the Amanda plan, would that mean anything to you?"

"There wasn't ever any plan to kill Amanda. She never said she'd kill her, not to me."

Henry turned the tape recorder off, he produced Kristie's letters to Kelly Downs, Kristie acknowledged her handwriting, and the recorder was turned on again.

"Okay, we'd like to discuss some letters you possibly wrote indicating that Melinda Loveless had a plan to kill Amanda Heavrin."

"She said she'd just like to scare her real bad. I didn't know if she was serious or not about killing her. I wasn't real sure then. I'm not real sure now. And she said something. Beat her up real bad or she'd die or something, like, 'Then Shanda couldn't have her, but neither could I. Neither one of us wouldn't have to worry about Shanda.' She wanted to sneak out one night and go do it, but Amanda was asleep . . ."

"Where was Amanda when she was asleep?"

"At home."

"At Amanda's house. Did you go to Amanda's house?"

"Yeah."

"What happened?"

"All the lights were out so we left."

Kristie told Henry that one of Melinda's friends was driving that night, an eighteen-year-old guy called "T" who had his friend, Eric, along. The guys didn't realize what was going on, Kristie claimed. Melinda was supposed to have an unloaded gun with her but Kristie said Melinda "couldn't get ahold of one."

"She was going to hide up behind the seat and jump up and scare her to death," Kristie told police. "Melinda was going to do that, or else just scare her. I don't know if she was going to beat her up or scare her or not. The plan wasn't really perfect. It was just kind of . . . one of the things she said, we ought to scare her real, real bad and then take her home . . ."

"Is that the only time she ever discussed that with you?" Shippley asked.

"That's the only time. And the more she got to thinking about it, she said she couldn't do anything to Amanda."

"Prior to that night, when was the first time that she talked about wanting to harm Amanda?" Henry asked.

"She didn't say anything about . . . that she wanted to do anything to Amanda. I told her at Harvest Homecoming, I told her to leave Shanda alone. Leave Shanda out of it because, I mean, she's allowed to have friends and I said 'she can be friends with whoever she pleases. If you're going to get on anybody, get on Amanda's case. That's between you and Amanda.' I said, 'You shouldn't take that up with Shanda.' "

Kristie described the night when she and Melinda called Shanda's, discovering that Shanda had been to the haunted house with Amanda. She explained that when they called Amanda, Amanda was dishonest about it, which made Melinda furious.

"Melinda's upset with Amanda for lying, is that correct?" Henry asked.

"Yeah."

"Now as close as you can remember, what all did the conversation between you and Melinda consist of from the time that you hung up the phone from talking to Shanda?"

"She was like, 'God, how can I get back at her,' I don't know, she said scare her. I said, 'She doesn't know you're with me. She thinks you went home.' She said, 'Okay, I'll hide behind the seat.' I said, 'You have anything here that you could jump on and scare her with?' "

"At first we said she could dress up like somebody else, like a guy or something, one of Eric's friends," Kristie explained, "but then she said, 'No, it's too obvious.' So we sat around trying to think of a way that we could get Melinda hidden enough for Amanda to be able to get in the car. I mean we sat around trying to figure out how to do this. And then finally we just decided to just jump up from behind the seat. And she said, 'You don't have a gun, get one.' I said, 'No I don't think so.' She said, 'Are you sure?' I said, 'No, I don't think I can get a gun." So then she said, 'We'll get a knife.' I said, 'no, we're not going to take a knife cause my mom might wake up.' So we didn't get a knife, we didn't get a gun, then she said, 'well, we could just beat her up.' "

It was about 5:00 in the morning in late October 1991, when Kristie went to Amanda Heavrin's door, knocking at the window to try to wake her. Kristie was having no luck, however, and after a few minutes, she was scared away by a shadowy figure she perceived from the corner of her eye. It was some man, a neighbor, Kristie guessed, and she ran back to the car, telling Melinda that their plans had been foiled.

The day after they talked with Kristie, police got a lead that Mikel Pommerehn, a close girlfriend of Toni Lawrence's, had information about the murder. By 5:15 P.M. in the afternoon, they sat down with Pommerehn and her mother, interviewing the fifteen-year-old at her comfortable middle-class home in Madison. Mikel reiterated the phone conversation she had with Toni on the morning of the eleventh.

"She was talking real fast and said she was on her way home," Pommerehn said. "And I said Toni what's wrong, and she said she went out with Laurie and Hope and Melinda and something bad happened. She told me the little girl's name and she said they beat her with a crowbar and tried to slit her throat. Because she was talking real fast, I could hardly understand her."

Pommerehn went on:

"She said that they made her look in the trunk to see this girl's body, and she said there was blood everywhere, and she said that they had taken and they had burned her."

"Okay, just for the record, you said this was Friday or Saturday, what date was it when you talked to her? The body was found on the eleventh. Now, is this Friday or Saturday you're referring to?" Shippley asked.

"Saturday morning at 9:30 A.M. She called me."

"The times are very important here. You said she called you from McDonald's about 9:30 A.M., is that pretty close?"

"That's exactly close."

"9:30 A.M. on Saturday the eleventh?"

"Yes."

"How did she know that they burned her?"

"She just said they burnt her. I don't know if they were in the car, if Hope and Toni were in the car or not, but Toni just said they burnt her. Melinda and Laurie burnt her."

"And you say she told you this from McDonald's, or later on?"

"She told me, she said they burned her and they left. They just left her there."

"This is real important, now," Henry interjected, "that conversation took place at 9:30 A.M. in the morning from McDonald's? We've got to get that straight. Is that when she told you that?"

"All she told me at McDonald's was, they burned her. She said I've got to go because they're waiting and they're going to get suspicious, then later on she talked to me and told me about it."

Seventeen

By the end of January, a few weeks after Shanda was buried, her mother started cleaning out her baby's closet. Back behind a pile of clothes and toys, she found a shoebox, tied shut with a string. Written on the top, in Shanda's handwriting, was a warning: "For My Eyes only. Please do not open."

"I knew what it was," Jackie later told the press. "It was something that she was so ashamed of that she had to hide it from me."

Reportedly, the box contained the letters that Amanda Heavrin had written to Shanda. Jackie sat down, it took her hours, and she read every note, in the order that they were written.

"She would compliment Shanda and tell her how pretty her hair was and how pretty her clothes were. An overabundance of compliments," Jackie told one reporter. "You could just see how manipulative she was and how she was just working her and reeling her in."

The letters included the professions of love that Amanda made, the jealousies that she articulated, and finally, the warning to Shanda about Melinda's wrath.

"It was all right there," Jackie was quoted as saying, "it was everything."

At around the same time, toward the end of January, over at the Indiana Women's Prison, the initial results of Laurie Tackett's psychological report were complete.

When she was first seen on January 21, Laurie was dressed in a paper gown. She was quite uncomfortable about that, but soon thereafter, she was given her clothes back, was told that she would not have to wear handcuffs, and she became more responsive and accepting of the process. Overall, Laurie seemed to be well adjusted to the housing unit. Her behavior had stabilized. (The first week Laurie had a number of fainting spells and was also found scratching her wrist.) When Laurie was seen by the psychiatrist, it was determined that there was no need for medication and that there was no psychosis.

Laurie described herself as basically a helpful and caring individual who, for the most part, was pleasant, easygoing, and agreeable. She expressed a great deal of anxiety about her upcoming court case and its outcome. She talked openly about her hallucinations and delusions, claiming that she constantly heard voices, but was unable to understand what they were saying.

"It sounds like they're chanting," Laurie said.

Laurie also claimed that she was seeing visions of people who were inside her who were talking to her. She told the psychologist that the individuals inside her were people that she might have known, but never met personally. She stated that on some occasions there was a vampire inside of her that was "coming through" her, saying there were three other dead people "coming through" her as well.

When asked if she was seeing anything or hearing voices while sitting with the psychological examiner, Laurie said she could see a burning fire with trees, and could hear small children calling for help, but there were no parents around, and she was unable to help them. All she could do was sit and watch. When asked about suicidal ideations or plans, Laurie admitted that she thought about suicide in the past, telling the examiner, "I think it would have been better for me."

The only time Laurie got emotional was when talking about her parents' alleged abuse of her, breaking down into tears, saying that she wanted help.

The initial diagnosis: Laurie was of average to high intelligence, suffered from chronic depression, displayed antisocial and paranoid features, she was delusional and perhaps had an alcohol abuse problem. The consulting IWP psychologist, Dr. Paul Smith, determined that he could not ascertain treatment until the disposition of Laurie's case was reached. He recommended that Laurie's behavior be monitored, but did not assess her as being prone to violence or a risk for escape.

A second report, completed on February 4, by Dr. Paul Shriver, the staff psychologist at IWP, responded to the court-requested pretrial evaluation and would specify Laurie Tackett's competency to stand trial. For that purpose, Laurie was interviewed in-depth for a period of five hours on two separate occasions by a team of three examiners. In his report, Dr. Shriver promised to draw reasonable conclusions given the information available from the two other examiners and from his own analysis of Laurie Tackett.

The summary of the claims Laurie was making were as follows:

1. She experienced blackouts, including a period of amnesia during the time of the offense.

2. She experienced visual and auditory hallucinations throughout her life.

3. She suffered a multiple personality disorder, during which time she has little or no control.

4. She suffered chronic depression, becoming suicidal and self-mutilating.

5. She believed herself to be "psychic," having "powers" of ESP beyond the average person.

The clinical interview data observed that Laurie always claimed to be "herself" throughout the examination process. Her manner was guarded and defensive, her answers often appeared forced. She was sad and anxious most of the time, becoming animated and enthusiastic only when humored about her several personalities and psychic powers. Her New Age philosophy, it was determined, seemed to be a blend of "spiritualism" and "hippyism," with a heavy emphasis on ESP. She spoke most typically in a low expressionless monotone, with frequently downcast or side-cast eyes, not making eye contact. She was observed to be right-handed, and claimed that two of her personalities were left-handed, but she was unable to demonstrate that.

The examiner noted four important observations in his report, the first having to do with Laurie's eye movements, which did not shift positions in a way that would be expected when Laurie was recalling either past events, reality, or fantasy. This implied a "purposeful control" designed for "impression manipulation," or deceit. "There were also few eye blinks or flutters, which has the same implication of conscious control," the report stated, "conscious attempts to control eyes and mouth are seen during lying."

The second significant observation was that Laurie, when asked to produce one of her personalities, chose "Deanna." She was observed first dropping her eyes as if meditating, then raising her face with a very different expression, but her degree of animation and manners were "not vastly different" from the qualities already attributed to Laurie. Her voice did not change, her "altered" state was present wholly in her face, in her eyes and mouth. "She both reported and was observed to be maintaining this personality's presence with effort and acted exhausted afterward," the report noted, adding, "none of this behavior is typically reported in studies of multiple personalities."

A third observation was that, while Laurie claimed to be experiencing both visual and auditory hallucinations during the interviews, she did not observably respond to them, nor did she ever appear to be distracted by them, nor could she ever report their content, nor did she ever report any compulsion to obey them.

A final observation was that Laurie seemed relatively unemotional when discussing her past traumatic experiences.

Included in the psychological report was Laurie's own summary of the various "personalities" that inhabited her throughout her life: "Sissy" at age three; "Sarah" at age four; "Darlene" at age nine; "Geno" (a male) at age fifteen; and "Deanna" (age 23) at age sixteen. She claimed that the only way she was aware of the names and ages of these personalities was through the reports of friends who observed her in what she described as a state of partial "amnesia."

Laurie told one psychologist that she believed that "Darlene," "Geno," and "Deanna" were all alternatively "present" at the time of the offense. She claimed that she, herself, after realizing that "something" terrifying was going on, was not consciously present that night. However, she did remember fragments of what went on, but she contended that these returned to her gradually and were piecemeal.

All of the personalities, the report indicated, "shared in common" the basic knowledge that knives are dangerous, that one can die from the loss of blood, that it is dangerous to play with matches, especially around gasoline, and that harming and killing others is morally and legally wrong.

The report noted that Laurie described her inner voices as "personalities" to one examiner, then as "transfers" or "spirits" to a second and third examiner, barely mentioning her "personalities" at all.

In discussing her psychic experiences, Laurie claimed to have a personal "teacher" in 1991 who "demonstrated" more advanced "powers" (such as psychokinesis) and who sought to encourage Laurie's "gifts." She said she herself had been known to "interpret auras," to do "psychic healing," and to "hold seances."

During the course of her examination, Laurie said, "I love to make up wild stories and put people on," yet she clung to her several "identities" complaining bitterly that no one has ever believed her. She begged for psychiatric help, telling the examiners that she would commit suicide if the jury and court did not believe in her mental illness. Because of her illness, she told examiners, she expected to be acquitted of the charges.

The overall summary of test findings: "Laurie is a bright articulate adolescent whose intellect is clear and unimpaired and who achieves appropriately at her ability level. She has a strong, even punitive conscience and is currently feeling guilty, depressed, ashamed, and very anxious about her future, rather than helpless and doomed. She is seeking 'rescue' and treatment with a strong sense of desperation and invention and enumerating every symptom she can think of or ever heard of to obtain both, in a very naive manner."

The report concluded that Mary Laurine Tackett was desperately trying to avoid conviction and a prison sentence, and was fabricating symptoms "in order to support a defense of insanity." The unanimous consensus was that her responses appeared to be calculated, "to produce an impression of severe psychosis and achieve commitment to a mental institution."

In the examiner's opinion, Laurie had a precise appreciation of the charges against her, and the consequences of being found guilty of them; she had a thorough awareness of the possible pleas and the degrees of guilt; she believed in punishment of the guilty, and she had an adequate understanding of courtroom and judicial procedure.

"In no case," the report stated, "has a defense of 'not guilty by reason of the presence and actions of an alternative personality' ever been accepted in court as valid, and the syndrome itself is controversial."

Meanwhile, the investigation continued. On Monday, February 10, about a week after the interview with Pommerehn, Steve Henry was able to track down Candy Holcroft, interviewing her at her home in Madison. Holcroft was a counselor at Madison Junior High School, and she happened to be having breakfast at McDonald's the morning of January 11. Holcroft told Henry that she saw Laurie, Hope, and Toni there at approximately 9:30 A.M. They were with a girl she didn't recognize. Holcroft didn't notice anything unusual about the girls' actions, but she did remember seeing Toni on the phone at the McDonald's counter.

Ten days later, the Clark Oil Station on Clifty Drive was ordered to produce the cash register tape from their place of business for Saturday, January 11, 1992. The station manager was able to pinpoint the exact amount the girls spent that morning, recalling that she first charged them for a two-liter of Coke, which was on sale, then she had to void the receipt because the girls insisted on purchasing Pepsi, which cost a few cents extra. There was no transaction that matched their purchase at the time Toni Lawrence said they were there. The tape receipt placed the girls at the station at 8:40 A.M.

On February 21, at a garbage dump located on the logging road near the Tackett house, Steve Henry located a pair of fairly new light brown suede shoes, with the brand name, Pinecones. The shoes were found side by side, still tied. Henry contacted Jackie Vaught, who said that she had purchased Shanda a pair of shoes matching that description for Christmas.

Also on that day, at 6:15 P.M. in the evening, Henry and Shippley interviewed Carrie East at the Sellersburg Post. The eighteen-year-old told them that in the fall of 1991, Amanda Heavrin had threatened her because she was seeing Melinda. It was just talk, East said. Amanda would call her and threaten to damage her car and do other minor things to her. East described her connection with Melinda, explaining that they met through Melinda's older sister, Melissa, telling the officers that Melinda and her sisters were strictly gay.

"I want to read something and you can tell me if you either agree or disagree," Shippley said.

"Okay."

" 'I hate that little bitch. I'm going to kill her. Take me to Shanda's house so I can beat her up.' "

"I never heard her say anything like that."

"You made a statement that anybody, you know, that Melinda's friends should stand behind her now," Henry mentioned.

"Yeah, I'll stand by her."

"Why?"

"Because I just feel that Laurie Tackett has more to do with this than Melinda does."

"Why do you think Shanda was killed?"

"I think Shanda was killed because, this is just what I've heard through the grapevine somehow, Laurie needed to get into an occult group and she had to kill somebody, and it was more or less a perfect setup to put it on Melinda because, you know, Melinda had a lot of hate for Shanda."

"Did anybody say anything about Laurie cutting one of her own nipples off?"

"Cutting one of her own?"

"I got a call at home that said you had told someone at the Sports Club or Fitness Club, wherever you work, that Laurie Tackett had cut one of her nipples off and that she had to kill Shanda in order to join a satanic cult."

"I didn't say that."

In discussing her relationship with Loveless, East acknowledged that she and Melinda broke up, it was a mutual agreement, she said, because Melinda was seeing Amanda again. She claimed the last time she spoke to Melinda was three weeks before the murder, at which time they had a casual conversation and decided to be friends. She said Shanda's name never came up.

On March 6, Steve Henry reinterviewed Peggy Tackett, who told him that at 7:30 A.M. on January 11, Laurie and Melinda came through the front door, and her daughter asked for some matches, but she didn't give her any. She said the girls then went back outside, and she saw the four girls standing around Laurie's car. The four got into the car and pulled up to the house, at which time she argued with Laurie about being out late. The girls said they were going to McDonald's to get something to eat, and a little while later, Laurie and Melinda came back, hanging around the house, waiting for her husband to get off work so he could repair the muffler on Laurie's car.

Peggy told Steve Henry that Melinda was sitting at the kitchen table, picking at her fingernails. She told Melinda how pretty her hair was, and Melinda made a comment about how much dirt was under her nails, then going to the bathroom to wash her hands. She said that none of the girls gave her any indication about what was going on, telling Henry that if any of them just said something, she could have possibly saved the little girl that died.

One week later, Kary Pope was voluntarily polygraphed at the Sellersburg Post by Sergeant David Motsinger. She was given three tests, during which she was asked if she was with Melinda and Laurie on January 11, if she was there when Shanda was set on fire, and if she knew that Shanda was dead before she heard about it from newscasts.

Kary Pope failed the polygraph concerning the prior knowledge issue.

On March 16, 1992, the Jefferson County Juvenile Court held a probable cause hearing for juvenile delinquency regarding Toni Lawrence and Hope Rippey. The prosecutor filed identical charges against both girls: Count I, Murder; Count

II, Criminal Confinement; Count III, Criminal Deviate Conduct; Count IV, Aggravated Battery; Count V, Arson; Count VI, Intimidation; Count VII, Battery by means of a Deadly Weapon. On the same date, in a separate hearing, it was further determined that the charges against both Toni Lawrence and Hope Rippey would be waived from the juvenile court system. The two fifteen-year-olds would be tried as adults. Rippey's trial date was set for September 8; Lawrence's for September 22. Immediately following the lengthy hearings, which were closed to the public, Rippey and Lawrence were put behind bars at the Jefferson County Jail. Because the four girls had to be kept separated, Toni Lawrence was soon moved to the Scott County Jail.

Also on March 16, seven additional charges were filed against Melinda Loveless and Laurie Tackett, all of them identical to those filed against Rippey and Lawrence, with one further charge: child molesting. (A crime for which Rippey and Lawrence could not be charged since they themselves were under the age of sixteen at the time of the offense.)

During Tackett's arraignment, her attorney, Rob Barlow, told the court that he was considering an insanity plea and asked the court to pay for a supplementary psychological evaluation. Judge Ted Todd said he would consider Barlow's request, and eventually, before her sentencing, Tackett did have the benefit of further psychological testing.

Hope Rippey remained in the Jefferson County Jail in Madison, and she posed no difficulties to the jailers there. The only problem they had with Hope was that she was reluctant to keep her living area clean. At times, she shared a cell with as many as four other inmates, and there were a couple of complaints about Hope's failure to clean the commode and the shower.

On April 2, police learned that Jeannie Whitson, an inmate who shared a cell with Hope Rippey, had been given some information by Hope in reference to the case. Steve Henry interviewed Whitson that same day, only to conclude that Whitson had nothing useful to offer him. Most of what she said was generic information, things that had been highlighted on the news months before.

One week later, April 8, Henry conducted a similar kind of interview with an inmate who had shared a cell with Melinda at the Clark County Jail. Tracy Plaskett, a twenty-one-year-old who was in jail for forgery and theft, said that she and Melinda discussed the details of Melinda's case, and proceeded to tell Henry what she claimed was Melinda's version of the night on January 10 and the morning of January 11.

"When she would relate the details of this crime, would she become upset?" Henry asked.

"No. When she would talk she would say stuff, like, 'Well we'll be driving down the road and Shanda would come to, and yell for help. We'd pull over, we'd go back, we'd beat her or stab her, then we'd get back in the car.' Then all of a sudden she'd start laughing."

"Melinda would start laughing?"

"Yes, Melinda would start laughing, thinking the whole ordeal was funny. When they showed Shanda's funeral on TV, and at the same time they had Melinda's mother on TV, you know, and when she sees Shanda's casket come out, she didn't say anything. She didn't cry or anything when she saw the casket, but when she saw her mother on TV, she cried."

"Going back a minute, did she give you any indication at all as to who actually set Shanda on fire?"

"Yes, she said Tackett actually set Shanda on fire."

"But one of the other little girls poured the gas?"

"Yes."

The next day, April 9, prosecutor Guy Townsend filed the additional count of felony murder against both Melinda Loveless and Laurie Tackett.

On April 13, because of the heavy publicity the case had received, a motion for change of venue was presented to the court by Mike Walro on behalf of Melinda Loveless. Judge Ted Todd granted the motion, not by allowing the case to be moved out of Jefferson County, but by deciding to select a jury from another county, which remained undisclosed. At the same hearing, new trial dates were set; Loveless would be tried on August 10, Tackett on August 25.

Eighteen

On April 17, Toni Lawrence was interviewed for the second time. Present in the library of the Scott County Jail were Steve Henry and Buck Shippley, Toni, and her attorney, Paul Baugh.

Henry asked Toni to start from the beginning and tell the whole story as if none of them had ever heard it. Toni described the days preceding their trip to Louisville and the arrangements she made to sneak away from town. Before they left Madison, Toni said the three of them went to Radio Shack, then to Burger King, and then Laurie and Hope went into Wal-Mart and stole batteries for Laurie's jam-box.

She said that on the ride to New Albany, just as they were arriving in town, Laurie asked Hope whether Toni "knew about it." Laurie then told Toni, "We're going to kill a little girl."

The two officers asked repeated questions about why Toni went to Shanda's door, but for a while, it was like pulling teeth.

"So, Melinda was explaining to you what all the problem was? What did she say?" Henry asked.

"She said that she was going with a girl named Amanda and Shanda had been flirting with her and had been trying to steal her away and they've got into a lot of fights and she wanted to kill her."

"So the purpose, when you went to the door, was to entice her out of the house," Shippley said.

Toni said nothing.

"To get her to come with you all?" he asked.

"Yeah."

230

Toni ran through their adventure at the skate park in Louis-ville, detailing the trip back to Shanda's, and the drive to The Witches' Castle. She said Hope was driving, and she believed that Hope had been there before.

At the castle, Toni told them, Laurie took a rope out of her pocket, and Laurie and Melinda tied Shanda's feet and wrists. Toni claimed that Shanda didn't resist in any way. She said that when cars passed by, they all got scared, and Melinda and Laurie untied Shanda, leading her back to the car. Shanda did not try to break free from them.

Toni explained that before going to Madison, they stopped at two gas stations. At the first station, Five Star, she and Hope met two guys, and in a joking way, Toni told them that she wanted to go with them to Madison, but the boys weren't headed that way. At the next station, Hope stopped for direc-tions, and Toni said she made a phone call to Louisville, speak-ing to her friend, Mike. She had no reason for calling him, really, their five-minute conversation was just small talk.

Once in Madison, at the wooded logging road by Laurie's house, Toni said Hope went out and joined Laurie, Melinda, and Shanda, and "it looked like she was helping."

"Looked like who was helping?" Baugh asked.

"Hope was helping her."

"Helping Melinda and Laurie?"

"Yeah, but then she let her go and got back in the car."

"Okay, and did you say anything to Hope?"

"I asked her why she was helping them."

"And what did she say?"

"She said she wasn't helping her, she was helping Shanda."

Toni continued her tale, reporting that Melinda and Laurie strangled Shanda and then put her in the trunk. She said she heard Shanda moaning.

Over at the Tacketts, just about sunrise, all four girls went out to the car. Toni got into the car because the trunk was open and she didn't want to see Shanda. The other three girls stared into the trunk, "looking." Then Laurie went back to the house to get some matches.

"Okay, why did she need matches?" Baugh asked.

"To set a pair of pants on fire."

"Okay, whose pants?"

"Hers."

"What was she going to do that for?"

"Because she was going to put Shanda there."

"Okay, she said that?"

"Yeah."

But Laurie never had the chance to burn Shanda then and there. She lit the pants on fire, Toni said, and then her mom came outside and, unaware of what was happening, told the girls not to start a fire.

At the place on Lemon Road, after Toni purchased the two-liter bottle which Laurie then filled with gas, the other girls took Shanda out of the trunk. They poured the gas, and Shanda caught on fire. Toni said she didn't really see who did what.

"Okay, who poured the gas?" Baugh asked.

"Supposedly Hope."

"Why do you say supposedly?"

"Because she told me that on the phone. She told me not to tell the cops."

That pretty much concluded the one-hour-and-forty-minute interview with Toni Lawrence.

On April 20, Prosecutor Guy Townsend agreed to drop six charges against Lawrence, including murder, arson, and aggravated battery. The plea agreement would allow Toni to plead guilty to a single count of criminal confinement, a class B felony, which carried a sentence of ten years that could be increased by up to ten years or reduced up to four years, based on aggravating or mitigating circumstances. The acceptance of the agreement by the court was made contingent upon Toni Lawrence passing a polygraph.

Before taking the lie detector test, Toni asked to make another statement to police, telling them that there were a few things she hadn't been truthful about, that she needed to have everything off her chest.

On April 21, Henry, Shippley, Baugh, and Lawrence went through the events of the crime once again. The main thing that

Toni wanted known was that when she looked on at the kill site, Shanda was laid on the ground wrapped in a blanket.

"Okay, at any point in the evening did Shanda ask you or anyone else to make them quit hurting her?" Henry asked.

"Shanda asked me to tell them to stop."

"Where? At what point in the evening?"

"At the woods."

"That was before they took her clothes off?"

"Yeah. And I told Melinda to take her back home and she said no, because she knew everybody's name."

"Were you scared after this girl was burned?"

"Yes."

"Okay, how scared were you?" Henry prodded.

"I bit my hand."

"Was there any concern expressed about anybody finding the body?"

"Melinda said, well what if somebody finds the body, and Hope said that nobody comes down this road."

"Did they say anything about anybody going back later and doing anything with the body?"

"They said they were going to go back later on that night."

"Who said they were going back?"

"Laurie. She said they were going to take a shovel with them."

"So throughout this whole episode, you did nothing to help?" Shippley asked.

"No."

"Other than go and buy a two-liter bottle of Pepsi."

"Yeah."

Between April 22 and April 27, Toni Lawrence was given three lie detector tests. After careful analysis and numerical scoring, the examiner was unable to form a conclusive opinion.

On June 4, Steve Henry finally would get what he believed to be the whole truth out of Toni Lawrence. On that date, having gained consent to search the property from the owner, Henry and Baugh did a taped interview with Toni on the grounds of The Witches' Castle.

(In Madison) Me and Hope turned both radios on and I looked out the window and Melinda had one arm and Laurie had one arm and Melinda had the knife in her other hand and she was trying to slit her throat but the knife was too dull. Hope got out of the car and went over and grabbed Shanda and they stumbled back and then Hope came back to the car and I asked her why she was helping them. She said that she tried to pull Shanda away from them and then I looked out the window and Laurie was sitting on Shanda's stomach and Melinda was on her legs and Laurie was strangling her so I looked back out the windshield and listened to the radio. A few minutes later Laurie knocked on the window and rolled it down and she said that Shanda was knocked out and that she needed the keys to the trunk Hope handed them to her and she said she needed help and neither us would help. Hope started to cry and I just stared out the windshield.

We drove over to the "burnpile" and we all got out and walked around and then Laurie said she was gonna open the trunk so I get back in the car. She opened the trunk and Hope brought me the keys and I turned on the car so I could turn the heat on. Laurie came and told me to press the accelerator so nobody would hear Shanda scream if she screamed so I did and I looked through the rearview mirror and I seen the blood on the car.

Went to Clark and I went in to buy a Pepsi and Laurie came in and said to buy a 2-liter so I did. Hope pulled the car up to the station and Laurie said shit and we went outside and Hope said she (Shanda) was making noises and the guy that was getting gas behind the car was looking at them weird.

We drove for a little bit and Laurie stopped and backed into this little patch of gravel. We all got out and walked around and I walked out into the road and put out my cigarette and then I got back in the car and they opened the trunk and got her out and closed the trunk. Laurie pulled the car out into the street and she got out and went over to Shanda. I glanced over and she was wrapped in a agreed to remortgage her house to that end.

The grounds Townsend listed as the basis for the change of judge rested largely on his contention that Ted Todd was favoring the defense. Ted Todd had been elected to the Fifth Judicial Circuit in 1988; he had been an attorney since 1964, and never before had he been confronted with this type of allegation.

Townsend determined that because Ted Todd had at one time been in law practice with Mike Walro, he was biased against the state. He argued that the decision to hire Russell Johnson was made in closed chambers, without his presence, which, he contended, was a violation of professional ethics. Townsend requested that a "special judge" be selected to replace Todd. However, it would be determined during the hearing that Townsend had no legal basis to question the judge about what was really an administrative decision.

"You have made a very strong accusation against this court and you're not substantiating it," Judge Todd said toward the end of the hearing. "Now, if you could give me some law that I could not have a conversation to clarify an Order with another party involving an administrative matter, I want to know it."

"Your honor, I don't know the answer to that question," Townsend responded.

Townsend admitted that in administrative matters, a judge was permitted to have ex parte communications, yet he still proceeded with his argument, insisting that the judge was not being impartial.

Russell Johnson pointed out that the request for co-counsel was not material as to the guilt or innocence of the defendant. In his twelve years of experience as an attorney, Johnson had never been involved with anything quite like this.

"This motion for change of judge is just totally without merit and I don't know of any case law to support this," Johnson told the court. Mike Walro, who had been in practice for sixteen years, also took the stand, citing case law which supported a judge's discretion in ruling on administrative matters.

In the end, Judge Ted Todd overruled the motion.

As the prosecution continued to prepare for trial, on June

26, Curtis Wells and Buck Shippley personally delivered evidence specimens to the FBI laboratory in Washington. They included numerous specimens from Shanda's body such as pubic hair combings, vaginal swabs, debris from her hands, and a hair clump.

Nineteen

In the summer of 1992, Kary Pope kept close contact with Laurie through visits and letters. For some reason, after the murder, Kary felt more drawn to her. She even went so far as to move to Indianapolis for a few weeks that summer, visiting Laurie every day.

In return, Laurie expressed her feelings to Kary in a series of letters and poems. In a letter written on the first of June, Laurie said she always had Kary in her heart, promising, "About Melinda, no, I *never* loved her. *Only* as a friend. After you had Tracy, I just sort of clung onto the first person that came around, and the emotions and feelings I had for you never left. In my mind, I substituted Melinda in your place."

Laurie went on professing her love for Kary, at one point wondering why Kary never before mentioned that Laurie's psychic powers scared her. Initially, when Kary learned of the murder, she was telling people that Laurie was obsessed with death and was freaking her out. Evidently, the seances even scared Laurie "sometimes." She mentioned being frightened by her own powers the night at Amanda Sommerville's house, claiming, "Half of that night, Kary, I don't remember *because* of all channeling I was doing." Laurie wrote, *"That* lets me know it was real. Sometimes even I wondered whether is was real or not, but when you go into something and can't remember it afterwards, something there tells you it's not fake. Maybe in a way it was an attention getter — but *never* fake. *Please* believe that."

Laurie pictured herself as someone who was "fallen," telling

Kary, "I'm so scared," explaining that she never felt there was anybody she could ever go to to discuss her problems. Even as she wrote, Laurie was in "lockup," where she remained for some time. She had been placed in a segregated area because she had violated prison rules and had posed a danger to herself and others.

"You *know* I was never violent," Laurie wrote. "I got in trouble about 2 nights ago. I was sleeping and was reliving that night with Shanda in a dream, only in the dream there were people all around us and they weren't alive but they were crying and watching and I felt like one of those people, helpless. Anyways I started yelling in my sleep and the police came in. It was a crazy dream."

That same week, in early June, Laurie wrote another letter to Kary, complaining about jail life, in particular she talked about having to call the "police" (jailers) just to go to the bathroom, claiming that she would then sometimes have to wait upwards of thirty minutes to an hour before a jailer would respond. She also griped about being locked up in a room "no bigger than a stable 24/7."

"I hope your life is better and you never have to go thru this. You won't!" Laurie signed off, adding, "BE HAPPY! TOMORROW IS A NEW DAY!"

Also in the envelope, Laurie included a packet of poems she had written, including one new poem, written especially for Kary, "God Made Friends," which spoke of their "special relationship." In Laurie's view, Kary was "Someone who would love without judgment and believe, regardless of the circumstances."

"God did not create us to laugh or cry alone," Laurie wrote. "That's why he made friends."

Among the other poems included in the packet were a series of poems Laurie had written in the first few months following the murder. She made a point of explaining that the poems focused on death because she felt suicidal when she wrote them, telling Kary, "don't be alarmed," assuring her that she didn't feel like killing herself any more.

"There, just so you'd know, and not think I *am* some kind of crazy killer—because for real—I'm not. *Please* believe me!" she told Kary.

Kary Pope read the poems and felt they should be seen by others. Eventually, they wound up in the hands of the authorities, but they were never entered as evidence.

I do not expect any person to understand, to believe, to see inside this perfect, yet, deformed shell which is my own. My mind crumbles more every second of every day. . . . Death calls to me . . . Things that have kept my mind tormented, my thoughts confused, are now coming at me in bounds. Set me free, set my soul free. My mind is not stable enough to be imprisoned any longer. My life has been a confusing, hurting, and lonely mission, but now, even more so.

By the second week in June, Laurie suddenly had a complete change of heart about Kary, writing to tell her things would never work out between them. Laurie had found herself a girlfriend at the prison, April, whom she had "married." She was also being confronted by her attorney with the possibility that she might face the death penalty if she didn't agree to a plea bargain. Laurie was under too much pressure, trying to deal with her guilt in her own way, and she didn't need Kary Pope complicating matters.

Laurie told Kary that their relationship was too painful for her, explaining why she was pulling Kary off her visiting list. "I'm sorry!" Laurie wrote. "I deserve this, everything I'm getting I deserve. I want to die, so the death sentence really doesn't matter."

Laurie told Kary that she was tired of fighting, that she had no fear of death, signing off, "Be careful—Life is too short. Everything has changed because of me. Please forgive what I've done."

Kary responded to Laurie a lengthy letter, filled with both anger at Laurie's rejection, and understanding of her fear and guilt.

In June and July, as the local news coverage continued to divulge bits of new information about the four girls, Laurie wrote Kary a few angry letters, telling Kary to stay away, enraged that Kary had caused problems between Laurie and her "wife," April.

"You have made me *lose* the only person I had and the only person who I know loved me and was real!" she told her. "You lied to the police about me. And who knows what else you said about me that I don't know about. Just please stay out of my life. I don't want anything else to do with you!"

By the end of June, the torture-slaying of Shanda Sharer began to get national attention. On Sunday, June 21, the *Los Angeles Times* ran a two-page Associated Press story on the stunned town of Madison. Townspeople from the quiet Ohio River town spoke about their horror and disbelief. In response, the article quoted Madison Mayor Morris Wooden, who tried to smooth things over as much as possible.

"I think Madison has such a good image in the area, people will see that what happened is a fluke," Wooden told the Associated Press. "The people here know it's not typical of their town. They'll just go about their business and hope for a better day."

Also quoted was seventeen-year-old Tina Rippey, Hope's older sister, who, after a brief courthouse visit with Hope, struggled to comprehend the charges.

"She says she didn't do it, other girls say different," Tina told the reporter. "When she's put on trial for murder, what am I supposed to do? Say she's guilty like everyone else? She's my baby sister and I'll stand by her."

"Hope was real shy," Tina's boyfriend, Roy Newby, chimed in. "From what I know, this was the first time she'd met this girl [Shanda] and she tried to kill her? I can't believe that. And Toni Lawrence, she's scared of a bug. I can't believe she would even be in the car. You throw a frog at her and she'd scream."

A few weeks later, on Thursday, July 9, *USA Today* ran a lead story on "teen girls and crime" which covered the Shanda Sharer murder and addressed the problem of kids killing kids. Some Madison residents told *USA Today* that they were certain satanism was connected to the murder, unable to conceive of fifteen- and sixteen-year-old girls doing something like this on their own.

"This is supposed to be an area protected by the values system," the principal of Madison High School, Roger Gallatin, told the *USA* reporter. "When this happens, where do we have a safe place to raise a family?"

The public pressure was mounting, and still, Guy Townsend had gotten no cooperation from any of the girls or their attorneys. He was in a hurry for them to agree to a plea bargain, and to that end, the prosecutor began taking the steps necessary toward filing the death penalty against both Loveless and Tackett. For Rippey, who was just fifteen, the death penalty was not a possibility under Indiana case law.

"It now appears likely that the cases will go to trial," Townsend told the *Madison Courier* in early July. "The state intends to use whatever means are available to it to see that justice is done."

"I didn't want to file the death penalty," Townsend later said. "It was because they wouldn't take the deal, even when they knew everything. By the second day we knew basically what had happened as related to Tackett and Loveless. We knew they were guilty of murder, no question. And the evidence was there."

On July 13, 1992, Townsend dropped the legal bombshell. The death penalty specifications were filed against Melinda Loveless and Mary Laurine Tackett. Also on that day, Townsend filed the additional charge of conspiracy to commit murder against both girls. Each was charged with ten crimes in all.

In order for Townsend to impose the death penalty, Indiana law required that he prove at least one aggravating circumstance. In his motions, Townsend had already cited seven aggravating circumstances. Among them, the girls committed the murder by "lying in wait"; and they committed the murder "intentionally," while attempting to commit arson.

Days later, a pretrial conference was held on behalf of Loveless and Tackett, and motions were filed to continue trial. It was determined that a new trial date would be set on September 21, at which time pending matters would be heard.

By July 15, the news that execution was being sought for the two teens hit the local airwaves and area newspapers. By the end of the month, it was splashed across the front page of the "Tempo" section of *The Chicago Tribune* in a piece entitled "Fatal Affection?"

"The age of innocence here ended at about 10:45 A.M. last January 11 on a dirt road 15 miles north of town," the article began. It went on to describe the burned corpse that the hunters found, saying that the people in Madison never dreamed that their "picture-book village" would ever suffer such a tragedy.

For conservative Madison folks, the most difficult thing to deal with by far, was the homosexual aspect of the Shanda Sharer murder. Most of the adults in the town were uncomfortable with the idea that children of the age of twelve, or even sixteen, might be sexually active in heterosexual relationships, no less in homosexual affairs.

Until the Sharer case, the adults in Madison seemed to be unaware that the sexual revolution had reached their town. But the teenagers in Madison, the contemporaries of Hope, Toni, and Laurie, all knew differently. Many of them hung out nightly at a strip-mall parking lot, which they referred to as "The Lot." There, kids secretly enjoyed a world free of societal constraints.

By early August, local news focused on the public cost involved in prosecuting the four girls in Madison. Already, Jefferson County had spent $15,000 to keep the girls in jail, and the costs were rising at exorbitant rates. Weeks before, the Jefferson County Council had transferred $147,000 out of its general fund to the Jefferson Circuit Court in anticipation of the trial expenses. Among other things, that comprised $75,000 for the eight public defenders representing the four girls; $45,000 for food and lodging of sequestered juries; $15,000 for witness fees, and $2000 in travel expenses for transporting the girls to and from Madison.

Because the death penalty was being sought against Loveless

and Tackett, and state law required that lead counsel in such cases be "death penalty certified," co-counsel for both Loveless and Tackett was automatically employed. For Loveless, Bob Hammerle, one of the most prestigious attorneys in the state, had been brought on board. For Tackett, Madison attorney Wil Goering and Indianapolis attorney Ellen O'Connor stepped in. In addition, Judge Todd elected to have the original counsel (Walro and Barlow) remain on the case to insure the continuity of the girls' defense. Guy Townsend would later complain bitterly about the "team" of attorneys each girl had.

On Sunday, August 16, the *Los Angeles Times* did a follow-up piece on the alarming number of "kids who kill." The article made reference to the most recent FBI crime statistics, reporting that children were killing more than ever. "The number of juveniles arrested for homicide between 1981 and 1990 increased 60 percent nationwide, far outpacing the 5.2 percent increase among adults," the article revealed. A photograph of Melinda Loveless being escorted from the Jefferson County Courthouse covered a full half page of the *Los Angeles Times*. She was the only teen killer singled out from anywhere in the country other than New York and Los Angeles.

The newspaper discussed the influence of Hollywood violence on teens, delving into the issue of TV violence, which, it reported, seemed to make kids more accepting of violence.

"We have kids growing up who treat violence as if it is an ordinary fact of life, from the Ninja Turtles to Arnold Scwhwarzenegger movies," one expert said.

The article also laid blame on domestic violence, citing statistics and using graphs to prove that the vast majority of condemned teen killers were themselves subject to households rife with abuse. It quoted a psychiatric study published in 1988 (based on fourteen juveniles condemned to death) which found that eighty-five percent had been brutally abused in their homes and thirty percent had been sodomized by older male relatives.

On August 17, Monday afternoon at about 5:00 P.M., a jailer found Toni Lawrence slumped over in her cell. Lawrence was taken to Scott Memorial Hospital in Scottsburg, and then heli-coptered to Kosair Children's Hospital in Louisville. She was reported as being in critical condition upon her arrival, in a state of a coma after an apparent suicide attempt. Lawrence was given little hope of survival. In the emergency room, in an attempt to revive her, Lawrence had been aspirated with char-coal and intubated three times, but she still remained uncon-scious.

According to one newspaper account, jailers found two tab-lets of the antidepressant Lorazepam in her cell and "four or five" more in the bottom of an empty soft drink can.

Scott County Sheriff John Lizenby described Lawrence as someone who had shown no particular depression, although he did mention that jailers had taken Lawrence to the hospital three months before when they found her hyperventilating in her cell.

In the Scott County Jail, Lawrence had been kept in a hold-ing cell that was separate from other prisoners. Lizenby told the press that the cell had a video camera, and said that Lawrence spent most of her time on the floor near the cell door, looking through the little peephole through which food was delivered to her.

Because of her serious suicide attempt, Lawrence developed Adult Respiratory Distress Syndrome, and she remained in the Intensive Care Unit for eleven days. On August 29, a spokes-woman for the Kosair Children's Hospital told the press that Lawrence had been upgraded from a status of "critical" to "seri-ous." She was transferred to a regular hospital bed, where she was pleasant and cooperative but very reserved. Lawrence was placed on strict "elopement" precautions and was not allowed to attend group activities while hospitalized. In addition, Jef-ferson County sent officers to guard Lawrence's floor.

After two weeks, Lawrence had recovered from the suicide attempt, while still suffering from postpneumonia symptoms; however, she had no other medical problems.

On Tuesday, September 1, Judge Todd issued an order that Lawrence be transferred to the Lifespring mental health facility in Jeffersonville for observation and treatment.

On that date, the Lifespring facility did a physical and medical background evaluation on Toni. They discovered that it was the first time that Lawrence had ever been admitted into a mental care unit, even though she had been depressed for some time and had tried to slash her wrists in the past. They also learned that in recent months, while in jail, Lawrence had been trying to slash her wrists, burn herself, and overdose.

In an interview with mental heath care examiners, Lawrence discussed her involvement with the Shanda Sharer murder, saying that she was simply "in the wrong place at the wrong time." Although she was facing the possibility of being sentenced somewhere between six to twenty years, she expressed hope that the judge would show her leniency because of her willingness to testify against the others. She claimed that her family was being supportive and that they unquestionably believed in her innocence.

On September 2 and 3, Lawrence was referred by Dr. Ghada Al-Asadi to the Ball Psychological Clinic in Jeffersonville, where she underwent a personality assessment test. Lawrence was given the Minnesota Multiphasic Personality Inventory, and was diagnosed as suffering from posttraumatic stress disorder and antisocial personality disorder. The most prominent characteristic of her personality showed that she had a marked disregard for social standards and values, that she acted without considering the consequences of her actions.

At that time, based on her test performance, Lawrence was not considered to be potentially dangerous to herself or others; there was no clinical evidence of severe depression. Nevertheless, in view of what had just taken place, William Ball, the clinical psychologist who administered the assessment, recommended that she be kept on a "constant suicide alert." He also recommended that psychotropic medication be prescribed to relieve some of Lawrence's anxiety.

Lawrence remained at Lifespring through September 21, during which time she was described as being "cheerful" and "conversive," although she still had sporadic periods of increased anxiety and agitation at times. During her stay at Lifespring, for the most part, she responded well to staff members, was able to express her feelings, and had shown a lot of insight. Lawrence was visited by her family, was allowed to participate in group activities, and was encouraged to do a lot of self-evaluation, all of which seemed to be helping her state of mind. According to Toni's Clark Memorial Hospital patient progress report, Toni told her therapist that her mother confessed to her that she herself tried to commit suicide when she was a teenager. Her mother admitted that she had been hospitalized for one month in 1973 or 1974, "for psychiatric problems."

In a daily therapeutic exercise, which she had participated in throughout her hospitalization, called "Room Reflect," Toni wrote many of her innermost wishes and thoughts. She described the things in her life that helped her to feel secure: "My boyfriends picture, my teddy bears, my Oscar the Grouch, my baby blanket that my granny made, and jail."

She talked about death: "My philosophy on life is it could be alot better. Like I would've never gotten into this mess if I wouldn't have tried to commit suicide. Actually I was just trying to make myself sick. But then again it could be *alot* worse! I could've been the one who got killed and I could have died when I ODed or it could have left me paralyzed or brain dead."

She enumerated her belief in "God, love at first sight, premarital sex, having babies out of wedlock, and peace," and her disbelief in "abortion, war, drugs, shooting up with needles, and anything that can kill someone."

She reflected on what her life would be like in the future:

In 10 years I hope to be very happily married! I want to have 1 kid and adopt 2. I want to have a well paying job and I want my husband to have a well paying job! I want to live in a big house in the county with 10 mustangs. I also want a vacation home in the Bahamas! I want to go to France for 2 years. I studied it (French) for 2 years (going on my 3rd year). I hope to have gotten *all* of this mess behind me and be finished with it all! And I want to stay close to *all* of my family!

On September 21, Lawrence was transferred to LaRue

Carter, a criminal psychiatric hospital where she remained for two weeks. At that institution, it was determined that Lawrence was in need of long-term treatment; however, that would be left to the judge to decide. At LaRue Carter, once Lawrence was taken off all medication, she was diagnosed as being able to return to jail, and in early October, she was transferred to the Jefferson County Jail. It would be weeks before Toni would make any more trouble for the folks in Madison again.

Twenty

On a near-perfect autumn day, while Madison farmers were busy selling pumpkins at the nearby farmer's market small groups of people gathered around the courthouse steps, hoping to catch a glimpse of Loveless and Tackett. At about 2:00 P.M., the girls were escorted from the jail by police, under the scrutiny of a half-dozen television cameras, still photographers, reporters, and interested bystanders. Looking every bit a teenager, Melinda wore a dark vest over gray pants. Laurie took a different tack, wearing a prim and proper blue-and-white striped dress.

It was September 21, 1992. Judge Todd, sounding more like a schoolteacher than a judge, leaned over the bench, urging first Loveless, then Tackett, to ask questions if they didn't understand something about the proceedings.

On that day, Melinda Loveless and Laurie Tackett signed plea agreements with the Jefferson Circuit Court, pleading guilty to the murder and torture of Shanda Sharer. In exchange, the state of Indiana agreed to withdraw the death penalty specifications against each girl. The plea agreements called for both Loveless and Tackett to cooperate fully with the state, including testifying at all hearings or trials at which their presence would be required. Both pleaded guilty to murder, arson, and criminal confinement. In exchange, the seven other charges against the two were dropped. The agreement stipulated that the sentences on the three charges would run concurrently, meaning that each would face a maximum of thirty to sixty years for the most serious charge: murder while aiding in an attempt to commit arson. As their plea agreements were read aloud, Loveless maintained her composure and Tackett occasionally sobbed. A formal plea hearing, at which Judge Todd would decide to accept or reject the pleas, was set for October 6.

The next day, the news of the guilty pleas received heavy coverage in local papers. Melinda Loveless was pictured holding the arm of her handsome lead counsel, Russell Johnson, who, with Bob Hammerle, walked her through a throng of angry onlookers.

"I've been through this numerous times, through it on cases where you've got a lot of press covering it and that type of reaction," Hammerle later said, "but I'm telling you, that walk with her from the jail to the Courthouse door, which can't be more than sixty yards, I got inside, I had to go to a side room. I was out of breath. The intensity from the media, from the people yelling at her, from the people screaming obscenities at her, I felt like I had run a mile."

Instead of concentrating on the girls, much of the local news focused on the reaction of Shanda's parents, who both felt that the death penalty was never the right answer.

"The death penalty is too easy," Jackie Vaught told *The Courier Journal*. "I want them to go up for a very long time. I want this to haunt them every night . . . I think it's gone on long enough. It needs to be over with. Shanda needs to rest, and so do we."

"I just hope that some good comes out of this," Steve Sharer told a reporter. "Kids need to listen to their parents, and parents need to listen to their kids. I hope it never happens again to another child. No child deserves this. Not like this."

Wil Goering, Tackett's lead counsel, later told the press that his client accepted the plea, in part to avoid the death penalty, but also because she had a "sense of remorse" over the incident.

Under Indiana law, prisoners on good behavior can have their sentences reduced by one day for each day served, so there was a possibility that Loveless and Tackett could be out on the streets in just fifteen years, if they received the minimum sentence.

On October 6, the day that Judge Todd accepted Loveless's and Tackett's pleas, a two hour pretrial conference was held for Hope Rippey. Rippey's attorney, Darrel Auxier, rejected an agreement which would have Rippey plead guilty to murder, arson, and criminal confinement.

Auxier, a highly respected Madison attorney, refused to comment to the press. It was surmised that he maintained a "not guilty" plea in an attempt to get his client a better sentencing deal after the hearings for Loveless and Tackett were over.

Eight days after the plea agreements were accepted, Melinda Loveless made the news again, this time for allegedly having sex with a jail employee at the Clark County Jail. On October 14, newspapers reported that the employee resigned in an effort to evade a dismissal hearing. Apparently, a woman inmate told police investigators that Loveless had bragged about having sex with the correctional officer, which led to the employee's immediate suspension. The employee, who remained unidentified, emphatically denied having sex with Loveless, however, according to news sources, both were caught in a "security pod" minutes before midnight on the night in question. Having sex with an inmate is a class D felony in Indiana.

Michelle Loveless wanted the man's name to be printed in the newspaper. She was outraged at a legal system that employed people who, instead of behaving like caretakers, acted like animals.

"Melinda said he took her in a room, she said she was scared," Michelle recounted. "He told her not to cry, and he told her to turn around and drop her pants. She did and he had sex with her and it did not feel good, it was horrible. And then when it was over, she said, 'Did anyone make you do this? and he said, 'No, just pull 'em up and get back.' "

One week later, Melinda Loveless was transferred to the Indiana Women's Prison, where she remained until her sentencing.

On November 9, Toni Lawrence was readmitted into the behavioral unit at the Lifespring facility in Jeffersonville because she was openly threatening to commit suicide by either cutting or hanging herself.

At Lifespring, Lawrence was very tearful and frightened, and nurses' observations said she appeared distant and vague. She claimed that she was not suicidal, yet a week later, she was overheard having a phone conversation with her mother at which time she again threatened to kill herself.

On November 12, Dr. Al-Asadi conferred with Judge Todd, telling the judge that Lawrence was well enough to make a trip to Madison for the purposes of giving a deposition. When Lawrence was notified that she would be transported to Madison the next day, she started talking about suicide again. That afternoon, her parents went to visit her, voicing their concern about Toni's suicidal thoughts. The Lawrences were also concerned about the impending depositions Toni would have to go through.

The next morning, Paul Baugh and Steve Henry did a pre-deposition interview with Lawrence at the Lifespring facility in Jeffersonville. Once Toni realized that she would not have to make the trip to Madison, she became relaxed and cheerful for a while. The day after Henry and Baugh were there, Toni went to the recreational area where she rode an exercise bike and played a little pool. Toni said she was still depressed, but told her doctor that she couldn't cry because it would remind her of Shanda's crying.

Just days later, however, Toni appeared to be extremely apathetic about her defense. During an "expressive therapy" session, she told a counselor that she wanted to return to her family and pretend the murder didn't happen, and she was in complete denial about her criminal actions. She didn't seem to understand that she could have prevented the murder from happening that night.

On November 17, Toni opened up to a therapist, admitting that she was especially tearful because a few weeks prior, she learned that a close male friend of hers (who was on his way to see her in jail at the time) was killed in a car crash. Toni spoke at length about her feelings of loss, becoming extremely upset and emotional, saying that she felt it should have been her instead.

The next day, Toni was put on a suicide watch. She was restricted to the third floor, was put into a hospital gown, and was not permitted to go to any group activities. These restrictions were an attempt, on the part of the Lifespring team, to get Toni to stop using suicide as a way of gaining special treatment. And apparently it worked, because after a few days, Toni never mentioned suicide at all.

Within a week, Toni was placed back in the regular behavioral unit where she was observed as being subdued and brooding. A November 23 notation on Toni's progress record said that she still tended not to accept responsibility for her behavior: "When told by a peer that she seems 'unfriendly' and 'brattish' Toni commented 'Well, I'm a teenager' and 'I learned it from my mother.' "

On November 24, having been told that she would receive a discharge from the hospital the next day, Toni was tearful and angry. She attended a "general art" therapy session in a "huff," painting the word "DIE" in an artwork.

Just hours before she was transported back to the Jefferson County Jail, Toni was confronted by her family in a group session at Lifespring. When asked how she felt about Shanda, Toni screamed like an animal, began hyperventilating and pulling out handfuls of her hair, saying she would rather that Shanda be alive, and she herself be dead, but promised her family that she would not kill herself.

On November 16, Curtis Wells received a report from the FBI lab which determined that the blood sample from the victim matched the human blood identified on one of the specimens. Results from the fingerprint examinations were still pending.

On November 23, a plea agreement hearing for Melinda Loveless was held in Madison. In a trembling voice, Loveless admitted that she had poured gasoline on Shanda Sharer's already burning body. She didn't say who struck the match, but she did admit that she knew Shanda was alive prior to the time that the initial fire was set. Shanda's mother, Jackie, sobbed throughout the testimony.

Melinda's responses to the questions asked by Judge Todd were brief, but sufficient. Judge Todd accepted her guilty plea, and her sentencing hearing was set for December 14, 1992.

The following day, Laurie Tackett, looking wooden and somewhat disinterested, sometimes leaning her hand against her chin, acknowledged she was guilty of arson, murder, and criminal confinement. After Tackett answered a few questions, Steve Henry testified briefly, establishing a factual basis for the charges. Judge Todd accepted Tackett's guilty plea and ordered that her sentencing hearing would immediately follow the sentencing hearing for Loveless.

Ellen O'Connor, one of Tackett's attorneys, said that for months, Laurie wasn't responding to legal advice, and they were never sure that she was going to plea bargain. O'Connor explained that in order to get Laurie to plead guilty, she and the other attorneys had to become like "family" to her.

"We had to convince her that the best thing for her was not to go to trial and face a potential death penalty," O'Connor later said. "I mean, it got to a point that I saw her almost every day. We kind of had to become the dominant people in her life because that's who she responds to."

Also that day, in a separate hearing, a March 1, 1993, trial date was set for Hope Rippey, who continued to maintain a plea of "not guilty."

That same morning, over in the jury room of the Jefferson County courthouse, in the presence of two of her attorneys, Laurie Tackett made a full statement to Steve Henry and Buck Shippley.

Initially, Laurie talked about January 9, 1992, when she spoke to Melinda about going to the "hard-core" show. At that time, Melinda told her she wanted to beat Shanda up, that she wanted to kill her. Laurie said she had never met Shanda, that she didn't know who Melinda was referring to.

"She said she really wanted to kill her and I didn't, I thought she was just upset, and I thought she was just talking, you know, like most people do," Laurie told them.

Laurie claimed that on the ride to New Albany, Hope brought up the subject of killing someone, whereupon she and Hope gave Toni what details they had about Shanda. She delineated most of the same things Toni had already described, including the stop at The Witches' Castle, the trip to Louisville with the detour to Shanda's the first time, and the return to Shanda's after the hard-core show, at which time she helped Melinda cover herself with a blanket in the backseat before going up to Shanda's door. She described bringing Shanda to The Witches' Castle and admitted igniting a black T-shirt of hers while there, placing it within a circle of stones.

Laurie said she was "kind of scared" when they got lost after leaving the castle, stating that Shanda had given them directions to the Five Star gas station. When they got lost a second time, Laurie suggested they go up to Madison. "I kind of wanted to be close to my home," she explained. Laurie made the trip to Madison sound friendly.

"We all started off to Madison and we were all just, you know, we could have been friends," Laurie went on, "cause, you know nothing really was said, except for some threats made by Hope, she was really trying to scare Shanda . . . I mean, I don't know why we were trying to help Melinda."

Laurie described the scene at the woods by her house, saying that it was Melinda alone who grabbed Shanda by the hair, hitting the girl in the face with her knee, then forcing her to strip.

"Before all of this happened, Shanda hugged me and asked me, you know, not to let Melinda hurt her," Laurie told the authorities. "She asked me not to let Melinda kill her, and I can't remember what I said. I don't even remember what I thought."

Laurie claimed that after Shanda was unconscious, the four girls placed her in the trunk. When they went back to her house, Laurie poured them all a drink from a two-liter bottle of Pepsi, and then her dog started barking and they heard Shanda moaning outside, so Laurie went out there.

"I went out to the car, and I looked in on Shanda," Laurie said. "She was screaming and she was banging on the trunk and I opened the trunk up and I looked in at her and said, 'Shanda,' and she looked up, and her eyes rolled back into her head and it just scared me to death, and she was all bloody and there was blood everywhere. And I grabbed the red blanket out of the backseat of the car and put it over her, cause she was shivering and stuff, and I went back in and they asked me what was going on and I said, 'She can't talk.' I said, 'And if she can, she won't talk to me.' I said, 'I think she's dying.' "

Laurie went through the scene where she and Melinda took off driving, first stopping at the burn pile, at which time she went to the neighbor's trailer and acted like she was buying a Coke, because she wanted to "see if anyone could hear anything from up there." Then she and Melinda drove to Cannan. Laurie said she couldn't remember all that happened, except at one point, when Melinda was driving, Melinda wanted to get Shanda out of the trunk so she could run her over with the car. They stopped the car and opened the trunk, but "Shanda never got out," Laurie said. The trunk was closed and they kept on driving around. That's all she remembered about Cannan.

According to Laurie, back at her house, she and Melinda woke Hope and Toni. They all went out to the burn pile, and all four of them decided to open the trunk, to see what kind of state Shanda was in.

"We were trying to talk to her, to talk to Shanda, and she wouldn't talk or she couldn't," Laurie said. "I don't know if she couldn't or wouldn't, but I do know she was banging all in the trunk. I know she was able enough to bang the trunk and yell, but all of her words were slurred and I couldn't understand what she was saying when she yelled. And, except for when she said Mommy, that's all you could hear, that's all you could understand."

Laurie said that at the burn pile, Hope sprayed Windex on Shanda's leg and "it started sizzling." She stated that Melinda was the one who brought up the idea to burn Shanda, because her friend, Crystal Wathen, said that the best way to get rid of a body was to burn it.

"Melinda was the burner," Laurie told them, "and I think we were just scared."

When they went to the gas station, Laurie filled the two-liter Pepsi bottle with gas, and Hope gave her directions as she drove "out in the country somewhere." According to Laurie, all four girls lifted Shanda out of the trunk, she wasn't moving or making any noise, and they laid her on the ground.

"Melinda got the gas and poured it on Shanda, and Shanda

257

started crying and I was bending over her, you know, trying to see," Laurie said. "I was going to lift up the blanket, I guess I was going to try to talk to her again, and then the fire just went up to my face and it singed my bangs."

Laurie said she looked back and saw Melinda and Hope running to the car, and she followed them. They drove a little distance, then turned and drove back to the body, and Melinda got out and poured the rest of the gas, then they drove to McDonald's. Laurie claimed neither she, Hope, or Toni could eat, but Melinda "took our money" and ate well.

In the afternoon, once her dad fixed the muffler, they took off for New Albany. There, they were joined by Crystal and, later, Amanda. Laurie didn't remember everything about that day. She remembered going to Taco Bell to eat. She remembered going to the mall. She said that when she and Melinda tried to sleep that night, she couldn't, because she just kept hearing Shanda screaming.

Shippley asked Laurie who lit the match, but she didn't know for sure. She guessed that maybe Melinda did it.

Later in the interview, Laurie said that while at her house before her dog started barking, she got mad at Melinda for hurting Shanda, claiming she told her "it's not worth it."

"So why didn't it end there?" Shippley asked.

"I was scared."

"Scared of whom?"

"Nobody would understand unless they were in a situation like that. It could be, it didn't have to be us. It could have been the nicest people on Earth with one bad person. I went out under the impression that we were going to scare her and Melinda was going to beat her up. After Shanda went unconscious and all the blood and everything, they thought that she was dying. We were scared to take her anywhere. I was. I don't know about them. But I was scared because if I were to take her to the hospital, I mean, they would say to me, how did she get like this."

"How did she sustain these injuries?" Shippley asked.

"I don't know."

The sheriff reminded her of the statement she made about

Melinda striking Shanda with her knee. Laurie told him Shanda wasn't really hurt at the time. She had no idea how the lacerations occurred. Nothing like that happened, that she could remember.

"We sure didn't do anything," Laurie insisted. "We didn't molest her, we didn't do anything to her in any way, like molested her or anything. I mean, it wasn't like that."

"Now Laurie, what you're saying is that you don't know how she sustained the injury to her anus, right?" Henry interjected.

"Right."

"Did you see it?"

"What?"

"It was an obvious injury. Did you see it that night when she was on the ground?"

"No, she had underwear on the whole time."

Laurie surmised that Shanda might have had sex with somebody else that night. That was all she could think of that might explain it.

"At any point in time, did Shanda get on the road barefoot?" Henry asked.

"No."

"Okay, she's got stuff all over her feet, you know, that limestone from the road. Can you think of any time that she would have got on her feet? Did she ever try to run away?"

"No, she never did."

When Henry questioned her about how Shanda got the injuries to the back of her head, Laurie said she didn't know, but she speculated that it could have happened because "Shanda did a lot of banging around in the back of the trunk."

"It sounded like she was kicking the back of my car out," Laurie added. "I kept wondering myself how she had that much strength."

"So you're saying that neither you nor Melinda struck her in the head with a tire tool or anything?" Shippley asked.

Laurie shook her head yes.

Following a different line of questioning, Laurie denied having any conversations in the presence of Crystal and Amanda regarding her doing anything to harm Shanda.

259

"Melinda was not saying that I did it, she wasn't saying that at all. She was telling what happened. She told Amanda she killed her, she told Crystal she killed her, she told Leslie Jacobi she killed her. It was not until after we got arrested, she changed her story."

"What was Amanda's reaction when she found out that Shanda was, in fact, dead?" Henry asked.

"She just kind of looked into the car. And uh, I think the blood is what convinced her. She didn't say anything, she didn't smile, she was just quiet, and then she said, 'I can't look in there anymore,' and then shut the trunk."

"Did you open the trunk for her?"

"Yeah, I had the keys."

"When Shanda's on the ground, you're saying that Melinda poured the gas on her, okay. Was anybody smoking?"

Laurie shook her head yes.

"Who?"

"Me and Hope were."

"Somebody throw a cigarette on her?"

"I do not know how, I thought it caught on fire. I was bending over her, uh, if my cigarette fell, I wasn't aware of it. All I know is the flame just went up in my face. I mean, you know, the heat was right up in my face. I'm surprised I didn't get burned from it. It singed, it did singe my hair."

"Did she die right then?"

"I looked back and she was trying to get up. That's the last time I looked back."

"When you dropped off the two girls at your house, cruisin' or whatever you call it, did you have occasion to confront anyone? Run into anybody else? You did not see another soul?" Shippley interjected.

"Only seen like maybe three cars. One that we thought was following us."

Laurie said that during their "cruisin'" Melinda went back to the car by herself several times.

"How did she get in the trunk?"

"She took the trunk key off the ring."

"Is it safe to assume that if she had hit her, that you would have known it?"

"The muffler was louder than the screaming, and she was screaming pretty loud. I couldn't hear anything."

"If you couldn't hear, how did you know she was screaming?"

"Cause when you got into the car, you could hear it as plain as day. But when you were standing outside the car, you couldn't hear anything over the muffler."

"How did you get the blood on your coat?"

"Probably when I was looking in at her. 'Cause I leaned up against the back of my car and there was blood going all the way back down the back of my car, and the blood was kind of watery, I think from the dew."

"She was inside the trunk?"

"It was real cold outside and the trunk was heated and the blood on the outside of the car was real real watery. There was more water than there was blood. And me and Melinda washed all that off cause I couldn't stand it being on my trunk, washed all of that out, and I had my coat on the whole night, I mean, I wore the coat all of the time. I never took it off, only to sleep."

When Laurie was asked again about the drive to Cannan, she said all of it was blanked out.

"A lot of things could have occurred, you just don't remember?" Henry asked.

"Yeah, cause it was a long time from Cannan. I remember the time changing, it started getting light. When we left my house it was dark and when we came back it was light. That's how I know it was a long time. And it seems like an eternity when I try to remember it. It seems like we were out there forever."

"When you got back to the house, when Toni and Hope were in the bedroom, in some of the previous statements it indicated that you both had blood on you, and Melinda had some in her hair."

"I don't remember that."

"Other than spraying Windex on Shanda, what all was Hope's involvement?"

"Just threatening her, and going up to the door."

"Did she pour any gas on her?"

"No, she didn't."

"Did Melinda attempt to burn anything that you would consider to be evidence, like clothes or anything, there at the place where Shanda burnt?"

"I never saw her burn anything. I was wondering about that myself, cause in the statements, they said she was burning evidence. I'm not saying she didn't, but I really didn't pay much attention to Melinda."

The interview concluded with a few questions about the Leatherburys. Laurie said they were like brothers to her, and she talked a little about all of them going to The Witches' Castle, which, she said, was no big deal. When questioned about Larry Leatherbury's statement that claimed she had a fascination with burning people, Laurie said the only thing she had "a fascination with" was cutting herself.

Twenty-one

On November 30, at the Indiana Women's Prison, Melinda Loveless gave her statement to Henry and Shippley. Present in the room was Russell Johnson.

Initially, she talked about how it all got started, explaining all about how Shanda interfered in her relationship with Amanda. She talked about Amanda being at her house, having letters from Shanda in her pocket, some of which were perfumed, describing her anger at Amanda.

"I told Amanda to stay away from Shanda. I told her I just didn't think it was right, you know, just tell the little girl we're together, we've been together for two years, and just leave it at that. . . . And you know, I'm getting worried. I'd be at Amanda's house and she would call all the time, and she'd hang up when I'd answer. And just stuff like that started happening, so I was upset."

Melinda went through all the threats she made to Shanda, and the fights that went on, explaining that for a while, she and Amanda stopped seeing each other. She talked about the school dance when she slapped Shanda.

Later, when she finally got into the night of the murder, Melinda said she and Laurie planned to go to the slam dance, and Laurie suggested Melinda spend the weekend in Madison afterwards.

She told police that she just wanted to threaten Shanda, just beat her up. She said it was her idea to get this "old dull knife" out of the kitchen, that she stuck it in her purse, and then on the way to Louisville, they stopped at Shanda's house. She ran through Hope and Toni going to the door, then the events in Louisville, saying that Hope and Toni were having sex in the car with two boys, that they had even "switched partners."

After they got Shanda in the car, Melinda described putting the "dull side" of the knife to her throat.

"And I kept saying, 'I just want to talk to you. I'm not going to hurt you,' " Melinda told them. "And she was real upset, crying, choking, you know, sobs."

When they went to the castle, according to Melinda, Hope took the knife, and then started to threaten Shanda, taking her Mickey Mouse watch. By Melinda's account, Toni forced Shanda to turn over her sweatshirt, which she put on. There was nothing burned up at the castle, they all just went back to the car, because it was all "kind of silly," Melinda explained. "Nothing happened up there."

When the cars drove by the castle, Melinda claimed they all scattered and Shanda took off running by herself, getting into the car of her own accord. She said Shanda gave them directions to a gas station, telling them, "Oh, I'm going to get in trouble for being out so late," and "My brother's going to find out and be real mad at you all."

When they got to Madison, Melinda, Laurie, and Shanda got out of the car. Laurie told Melinda, "Do it now, um, hit her."

Melinda claimed that Laurie alone strangled Shanda, then asked her to get a rope from the car, which she did, thinking that Laurie was going to tie Shanda, "It wasn't really rope, it was like a shoe string almost.

"As soon as I handed it to her, she put it around her neck and started strangling her," Melinda told them. "That's when Shanda started choking for air, and just screaming, 'Melinda help me! Please don't let her do this!' She was yelling all kinds of stuff, and, um, I just started crying and I said, 'Shut the fuck up!' "

The next thing Melinda knew, Shanda was unconscious. She thought she was dead.

"That's when the knife showed up again," Melinda continued. "And, um, I hate talking about this. She just started cutting her. I think somewhere she told me to come help her. She said she just wanted to finish her for doing that to me, and she just kept saying, 'Let's finish her. Help me!'

"And she snatched my hand and put it on top of hers with the knife and just started stabbing. I was just, like, shocked. I'd never seen anything like that. I just freaked out. I couldn't move. I was actually, like, frozen."

Melinda told police that when Laurie asked her to help put Shanda in the trunk, she refused, so Laurie dragged Shanda's body by herself, placing her in the trunk on her own. They got back in the car, Hope and Toni never said a word, and they went to Laurie's house. Laurie was the only one who had blood on her hands, and she went to the bathroom to wash it off.

"I didn't have no blood on me at the time. None whatsoever, that I was aware of. Maybe from her mouth, could have gotten on my jacket or something, or on my pants from hitting her with my knee, but I wasn't aware of it."

Melinda went into the bedroom with Hope and Toni, and after a few minutes, off in the distance, she and the others heard a "low scream."

"Tackett must have heard it, because she said, 'I'll be right back. I'm going to go take care of this . . .' She didn't stay that long. And, um, the screaming and yelling stopped. Um, she came back and that's when she had blood on her."

Not long after, Laurie and Melinda went cruising in the country.

"So we're driving around and this is when, um, Shanda starts kicking again and yelling," Melinda recounted. "It's like, I know something was messed up with her throat. Something. Tackett had to do something, because it was like a gurgle. I mean, like, she couldn't really scream. I know at one time she was saying my name, and that's when Tackett told me, 'I want you to take over.' "

Melinda told police that the purpose of her driving was largely for her to keep her foot on the gas pedal to drown out Shanda's screams. At that point in the statement, she described a time when the two of them stopped the car and Laurie went

265

to the trunk.

"She said she'd be back. She's gonna do something. So I was aware that she opened the trunk, because you can see it, the little rearview mirror, the trunk opening. You can see, like, through the crack," Melinda told them. "And I was steady looking to see. I couldn't see much. I didn't hear nothing. There was a lot of silence at that time. I heard something thump. And it was real quiet. And there was like a weeping there. It was quiet. And then I heard something going on in the trunk. And then I hear this, it's like real loud, this big, like, just a hit. Like you would hear when someone hits you in your stomach."

Allegedly, Laurie got back in the car and showed her the tire tool, hitting it on the dashboard, asking her to smell it. Melinda took it from her and threw it down, telling her, "That's sick!" Then Laurie resumed the wheel.

"I asked her what she did, and she said, 'I went back there and hugged her,' and then she explained again about the hitting. She said, 'You got to see her, she's soaked with blood. She's red.' "

In Melinda's version of the crime, it was Laurie who had all the ideas about "what to do with her," saying Laurie suggested they put Shanda in a bag and throw her in a lake or maybe burn her.

According to Melinda, the four of them went to the gas station, Hope went and bought the soda, a two-liter bottle of Big Red, and Laurie filled it with gas. When Shanda started banging on the trunk, the four of them were present. Toni bit her hand when Laurie asked, "Where can we burn her?"

"That's when, out of the blue, Hope says, 'I know,' " Melinda reported.

At Lemon Road, Toni stayed in the car; the other three went to the trunk. Laurie wanted help getting Shanda out of the trunk, but Melinda refused, and Laurie talked Hope into it. Melinda said Shanda looked stiff as she watched them lay her onto the ground. She watched and "did nothing" as Hope poured the gas and Laurie struck the match.

When they got halfway up the road, Melinda said Laurie

266

stopped the car, turned back, and ordered her to go out and pour the rest of the gas. Hope reached over, screaming and crying, saying, "Just do it. Do what she says!"

"I threw the two liter of Big Red. I threw it and I know it went beside her and it hit the ground and it thumped. I guess it went in the fire. The flames were . . . then that's when they started going again. But when I looked at it, the flames had died down, and I seen her face. She was burnt to a crisp, you couldn't recognize her. Her tongue was sticking out of her mouth, you could see it."

From there, they went to McDonald's. Melinda ordered orange juice, and, allegedly, Laurie had some sausages which Laurie was making jokes about, saying, "Shanda looks like this."

Back at the Tacketts, after the other two were dropped off, her dad fixed the muffler, while Laurie and Melinda cleaned out the car. Melinda said she threw a lot of things onto the burn pile: clothes, paper bags, and whatnot. After Laurie's parents were out of sight, Laurie took a hose and sprayed out the trunk.

"I remember seeing two pair of white socks in there that had blood on them. They were Shanda's socks, I'm sure. Socks she had on. I remember a lot of handprints. Her hands, like, hitting the trunk. A lot of blood handprints all over the top of the trunk," Melinda told them, alleging, "And that's when Tackett was picking at something on the trunk she said, 'Look,' it was a hunk of, it was, like, blood, but it was, like, hard. By the way, she was touching it, and she said, 'Look, a piece of her skull,' and she was laughing. She said 'Smell it,' and I hit her hand, and it fell on the ground at her house. It fell on the grass."

Once they got down to New Albany, Melinda called Crystal, then Amanda, and Laurie showed both of them the trunk. After they dropped Amanda at home, Melinda said she begged Crystal not to leave her alone with Laurie.

"A few questions. What happened to Shanda's clothes?" Henry asked.

"I don't remember. I really don't know. I could have put them on that pile when I was cleaning the car out."

"How did Shanda get the injuries to the back of her head?"

"With a tire tool."

"On the back of her skull?"

"The tire tool."

"You're saying that you never saw Laurie Tackett hit her though. Did you?"

"Not with the tire tool."

"I mean, you're just basing that on . . ."

"With the knife, she hit her, yeah."

"I understand that. But you're basing what you're saying to me on what she told you when she came back in the car, not that you ever saw her."

"I never seen her. I couldn't."

"Okay, do you know how she got the injury to her anus?"

"No. I wasn't even aware until, you know, they said there was molestation."

Melinda believed that Laurie had the opportunity to inflict that injury on two separate occasions, when Laurie went back to the trunk by herself at her house, when the dog was barking, and also during their drive to Cannan.

Shippley asked how Laurie was able to get into the trunk if Melinda was in the car revving the engine to drown out the screams. Melinda said Laurie took the trunk key off the key ring.

Henry asked if Melinda had ever met Hope or Toni before. Melinda told him January 10 was the first time they met. When questioned about having a conversation with Jeffrey Stettenbenz, Melinda admitted to talking to him on numerous occasions, telling him she "could just kill" Shanda. Later in the interview, she was questioned about formulating a plan to kill Amanda, but said that was just "playing around." She did admit that she and Kristie Brodfuehrer went to Amanda's during Harvest Homecoming in 1991, that Kristie knocked on the door, but Amanda never came out.

Henry asked if she knew anything about Laurie's involvement with witchcraft, and she described a night when they were at some guy's apartment in Louisville, a guy, Steve, who had a pet pig, she remembered. Laurie and the Leatherburys were there.

"She would ask someone, 'Let me cut you,' or, she'd just want to see the blood. And they all used to say she would kill cats. I never witnessed this, so I can't say it's true. I know they would talk about the devil, and they had, like, books. I know Tackett had some books, too, on witchcraft," Melinda told them.

Apparently, Laurie had some kind of an "altar" in her room, where she would hold seances. At one point, after Shanda was burned, Laurie allegedly talked about having a seance to bring Shanda back.

"Okay, at any time during the night, did Hope Rippey do anything to hurt Shanda Sharer?" Henry asked.

"I seen her spray Windex."

"Okay, when did that occur?"

"It was in the trunk, and that's when they both laid her on the ground, and she sprayed Windex. That's when the steam was coming off her. She sprayed this Windex all over her legs. She said she wanted to see what it would do. It was like acid steaming off."

"What was Hope's attitude while she was spraying the Windex?" Shippley asked.

"You know how if you're very interested in something, or you're dissecting an animal, and you're like. . . . She's like that."

One of the questions Henry and Shippley were unable to answer throughout the course of the entire investigation was the limestone issue. The postmortem indicated that limestone powder was discovered on Shanda's feet, a component on the road next to the field where she was burned. At no point in any of the conducted interviews did anyone say that Shanda was out of the car barefoot, except at the "woods" scene when she was initially beaten up, but police found no limestone on that property.

On December 2, a progress report on the psychiatric evaluation of Laurie Tackett was submitted to the Jefferson Circuit Court by Dr. Edward Shippley, psychiatrist, and Dr. Paul Shriver, staff psychologist at IWP. It focused on Laurie's disorderly conduct and her possession of a deadly weapon, a razor blade, while in prison.

The report indicated that since she had been at the Indiana Women's Prison, Laurie had been placed on suicide watch on three occasions. The first was in January, after she made an overt suicide threat. The second was in March, when she was found to be in possession of a razor, which she used to mutilate herself by slicing her arm. The third time was in May, when she was accused of damaging state property and was also found to be in possession of a "suicidal item." Dr. Shippley saw her a few days after she was placed on suicide status and determined that she was not overtly suicidal, nor did she seriously mutilate herself. Laurie also received a disciplinary write-up in July, for disorderly conduct, having been rebellious against jailers and having yelled at the supervisor.

At the time the report was written, November 25, 1992, Laurie was optimistic about receiving a release from prison earlier than whatever time she would be sentenced to, hopeful that regardless of the sentence, further appeals would be made.

She spoke positively about herself, even in the wake of having broken up with her girlfriend, April, saying that the loss of love was not a good reason to kill herself. A discussion with April later revealed that she felt it was possible that Laurie would do something to retaliate, describing Laurie as extremely dominating, jealous, possessive, and a controlling person.

April stated that Laurie had made overt and implied threats against her, telling her that she was going to use the razor blade on her. Laurie also told April that they could be together spiritually if both of them were to die, saying that rather than let her go into a relationship with anyone else, she would continue to possess her, one way or another, even if she had to do that by sending them both to the afterlife. In discussing this problem with the IWP psychologist, April seemed "genuinely frightened." The report stated that the inmate seemed to "believe that Laurie was capable of such an act." April also stated that Laurie was practicing forms of "witchcraft and voodoo," and she was afraid that Laurie could possibly use mystical means to retaliate. (Officers of IWP would later report seeing Laurie engage in some kind of occult practice with other inmates, but had no "hard proof" of this.)

In an interview with Dr. Shriver, when questioned about threatening her former girlfriend, Laurie denied it. However, his report noted that she seemed "somewhat evasive" about it. She later said that in the past, when a relationship was over, she took some kind of overt retaliation against the person, including "verbal harassment and vandalism."

The report indicated that Laurie had recently been tested by the Beck Suicidal Inventory, which determined that she was no more of a threat to herself or others than anyone in the general population. "Mary has always been basically rather evasive and deceptive and is intelligent enough to be able to fake her answers, to some degree, if she chooses to do so," Dr. Shriver wrote. "She is a very secretive type person who has been known to lie overtly and who has also been very inconsistent at times in her self reports and very self contradictory. She appears to be somewhat indecisive and to not know her own mind and to often act on impulse."

She had been described as emotionally unstable, having identity problems, being insecure, irresponsible, depressed, introversive, and as having some neurotic features and features of mild character disorder. She was not found to be psychotic, nor was she found to suffer from a multiple personality disorder.

Also noted was the fact that Laurie maintained that she did not consciously take part in the offense against Shanda Sharer. She overtly professed her innocence with respect to the crime, denied having a fascination with blood or fire, and said she felt "nervous" while in the presence of knives or sharp objects. She admitted that she was uncertain whether she could control herself around such objects when they were available to her.

Tackett's defense attorney, Ellen O'Connor, would later see this self-mutilating behavior as part of Laurie's coping mecha-

271

nism, explaining that Laurie engaged in that kind of thing as a way to prevent being made fun of by other kids.

"When she was just a regular Pentecostal, people made fun of her, thought she was weird, and they stayed away, and that made her feel bad," O'Connor said. "But when she started talking about all these weird things, and wearing black, and dying her hair, people were in awe of her. They were a little bit scared of her. She was still the outsider but she felt like she had a little bit more control. She kind of liked that, making people scared of her."

The first week in December, Laurie Tackett did an exclusive interview with WKRC-TV in Cincinnati. A news reporter, Chris Yaw, was permitted to tape the interview at the Indiana Women's Prison; it was the only interview any of the four girls would ever give.

Throughout the five-minute segment, Laurie, who wore heavy eye makeup and whose blond hair had grown out a bit, kept insisting that Melinda was to blame for the murder.

"I didn't think she was gonna go that far," Laurie said in an innocent voice. "It wasn't really the fact that I can't believe I'm doing this. It was the fact that I can't believe this is happening. I told her it was stupid."

Laurie acted baffled, telling the reporter that she couldn't understand why Shanda was put through such an ordeal.

"Shanda hugged me. She asked me not to let Melinda do it. She was crying," Laurie said. "There wasn't anything I could do."

At the end of the interview, the WKRC broadcast reported that Tackett expected to beat the charges, that she had already enrolled in high school and was earning her GED, that she had plans to go on and pursue her college degree in child psychology.

That same week, on December 6, the front page story of *The Courier Journal* showed a color photograph of Jackie Vaught, posing with glass-encased mementos of Shanda. There were Shanda's red-and-white St. Paul jacket, her many "prize" ribbons, and a large photo-portrait of her beautiful smile.

"Parents blind themselves," Vaught told the newspaper. "They don't want to believe that this could happen to their child, or that their child could ever be subjected to this. Well, I'm here to tell you, as a mother who has had her child murdered, brutally murdered by girls, it did happen, and it could happen again to your child."

The article detailed the crime, the circumstances leading up to it, and the letters that Jackie found in her daughter's closet. It quoted Jackie describing her "scene" with Shanda regarding the letter she found in which Amanda told Shanda to forge a detention slip. She confronted her daughter about Amanda Heavrin, asking if Amanda "ever touched her in a way that she should not," but Shanda denied it.

"I said 'Shanda, we will always love you. Whatever you have done, it is not unforgivable,'" Vaught told the press. "I asked her if she wanted to talk to a counselor, but she insisted she was OK."

Vaught asserted that there was "no way" that Shanda intended to leave in the car with the girls that night. She was certain that the girls forced Shanda into the car.

"She'd left her purse and coat in the house," Vaught said. "It was cold that night, and Shanda never went anywhere without her purse."

On December 8, Amanda Heavrin received a subpoena ordering her to testify in the upcoming sentencing hearing for Melinda Loveless. Her attorney, Steve Lomeyer, motioned to quash the subpoena and notified the Jefferson Circuit Court that Amanda Heavrin intended to exercise her Fifth Amendment right against self-incrimination. A hearing was held on the matter that same week at which time it was ordered that the state of Indiana would grant Use Immunity to Heavrin. In other words, none of her testimony regarding the case would be held against her. Given that circumstance, Heavrin could not refuse to testify.

On December 10, Toni Lawrence appeared before Judge Todd, who accepted her plea of guilty to one count of criminal confinement in exchange for her testimony at the upcoming hearings of Loveless and Tackett. Lawrence also agreed to testify against Hope Rippey, who was maintaining a plea of not guilty and was scheduled to face trial on March 1.

Just before Melinda Loveless's sentencing hearing would begin, a motion was filed to quash a subpoena ordering Peggy Tackett to testify. The motion, including a statement by her physician, Dr. Robert Ellis, contended that the appearance and testimony of Mrs. Tackett would endanger her mental, emotional, and physical well-being.

Twenty-two

The morning of December 14, when Guy Townsend made his opening statement at the sentencing hearing for Melinda Loveless, the courtroom was jam-packed. For Loveless, who would be sentenced for the murder charge alone, the sentence could range anywhere from thirty to sixty years. First, she would be sentenced to the presumptive sentence for murder, which is forty years in the state of Indiana; then, based on information provided in her hearing, the judge could either subtract ten years for mitigating circumstances or add twenty years for aggravating circumstances.

Townsend gave the history of twelve-year-old Shanda Sharer, from Shanda's move to New Albany, her transfer to Hazelwood Junior High, through her fist fight with Amanda Heavrin. He talked about their subsequent friendship and referred to the letters written by Melinda expressing her jealousy.

The prosecutor described the concern of Shanda's parents, explaining how they moved her to a parochial school, Our Lady of Perpetual Help, in an effort to protect their daughter. He detailed the threatening letters written by Melinda Loveless, one of which stated, "I want Shanda dead." Townsend referred to the "Amanda plan," which he described in his effort to prove premeditation.

"Kids talk, kids make pompous announcements," Townsend told the court. "Kids say I'm going to kill you. In this case, a plan was made to kill Amanda Heavrin, and the plan was put into operation."

He described the meeting of Loveless and Tackett, their initial contact, and their eventual plan to go to a concert in Louisville on January 10, 1992. He explained that Hope and Toni went, by way of lying to their parents, and also gave the particulars involved in their initial departure: their trip to Wal-Mart where batteries were shoplifted, their stop at the car wash and Burger King; later, their long ride down highway 62 toward Melinda's house. He talked about their conversation on the way to New Albany, including their stop off at The Witches' Castle, and defined their initial contact with Melinda Loveless that night. Melinda directed them to Jeffersonville, Townsend said, and after getting directions at a McDonald's, they made their way over to Steve Sharer's address.

The whole offense was recreated, everything that transpired in Madison, from the "woods" scene by Tackett's house, through the drive to Cannan, to the decision to burn the body. He depicted the scene at the burn pile, when one of the girls revved the engine to drown out Shanda's screams. He recited the events which led to the Clark Station, where a two-liter bottle of gasoline was purchased.

The prosecutor told the court that at Lemon Road, the girls opened the trunk, took Shanda, who was clutching the blanket in her hand, and prepared to dispose of her. They doused the body with gas, and Tackett produced a match, allegedly throwing it on the body. But "the body is not burned enough to Melinda's satisfaction," Townsend said. "Melinda gets out of the car with the remaining gasoline in the bottle, walks over toward the body, which is still smoldering, and throws the gas bottle on Shanda."

Townsend described the crime scene and talked about the painstaking police operation of gathering the remains of the bottle that held the gasoline, of obtaining the tire tracks and footprints. He also recounted the early evening of January 11, 1992, when Toni Lawrence came in to report what happened. He described the arrest of Melinda Loveless and Laurie Tackett at the Loveless residence on January 12, and alluded to the autopsy report, which revealed that Shanda had died from smoke inhalation.

"People were talked to," Townsend summed up, "people that knew Melinda and Shanda and all the other individuals. Those people contributed to the picture that I tried to describe here, and those people will be called and asked to personally tell the court what they know about what happened."

The defense made a motion for the separation of witnesses, which was granted with the exception of Steve Henry and Shanda's family, Jackie Vaught, Steve Sharer, and Paige Boardman, who were all permitted to remain in the courtroom. For the defendants, Marjorie (Loveless) Donahue, Michael Donahue, and Michelle Loveless were permitted to remain. All other persons who knew themselves to be witnesses to the case were asked to leave the courtroom until after they had testified.

Townsend proceeded to bring forth the first witness, hunter Donn Foley, and Johnson raised an objection, reminding the court that there was already a guilty plea, that there was no question that the body was discovered, and that only aggravating and mitigating circumstances should be presented at the sentencing. Townsend argued that the testimony of every person who was a party to the scene was a part of the "circumstances," and Judge Todd allowed the testimony. The courthouse audience was able to hear every captivating detail, first from the hunter, then from the deputy, and again from the sheriff.

As Shippley described the initial arrest of Loveless and Tackett, the defense counsel objected, again reminding the judge that the court was hearing something that was not in question. After Shippley, Curtis Wells detailed the Saturday morning when he arrived at the crime scene. Wells handed over the photographs of the scene, which defense attorneys also objected to.

However the photos were admitted, but they were not publicly shown. Wells related the contents of each one in detail, stunning the courthouse audience with gruesome images. The photos not only showed Shanda's burnt and injured body, they also showed the blood in the trunk, the tire in the trunk, and the entire crime scene. At Townsend's prompting, Wells described it all.

Townsend then questioned him concerning the letters written and received by Melinda, Amanda and Shanda. The letters between Amanda and Shanda found in Jackie Vaught's home were admitted into evidence. Next, Wells testified about the letters between Melinda and Amanda which he received from chief probation officer Virgil Seay. However, when the prosecution questioned him about how Seay came into possession of these letters, Johnson objected on the grounds that Seay was not listed as an official witness and that the state was attempting to turn the sentencing into a trial.

"This is not a trial," Johnson told the court. "The state of Indiana wants to make this a trial, apparently. They want to go through every witness one by one, but they offered the plea agreement. This plea agreement was accepted. This is a sentencing hearing and we've got criteria to go by, which they want to ignore."

Townsend argued, "The statutes of the state of Indiana state that the trial court, the sentencing body, must consider the facts and circumstances of the crime and that is what we're trying to put before the court."

Judge Todd ruled that while Johnson's objection to the introduction of Seay as a witness would be sustained, he agreed with Townsend that all facts and circumstances of the crime must be considered by the court in order to impose sentence.

The state then offered the letters between Amanda and Melinda into evidence, at which point both Johnson and Bob Hammerle objected as to their relevancy and sensational content. Hammerle was concerned that the letters had been selected to "inject an element of homophobia" into the hearing which he considered an attempt to prejudice the court.

After a further response from the prosecution, Todd asked to read the letters and subsequently allowed them to be admitted into evidence.

Toward the close of the first day, Steve Henry was called to take the stand. Responding to Townsend's questions, he delineated all the specifics of the initial investigatory process, from the moment that Pyles walked into the jail with information he received at the bowling alley, through the arrest of Loveless and Tackett and the girls being taken into custody. He described the first night that Melinda was in jail, when he overheard Melinda say "It was Shanda" during a phone call.

Throughout Henry's testimony, the defense logged a continuing objection.

Henry gave details about the evidence collected, all of which was admitted into the record, along with the taped statement he had taken from Melinda Loveless two weeks earlier.

That night, the local airwaves buzzed with news that teen murderers, Loveless and Tackett, might have been dabbling in the occult, highlighting the "circle of stones" at The Witches' Castle which Detective Henry had discovered. The local media had a field day with the story, revealing all the grisly events of the night of the torture-slaying, informing the public that Shanda Sharer's murder may have been a "sacrifice."

Moments before the hearing resumed the next morning, Melinda broke down in gut-wrenching sobs. "I can't stand it," she wailed, grabbing Marjorie's arm for support.

The crowd was unmoved by her effort to gain sympathy.

It was Tuesday morning, December 15, and Toni Lawrence was called to the stand.

As the fifteen-year-old timidly sat down in the witness chair and began to speak, no one who was seated beyond the first few rows in the courtroom could hear her wispy voice. In a fatherly manner, Judge Todd asked her to speak up.

In her testimony, Lawrence went over being at Melinda's house and being shown the knife, she covered all of the same information that she had given in her three statements to police, sticking closely to her fourth and final handwritten statement. As her story reached its tragic end, a hush fell over the courtroom. Toni said she was in the car, watching, as the three other girls burned Shanda alive.

Under cross-examination, Lawrence testified that she never heard Loveless say anything about killing Shanda. She told the court that Melinda said, "I'm not going to cut her, I'm just go-

279

ing to run the knife down her body to tease her. I'm going to act like I'm going to hurt her, but I'm not going to kill her." This was something which had been corroborated in Toni Lawrence's polygraph.

The defense team asked Lawrence questions which tried to establish that Tackett was the person in control that night; their strategy was to show that Laurie was the aggressor, that Melinda and the other girls were Laurie's pawns. Their theory of defense entailed proving that Tackett was a dominant personality, that she was the dominator in the events of January 10 and 11, 1992.

Toni Lawrence provided them with a basis for that argument, consistently testifying that Tackett had most of the ideas on the night of the offense.

After a short recess, Laurie Tackett strutted into the courtroom with a defiant air. As she sat down in the witness chair, she made no eye contact with Melinda whatsoever. Tackett told essentially the same story that Lawrence did, differing only on some of the fine details. She gave the history of meeting Loveless for the first time, their plans to go to the concert in Louisville, and then detailed the events which led to Shanda's death.

At one point, when Tackett described seeing Shanda in the trunk out by her house when her dog was barking, she broke down into loud sobs and a five-minute recess was called. After her testimony resumed, the audience was so disgruntled that Judge Todd had to ask for silence in the courtroom.

Tackett testified that Shanda was shivering, that she got a blanket to cover her, and then she closed the trunk, "not all the way, but half enough to where it would stay." She also alleged that when she and Melinda went "cruisin'," Melinda wanted to run Shanda over with the car.

She told the court that she knew nothing about Shanda's injuries, saying that she didn't threaten Shanda, that she didn't burn anything at The Witches' Castle, that she didn't get any matches from her house that evening. She contended that it was Melinda's idea to burn her, that Melinda brought it up when they were "cruisin' " and later again at the burn pile, that

Melinda poured the gasoline on Shanda.

"Who set her on fire?" Townsend asked.

"I have no idea. I was bent over her. I was going to take the blanket away from her face because she was crying. I was bent over her and the fire went up to my face and singed my hair."

"Miss Tackett, when Shanda was lying on the ground with the blanket on her and the gasoline poured on her body, did you or anyone say anything to her?"

"No."

Townsend had no further questions and the court recessed for the day.

Local press continued to inform the public about the troubled teens, especially Laurie Tackett, who allegedly "masterminded" the slaying of Shanda Sharer. At the same time, the reactions of Shanda's parents were made public. For months, Jackie Vaught and Steve Sharer had been leery about talking to the press, but little by little, as the sentencing hearing progressed, both of them opened up. Jackie was particularly vocal, describing her pain and horror to throngs of local reporters out on the courthouse steps.

The next morning, day three of the hearing, the real sensationalism began when Laurie Tackett took the stand for cross-examination. Among other things, the seventeen-year-old was questioned about her problems at Indiana Women's Prison, her occult practices, and her fascination with killing and fire.

"Have you ever told Kary Pope you would kill her grandmother for her?" Johnson asked.

"Jokingly, yes."

"Have you ever told Kary Pope that you would like to take a knife and run it through somebody's heart, just to see what it feels like?"

"No."

"Isn't it a fact that you told Mr. Leatherbury ten or twenty different times that you would like to kill someone?"

"No, it isn't."

"Isn't it a fact that you have told Mr. Leatherbury that one of your biggest fascinations that you have, is to know what it feels like to see someone burn?"

"No, it isn't."

"Did you ever talk to Mr. Leatherbury about a consistent dream that you two have kind of shared about mutilated bodies of babies hanging in trees?"

"No. My dream never had babies hanging in trees."

"But mutilated bodies?"

"No."

"So that fact is incorrect?"

"The dream was of a forest burning, and that's all I could see, but there were people, there were little kids, it sounded like these little kids crying. And in the dream I got the impression that the parents couldn't help them and I woke up. It was one of the worst dreams I ever had."

Tackett was immediately followed by pathologist George Nichols, who took the stand to report the autopsy findings. Dr. Nichols, the chief medical examiner for the Commonwealth of Kentucky, testified that the postmortem examination of Shanda Sharer showed that fifty percent of Sharer's skin surface suffered third- and fourth-degree burns. He detailed the injuries to Sharer's head and legs, describing a three-inch scalp hematoma and lacerations and abrasions discovered in the legs and feet. Nichols surmised that the injuries to the head were the result of a blunt object.

He found no evidence of strangulation and no injury to account for unconsciousness. He testified that the injuries to the legs and feet were a result of incisional wounds, but said that there were no injuries to the legs, feet, or ankles which would have prevented the victim from walking or running. His testimony corroborated the theory that the body had been "dragged over a space." He stated that some of the contusions were consistent with "drag marks."

On direct examination by deputy prosecutor Donn Currie, Nichols discussed the injuries to the anus of the victim. The pathologist said that he initially observed what appeared to be a "superficial puncture wound" of the anal verge, explaining that further examination of these tissues showed a deeper injury to the anus.

"What, specifically, did you notice?" Currie asked.

"Examination of the tissue demonstrated it to be a deeper injury with a larger diameter."

"Could you determine, what, if anything, caused the injury?"

"A cylindrical firm object with some type of edge capable of passing through human skin. At least a somewhat sharp pointed cylindrical structure."

"Could it be consistent with a tire tool?"

"Yes."

The pathologist's findings concluded that there were "multiple insertions" made into the victim's anus, that an object had been inserted approximately 3.5 inches.

"In your opinion, Doctor, was the object inserted during life or after death?" Currie asked.

"During life."

"How can you tell that?"

"There is clear vital reaction, with bleeding into the injured tissues."

"So there was evidence, Doctor, of hemorrhaging in and around the anus, is that correct?"

"That is correct."

"What was the cause of death?"

"Smoke inhalation and burn."

At that time, the state asked to present the slides of Shanda Sharer's body. The judge allowed it, but refused the state's request to allow the public to view them. The deputy prosecutor approached the bench, requesting for the second time that the public be allowed to view the evidence, but Judge Todd again refused, ruling that only he and the pathologist view the actual photos.

The lights in the courthouse were turned down, the judge asked the audience to be quiet, and Nichols proceeded to describe the photographs of the injuries to Shanda Sharer.

"Can you tell us what this shows, please," Currie asked.

"It's a photograph of the right side of the body of Shanda Sharer."

The deputy prosecutor proceeded to question Nichols as to the content of each of the thirty-two photo exhibits, exacting specific details about Shanda's burned and bloodied corpse.

A photograph of the wrist injury was shown, showing what Nichols called "a contusion associated with binding or some other form of manacle."

A photograph of the urogenital tissues of the victim was shown, depicting the injury to the anus, and Nichols pointed out a tear into the soft tissues with "associated hemorrhaging."

Once the photographs were presented, the state had no further questions.

Upon cross-examination, Johnson asked Nichols questions which attempted to show that the injuries to Shanda were not as severe as the photo descriptions made them sound.

"Doctor, the anal laceration injuries that you observed did not pose risk of death, did it?" Johnson asked.

"No."

"Did it pose risk of serious permanent disfigurement?"

"No."

"It was your opinion in your deposition that the person was alive for just a very short time after the fire, but you can't tell how long?"

"It's my opinion that the interval of survival was short."

Upon redirect examination, Nichols was questioned about the anal lacerations a third time. Currie wanted the record to show that the anal wounds were not associated with the death of the victim. Dr. Nichols testified that the injuries Sharer received would have necessitated a colostomy, which would have meant a temporary disfigurement, however, Sharer would have survived.

Wearing baggy jeans under an oversized flannel shirt, Amanda Heavrin then took the stand. In a soft voice, the fifteen-year-old girl spoke about her friends Melinda Loveless and Shanda Sharer. "Amanda, how would you characterize your relationship with Melinda Loveless?" Townsend asked.

"Girlfriend relationship."

"I don't want to embarrass you, but would you be more explicit? Is it a physical relationship?"

"Yes, sir."

Amanda gave details about her romance with Melinda, her fight with Shanda, and the evolution of that friendship, which resulted in a love triangle. The love letters between Amanda and Melinda, and between Amanda and Shanda, were admitted into evidence.

Heavrin told the court that she received a phone call from Loveless the night of January 10, but said that nothing unusual was discussed. She described her day on January 11, when she was picked up at the River Falls Mall, taken to the Loveless residence in Tackett's car, and shown the blood in the trunk. In her testimony, she said nothing new. She merely reiterated her statement to police.

The next person to testify was fifteen-year-old Crystal Wathen. An extremely attractive blond-haired young lady, Wathen had arrived by police escort, claiming to authorities that she had no way of getting to the courthouse.

Crystal said she did not know Shanda Sharer. She testified only about the events on Saturday, January 11, after receiving a phone call from Melinda, telling the court that Laurie Tackett showed her the knife she had taken from her home in Madison, that Laurie took a tire tool out of the side pocket of her car door, tapping it against the dashboard in an attempt to brag about the crime.

"I looked over at Laurie and asked her what she was doing, and she was feeling on it," Crystal testified. "Laurie said she could remember what it felt like when she was hitting Shanda in her head. She said it was like taking hunks out of her head."

"And Laurie Tackett did something with that tire tool, didn't she?" Hammerle asked.

"Yes, she did."

"What did she do?"

"She stuck it in my face and told me to smell it."

"Isn't it a fact that at that time, Laurie Tackett started laughing and said that she did not feel bad anymore about killing Shanda?"

"Yes, she did."

"Isn't it a fact that on that evening, Laurie Tackett told you that she found a piece of Shanda's head in the trunk and threw it out in the yard for her dog to eat?"

"Yes, she did."

"Nothing further."

As Crystal stepped down from the stand, Leslie Jacobi was called forward. Jacobi testified that she and others heard Melinda say that she wanted to kill Shanda, but none of them ever took her seriously. She said they thought Melinda was joking around.

"How would you be inclined to take a statement from any of your friends who said I'm going to kill someone?" Townsend asked on redirect.

"Melinda never, she's not the type of person to kill somebody," Jacobi told him.

Kary Pope came next, her testimony being the most sensational when during cross-examination, she described Tackett's channeling phases, making reference to "Deanna the vampire" and detailing Tackett's enchantment with sucking blood. Telling the court about Tackett's desire to kill, Pope alleged that Tackett told her she'd like to go on a trip of acid, kill somebody, and then not remember it. She also asserted Tackett made the statement that it would be fun to kill somebody and get all the publicity.

At one point, when Kary described Laurie Tackett's power over other people, Kary broke down in tears, telling the court that she believed Tackett had managed to gain control over her mind.

Pope's appearance was followed by the testimony of petite, fifteen-year-old Kristie Brodfuehrer. Under oath, she admitted that the handwriting on an unsigned letter was hers, and the letter describing the "Amanda plan" was offered into evidence:

1-14-92

Kelley,
The thing about Melinda and Amanda is true in a way. See, Melinda and Amanda broke-up over Shanda a while back. When Amanda was fine w/out Melinda. She got jealous that Amanda was w/Shanda. See Shanda liked Amanda & I know it for a fact! Back during Har-

vest Homecoming Amanda & Shanda went up to one of the haunted houses & Melinda stay t. night w/me. When Amanda got home we asked where she went she said she just went "out." So we called Shanda and asked her if she went out w/Amanda and she said yes. So, we scared her half to death. Please don't tell anyone but Melinda and I were going to do just about the same stuff only to Amanda, way back in October. We didn't because Amanda had fallen asleep and when I went up to her house (some big, burly guy (not her dad)) came around the corner and chased me down the street, I hopped in the car & we got out fast!

W/B

"When did you formulate this plan involving taking Amanda in the car?" Townsend asked her.

"That same night," Brodfuehrer said.

"Did you talk to Melinda the next day or some subsequent time about the plan not going through?"

"Yes."

"And what did Melinda say?"

"She said she was glad she was asleep because she could never do anything to hurt Amanda and she was afraid that she might have."

Under cross-examination, Brodfuehrer told the court that she and her friends had watched accounts of the murder on television, acknowledging that she wrote the letter months after the fact. Brodfuehrer admitted that a few days after the "Amanda plan" failed, she had been admitted into a drug and alcohol rehabilitation center for cocaine abuse. Brodfuehrer also told the court that on the night of the "Amanda plan" she had done something that "posed as" cocaine, paying for it by having sex with one of the boys she was with.

"Melinda never said that she wanted to kill Amanda, did she?" Hammerle asked.

"No."

"Now, when you drove over to the house, the two boys that were in the car, was that Eric and T?"

"Yes."

"Okay, neither one of the two boys had ever been told about beating up Amanda, were they?"

"No."

On Thursday, December 17, after sitting quietly for three days, Steve Sharer took the stand to give the details about the two girls who called on Shanda the night of January 10, followed by his account of the attempt to locate Shanda the next day. After his testimony regarding those facts, Steve Sharer was asked to make a statement about how Shanda's death had affected him. The defense objected, reminding the court that Shanda's mother had been designated as the official victim's representative, arguing that in accordance with Indiana legislature, she was to be the only person to speak about family grief. Overruling the objection, Judge Todd allowed Steve Sharer to speak.

"As far as myself is concerned, I feel a great deep hole in my chest. My heart sags very sorrowfully," Sharer told the court. "This is my only child."

He searched for words as he went on to describe the simple pleasures he would miss, like watching his daughter graduate, go to college, and maybe have kids of her own one day.

Steve recalled Shanda's last day with him, when she helped him get some tools and supplies ready for the home improvement job he had planned. He called her "daddy's little girl" and said he "loved her to death."

Shanda's stepmother, Sharon, whose class ring Shanda had on when she was murdered, also made a statement about the heartache the family had suffered. She described Shanda as a loving girl who she felt was like a daughter of her own. "Shanda loved all of us," Sharon told the court in a choked-up voice.

Shanda's half sister, Paige Boardman, testified that her sister's death had ruined her life. She condemned Shanda's murderers, telling the court, "I don't see how they could live with theirself.

"They didn't cry when they were doing it to her. Why should

288

they cry now?" Paige said. "Because they're in trouble? My sister doesn't have a chance to cry. She didn't have a chance at anything. She didn't have a choice but to die."

Paige talked about the times when Shanda used to cry when she got into trouble. Now, each night when she went to bed, Paige could only hear her sister crying for help.

"My sister wasn't a mean person. She loved everybody. She wanted to be friends with everybody," Paige Boardman told the court. "She would have never hurt anybody. She didn't deserve to die."

Before the state rested its case, Tracy Lynn Plaskett, an inmate who shared a cell with Melinda at the Clark County Jail, was called to testify about Melinda's lack of remorse. Plaskett told the court that one week after Valentine's Day, Loveless discussed the murder and she literally "burst out laughing" over it.

Twenty-three

Throughout the week of testimony, the courtroom audience had been stunned by the manner and appearance of Melinda Loveless's friends who came to testify and observe. The teenagers acted in a way that many people thought inappropriate, hanging on each other in the courtroom, kissing each other openly in the halls. They seemed to revel in their notoriety as witnesses in a sensational murder trial, doing anything for attention, talking to as many reporters as possible.

However, when the defense began presenting evidence on Thursday afternoon, it was Larry Leatherbury who managed to shock and appall the onlookers more than any of his peers. Leatherbury came to court wearing all black, he had on a torn T-shirt with hundreds of safety pins fastened to it, a glove with the fingers torn out, and spiked jewelry around his neck and wrists. In his testimony, the eighteen-year-old confirmed Tackett's fascination with death and blood, admitting that he himself had drawn blood from his arm with a razor "for release of stress."

Under cross-examination, it was revealed that Larry Leatherbury had been in the Jefferson Circuit Court before, in January 1990, because of an altercation he had at school with another student.

"Would you tell the court what happened with that boy at school?" Townsend asked.

"Well, being that I wasn't really in the norm at school . . ."

"Let me interrupt your answer here to ask you what you mean by that?"

"Well, I had been ridiculed for many years for being so different. So, I went to school and I intended to intimidate someone."

"How did you intend to intimidate someone?"

"With a knife."

"And what did you do with that blade, Mr. Leatherbury?"

"It's not what I had done with the blade. I must stress that it was an accidental injury to that person."

"Where was the blade when the injury occurred?"

"It was to the person's neck."

"Okay, and did it cause some bleeding?"

"Yes."

Just when the courtroom audience thought they had heard it all, defense attorneys presented evidence of the violent sexually abusive atmosphere that Melinda had grown up in, further shocking and horrifying most of the onlookers and interested parties.

Teddy Barber, Melinda's twenty-eight-year-old cousin, was the first witness called to the stand.

Teddy told the court that she had become a part of the Loveless household when she was age ten, baby-sitting for Melinda who was a newborn at the time. She gave some details about her role in the house, about Margie's long work hours, saying that she spent nights and weekends at the Loveless house for a period of six years.

"Did there come a time when there occurred an incident in that home that Larry Loveless did something to you?" Hammerle asked.

"Yes."

"When did that happen?"

"It started right off, about when I was ten."

"Can you describe that?"

"It started where he would play with my feet and over time he worked his way up to the vaginal area, breast area."

"Besides Melinda being an infant at that time, where would the other Loveless girls be when Larry Loveless was doing this to you?"

"Sometimes they would be in bed or sometimes they would be right there in the living room."

"Was there a time where Mr. Loveless progressed further with you?"

"Yes, it got to where he would have vaginal and anal sex and oral sex."

"With who?"

"With me."

"How frequently did this occur?"

"All the time."

Teddy Barber described the routine she followed in the house. One of her responsibilities was to wake Larry Loveless, at which time he would pull her into the bed and have "all different kinds" of sex with her. It went on from the time she was ten to the time she was sixteen, Teddy told the court. She thought it was expected of her, explaining that she had seen Loveless doing the same kinds of things with his daughters.

"Can you tell the judge what you observed, and be specific, with the daughters?" Hammerle asked.

"There was one particular case in that he took me and the three girls, one at a time, into the garage, and would strip us of our nightclothes and lay us on the concrete floor, and he used, we were all laying there and he used some type of chain to I guess bind us together, I don't know."

"What would he do?"

"He worked his way down the line. We was all close together."

"Was Melinda in that line?"

"Yes."

"How old was she?"

"Three, maybe four."

Teddy said that after the incident, Larry let the girls up, they each got dressed and went to the living room. Melinda was whimpering, Teddy recalled, she crawled up into Teddy's lap and asked to be held.

Teddy also testified about Larry Loveless taking each girl into the bathroom, saying that when he had her in there, he would force her to submit to oral, anal, and vaginal sex.

"Did you ever see incidences in which he took his other daughters, including Melinda, into the bathroom?"

"Yes."

"Did the events you describe ever stop during the entire time you were baby-sitting in the Loveless house?"

"No."

When Teddy Barber left the stand, her sister, Edie Rager, a licensed practical nurse, age thirty-two, came forward. She testified that the last time she had seen her cousin Melinda was at her own mother's funeral in November 1990. Rager described spending weekends at the Loveless house when she was between the ages of eight and ten. At the time, Loveless had just come back from Vietnam. It was before Melissa and Melinda were born.

"Do you remember an incident that occurred between you and Larry Loveless?" Hammerle asked.

"Yes, I do."

"Describe that to the court, please?"

"On one occasion, I was spending the night with Margie, and I slept with Margie, and I thought I was having a nightmare, and I was trying to wake up out of it, and in the nightmare, it was like somebody was holding their hand over my mouth, and when I did wake up, Larry's hand was over my mouth. I was laying on my left side. His right hand and arm were around me, holding my arm, and his penis was in my rectum and Larry made some noises and moved around and he got up and walked out of the room. And then I got up and went into the living room and I curled up on the couch and went back to sleep."

"Who else was in bed at that time, anyone?"

"Margie."

Edie described a number of occasions when she was age eight and nine where Larry would fondle her, where Larry would take her panties out of her overnight bag and smell them, parading through the house with them while making rude remarks. When asked why she never reported it to adults, Edie said, "Because you didn't talk about things like that."

Friday morning, on the fifth day of the sentencing hearing, the courtroom listened in disbelief as Michelle Loveless revealed the appalling details about her brutal and abusive household.

She described her father as a "monster" who required all of them to be extremely submissive, stating that he was physically and mentally abusive toward every one of them, with the exception of Melinda.

Michelle told the court that her father punished her by locking her in her bedroom closet. She testified that she was sometimes locked in overnight; publicly admitting to urinating on the floor, then using her clothes to clean her mess up.

Michelle talked about Larry's fetish with guns, testifying about the time when, at five years of age, he showed her how to use and clean a gun.

"I was sitting beside my dad and he was trying to explain to me how to clean a gun, and he told me to never clean a loaded gun," she said. "And then he pointed it at my head and he shot but it missed and it hit the wall, and all I remember is seeing a bunch of little bullet holes on the wall and I peed on myself."

Michelle spoke of her parents' abusive relationship toward each other, saying that she and her sisters were subject to Larry's constant physical attacks on their mother. While their arguing was going on, Melinda would often crawl to her room and hold herself in a fetal position, crying and weeping.

She described the relationship of Melinda and Larry as "more like a husband and wife," telling the court that Melinda slept with Larry right up until the time that he moved out of the house.

She characterized Larry as a manipulator, who threatened suicide at times, going across the street from their house with a gun, kneeling at a tombstone with a gun to his head, but then always returning home.

"One time he fired the gun in the yard and the bullet didn't go off properly, and he said that was the bullet he was going to use and he told us about this over and over," Michelle said.

She enumerated the incidents involving the disappearance of their pets, and Larry's other cruel and unusual forms of discipline. "He'd spit tobacco on you for punishment," she said. "He'd pour cold water on us when we were taking a shower."

Michelle gave a portrayal of the lack of privacy in her house, of Larry walking around in the girls' underwear, sometimes wearing their makeup, sometimes using their perfume.

"My underwear, I was scared to death to throw them away because he would get them out of the garbage and smell them in front of everyone and tell me they stink," she testified. "He had a gym bag full of underwear. They were big bloomers. They didn't belong to any of us, I don't think, and he would masturbate in them and put them under the mattresses throughout the house, and on occasion, on the windowsill outside the house."

Michelle recounted the religious phase Larry went through, giving the details about Patty the doll being burned. She broke down in sobs as she recalled the time when five-year-old Melinda was left alone in a motel to be exorcised by a fifty-year-old stranger.

Michelle sketched the horrors of living in the Loveless home, giving particulars about incidents which seemed too cruel and warped to be true, ultimately admitting that she was sexually molested by her father.

Under cross-examination, Michelle told the court that she had no direct knowledge of Melinda having been abused by Larry Loveless. She stated only that she had seen them rub each other in inappropriate ways.

In her final words of testimony, Michelle broke down into tears, calling Shanda's death a horrible crime.

"So many people have been hurt. I don't know who to blame or what to do about it."

* * *

Amid a courtroom of stunned reporters and onlookers, the shy and reserved Melissa Loveless then came forward.

Even though she was highly uncomfortable about testifying, Melissa spoke candidly about the nature of her household, describing her father in much the same way as Michelle had. The defense attorney outlined the various forms of abuse Melissa suffered, and she acknowledged everything by answering "yes" to specific questions put before her.

"I always had a nervous stomach," Melissa told the court. "I was always a nervous wreck. I mean, you never knew when he was going to come in the bathroom or in your room. He would come into the bathroom when I was in there taking a shower and I would beg him to get out and leave me alone. I would cry and scream and he wouldn't listen. He would just laugh and stand there and stare at us."

Melissa said she had no self-esteem because she was always berated by Larry, often called a whore and a bitch. She said she was ashamed to have friends over because Larry would do disgusting things.

"One time, Melinda, I know, was there, he grabbed Mom's crotch. He put his hand in her pants and grabbed her crotch and smelled his hand and we were all standing there."

"Would you tell the judge whether while you were growing up in that household, that you were sexually abused by your father, Larry Loveless?" Hammerle asked.

"Yes, sir, I was."

There were no further questions.

Johnson called Mina Thevenin to the stand, the therapist who worked with the Loveless women at Lifespring Mental Health Services in New Albany. Thevenin testified that she met with Melinda in February 1991, that she was familiar with the family history and the problem of sexual abuse, that her notes reflected that she had reported the alleged abuse to the Welfare Department because, legally, that was her responsibility.

"So these were reported to which Welfare Department?" Johnson asked.

"Floyd County Department of Public Welfare."

"Were you ever contacted concerning these reports?"

"No."

Under cross-examination, Thevenin testified that Melinda was the only Loveless girl who didn't admit that she was molested by her father. However, it was Thevenin's opinion that all three girls were sexually abused by Loveless.

At 12:45 P.M. the hearing recessed for the day, scheduled to resume at nine o'clock the next morning.

Out on the Jefferson County Courthouse steps, Jackie Vaught and Steve Sharer spoke to the media, making no attempt to hide their bitterness.

"There is no excuse, no defense for our child's death," Vaught told reporters. "It was senseless and unforgivable."

"To me this was just another day of testimony," Sharer said. "I cannot see why this would give anybody any reason to do it."

"I felt nothing today. I feel no sympathy, no remorse," Vaught added. "I'm sorry, but they can bring out any defense, it is not good enough. My daughter is dead. What my daughter suffered through that night could not compare to what they suffered in their lives."

On Saturday December 19, the final day of the sentencing hearing, two psychologists were brought forward to describe their evaluations of Melinda Loveless. Dr. Richard Lawler, with the Riley Child Psychiatric Clinic, and Dr. Elgan Baker, Director of the Indiana Center for Psychoanalysis, both diagnosed Melinda as suffering from Borderline Personality Disorder and Posttraumatic Stress Disorder. Both doctors felt the court should address the need to provide psychological treatment for Melinda after her incarceration.

Lawler explained Posttraumatic Stress Disorder (PTSD) to be a psychiatric condition resulting from a person having been exposed to a circumstance so severe, to something beyond the normal human condition. Lawler diagnosed Melinda as suffering from both acute PTSD, resulting from her participation in the crime, as well as complex PTSD, the result of the abusive conditions Melinda lived in for a number of years.

The identity disorder that Melinda suffered from was described to the court, and in particular, Lawler made connections between Borderline Personality Disorder (BPD) and the crime itself. Melinda exhibited all the hallmarks of a borderline personality, Lawler testified, explaining that her sexual identity confusion, her constant mood swings, her unpredictable emotions, and her overdependency on others, all contributed to her criminal act.

"For a borderline person to feel that they're going to be abandoned, it's like they're falling apart," Lawler told the court. "For someone who's got basically a borderline personality structure, the threat to their own integrity, their ability to hold themselves together, is much greater when they feel that they are losing these [teenage] relationships."

Dr. Elgan Baker testified that Melinda Loveless functioned emotionally on the level of a three- or four-year-old, explaining that her "infantile dependency" was evident in her relationships with peers and authority figures. Baker characterized Melinda as suffering from depression, as having problems of impulse control, as having fluctuating attachments to others, and fluctuating self-expression, all of which are specific symptoms of Borderline Personality Disorder.

Baker told the court that Melinda was not a leader, that she had a limited intellectual level, that it would be difficult for her to organize or direct complicated activities. During Baker's testimony, the question of Laurie Tackett's psychological profile was brought up, and Baker commented on Dr. Shippley's report on Tackett, from the Indiana Women's Prison. While the report indicated that Tackett was a sociopath, Baker testified that he viewed her as a strong-willed individual who was somewhat oppositional and easily prone to violence.

In comparing the two girls, Baker said that Tackett was at much greater risk for violent acting out than Loveless.

"I wouldn't say that one of them is 'sicker' than the other," Baker testified. "I think they both have significant emotional problems, but I think Melinda's largely have to do with things going on inside of her in terms of her ability to think, to deal with her emotions, whereas Miss Tackett has more to do with her involvement in the world, her impulsivity, her acting out, and her capacity for violence."

At the conclusion of Baker's testimony, the defense rested. All that remained was the closing arguments and the victim's representative statement from Jackie Vaught.

Before she spoke, Jackie showed Judge Todd some shadow boxes representing what Shanda's life was like. Holding back tears, she described each collage to the court; there was Shanda's school jacket, there were her hair barrettes, her cheerleading pictures, her awards. There was also a picture of Shanda's tombstone which had an engraving of hands cupped together holding a butterfly. Vaught explained that the butterfly represented something beautiful which you can catch in your hand, but then must let go. Jackie asked to show a video of Shanda's scrapbook which contained pictures of her when she was a baby, of her with her family, of her at Christmas time.

Melinda's attorney told the judge that Melinda would watch the video if the family wished it, and the lights were turned down in the courtroom. Jackie narrated Shanda's short life, telling the court that her grandmother spoiled Shanda rotten, showing the judge that Shanda really did enjoy life, describing pictures of her in her Easter dress, at a pool party. There was a video of Shanda at a birthday party, and Jackie pointed out that Shanda's laughter was something she would always cherish.

Once Jackie's presentation was finished, her statement took about forty-five minutes. She began by talking about how compassionate Shanda was, by saying that Shanda was someone who everybody gathered around because Shanda mothered and took care of people. She described Shanda's dreams and hopes for the future.

"It has obviously shattered all of our lives," Jackie told the court. "I speak for all of us when I say I don't think there's anything worse than burying your own child."

Jackie described coming home from work with nobody to

cook for, nobody to wash clothes for, nobody to kiss good night. She said that after Shanda's death, she avoided all of her family and friends because she couldn't stand to see their pain or to hear anyone speak of Shanda's memory. She testified that since Shanda's death, she was unable to work, that she had been admitted into Jefferson Hospital because she was suicidal. Jackie said that she was under the care of both a psychiatrist and a psychologist, taking antidepressants to get through the day, sleeping pills to get through the night.

"I can't control my emotions most of the time and I cry because I want my baby back," Jackie told the judge. "I want her home for Christmas this year but I can't have her. This year I didn't get to buy Shanda any presents. There are no presents for her under my tree."

Vaught blamed Melinda, who, she said, "has cheated me out of being with my daughter during this life," and, directing a piercing gaze at Melinda Loveless, Jackie Vaught finished her statement, lashing out at her daughter's murderer.

"It is my wish for you that you live your life with the memories of her screams and the sight of her burned and mutilated body. I'm not sure who you love most in life, Melinda, whether it be your mother or father, but I want you to imagine that person being Shanda that night. I want you to imagine them in the trunk of that car. I want you to imagine the person that you love the most begging and screaming for their life. I want you to imagine that person being the person laying on that ground that was burned and mutilated. Maybe then, and I doubt this seriously, you could feel a small portion of the pain our family feels."

Vaught told the court that in her eyes, Melinda Loveless had put herself in the same category with Charles Manson and Jeffrey Dahmer, and asked for the maximum sixty-year sentence.

"Anything less would be a crime equal to the murder of my daughter," she told the judge.

Allowing herself to cry for the first time, Jackie Vaught ended her testimony by turning toward Melinda, saying, "May you rot in hell."

Melinda Loveless never testified on her own behalf; however, she asked to make a brief statement before the closing arguments would be heard.

Looking directly at Shanda's relatives, who were seated in the front two benches of the courtroom, Melinda's voice quivered as she spoke.

"I know there's nothing, I know I can't take away your pain and I can't bring Shanda back, but I am sorry. I truly am sorry and I do feel your pain and if I could trade places with your daughter, I would. I'm so sorry."

When she stopped speaking, Melinda fell, weeping and moaning, into Russell Johnson's arms.

In his closing argument, Guy Townsend addressed some specific aggravators, beginning with Melinda's motive and intention to commit the crime, ending with her unspeakable acts of terror and violence and her lack of remorse.

Townsend asked the court to weigh the believability of all the testimony regarding acts of molestation against Melinda.

"As to these people who were allegedly molested by Larry Loveless, there are aspects of that testimony that do raise questions as to its credibility," he told the court.

Townsend questioned the integrity of Teddy Barber's testimony regarding the scene in the Loveless garage, asking why, if in fact that did happen, did neither Michelle nor Melissa Loveless bring it up in their testimony which followed.

He disregarded Loveless's alleged sexual abuse as a possible mitigating factor, insisting that Melinda Loveless was, in fact, aggressive, assertive, and threatening, that she was not a meek girl who happened to be Laurie Tackett's pawn.

He dwelled on the fact that Melinda asked Shanda to strip, which he said was proof that Melinda knew Shanda was not going to come out of the ordeal alive.

"The one and only reasonable explanation for taking Shanda's clothes was that Melinda Loveless knew and intended at that point, if not all along, that Shanda was not going to need any clothes in a short time because she was going to be dead," Townsend argued.

Townsend pointed to a number of things upon which Tackett and Lawrence's testimony agreed, all of which incriminated Melinda Loveless. Both Toni and Laurie testified that it was Melinda who beat up the naked Shanda Sharer on the logging road near Tackett's house; it was Melinda who helped toss Shanda's body into the trunk; it was Melinda who went "country cruisin' "; it was Melinda who ordered the car be stopped after Shanda was initially set on fire; it was Melinda who poured the rest of the gasoline on Shanda's smoldering body; it was Melinda who said she was glad Shanda was dead.

"If Melinda Loveless had been tried and convicted only of the crimes that she is presently pleading guilty to, not all the crimes that were charged against her, then the jury would have to consider the question of whether to impose upon Melinda Loveless a punishment only remotely related to the punishment that Melinda Loveless imposed upon Shanda Sharer. That punishment is the death penalty," Townsend told the court.

"Melinda Loveless cut short Shanda Sharer's life when she was only twelve years old, but in one sense, Melinda Loveless made Shanda Sharer's life very long indeed," Townsend said. "Can anyone doubt that the hours between eleven o'clock on the night of January 10, 1992, and nine o'clock on the morning of January 11, took an eternity to pass for Shanda Sharer? The hours locked in the trunk punctuated only by brief episodes of being beaten and tortured and sodomized must have gone on forever for her."

Townsend spoke of the heinousness of the crime, of the brutal manner in which it was committed, of the fact that an object was inserted three and a half inches up the child's anus, saying that all of the abominable acts of torture were committed because Melinda Loveless wanted Shanda Sharer punished.

He asked the court to consider the extreme physical, mental, and emotional harm done to the victim in setting a sentence, requesting that the court ignore any mitigating circumstances, pressing for the maximum penalty of sixty years.

Mike Walro was the first attorney to speak on Melinda's behalf, citing the vulnerability of his client, a girl who, when he first met her on January 12, 1992, was honest and remorseful about the crime. He called Melinda a "handicapped person" who came from an abnormal home. He argued the crime occurred because Melinda ran into Laurie Tackett, who took Melinda's threats and put them into action.

Bob Hammerle spoke next, first addressing the parents of Shanda, telling them that he had never once forgotten their anguish and inconsolable pain. He also addressed Melinda's sisters, whom he called "two of the braver people I've ever met in my life," commending them for testifying to the acts of terror that they and their sister Melinda suffered at the hands of Larry Loveless.

"I don't know that I can admire two people more or ever will again, but to have them be cross-examined as they were, and approached by Mr. Townsend as if they had come in here and fabricated, makes me ashamed of my profession," Hammerle told the judge. "To have them come in here and Mr. Townsend to stand up and question their credibility when he knows at this very minute a detective is investigating the truth of their measures to go ahead and arrest their father, is an exercise in hypocrisy."

Hammerle made reference to the Salem witch trials of 1692, at which time hysterical young teenage girls faced an inflamed community and everybody responded to emotion, not to reason. As a result, people wound up being executed for being witches. He asked that the court set aside emotion and decide the case on the facts and the law.

Russell Johnson was the last to speak, outlining the mitigating circumstances, the most significant of those being the age of the defendant, the fact that she had no past criminal record, the remorse of the defendant, the contribution of her dysfunctional home life, and the contention that Melinda acted under the domination of Laurie Tackett. In all, Johnson listed twenty-three mitigators and only three aggravators. He contended that a sixty-year sentence was not appropriate, and stated that Loveless should receive the sentence normally prescribed for felony murder by Indiana law, forty years. Johnson also asked the court to consider a split sentence, whereby Melinda Loveless would serve part of her sentence in prison and part of her sentence on probation, living back in the community, being supervised by the court.

Judge Ted Todd advised that he would make a ruling within forty-eight hours, telling the courtroom that he would seal that decision with the court clerk and would not make his sentence for Loveless public until after the sentencing hearing for her co-defendant, Tackett, scheduled to begin the following Monday, December 28.

Twenty-four

It was the first white Christmas Indiana had seen in seven years, but it was a dismal holiday for Laurie Tackett, spent in the harsh reality of the Indiana Women's Prison. When she appeared in court three days later, she sat silently brooding, watching as Steve Henry testified about the arrest and the collection of evidence. The business of entering physical evidence, slides, photographs, police reports and records was not necessary; all of that was stipulated into the record since it had been presented and testified to during the hearing for Melinda Loveless.

Toni Lawrence testified, narrating the entire course of action, from the moment she left Madison on January 10 to the time that she confessed in four separate statements to police. Under cross examination, Wil Goering tried to establish that many things which occurred on the night of the offense were Melinda's idea, but no matter how much Goering tried to implicate Loveless, Lawrence's responses did not differ from her police statements. Tackett looked no less guilty once her defense attorney was through.

Then, for the first time in the court proceedings, Melinda Loveless was called to the witness stand. Her testimony would last for two days, throughout which she would lay as much blame on Tackett as possible. According to Melinda, it was Laurie who made Shanda strip, who put Shanda in the trunk, who "quieted" Shanda. Because Loveless was all but denying her presence at the scene, Tackett's attorneys could do nothing

305

more than point out how many times Melinda could have prevented the murder.

At the end of the first day, Goering and O'Connor made a motion to the court, requesting that the prosecution look into a withdrawal of Loveless's plea of guilty. Since Loveless was denying responsibility, they wanted the court to consider setting a trial date. In essence, Loveless testified that she did not participate in the offense willingly, that she participated under duress. O'Connor made a motion to strike all of Melinda Loveless's testimony, which Todd denied.

On day two of Tackett's hearing, O'Connor cross examined Loveless for hours. She went over Melinda's plea agreement, asking if Melinda understood that the state had agreed to dismiss all of the original charges, reminding her that she was pleading guilty to felony murder (murder by arson) in exchange for the dismissal of the death penalty specifications.

"You claimed yesterday, if I remember right, you said of all these circumstances that you talked about, that you really weren't involved in them, but that you didn't do anything to stop it? Is that pretty much the gist of your testimony?" O'Connor asked.

"No, I'm not saying that I wasn't involved. I mean I was there and I didn't stop it," Melinda told her.

"And specifically, you said that at the very end of these events, that when Shanda was on fire, that by the time you saw her up close she was already dead?"

"Yes."

"And that you threw a two-liter bottle of something?"

"Yes."

"So you're saying that you did not participate in the arson?"

"No, I'm not saying that."

"Basically what you're saying is you pled guilty to all these things to save yourself the death penalty?"

"No."

O'Connor asked Loveless about her girlfriend, Amanda, about the letter she wrote stating "I want Shanda dead," and about the "Amanda plan." The questioning lasted for a grueling three hours.

Melinda claimed that she never used the word "kill" on the night of the offense, that she never directed the car to Shanda's, that they "just happened" to go there, that Hope and Toni volunteered to go up to Shanda's door.

"You put the knife to Shanda's throat?" O'Connor asked.

"Yes, I did."

"You pulled her hair back?"

"Yes."

"Did you hold it real tight?"

"No, I did not."

"You had the knife to her throat?"

"Yes, I did."

"The whole way to The Witches' Castle?"

"Yes, I had the dull side to her neck."

"That's when you said that you weren't going to hurt her, but in reality you were going to beat her up?"

"I was just going to scare her."

"You said yesterday that you were going to beat her up."

"I was going to."

"And that wouldn't hurt her?"

"I thought she'd fight me back. That's what I wanted."

"You wanted a fight?"

"I just wanted a fight, that's it."

"Well, apparently she wasn't capable of fighting you back because you killed her. Is that true?"

"I did not kill her."

"Did you plead guilty to felony murder?"

"Yes, I did."

"Then you're responsible for killing Shanda Sharer, aren't you?"

"Yes. I believe I am to blame that she died. Yes."

Throughout her testimony, Melinda's memory seemed to be very convenient; she remembered only the things that took the blame away from her. She alleged that Laurie strangled Shanda, that Laurie forced her to help stab Shanda.

"She had her hand on the knife," Melinda told the court. "She took my hand and put it on top of hers and held my hand and stabbed Shanda and I pulled my hand away."

After a ten-minute recess, O'Connor brought out the photographs of Shanda's stab wounds, asking Melinda to look at them and identify which wounds she inflicted. Melinda twice refused to look at the photos, but then realized that she would have to submit to the attorney's request. When viewing them, Melinda broke down into tears.

Melinda continued to deny her involvement in the crime, insisting that she never saw Shanda get hit with a tire tool, that she had no knowledge of how Shanda got the wound to her anus, that she did not see any injuries perpetrated upon Shanda after the initial "beat up" (the choking and stabbing) that she helped Laurie perform during the "woods" scene at the logging road.

When the defense attorney questioned Loveless about what transpired at the Clark gas station, Melinda confirmed that Laurie filled a two-liter bottle with gas and handed it to her to hold between her legs.

"Now, wasn't it true all four of you girls discussed how wounded Shanda was at that point," O'Connor asked.

"No."

"And you said she was like a little animal, she might as well be dead, we might as well make her dead and put her out of her misery?"

"No."

"You didn't say that?"

"I never said that."

Melinda told the court that she did whatever Laurie told her to do because she was afraid of her. O'Connor pointed out that Melinda wasn't afraid enough to refuse to go "cruisin' " with Laurie alone. She wasn't afraid to sleep with Laurie that next night, when police arrested them at her home.

O'Connor questioned Melinda about the events of Saturday, January 11, when she and Laurie went back to New Albany and showed Crystal and Amanda the trunk, telling them all the grisly details of their crime.

"You told Crystal all these things later, didn't you?" O'Connor asked.

"I did not tell Crystal, Laurie did."

"Crystal is one of your best friends, right?"

"Yes."

"She had told you once that if you wanted to get rid of somebody, you should burn the body?"

"Crystal never said that to me."

Entered into evidence were pages and pages of reports on Melinda's conduct at the Clark County Jail and at the Indiana Women's Prison, most of which showed that Melinda expected special treatment, that she tried to get her way by writing grievance notes to the jailers. The reports also indicated that she had violated prison rules by having more than one inmate in her cell, and that she was put in "lock-down" for threatening another inmate.

The state called Crystal Wathen to the stand, who told the court that she never heard Melinda say that she wanted to kill Shanda, that she knew nothing about a plan to kill Shanda.

Amanda Heavrin was next to testify, detailing the relationship she had with Melinda and the friendship she grew to have with Shanda.

"You knew that your breakup with Melinda put Shanda Sharer at some risk, didn't you? You knew there was danger to Shanda Sharer because you had broken up with Melinda?" Goering asked.

"Not really," Amanda said.

'You knew that Melinda blamed Shanda Sharer for your breakup, didn't you?"

"Yes, sir."

"Alright. And don't you think that caused her any problems? You didn't think that was going to cause her problems?"

"It didn't for Shanda."

Goering reminded Amanda of the letter she had written, warning Shanda that Melinda might kill her. He asked her about other letters to Shanda, in particular, he wanted to know what the number "23" meant, but Amanda insisted that she didn't know. He pointed to a number of letters, showing Amanda the number "23," but she still claimed she hadn't written it.

"You wrote the note?"

"Yes, sir."

"And you gave the note to Shanda?"

"Yes, sir, I did."

"But you didn't write the 23s on there?"

"No, sir, I didn't."

"Did you have a physical relationship with Shanda?"

"Yes, sir."

"When did that start?"

"About two or three months after we had known each other for a while."

The defense attorney had Amanda confirm that in late October 1991, Kristie Brodfuehrer called her house, telling Amanda that she was going to come pick her up, to wait up for her. Amanda admitted that she was afraid of Melinda at the time, that she knew Melinda wanted to beat her up.

When Amanda stepped down, Kary Pope testified, responding to Townsend's questions about Tackett's involvement with witchcraft. O'Connor objected, saying the line of questioning was inappropriate because there was no evidence that the murder was linked to occult practices. The objection was sustained, and at that point, Judge Todd adjourned for the day.

At 9:00 A.M. on December 30, Kary Pope took the stand, enthralling onlookers with the story of Laurie Tackett's fascination with death and fire, repeating her testimony given at the Loveless hearing.

Under cross-examination, Kary told O'Connor that she had been in touch with both Loveless and Tackett since their incarceration. She testified that she had submitted to a polygraph, concerning her involvement with the death of Shanda Sharer, which she failed.

Arlinda Randle, an inmate at Clark County Jail, was brought forward to testify about her contact with Melinda Loveless, telling the court that she shared the same cell block with Loveless in April. The inmate said that she witnessed no remorse in Melinda, that Melinda seemed to celebrate her crime, and that, on one occasion, Melinda signed an autograph for someone.

Randle testified that Melinda showed her a copy of the Hazelwood Junior High yearbook, which had a circle and other marks around the picture of Shanda Sharer. The inmate said that underneath Shanda's picture, Melinda had written, "So young. So pretty. Had to die early."

"Did Melinda put anything up on the walls of the cell?" Goering asked.

"At one time she had a picture of Shanda."

"Did you write anything about it?"

"Not on Shanda's. She had a picture of herself on the wall. She put 'most wanted' under it."

The next witness was Laurie Tackett, who opted to testify on her own behalf, trying to gain the sympathy of the court by recounting a life full of pain. Throughout her four hours of testimony, she related the "horrors" of her young life, contending that her mother beat and choked her, that she was forced to submit to her mother's religion, that she was sexually molested at the ages of six and eleven. She said that "being born" was the worst thing that ever happened to her.

Tackett and her attorneys tried to show that Laurie accepted responsibility for what she had done, that she was remorseful, that she had a troubled past. They also tried to attack the credibility of Melinda's testimony.

After reiterating the course of events on January 10 and 11, Tackett all the while claiming that Loveless was the aggressor, Goering asked Tackett to describe how she felt about the night of the murder.

"I don't feel human," Tackett said. "I don't know. I just can't believe it happened. I just know how terrible it would be to lose somebody. I'll live with that night for the rest of my life. I know I will. It's never going to leave. I think about it every day. I can't help it."

Under cross-examination, Laurie balked at giving the names of the males who allegedly molested her. A short recess was taken, during which time Tackett wrote the names on a piece of paper and handed it to the judge.

She also claimed that she had been raped by a classmate just months before the murder. Townsend later called fifteen-year-old Grant Pearson to the stand, who contradicted Laurie's testimony, telling the court that Laurie didn't say "no," and that in his eyes, her physical presence equalled consent. He was granted immunity from rape charges for his cooperation.

Most of Tackett's responses regarding the crime raised doubts about the truthfulness of her previous testimony. When Townsend would back her into a corner on some particular detail, Laurie would either contradict herself or claim that she couldn't remember. Her voice sounded choked and strained at times, and at one point, she broke down in soft sobs.

"As far as securing the trunk, all you did was close the lid real lightly?" Townsend asked.

"Yes."

"Now do you recall yesterday testifying that when you went back into the house, the thought that was going through your mind was that you had to get the car going?"

"Yes."

"What did you mean by that?"

"Muffler so the dogs and screams would be drowned out."

"Why was it important that that happen?"

"I don't really remember. Probably because of not wanting to wake the neighbors and my parents."

"And why didn't you want them waking up?"

"I was afraid Shanda was dying and I was afraid they'd find—"

Townsend interrupted.

"Okay, if you were afraid, were you concerned with whether she was dying or not?"

"I didn't want her to die."

"So you went to get help for her?"

"I was afraid to."

"Why is that?"

"Cause I don't really know. I was just afraid. I didn't want anyone to know that I had a dying baby in my car."

The prosecutor questioned Tackett about the events at the kill site, asking her to give specifics about what went on there. Then, in the most dramatic moment of the court proceedings, Townsend took a book of matches from his pocket and struck a match, holding the flame to Laurie Tackett's face.

"Isn't it true, Laurie, that you went up to Shanda's body after Hope had soaked it with gasoline and took that book of matches out of your pocket and took one of those matches and you were going to show that match to Shanda Sharer before you set her afire?"

"No."

"Somehow, she just spontaneously combusted, is that right?"

"I'm not saying that. I don't know how the fire started."

"But you were there beside her, weren't you? You were so close to her, were you not? You were getting ready to talk to her?"

"I had just bent down when the fire went in my face."

At that point, the prosecutor got down on one knee, recreating the scene at the kill site, pretending to kneel over Shanda.

"Okay, and you're kneeling down beside Shanda's still living body and you want to say something to her?" he asked.

"I wasn't kneeling like that."

"Like this?" (He shifted his position.)

"Yes."

"And you're getting ready to talk to Shanda Sharer?"

"I had just gotten down on my knees."

"What were you going to say to her? What do you say to somebody that you're about to burn to death?"

"I don't know what I was going to say. I was just going to get her to talk to me."

"Some famous last words you wanted?"

The last witness to testify at Tackett's hearing was Dr. Eric Engum, a clinical psychologist who said that Laurie had no sense of "self," that she literally intertwined her personality with others, like a "chameleon." He told the court that Tackett was a follower, that in his opinion, she was not the ringleader on the night of the offense, she was taking direction from others.

Engum testified that Tackett suffered from paranoia and schizophrenia, not psychosis. He stated that Tackett's anger was predominantly directed inward, that because of her bottled-up emotions, she was a walking "time bomb."

He told the court Laurie was in denial about the crime because it was "too big a truth to swallow," and explained that she had to "erect a barrier" between the reality of the event and herself as a way of maintaining whatever integrity she had.

"Is she able to have empathy?" Goering asked.

"She doesn't have empathy for herself. It's going to be very difficult for her to have empathy for somebody else."

"What effect, then, would that have on a person's ability to express remorse?"

"If you don't experience pain yourself, and you don't recognize that other people experience pain, what do you have to be remorseful for?"

"In your view, does Laurie Tackett view the world as a dangerous and hostile place?"

"Terribly, terribly dangerous and hostile. Very little that she can trust, and even when she does manage to enmesh herself in somebody else's personality, she's so unsure that they're going to remain true to her that she's frantically fearing abandonment all the time. And then when they do abandon her, her only response is one of anger, aggression, and hostility."

Before Dr. Engum left the stand, he told the court about the dynamics of group violence, stating that research literature showed that group crimes were usually more violent than crimes committed by an individual.

"It's almost like one person feeds off the other," Engum said. "The best example I can give you is kind of a shark feeding frenzy. One shark can be fairly destructive, but when you get a pack of them, they feed off each other. It's almost like they sense the increased tension in the air and they feed off of that."

"Melinda Loveless wanted somebody killed and Laurie Tackett wanted to kill somebody," Townsend said in his closing argument. "They each had a need that was met by the other. They each got what they wanted. Melinda Loveless's hatred alone did not lead to the death of Shanda Sharer. It wasn't until Melinda Loveless's hatred combined with Laurie Tackett's blood lust that Shanda Sharer's fate was sealed."

The prosecutor told the judge that it didn't matter who struck the blows to Shanda's head, who stuck the tire iron up Shanda's anus, or who struck the match. The fact was that the girls both acted in concert, and were guilty of murder by arson.

He talked about the horror of Laurie Tackett's willingness to take a life of a complete stranger, which, he suggested, made her a much more frightening character than Melinda Loveless, who at least had a motive.

"Melinda Loveless is a murderer and she deserves the maximum sentence this court can impose upon her for her crimes," Townsend argued. "But the threat of Melinda Loveless is limited to those who incur her enmity. Laurie Tackett is a different kind of murderer altogether. Laurie Tackett murders, not for vengeance, but for pleasure, and the identity of her victim does not matter to her."

Townsend implored the judge to sentence Laurie Tackett to the maximum penalty: sixty years.

In Goering's closing statement, the defense attorney called Laurie Tackett "an impaired, dysfunctional person, a weapon, used by Melinda Loveless," asking, "Who's more responsible for that tiger in the house and the damage that it does? The tiger, or the person that places the tiger in the house?"

Goering argued that Tackett's damaged psychological state was the greatest mitigator to be considered, and asked the court to demonstrate the mercy that Tackett herself could not comprehend.

O'Connor said that the case wasn't some tabloid story about "lesbo bitches on acid." She reminded the court that it was the story of a girl who had been terrorized at home and considered an outsider at school. Going over Tackett's history, the defense attorney called for authorities in schools and other institutions to reach out and help troubled teens like Laurie.

Outside the courthouse, in the cold winter weather, with the high reaching only thirty degrees, Madison townsfolk gathered in increasing numbers, waiting to lambast the girls as they were escorted to and from the jail.

"People would heckle. They'd sit at the bar and then come to the courthouse at the end of the day, when we'd bring the girls out," Henry recalled. "They'd jeer at the girls, saying, 'Why don't you get the electric chair!' "

"I hope you burn in hell!" one woman yelled at Tackett on her final day of testimony.

The hearings ended the afternoon of Thursday, December 31, on a cloudy New Year's eve.

Twenty-five

The morning of January 4, 1993, when Judge Todd pronounced sentence for Loveless and Tackett, there were so many spectators lining the walls of the courtroom that the condensation from their hands and heads left a black streak of human grime. An assembly of more than two dozen people waited outside the doors, standing on their toes to get a better view through the narrow windows. In the jury room, another crowd listened on a speaker system.

When Todd sentenced Melinda Loveless to sixty years, Marjorie, seated in the front row, collapsed against Michelle, sobbing bitterly, while cheers rang out from the rest of the courthouse audience. The shout and applause was so loud that the judge broke his gavel stand in quieting them down.

The judge cited the gruesome nature of the crime, the period of confinement of the victim, and premeditation as the most compelling aggravating circumstances. Melinda cried as Todd told her that she still had the power to turn herself around and do something useful with her life after being released from prison.

A few minutes later, after Loveless was taken out of the room, Judge Todd sentenced Mary Laurine Tackett to the maximum sixty years, bringing subdued sobs from some of Tackett's family members. George Tackett, seated in the row behind the Loveless family, stared straight ahead and appeared to blush. Laurie shook her head slowly, showing no emotion as her sentence was announced.

Both Loveless and Tackett asked to appeal their sentences. In Loveless's case, Russell Johnson would handle it; in Tackett's, the court appointed new counsel, Eugene Hollander, to represent her.

Under the Indiana Department of Corrections "good time" policy, for every "good day" an inmate serves, one in which he or she commits no offenses against prison rules, the inmate is credited with an additional day not actually served. In other words, if both girls exhibited good behavior, they would be released from prison in thirty years. Since the two had already been behind bars for one year prior to sentence, there remained twenty-nine years for them to serve.

Outside the Jefferson County Courthouse, despite the pouring rain, the hostile courtroom crowd followed the girls as they were taken back to the jail, calling them "murderers" and shouting obscenities.

Out on the courthouse lawn, an army of media descended upon Jackie Vaught and Steve Sharer, asking for their reaction to the sentences, and, although the sentences were as much as Shanda's parents could expect, they couldn't hide their heartbreak.

"I'll never be satisfied, because I want my baby back," Jackie told reporters. "I hope they stay in jail forever."

Both Vaught and Sharer felt that the system had done the right thing by accepting the guilty pleas, telling the press that if the cases had gone to trial, either girl could have been found not guilty by just one juror and been let out on the street, able to victimize someone else.

"I feel like I've been walking on eggshells for the past few weeks," Steve Sharer said. "I feel so much better now that they got the maximum. I feel like I can breathe again. I feel no sympathy for the families of those girls. They can still visit their child in jail. We'll never see Shanda again."

The following day, newspapers and television stations in Louisville, Indianapolis, and Cincinnati gave accounts of the sentences and the reaction of Shanda's family. By then Jackie Vaught had become something of a celebrity, having changed her hairstyle a number of times, she was evolving into a figure that people were interested in listening to. Vaught told the public that the last few weeks of graphic testimony were tough on her and her family, but said, "People need to know how gruesome our daughter's murder was, and what kids are capable of."

The shock and dismay of the public was expressed in editorials which appeared throughout the region. One Louisville columnist, Jim Adams, addressed the outward appearance of Melinda Loveless, describing her as an "immaculate" murderess, "whose hair could have been painted by Botticelli, whose wardrobe is the sort compiled only through serious mall time."

The column focused on the four "normal" seeming teenagers who committed the crime against Sharer, pointing out that in the same week, a fifteen-year-old girl, B.J. Quire, was found dumped in nearby Oldham County, police having discovered that she was murdered by her boyfriend; in western Louisville, a fifteen-year-old boy was shot and killed, allegedly by an eighteen-year-old girl he'd never met.

"The teen years as I knew them 20 and 25 years ago are long dead," Adams wrote. "The level of parental control we knew is gone. Twenty-five years ago, I'd never heard of four girls in their mid-teens who actually stayed out all night; even the wildest girls in school had curfews, and no one ever heard them talk the next day about murdering any small children while they were out on the town."

Another editorial, written by a concerned citizen from Corydon, Indiana, responded to Adams's column, asking that the government give some serious consideration to preventive programs for children.

"Our society is much more effective at doling out punishment after a crime has been committed than taking preventive measures to insure that children do not grow into persons capable of committing such a crime," the woman from Corydon wrote. "It is difficult, if not impossible, for some to feel sympathy for Loveless and Tackett. Would it have been as difficult to understand and treat their victimization when they were 8 or 10 or 12 — before their rage reached the point of no return?"

Over in Madison, however, the public wasn't concerned

about treatment for children; for the most part, citizens were still complaining about their picture-perfect city being forever tarnished. Only the people directly involved in the case seemed to accept the reality. "We're branded now as the town that spawned the murderers," Mike Walro candidly told reporters. "Stephen King couldn't come up with a plot like this," Walro said, trying to get people to realize that it was not a crime that would soon be forgotten, that the Madison community could no longer shelter itself from the violence and sexual immorality that plagued big cities.

There were many people who refused to even talk about the Shanda Sharer case, who wanted to look the other way and retreat into their own private bubble.

"What they did were really monstrous acts and people don't want to admit that these young girls are from here," one Madison resident said. "This area has been virtually crime-free. To have something like this is like dropping a bomb. The girls who did this to Shanda also did it to this town. It was almost as if the town about died."

Local TV news coverage included the reaction of two of Peggy Tackett's cousins, Mary Blair and Francis Carter, who both said the girls' sentences were too short. They told the press that they knew Laurie was involved with witchcraft, but "never dreamed it would go so far." Blair blamed Tackett's parents for their daughter's criminal behavior, claiming that Tackett was an unloved child who was "practically raised by her grandmother." Laurie spent a lot of time there because her grandmother allowed her to watch TV and do other "normal" things. Blair said Tackett's grandmother died when Laurie was thirteen or fourteen, and that's when Laurie went wild.

The media blitz on the Shanda Sharer case continued, with calls coming in from around the world. Journalists, TV talk show hosts, and Hollywood producers contacted Shanda's parents and the four girls' attorneys. Because no one was willing to talk on national television, TV shows such as "Hard Copy," "Inside Edition," "Larry King Live," "Donahue," "Maury Povitch" and "Sally Jessy Raphael" were turned down by both sides.

On January 6, after a local television station reported that Tackett was negotiating to sell her story to TV and movie producers, Steve Sharer and Jackie Vaught filed a lawsuit seeking $1 billion in damages, attempting to prevent any of the girls from capitalizing on their crime.

"During her testimony, Tackett couldn't remember a thing that happened," Sharer told *The Courier Journal*. "Now all of a sudden, she remembers everything and wants to sell her story. It's a slap in our faces."

Bob Donald, the attorney Vaught and Sharer had hired to file suit, told the newspaper that the family wasn't against the possibility of a book or movie; however, they wanted control over any portrayal of the case.

"If something is going to be done," Donald said, "the family wants to make sure that it's done tactfully and is not exploitive like the Amy Fisher movies."

Indiana law mandates that any money a felon receives for broadcast or publication rights would be deposited in a violent-crime victim's fund. A felon can only collect ten percent of that money, to be used exclusively for legal costs, with the remaining ninety percent going to the victim's family. Therefore, it is highly unlikely that any of the girls could profit from any commercial treatment of their case.

On January 19, Darrel Auxier asked the Jefferson Court to move Hope Rippey's trial out of Madison because of the extensive news coverage. Eventually a change of venue was granted. Rippey's case was assigned to St. Joseph Superior Judge Jeanne Jourdan of South Bend, Indiana, and a new trial date would be set.

On January 26, the sentencing hearing for Toni Lawrence began. Even though most of the prior testimony was stipulated into the record, it would last for two-and-a-half days.

Steve Henry was called to the stand, telling the court that Lawrence's statements were instrumental in getting Loveless and Tackett to plead guilty.

Melinda Loveless came forward, admitting that she didn't enter into a plea agreement until after she read the four statements that Toni Lawrence made to police.

Laurie Tackett testified, answering questions from Lawrence's defense attorney, Paul Baugh, a young Madison lawyer who hadn't much experience with murder cases. Baugh's line of questioning tried to get Tackett to minimize Lawrence's role in the event, but he did not really get the responses he wanted out of Tackett. She basically told the court that Lawrence did not take any clothing from Shanda, that she did not pour the Pepsi out of the two-liter at the gas station, that she did not get out of the car at the burn pile or at the kill site, all of which was already known.

Clifton Lawrence came forward to testify about the events of January 11, when he brought his daughter into the Sheriff's Department to report her knowledge of the crime. He also talked about Toni's pain and suffering since the murder, describing Toni's incarceration at the Scott County Jail, her suicide attempt, and the psychological assessment of his daughter which was done at the Lifespring facility in Jeffersonville.

Following Mr. Lawrence, a string of character witnesses were presented on Toni's behalf, including four of her teachers and a number of her closest friends. The gist of their testimony was that Lawrence was an easygoing girl, someone who was well liked and respected.

"She was an average student, behaved well in class, paid attention and cooperated," Barbara Hill, a French teacher, told the court.

"Toni was a typical academic student. She came from a good home. She did her homework, did well on tests, and cooperated well," Beverly Cook testified.

Mikel Pommerehn told the court that she was worried about her friend, saying, "She's an emotional person and doesn't handle things like this very well."

"She said she was real scared of Laurie Tackett, and that's why she didn't do anything to stop it," another friend of Lawrence's, Kelly Tullis, testified.

Dana Varble got on the stand to give details about Lawrence's alleged rape which occurred at Varble's house. Varble testified that her friend Toni was "crying" and upset after the incident; however, the defense was unable to produce police records to corroborate Lawrence's claim.

On day two of Lawrence's hearing, Toni Lawrence took the stand in an attempt to prove that she acted out of fear on the night of the murder. Under cross-examination, Townsend questioned Lawrence repeatedly about whether she did anything to stop the progress of the offense, asking if she ever attempted to warn adults while there was still time to save Shanda Sharer's life. Over and over again, Lawrence admitted that she did nothing to prevent the crime.

Then, in an emotionally charged moment at the close of her testimony, Toni Lawrence read a statement of apology to Shanda's parents:

> "Mrs. Vaught, Mr. Sharer, I'm so sorry about your little girl. I know that you can never forgive me for being with those girls on January 10th and 11th but I would like to explain some things to you.
>
> "I tried to help Shanda. After I gave her a hug and said I was sorry I asked Melinda to please take her home but Melinda told me to shut up, so I did. I was terrified of Melinda and Laurie. Melinda had a knife and was going to kill Shanda. I know I should be punished but in my heart, seeing Shanda tortured and burnt was punishment in itself. I didn't get help because I was scared they would kill me, too.
>
> "That night and morning will live visibly in my mind for the rest of my life. Mrs. Vaught, Mr. Sharer, I know you have the right to hate me. I wished there was something I could do for you but all I can say is how very sorry I am."

Once Toni finished her statement, the defense rested.

Jackie Vaught responded to Lawrence by reading a statement which refused Lawrence's apology. She commented about all the sympathy the defense tried to elicit for Toni, disgusted that the defense had brought forward Toni's teachers to say what a model student she was, had brought forward friends and family who testified unanimously about their disbelief at Lawrence's involvement in such a crime.

"Toni is apparently haunted by nightmares of Shanda's burned body which she claims she never saw," Vaught told the court. "She claims that she has nightmares of the burned body coming to her and asking her to help her. I'm sure that must be horrible for her. I pray her nightmares continue to haunt her for the rest of her entire life, and may her life be very long.

"I have seen no evidence of remorse whatsoever. What I have seen is a spoiled rotten child who is totally put out with having to be here, a child who takes no responsibility for her actions and expects everyone else around her to shoulder the blame.

"I sat through three sentencing hearings and had to look and listen to my daughter's murderers day after day while they have lied and put on acts that are worthy of an Oscar. I have listened while each and every one cried child abuse and rape. I see attorneys trying to convince everyone that these girls were all victims. The victim here is Shanda Renee Sharer and her family and friends."

Toni Lawrence wept during most of Vaught's statement.

Vaught asked the court to sentence Lawrence to the maximum, which, under her plea agreement, would be twenty years. She told the judge if the maximum penalty was not levied, a message would be sent to the world that it was okay to watch while another human was being tortured and murdered.

On the morning of January 28, when she walked into the courtroom to be sentenced, Toni Lawrence looked very much a preppy, donning a cable-knit sweater and wire-rimmed glasses. While he could have sentenced her anywhere from six to twenty years, Judge Todd ruled that Lawrence would serve the ten-year presumptive sentence for the charge of criminal confinement, and an additional ten years for aggravating circumstances. The judge told Lawrence that any less than a twenty-year sentence would depreciate the seriousness of the crime committed.

Counting the time that Lawrence had already served, she would be eligible for parole in nine years.

* * *

On April 19, Hope Rippey was driven five hours north to appear before Judge Jeanne Jourdan in South Bend, at which time she signed a plea agreement that was identical to those of Melinda Loveless and Laurie Tackett, pleading guilty to murder, arson, and criminal confinement. Depending upon the mitigating and aggravating circumstances, Rippey was facing a sentence between thirty to sixty years.

Answering "yes" to questions asked by Auxier, Rippey told the court that she helped lure Shanda from her home and eventually poured gasoline on her before she was set ablaze.

Her sentencing hearing took place in the St. Joseph County Superior Court on June 1, 1992. Auxier cited Rippey's lack of prior criminal record, the strong provocation that she acted under, and the unlikelihood that she would commit another crime as the mitigating factors which, he argued, should reduce her sentence to the minimum thirty years.

Appearing in a navy blue jail uniform, Hope showed no emotion on the first day of the hearing. Unlike the hearings in Madison, there was no angry crowd, no packed courtroom for her to contend with. Apart from the families of Sharer and Rippey, the audience was made up of reporters and a few curious onlookers. The hearing, which lasted just two days, did not dwell on the agonizing details of the death of Shanda Sharer, those having been stipulated into evidence.

Steve Henry was the first to take the stand, testifying that in a statement Hope Rippey made on May 7, 1993, she admitted that she watched Shanda sit up "Indian-style" when they were at the burn pile, with "one hand on her head and one hand on a tire.

"I mean, her eyes weren't really open but they were sort of rolled back in her head," Rippey told police. "She wasn't moving, I mean she was sort of swaying, but she wasn't talking, and Laurie said we had to start a fire."

Rippey's statement indicated that at the burn pile, Melinda asked where someone's heart would be located because she wanted to know how to get a knife to go into Shanda's heart. Rippey admitted that she showed Melinda where her own heart was, telling her to just "jab" the knife in.

Henry told the court that in Rippey's statement, Hope admitted that she provided directions to the kill site, then helped Laurie take Shanda's body out of the trunk.

"I didn't pour all the gas," Rippey told police in her recorded statement. "After I poured the gas, I went back in the car. Melinda came and asked for a lighter, and we all smoked, and Toni grabbed a lighter from the dashboard and gave it to her."

Once Steve Henry answered questions regarding Hope's guilt, Carl Rippey took the stand. In a low voice, barely audible in the courtroom, he told the judge that his daughter was a caring, friendly girl who often played the role of "peacemaker" in household fights.

"She would try and be a mediator and separate us and send us to our rooms," Carl testified. "Then she would talk to Gloria and I separately. She would tell me to drop it, and I'm sure that's what she told Gloria."

He described Hope as a child who was generally obedient, who was helpful at home, who enjoyed taking care of her sister's young son. Her father said Hope was a happy girl who, after the offense, had constant nightmares, no longer laughed, and had to be forced to eat.

Later that day, Dr. Michael Sheehan, a psychologist who had evaluated Hope Rippey in four separate sessions over a ten-hour period, testified that Rippey was caught up in a situation of peer pressure and group dynamics. He described Hope as a child who did not even understand that she had participated in a murder, using the analogy to the film *The Night of the Living Dead* to explain why Hope did not believe that Shanda would really die. He said Hope was "living" the horror movie, which depicts dead people who get up and walk, that she operated in "a state of shock," unable to function rationally.

"Panic caused Hope to resort to her habitual state of avoidance," Sheehan told the court. "She became very numb. She had an inability to think or reason. It was not in her awareness that she had a choice. It just did not occur to her."

Sheehan testified that Hope was an unwilling participant who went along with menacing Shanda rather than risk falling out with Tackett, who was an older sister figure to her. He stated that, as the youngest of the four girls that night, Rippey was "out of her element" in the face of the shocking aggressiveness of Loveless and Tackett.

The psychologist asserted that Hope Rippey's knowledge of the true intentions of Loveless and Tackett was no greater than Toni Lawrence's, and said that Hope expressed a wish that other teens could learn from her mistakes, saying that she would tell others, "Don't go along when you know people are doing wrong."

On the second day of Rippey's hearing, Steve Sharer was the first to take the stand, choking back the tears as he addressed Hope Rippey about his personal loss.

"You have no idea the problems you have started in our family as we try to cope with this. It's very hard to understand why you did not try to stop this from happening," Sharer testified. Then, directing a steely look at Hope, he said, "May you rot in hell with the rest of your murdering friends."

Rippey cried throughout Sharer's statement, showing emotion for the first time.

After Steve Sharer's statement, Jackie Vaught showed the video tape of Shanda, and noticing that Hope was hanging her head down, she requested that the judge order Hope to watch it. The tape brought Rippey to tears once more.

Hope never testified on her own behalf; she had been spared the grueling interrogation.

After a short recess, Judge Jourdan sentenced Hope Rippey to the maximum sixty years, then suspended ten years for mitigating circumstances, ordering the defendant to be placed on probation for ten years under medium supervision at the time of her release. The fifty-year prison sentence brought sobs from Gloria Rippey, who sat in silence throughout the two days of testimony.

"Hope Rippey had choices," Judge Jourdan said in her sentencing memorandum. "There were avenues of escape, ways to help herself, ways to help Shanda. She poured the gasoline so no one would get caught, even though she knew it would kill Shanda. Her lack of mercy, of tender courage, is a horrifying lesson to us all."

"I don't know what normal is anymore, I'm not the person I was when Shanda was here," a tearful Vaught told reporters after the sentencing. "I'm going home to my grandbaby that was just born. You have to go on. Shanda's with God."

Epilogue

The ABC affiliate in Louisville, WHAS, covered the story in a five-day news special designed to warn parents to look for the signs that might indicate their kids are in trouble.

"What we tried to show in the series was that this could happen to your child if you're not careful," newscaster Lawrence Smith said. "If you see something that raises a red flag in your head, don't ignore it. Look into it. Something as simple as watching who your kid is hanging around with. Do you know their parents? What kind of family they are? Those kinds of things parents used to do all the time but sometimes it's not done anymore."

The reporter gave credit to Shanda's parents, whom he thought had made some mistakes, but who he admired for being able to endure the horrible death of their child under the scrutiny of the public spotlight.

Looking back, Bob Hammerle said that nothing in the outcome of the hearings could possibly satisfy anyone or relieve the Sharer family.

"Here was a case where, in many ways, Melinda was an average little girl, a product of an aberrational home and a brutal father, Hammerle asserted. "It's an unresolved tragedy because this little girl reached out for help repeatedly, she went to her school teachers, to counselors. There are other little Melinda Lovelesses out there that might not respond as violently, but we are just not addressing kids. Madison, Indiana, is no closer to addressing the problems of these kids than it was before they discovered the problem."

Hammerle attacked the New Albany school system for not dealing with Loveless's predicament, insisting that teachers should become properly funded and trained to help kids who come from extreme dysfunctional homes. He also laid blame on the Department of Welfare, which, he said, should have provided some intervention early on and possibly have prevented Melinda from becoming a criminal.

"It's a ringing indictment of the institutions that are supposed to respond to kids who are not part of the mainstream," the attorney argued.

Russell Johnson said the situation in Madison, a mid-west corn-fed town, offered proof that the juvenile sub-culture was getting out of hand all across the country. The attorney likened the teen witnesses directly involved in the case to wounded soldiers on a battlefield, saying that as he was interviewing these kids, he discovered each one had large chunks of their lives out of order, that none of them seemed to have any guidance or love from home.

"Everywhere I looked there was a casualty, but no medics around to help," Johnson said. "I saw all these children come into the courtroom day after day and testify in a very high-profile death penalty case, yet none of their parents were around. I saw troubled kid after troubled kid, but no one wanted to focus on these kids coming in and talking about lesbian affairs and drinking people's blood. The community just ignored the children and their problems."

Tackett's lead counsel, Wil Goering, pointed out that most of the juvenile criminals he represented had an attitude about their crimes which was almost fantasy-like, saying that in some ways, his client was no different than many other teen criminals he had represented.

"I think that this is pretty common with young people today. They want a white knight," Goering said. "They want someone who is going to ride in there and rescue them. I think Laurie was looking for that, just like most of the younger people I have encountered who have been charged with serious crimes."

"Your generation has dropped all the load on us," Crystal Wathen complained. "We had no idea what murder was until adults showed us what it was. All the adults have screwed this nation up so bad, we have nothing to live for anymore. Violence went from mild to deeper and deeper, to where we don't give a hoot any more."

"Nowadays is different," Amanda Heavrin chimed in. "You have to be violent to get yourself across to people."

One week after Melinda was sentenced, on January 11, 1993, Larry Eugene Loveless, age 46, was arrested in Avon Park, Florida, charged with three counts of rape, six counts of sodomy, and two counts of class D sexual battery, stemming from actions that allegedly took place between 1968 and 1989. He was held in Florida on $300,000 bond pending extradition.

The Floyd prosecutor, Stan Faith, told reporters that the victims were identified in court documents from Melinda Loveless's hearing, stating that one of the charges included a claim that Larry Loveless had molested a twelve-year-old with a loaded pistol. The prosecutor explained that an Indiana Supreme Court ruling had recently dissolved the statute of limitations in cases where juveniles were threatened with a deadly force.

After deputy prosecutor Cindy Winkler made it clear that the Floyd Circuit Court would spend the money to extradite him, Larry Loveless agreed to waive extradition and was returned to Southern Indiana in early February. A photo of Larry Loveless, dressed in orange prison garb and shackles, appeared in newspapers across the state.

On February 8, Loveless appeared in Floyd Circuit Court for an initial hearing, at which time his attorney, Michael McDaniel, entered a plea of not guilty. McDaniel asked that Loveless be housed somewhere other than the Floyd County Jail, in order that he receive treatment for post traumatic stress disorder. Judge Henry Leist ordered that Loveless be held on $200,000 cash bond, and complying with McDaniel's request, had Loveless transported to the Clark County Jail, where he remains in custody. His trial date will not be set until sometime in 1994.

"He would say, if you want to be a big girl, big girl's don't cry," Teddy Barber recalled Larry telling her, choking back the tears. "He would pull me on the bed and do different things. Sometimes it was Michelle, Melissa, or Melinda. There was a pistol involved once when I was probably thirteen. He pistol-fucked me and then made me sit there and watch him clean the gun after it was all over. He said if I told anybody, he'd kill me like he killed the babies in Vietnam."

"When he was sexually molesting me he wore a ski mask so I couldn't see his face," Michelle tearfully admitted. "I remember I used to tell him, just don't hurt Melinda or Melissa. I told him he could do whatever he wanted to me if he just left the girls alone. I asked him not to use guns, because I was scared they would go off. He would put them in you, the barrels."

Throughout the ordeal, people noticed the "metamorphosis" of Jackie Vaught, who started off as a demure figure and eventually became a media master. TV reporter Kevin Roy felt that Vaught was doing a good job of warning parents to keep a closer watch on their children. She had become a crusader, appearing on local talk shows and news broadcasts, conversing about "Justice for Shanda."

"I think she realized the power through the media to get her message out," Roy said. "She has become the person who orchestrates the media, like a celebrity would."

But not everyone would agree with that position.

"A lot of this was happening during the Amy Fisher thing," Ellen O'Connor noticed, "and I think Jackie saw Mary Jo Buttafuco on the tabloid shows on TV and she wanted that for herself. She wanted movie deals and wanted to be on TV, but she wasn't there at the scene of the crime. She didn't know anything."

Melinda, Laurie, Hope, and Toni all reside together at the Indiana Women's Prison in Indianapolis. Toni has managed to keep her distance from the other three, relying on her parents' money to buy herself small "favors" on the inside. Melinda and Laurie say they are keeping an eye out for Hope, treating her like a baby sister who they both feel responsible for.

"I believe there is a place called hell," Laurie said in a telephone call she made from the prison, "I murdered somebody, but I can ask for forgiveness and not go to hell."

"This should not have happened. This is not me," Melinda contended. "It's so stupid when you think about it. It shouldn't have caused a death. I don't blame me. We just need a little growing up. We were young, and we still are."

Below is a preview excerpt from *A Perfect Husband,*
the next exciting Aphrodite Jones true crime
available from Pinnacle.

On December 9, 2001, just after 2:40 in the morning, a
frantic man dialed a 911 operator to report an emergency.
The caller was breathing heavily as he told a Durham, North
Carolina emergency operator that his wife had an accident at
their Cedar Street home. The caller was bordering on hyste-
ria. His wife, he said, had fallen down the stairs. She had an
accident, he reported, his wife was not conscious . . . but she
was still breathing.

> *9-1-1 Operator: Okay. How many stairs did she fall
> down?*
> *Caller: What? Huh?*
> *9-1-1 Operator: How many stairs?*
> *Caller: Stairs?*
> *9-1-1 Operator: How many stairs?*
> *Caller: Ah . . . Oh . . .*
> *9-1-1 Operator: Calm down, sir. Calm down.*

The caller seemed confused. He kept repeating that his
wife wasn't conscious. He wanted an emergency crew to
come over immediately. He had already given the address.
But the operator wanted the man to calm down. She could
hardly understand him, his voice was so shrill and his
breathing so loud. The emergency operator assured him that